James Sully

Illusions

A psychological study

James Sully

Illusions
A psychological study

ISBN/EAN: 9783742842893

Manufactured in Europe, USA, Canada, Australia, Japa

Cover: Foto ©Andreas Hilbeck / pixelio.de

Manufactured and distributed by brebook publishing software
(www.brebook.com)

James Sully

Illusions

A PSYCHOLOGICAL STUDY

BY

JAMES SULLY

AUTHOR OF "SENSATION AND INTUITION," "PESSIMISM," ETC.

THIRD EDITION

LONDON

KEGAN PAUL, TRENCH & CO., 1, PATERNOSTER SQUARE

1887

PREFACE.

THE present volume takes a wide survey of the field of error, embracing in its view not only the illusions of sense dealt with in treatises on physiological optics, etc., but also other errors familiarly known as illusions, and resembling the former in their structure and mode of origin. I have throughout endeavoured to keep to a strictly scientific treatment, that is to say, the description and classification of acknowledged errors, and the explanation of these by a reference to their psychical and physical conditions. At the same time, I was not able, at the close of my exposition, to avoid pointing out how the psychology leads on to the philosophy of the subject. Some of the chapters were first roughly sketched out in articles published in magazines and reviews; but these have been not only greatly enlarged, but, to a considerable extent, rewritten.

J. S.

Hampstead, April, 1881.

CONTENTS.

CHAPTER I.

THE STUDY OF ILLUSION.

CHAPTER II.

THE CLASSIFICATION OF ILLUSIONS.

CHAPTER III.

ILLUSIONS OF PERCEPTION : GENERAL.

CHAPTER IV.

ILLUSIONS OF PERCEPTION—*continued.*

A. Passive Illusions (a) as determined by the Organism.

CHAPTER V.

ILLUSIONS OF PERCEPTION—*continued.*

A. Passive Illusions (b) as determined by the Environment.

CHAPTER VI.

ILLUSIONS OF PERCEPTION—*continued.*

B. Active Illusions.

CHAPTER VII.

DREAMS.

CHAPTER VIII.

ILLUSIONS OF INTROSPECTION.

CHAPTER XI.

ILLUSIONS OF BELIEF.

CHAPTER XII.

RESULTS.

ILLUSIONS.

CHAPTER I.

THE STUDY OF ILLUSION.

COMMON sense, knowing nothing of fine distinctions, is wont to draw a sharp line between the region of illusion and that of sane intelligence. To be the victim of an illusion is, in the popular judgment, to be excluded from the category of rational men. The term at once calls up images of stunted figures with ill-developed brains, half-witted creatures, hardly distinguishable from the admittedly insane. And this way of thinking of illusion and its subjects is strengthened by one of the characteristic sentiments of our age. The nineteenth century intelligence plumes itself on having got at the bottom of mediæval visions and church miracles, and it is wont to commiserate the feeble minds that are still subject to these self-deceptions.

According to this view, illusion is something essentially abnormal and allied to insanity. And it would seem to follow that its nature and origin can be best

B

studied by those whose speciality it is to observe the phenomena of abnormal life. Scientific procedure has in the main conformed to this distinction of common sense. The phenomena of illusion have ordinarily been investigated by alienists, that is to say, physicians who are brought face to face with their most striking forms in the mentally deranged.

While there are very good reasons for this treatment of illusion as a branch of mental pathology, it is by no means certain that it can be a complete and exhaustive one. Notwithstanding the flattering supposition of common sense, that illusion is essentially an incident in abnormal life, the careful observer knows well enough that the case is far otherwise.

There is, indeed, a view of our race diametrically opposed to the flattering opinion referred to above, namely, the humiliating judgment that all men habitually err, or that illusion is to be regarded as the natural condition of mortals. This idea has found expression, not only in the cynical exclamation of the misanthropist that most men are fools, but also in the cry of despair that sometimes breaks from the weary searcher after absolute truth, and from the poet when impressed with the unreality of his early ideals.

Without adopting this very disparaging opinion of the intellectual condition of mankind, we must recognize the fact that most men are sometimes liable to illusion. Hardly anybody is always consistently sober and rational in his perceptions and beliefs. A momentary fatigue of the nerves, a little mental excitement, a relaxation of the effort of attention by which we continually take our bearings with respect to the real world about us, will produce just the same kind of confusion of reality and phantasm which we observe in the insane. To give but an example: the play of fancy which leads to a detection of animal and other forms in clouds, is known to be an occupation of the insane, and is rightly made use of by Shakespeare as a mark of incipient mental aberration in Hamlet; and yet this very same occupation is quite natural to children, and to imaginative adults when they choose to throw the reins on the neck of their phantasy. Our luminous circle of rational perception is surrounded by a misty penumbra of illusion. Common sense itself may be said to admit this, since the greatest stickler for the enlightenment of our age will be found in practice to accuse most of his acquaintance at some time or another of falling into illusion.

If illusion thus has its roots in ordinary mental life, the study of it would seem to belong to the physiology as much as to the pathology of mind. We may even go further, and say that in the analysis and explanation of illusion the psychologist may be expected to do more than the physician. If, on the one hand, the latter has the great privilege of observing the phenomena in their highest intensity, on the other hand, the former has the advantage of being familiar with the normal intellectual process which all illusion simulates or caricatures. To this it must be added that the physician is naturally disposed to look at illusion mainly, if not exclusively, on its practical side, that is, as a concomitant and symptom of cerebral disease, which it is needful to be able to recognize. The psychologist has a different interest in the subject,

being specially concerned to understand the mental
antecedents of illusion and its relation to accurate
perception and belief. It is pretty evident, indeed,
that the phenomena of illusion form a region common
to the psychologist and the mental pathologist, and
that the complete elucidation of the subject will need
the co-operation of the two classes of investigator.

In the present volume an attempt will be made to
work out the psychological side of the subject; that
is to say, illusions will be viewed in their relation to
the process of just and accurate perception. In the
carrying out of this plan our principal attention will
be given to the manifestations of the illusory impulse
in normal life. At the same time, though no special
acquaintance with the pathology of the subject will be
laid claim to, frequent references will be made to the
illusions of the insane. Indeed, it will be found that
the two groups of phenomena—the illusions of the
normal and of the abnormal condition—are so similar,
and pass into one another by such insensible grada-
tions, that it is impossible to discuss the one apart
from the other. The view of illusion which will be
adopted in this work is that it constitutes a kind of
borderland between perfectly sane and vigorous mental
life and dementia.

And here at once there forces itself on our attention the question, What exactly is to be understood by
the term "illusion"? In scientific works treating of
the pathology of the subject, the word is confined to
what are specially known as illusions of the senses,
that is to say, to false or illusory perceptions. And
there is very good reason for this limitation, since such

illusions of the senses are the most palpable and striking symptoms of mental disease. In addition to this, it must be allowed that, to the ordinary reader, the term first of all calls up this same idea of a deception of the senses.

At the same time, popular usage has long since extended the term so as to include under it errors which do not counterfeit actual perceptions. We commonly speak of a man being under an illusion respecting himself when he has a ridiculously exaggerated view of his own importance, and in a similar way of a person being in a state of illusion with respect to the past when, through frailty of memory, he pictures it quite otherwise than it is certainly known to have been.

It will be found, I think, that there is a very good reason for this popular extension of the term. The errors just alluded to have this in common with illusions of sense, that they simulate the form of immediate or self-evident cognition. An idea held respecting ourselves or respecting our past history does not depend on any other piece of knowledge; in other words, is not adopted as the result of a process of reasoning. What I believe with reference to my past history, so far as I can myself recall it, I believe instantaneously and immediately, without the intervention of any premise or reason. Similarly, our notions of ourselves are, for the most part, obtained apart from any process of inference. The view which a man takes of his own character or claims on society he is popularly supposed to receive intuitively by a mere act of internal observation. Such beliefs may not, indeed, have all the overpowering force which belongs to illusory perceptions, for the intuition of something by the senses is commonly looked on as the most immediate and irresistible kind of knowledge. Still, they must be said to come very near illusions of sense in the degree of their self-evident certainty.

Taking this view of illusion, we may provisionally define it as any species of error which counterfeits the form of immediate, self-evident, or intuitive knowledge, whether as sense-perception or otherwise. Whenever a thing is believed on its own evidence and not as a conclusion from something else, and the thing then believed is demonstrably wrong, there is an illusion. The term would thus appear to cover all varieties of error which are not recognized as fallacies or false inferences. If for the present we roughly divide all our knowledge into the two regions of primary or intuitive, and secondary or inferential knowledge, we see that illusion is false or spurious knowledge of the first kind, fallacy false or spurious knowledge of the second kind. At the same time, it is to be remembered that this division is only a very rough one. As will appear in the course of our investigation, the same error may be called either a fallacy or an illusion, according as we are thinking of its original mode of production or of the form which it finally assumes; and a thorough-going psychological analysis of error may discover that these two classes are at bottom very similar.

As we proceed, we shall, I think, find an ample justification for our definition. We shall see that such illusions as those respecting ourselves or the past arise by very much the same mental processes as those which are discoverable in the production of illusory perceptions ; and thus a complete psychology of the one class will, at the same time, contain the explanation of the other classes.

The reader is doubtless aware that philosophers have still further extended the idea of illusion by seeking to bring under it beliefs which the common sense of mankind has always adopted and never begun to suspect. Thus, according to the idealist, the popular notion (the existence of which Berkeley, however, denied) of an external world, existing in itself and in no wise dependent on our perceptions of it, resolves itself into a grand illusion of sense.

At the close of our study of illusions we shall return to this point. We shall there inquire into the connection between those illusions which are popularly recognized as such, and those which first come into view or appear to do so (for we must not yet assume that there are such) after a certain kind of philosophic reflection. And some attempt will be made to determine roughly how far the process of dissolving these substantial beliefs of mankind into airy phantasms may venture to go.

For the present, however, these so-called illusions in philosophy will be ignored. It is plain that illusion exists only in antithesis to real knowledge. This last must be assumed as something above all question. And a rough and provisional, though for our purpose sufficiently accurate, demarcation of the regions of the real and the illusory seems to coincide with the line which common sense draws between what all normal men agree in holding and what the individual holds, whether temporarily or permanently, in contradiction to this. For our present purpose the real is that which is true for all. Thus, though physical science may tell us that there is nothing corresponding to our sensations of colour in the world of matter and motion which it conceives as surrounding us; yet, inasmuch as to all men endowed with the normal colour-sense the same material objects appear to have the same colour, we may speak of any such perception as practically true, marking it off from those plainly illusory perceptions which are due to some subjective cause, as, for example, fatigue of the retina.

To sum up: in treating of illusions we shall assume, what science as distinguished from philosophy is bound to assume, namely, that human experience is consistent; that men's perceptions and beliefs fall into a consensus. From this point of view illusion is seen to arise through some exceptional feature in the situation or condition of the individual, which, for the time, breaks the chain of intellectual solidarity which under ordinary circumstances binds the single member to the collective body. Whether the common experience which men thus obtain is rightly interpreted is a question which does not concern us here. · For our present purpose, which is the determination and explanation of illusion as popularly understood, it is sufficient that there is this general consensus of belief, and this may provisionally be regarded as at least practically true.

CHAPTER II.

IF illusion is the simulation of immediate knowledge, the most obvious mode of classifying illusions would appear to be according to the variety of the knowledge which they simulate.

Now, the popular psychology that floats about in the ordinary forms of language has long since distinguished certain kinds of unreasoned or uninferred knowledge. Of these the two best known are perception and memory. When I see an object before me, or when I recall an event in my past experience, I am supposed to grasp a piece of knowledge directly, to know something immediately, and not through the medium of something else. Yet I know differently in the two cases. In the first I know by what is called a presentative process, namely, that of sense-perception; in the second I know by a representative process, namely, that of reproduction, or on the evidence of memory. In the one case the object of cognition is present to my perceptive faculties; in the other it is recalled by the power of memory.

Scientific psychology tends, no doubt, to break down some of these popular distinctions. Just as the zoologist sometimes groups together varieties of animals which the unscientific eye would never think of connecting, so the psychologist may analyze mental operations which appear widely dissimilar to the popular mind, and reduce them to one fundamental process. Thus recent psychology draws no sharp distinction between perception and recollection. It finds in both very much the same elements, though combined in a different way Strictly speaking, indeed, perception must be defined as a presentative-representative operation. To the psychologist it comes to very much the same thing whether, for example, on a visit to Switzerland, our minds are occupied in *perceiving* the distance of a mountain or in *remembering* some pleasant excursion which we made to it on a former visit. In both cases there is a reinstatement of the past, a reproduction of earlier experience, a process of adding to a present impression a product of imagination—taking this word in its widest sense. In both cases the same laws of reproduction or association are illustrated.

Just as a deep and exhaustive analysis of the intellectual operations thus tends to identify their various forms as they are distinguished by the popular mind, so a thorough investigation of the flaws in these operations, that is to say, the counterfeits of knowledge, will probably lead to an identification of the essential mental process which underlies them. It is apparent, for example, that, whether a man *projects* some figment of his imagination into the external world, giving it, present material reality, or whether (if I may be allowed the term) he *retrojects* it into the dim region of the past, and takes it for a reality that has been he is committing substantially the same blunder. The source of the illusion in both cases is one and the same.

It might seem to follow from this that a scientific discussion of the subject would overlook the obvious distinction between illusions of perception and those of memory; that it would attend simply to differences in the mode of origination of the illusion, whatever its external form. Our next step, then, would appear to be to determine these differences in the mode of production.

That there are differences in the origin and source of illusion is a fact which has been fully recognized by those writers who have made a special study of sense-illusions. By these the term illusion is commonly employed in a narrow, technical sense, and opposed to hallucination. An illusion, it is said, must always have its starting-point in some actual impression, whereas a hallucination has no such basis. Thus it is an illusion when a man, under the action of terror, takes a stump of a tree, whitened by the moon's rays, for a ghost. It is a hallucination when an imaginative person so vividly pictures to himself the form of some absent friend that, for the moment, he fancies himself actually beholding him. Illusion is thus a partial displacement of external fact by a fiction of the imagination, while hallucination is a total displacement.

This distinction, which has been adopted by the majority of recent alienists,[1] is a valuable one, and

---

[1] A history of the distinction is given by Brierre de Boismont, in his work *On Illusions* (translated by R. T. Hulme, 1859). He says that Arnold (1806) first defined hallucination, and distinguished it

must not be lost sight of here. It would seem, from a psychological point of view, to be an important circumstance in the genesis of a false perception whether the intellectual process sets out from within or from without. And it will be found, moreover, that this distinction may be applied to all the varieties of error which I propose to consider. Thus, for example, it will be seen further on that a false recollection may set out either from the idea of some actual past occurrence or from a present product of the imagination.

It is to be observed, however, that the line of separation between illusion and hallucination, as thus defined, is a very narrow one. In by far the largest number of hallucinations it is impossible to prove that there is no modicum of external agency co-operating in the production of the effect. It is presumable, indeed, that many, if not all, hallucinations have such a basis of fact. Thus, the madman who projects his internal thoughts outwards in the shape of external voices may, for aught we know, be prompted to do so in part by faint impressions coming from the ear, the result of those slight stimulations to which the organ is always exposed, even in profound silence, and which in his case assume an exaggerated intensity. And even if it is clearly made out that there are hallucinations in the strict sense, that is to say, false perceptions which are wholly due to internal causes, it must be conceded that illusion shades off into hallucination by steps which it is impossible for science to mark. In

from illusion. Esquirol, in his work, *Des Maladies Mentales* (1838), may be said to have fixed the distinction. (See Hunt's translation, 1845, p. 111.)

many cases it must be left an open question whether the error is to be classed as an illusion or as a hallucination.[1]

For these reasons, I think it best not to make the distinction between illusion and hallucination the leading principle of my classification. However important psychologically, it does not lend itself to this purpose. The distinction must be kept in view and illustrated as far as possible. Accordingly, while in general following popular usage and employing the term illusion as the generic name, I shall, when convenient, recognize the narrow and technical sense of the term as answering to a species co-ordinate with hallucination.

Departing, then, from what might seem the ideally best order of exposition, I propose, after all, to set out with the simple popular scheme of faculties already referred to. Even if they are, psychologically considered, identical operations, perception and memory are in general sufficiently marked off by a speciality in the form of the operation. Thus, while memory is the reproduction of something with a special reference of consciousness to its past existence, perception is the reproduction of something with a special reference to its present existence as a part of the presented object. In other words, though largely *representative* when viewed as to its origin, perception is *presentative* in relation to the object which is supposed to be im-

---

[1] This fact has been fully recognized by writers on the pathology of the subject; for example, Griesinger, *Mental Pathology and Therapeutics* (London, 1867), p. 84; Baillarger, article, "Des Hallucinations," in the *Mémoires de l'Académie Royale de Médecine*, tom. xii. p. 273, etc.; Wundt, *Physiologische Psychologie*, p. 653.

mediately present to the mind at the moment.[1] Hence the convenience of recognizing the popular classification, and of making it our starting-point in the present case.

All knowledge which has any appearance of being directly reached, immediate, or self-evident, that is to say, of not being inferred from other knowledge, may be divided into four principal varieties: Internal Perception or Introspection of the mind's own feelings; External Perception; Memory; and Belief, in so far as it simulates the form of direct knowledge. The first is illustrated in a man's consciousness of a present feeling of pain or pleasure. The second and the third kinds have already been spoken of, and are too familiar to require illustration. It is only needful to remark here that, under perception, or rather in close conjunction with it, I purpose dealing with the knowledge of other's feelings, in so far as this assumes the aspect of immediate knowledge. The term belief is here used to include expectations and any other kinds of conviction that do not fall under one of the other heads. An instance of a seemingly immediate belief would be a prophetic prevision of a coming disaster, or a man's unreasoned persuasion as to his own powers of performing a difficult task.

It is, indeed, said by many thinkers that there are no legitimate immediate beliefs; that all our expectations and other convictions about things, in so far as they are sound, must repose on other genuinely immediate

---

[1] I here touch on the distinction between the psychological and the philosophical view of perception, to be brought out more fully by-and-by.

knowledge, more particularly sense-perception and memory. This difficult question need not be discussed here. It is allowed by all that there is a multitude of beliefs which we hold tenaciously and on which we are ready to act, which, to the mature mind, wear the appearance of intuitive truths, owing their cogency to nothing beyond themselves. A man's belief in his own merits, however it may have been first obtained, is as immediately assured to him as his recognition of a real object in the act of sense-perception. It may be added that many of our every-day working beliefs about the world in which we live, though presumably derived from memory and perception, tend to lose all traces of their origin, and to simulate the aspect of intuitions. Thus the proposition that logicians are in the habit of pressing on our attention, that "Men are mortal," seems, on the face of it, to common sense to be something very like a self-evident truth, not depending on any particular facts of experience.

In calling these four forms of cognition immediate, I must not, however, be supposed to be placing them on the same logical level. It is plain, indeed, to a reflective mind that, though each may be called immediate in this superficial sense, there are perceptible differences in the degree of their immediacy. Thus it is manifest, after a moment's reflection, that expectation, so far as it is just, is not primarily immediate in the sense in which purely presentative knowledge is so, since it can be shown to follow from something else. So a general proposition, though through familiarity and innumerable illustrations it has acquired a self-evident character, is seen with a very little inspection to be less fundamentally and essentially so than the proposition, "I am now feeling pain;" and it will be found that even with respect to memory, when the remembered event is at all remote, the process of cognition approximates to a mediate operation, namely, one of inference. What the relative values of these different kinds of immediate knowledge are is a point which will have to be touched on at the end of our study. Here it must suffice to warn the reader against the supposition that this value is assumed to be identical.

It might seem at a first glance to follow from this four-fold scheme of immediate or quasi-immediate knowledge that there are four varieties of illusion. And this is true in the sense that these four heads cover all the main varieties of illusion. If there are only four varieties of knowledge which can lay any claim to be considered immediate, it must be that every illusion will simulate the form of one of these varieties, and so be referable to the corresponding division.

But though there are conceivably these four species of illusion, it does not follow that there are any actual instances of each class forthcoming. This we cannot determine till we have investigated the nature and origin of illusory error. For example, it might be found that introspection, or the immediate inspection of our own feelings or mental states, does not supply the conditions necessary to the production of such error. And, indeed, it is probable that most persons, antecedently to inquiry, would be disposed to say that to fall into error in the observation of what is actually going on in our own minds is impossible.

With the exception of this first division, however, this scheme may easily be seen to answer to actual phenomena. That there are illusions of perception is obvious, since it is to the errors of sense that the term illusion has most frequently been confined. It is hardly less evident that there are illusions of memory. The peculiar difficulty of distinguishing between a past real event and a mere phantom of the imagination, illustrated in the exclamation, "I either saw it or dreamt it," sufficiently shows that memory is liable to be imposed on. Finally, it is agreed on by all that the beliefs we are wont to regard as self-evident are sometimes erroneous. When, for example, an imaginative woman says she knows, by mere intuition, that something interesting is going to happen, say the arrival of a favourite friend, she is plainly running the risk of being self-deluded. So, too, a man's estimate of himself, however valid for him, may turn out to be flagrantly false.

In the following discussion of the subject I shall depart from the above order in so far as to set out with illusions of sense-perception. These are well ascertained, forming, indeed, the best-marked variety. And the explanation of these has been carried much further than that of the others. Hence, according to the rule to proceed from the known to the unknown, there will be an obvious convenience in examining these first of all. After having done this, we shall be in a position to inquire whether there is anything analogous in the region of introspection or internal perception. Our study of the errors of sense-perception will, moreover, prove the best preparation for an inquiry into the nature and mode of production of the remaining two varieties.[1]

I would add that, in close connection with the first division, illusions of perception, I shall treat the subtle and complicated phenomena of dreams. Although containing elements which ought, according to strictness, to be brought under one of the other heads, they are, as their common appellation, "visions," shows, largely simulations of external, and more especially visual, perception.

Dreams are no doubt sharply marked off from illusions of sense-perception by a number of special circumstances. Indeed, it may be thought that they cannot be adequately treated in a work that aims primarily at investigating the illusions of normal life, and should rather be left to those who make the pathological side of the subject their special study. Yet it may, perhaps, be said that in a wide sense dreams are a feature of normal life. And, however this be, they have quite enough in common with other illusions of perception to justify us in dealing with them in close connection with these.

---

[1] It might even be urged that the order here adopted is scientifically the best, since sense-perception is the earliest form of knowledge, introspected facts being known only in relation to perceived facts. But if the mind's knowledge of its own states is thus later in time, it i earlier in the logical order, that is to say, it is the most strictly presentative form of knowledge.

CHAPTER III.

THE errors with which we shall be concerned in this chapter are those which are commonly denoted by the term illusion, that is to say, those of sense. They are sometimes called deceptions of the senses; but this is a somewhat loose expression, suggesting that we can be deceived as to sensation itself, though, as we shall see later on, this is only true in a very restricted meaning of the phrase. To speak correctly, sense-illusions must be said to arise by a simulation of the form of just and accurate perceptions. Accordingly, we shall most frequently speak of them as illusions of perception.

In order to investigate the nature of any kind of error, it is needful to understand the kind of know-ledge it imitates, and so we must begin our inquiry into the nature of illusions of sense by a brief account of the psychology of perception ; and, in doing this, we shall proceed best by regarding this operation in its most complete form, namely, that of visual per-ception.

I may observe that in this analysis of perception I shall endeavour to keep to known facts, namely, the psychical phenomena or events which can be seen by the methods of scientific psychology to enter into the mental content called the percept. I do not now inquire whether such an analysis can help us to understand all that is meant by perception. This point will have to be touched later on. Here it is enough to say that, whatever our philosophy of perception may be, we must accept the psychological fact that the concrete mental state in the act of perception is built up out of elements, the history of which can be traced by the methods of mental science.

Psychology of Perception.

Confining ourselves for the present to the mental, as distinguished from the physical, side of the operation, we soon find that perception is not so simple a matter as it might at first seem to be. When a man on a hot day looks at a running stream and " sees " the delicious coolness, it is not difficult to show that he is really performing an act of mental synthesis, or imaginative construction. To the sense-impression [1] which his eye now gives him, he adds something which past experience has bequeathed to his mind. In perception, the material of sensation is acted on by the mind, which embodies in its present attitude all the results of its past growth. Let us look at this process of synthesis a little more closely.

When a sensation arises in the mind, it may, under

---

[1] Here and elsewhere I use the word "impression" for the whole complex of sensation which is present at the moment. It may, perhaps, not be unnecessary to add that, in employing this term, I am making no assumption about the independent existence of external objects.

certain circumstances, go unattended to. In that case there is no perception. The sensation floats in the dim outer regions of consciousness as a vague feeling, the real nature and history of which are unknown. This remark applies not only to the undefined bodily sensations that are always oscillating about the threshold of obscure consciousness, but to the higher sensations connected with the special organs of perception. The student in optics soon makes the startling discovery that his field of vision has all through his life been haunted with weird shapes which have never troubled the serenity of his mind just because they have never been distinctly attended to.

The immediate result of this process of directing the keen glance of attention to a sensation is to give it greater force and distinctness. By attending to it we discriminate it from other feelings present and past, and classify it with like sensations previously received. Thus, if I receive a visual impression of the colour orange, the first consequence of attending to it is to mark it off from other colour-impressions, including those of red and yellow. And in recognizing the peculiar quality of the impression by applying to it the term orange, I obviously connect it with other similar sensations called by the same name. If a sensation is perfectly new, there cannot, of course, be this process of classifying, and in this case the closely related operation of discriminating it from other sensations is less exactly performed. But it is hardly necessary to remark that, in the mind of the adult, under ordinary circumstances, no perfectly new sensation ever occurs.

When the sensation, or complex sensation, is thus defined and recognized, there follows the process of interpretation, by which I mean the taking up of the impression as an element into the complex mental state known as a percept. Without going into the philosophical question of what this process of synthesis exactly means, I may observe that, by common consent, it takes place to a large extent by help of a reproduction of sensations of various kinds experienced in the past. That is to say, the details in this act of combination are drawn from the store of mental recollections to which the growing mind is ever adding. In other words, the percept arises through a fusion of an actual sensation with mental representations or "images" of sensation.[1] Every element of the object that we thus take up in the act of perception, or put into the percept, as its actual size, distance, and so on, will be found to make itself known to us through mental images or revivals of past experiences, such as those we have in handling the object, moving to and from it, etc. It follows that if this is an essential ingredient in the act of perception, the process closely resembles an act of inference; and, indeed, Helmholtz distinctly calls the perception of distance an uncon-

---

[1] Psychological usage has now pretty well substituted the term "image" for "idea," in order to indicate an individual (as distinguished from a general) representation of a sensation or percept. It might, perhaps, be desirable to go further in this process of differentiating language, and to distinguish between a sensational image, *e.g.* the representation of a colour, and a perceptional image, as the representation of a coloured object. It may be well to add that, in speaking of a fusion of an image and a sensation, I do not mean that the former exists apart for a single instant. The term "fusion" is used figuratively to describe the union of the two sides or aspects of a complete percept.

scious inference or a mechanically performed act of judgment.

I have hinted that these recovered sensations include the feelings we experience in connection with muscular activity, as in moving our limbs, resisting or lifting heavy bodies, and walking to a distant object. Modern psychology refers the eye's instantaneous recognition of the most important elements of an object (its essential or " primary " qualities) to a reinstatement of such simple experiences as these. It is, indeed, these reproductions which are supposed to constitute the substantial background of our percepts.

Another thing worth noting with respect to this process of filling up a sense-impression is that it draws on past sensations of the eye itself. Thus, when I look at the figure of an acquaintance from behind, my reproductive visual imagination supplies a representation of the impressions I am wont to receive when the more interesting aspect of the object, the front view, is present to my visual sense.[1]

We may distinguish between different steps in the full act of visual recognition. First of all comes the construction of a material object of a particular figure and size, and at a particular distance ; that is to say, the recognition of a tangible thing having certain simple space-properties, and holding a certain relation to other objects, and more especially our own body, in space. This is the bare perception of an object, which always takes place even in the case of perfectly new

---

[1] This impulse to fill in visual elements not actually present is strikingly illustrated in people's difficulty in recognizing the gap in the field of vision answering to the insensitive " blind " spot on the retina. (See Helmholtz, *Physiologische Optik*, p. 573, *et seq*)

objects, provided they are seen with any degree of distinctness. It is to be added that the reference of a sensation of light or colour to such an object involves the inclusion of a quality answering to the sensation, as brightness, or blue colour, in the thing thus intuited.

This part of the process of filling in, which is the most instantaneous, automatic, and unconscious, may be supposed to answer to the most constant and therefore the most deeply organized connections of experience; for, speaking generally, we never have an impression of colour, except when there are circumstances present which are fitted to yield us those simple muscular and tactual experiences through which the ideas of a particular form, size, etc., are pretty certainly obtained.

The second step in this process of presentative construction is the recognition of an object as one of a class of things, for example, oranges, having certain special qualities, as a particular taste. In this step the connections of experience are less deeply organized, and so we are able to some extent, by reflection, to recognize it as a kind of intellectual working up of the materials supplied us by the past. It is to be noted that this process of recognition involves a compound operation of classifying impressions as distinguished from that simple operation by which a single impression, such as a particular colour, is known. Thus the recognition of such an object as an orange takes place by a rapid classing of a multitude of passive sensations of colour, light, and shade, and those active or muscular sensations which are supposed to enter into the visual perception of form.

A still less automatic step in the process of visual recognition is that of identifying individual objects, as Westminster Abbey, or a friend, John Smith. The amount of experience that is here reproduced may be very large, as in the case of recognizing a person with whom we have had a long and intimate acquaintance.

If the recognition of an object as one of a class, for example, an orange, involves a compound process of classing impressions, that of an individual object involves a still more complicated process. The identification of a friend, simple as this operation may at first appear, really takes place by a rapid classing of all the salient characteristic features which serve as the visible marks of that particular person.

It is to be noted that each kind of recognition, specific and individual, takes place by a consciousness of likeness amid unlikeness. It is obvious that a new individual object has characters not shared in by other objects previously inspected. Thus, we at once class a man with a dark-brown skin, wearing a particular garb, as a Hindoo, though he may differ in a host of particulars from the other Hindoos that we have observed. In thus instantly recognizing him as a Hindoo, we must, it is plain, attend to the points of similarity, and overlook for the instant the points of dissimilarity. In the case of individual identification, the same thing happens. Strictly speaking, no object ever appears exactly the same to us on two occasions. Apart from changes in the object itself, especially in the case of living beings, there are varying effects of illumination, of position in relation to the eye, of distance, and so on, which very distinctly affect the visual impression at different times. Yet the fact of our instantly recognizing a familiar object in spite of these fluctuations of appearance, proves that we are able to overlook a very considerable amount of diversity when a certain amount of likeness is present.

It is further to be observed that in these last stages of perception we approach the boundary line between perception and inference. To recognize an object as one of a class is often a matter of conscious reflection and judgment, even when the class is constituted by obvious material qualities which the senses may be supposed to apprehend immediately. Still more clearly does perception pass into inference when the class is constituted by less obvious qualities, which require a careful and prolonged process of recollection, discrimination, and comparison, for their recognition. Thus, to recognize a man by certain marks of gesture and manner as a military man or a Frenchman, though popularly called a perception, is much more of an unfolded process of conscious inference. And what applies to specific recognition applies still more forcibly to individual recognition, which is often a matter of very delicate conscious comparison and judgment. To say where the line should be drawn here between perception and observation on the one hand, and inference on the other, is clearly impossible. Our whole study of the illusions of perception will serve to show that the one shades off into the other too gradually to allow of our drawing a hard and fast line between them.

Finally, it is to be noted that these last stages of perception bring us near the boundary line which separates objective experience as common and universal, and subjective or variable experience as confined to one or to a few. In the bringing of the object under a certain class of objects there is clearly room for greater variety of individual perception. For example, the ability to recognize a man as a Frenchman turns on a special kind of previous experience. And this transition from the common or universal to the individual experience is seen yet more plainly in the case of individual recognition. To identify an object, say a particular person, commonly presupposes some previous experience or knowledge of this object, and the existence in the past of some special relation of the recognizer to the recognized, if only that of an observer. In fact, it is evident that in this mode of recognition we have the transition from common perception to individual recollection.[1]

While we may thus distinguish different steps in the process of visual recognition, we may make a further distinction, marking off a passive and an active stage in the process. The one may be called the stage of preperception, the other that of perception proper.[2] In the first the mind holds itself in a passive attitude, except in so far as the energies of external attention are involved. The impression here awakens the mental images which answer to past experiences according to the well-known laws of association. The interpretative image which is to transform the impres-

---

[1] This relation will be more fully discussed under the head of "Memory."

[2] I adopt this distinction from Dr. J. Hughlings Jackson. See his articles, "On Affections of Speech from Diseases of the Brain," in *Brain*, Nos. iii. and vii. The second stage might conveniently be named apperception, but for the special philosophical associations of the term:

sion into a percept is now being formed by a mere process of suggestion.

When the image is thus formed, the mind may be said to enter upon a more active stage, in which it now views the impression through the image, or applies this as a kind of mould or framework to the impression. This appears to involve an intensification of the mental image, transforming it from a representative to a presentative mental state, making it approximate somewhat to the full intensity of the sensation. In many of our instantaneous perceptions these two stages are indistinguishable to consciousness. Thus, in most cases, the recognition of size, distance, etc., takes place so rapidly that it is impossible to detect the two phases here separated. But in the classification of an object, or the identification of an individual thing, there is often an appreciable interval between the first reception of the impression and the final stage of complete recognition. And here it is easy to distinguish the two stages of preperception and perception. The interpretative image is slowly built up by the operation of suggestion, at the close of which the impression is suddenly illumined as by a flash of light, and takes a definite, precise shape.

Now, it is to be noted that the process of preperception will be greatly aided by any circumstance that facilitates the construction of the particular interpretative image required. Thus, the more frequently a similar process of perception has been performed in the past, the more ready will the mind be to fall into the particular way of interpreting the impression. As G. H. Lewes well remarks, " The artist sees details where to other eyes there is a vague or confused mass ; the naturalist sees an animal where the ordinary eye only sees a form." [1] This is but one illustration of the seemingly universal mental law, that what is repeatedly done will be done more and more easily.

The process of preperception may be shortened, not only by means of a *permanent* disposition to frame the required interpretative scheme, the residuum of past like processes, but also by means of any *temporary* disposition pointing in the same direction. If, for example, the mind of a naturalist has just been occupied about a certain class of bird, that is to say, if he has been dwelling on the *mental image* of this bird, he will recognize one at a distance more quickly than he would otherwise have done. Such a simple mental operation as the recognition of one of the less common flowers, say a particular orchid, will vary in duration according as we have or have not been recently forming an image of this flower. The obvious explanation of this is that the mental image of an object bears a very close resemblance to the corresponding percept, differing from it, indeed, in degree only, that is to say, through the fact that it involves no actual sensation. Here again we see illustrated a general psychological law, namely, that what the mind has recently done, it tends (within certain limits) to go on doing.

It is to be noticed, further, that the perception of a single object or event is rarely an isolated act of the mind. We recognize and understand the things that

---

[1] *Problems of Life and Mind*, third series, p. 107. This writer employs the word " preperception " to denote this effect of previous perception.

surround us through their relations one to another. Sometimes the adjacent circumstances and events suggest a definite expectation of the new impression. Thus, for example, the sound of a gun heard during a walk in the country is instantly interpreted by help of suggestions due to the previous appearance of the sportsman, and the act of raising the gun to. his shoulder. It may be added that the verbal suggestions of others act very much like the suggestions of external circumstances. If I am told that a gun is going to be fired, my mind is prepared for it just as though I saw the sportsman.[1]

More frequently the effect of such surrounding circumstances is to give an air of familiarity to the new impression, to shorten the interval in which the required interpretative image is forthcoming. Thus, when travelling in Italy, the visual impression answering to a ruined temple or a bareheaded friar is construed much more rapidly than it would be elsewhere, because of the attitude of mind due to the surrounding circumstances. In all such cases the process of preperception connected with a given impression is effected more or less completely by the suggestions of other and related impressions.

It follows from all that has been just said that our minds are never in exactly the same state of readiness with respect to a particular process of perceptional interpretation. Sometimes the meaning of an impression flashes on us at once, and the stage of pre-

---

[1] Such verbal suggestion, moreover, acting through a sense-impression, has something of that vividness of effect which belongs to all excitation of mental images by external stimuli.

perception becomes evanescent. At other times the same impression will fail for an appreciable interval to divulge its meaning. These differences are, no doubt, due in part to variations in the state of attention at the moment; but they depend as well on fluctuations in the degree of the mind's readiness to look at the impression in the required way.

In order to complete this slight analysis of perception, we must look for a moment at its physical side, that is to say, at the nervous actions which are known or supposed with some degree of probability to accompany it.

The production of the sensation is known to depend on a certain external process, namely, the action of some stimulus, as light, on the sense-organ, which stimulus has its point of departure in the object, such as it is conceived by physical science. The sensation arises when the nervous process is transmitted through the nerves to the conscious centre, often spoken of as the sensorium, the exact seat of which is still a matter of some debate.

The intensification of the sensation by the reaction of attention is supposed to depend on some reinforcement of the nervous excitation in the sensory centre proceeding from the motor regions, which are hypothetically regarded as the centre of attention.[1] The classification of the impression, again, is pretty certainly correlated with the physical fact that the central excitation calls into activity elements which have already been excited in the same way.

The nervous counterpart of the final stage of per-

---

[1] See Wundt, *Physiologische Psychologie,* p. 723.

ception, the synthesis of the sensation and the mental representation, is not clearly ascertained. A sensation clearly resembles a mental image in quality. It is most obviously marked off from the image by its greater vividness or intensity. Agreeably to this view, it is now held by a number of eminent physiologists and psychologists that the nervous process underlying a sensation occupies the same central region as that which underlies the corresponding image. According to this theory, the two processes differ in their degree of energy only, this difference being connected with the fact that the former involves, while the latter does not involve, the peripheral region of the nervous system. Accepting this view as on the whole well founded, I shall speak of an ideational, or rather an imaginational, and a sensational nervous process, and not of an ideational and a sensational centre.[1]

The special force that belongs to the representative element in a percept, as compared with that of a pure "perceptional" image,[2] is probably connected with the fact that, in the case of actual perception, the nervous process underlying the act of imaginative construction is organically united to the initial sensational process, of which indeed it may be regarded as a continuation.

For the physical counterpart of the two stages in the

---

[1] For a confirmation of the view adopted in the text, see Professor Bain, *The Senses and the Intellect*, Part II. ch. i. sec. 8; Herbert Spencer, *Principles of Psychology*, vol. i. p. 234, *et passim*; Dr. Ferrier, *The Functions of the Brain*, p. 258, *et seq.*; Professor Wundt, *op. cit.*, pp. 644, 645; G. H. Lewes, *Problems of Life and Mind*, vol. v. p. 445, *et seq.* For an opposite view, see Dr. Carpenter, *Mental Physiology*, fourth edit., p. 220, etc.; Dr. Maudsley, *The Physiology of Mind*, ch. v. p. 250, etc.

[2] See note, p. 22.

interpretative part of perception, distinguished as the passive stage of preperception, and the active stage of perception proper, we may, in the absence of certain knowledge, fall back on the hypothesis put forward by Dr. J. Hughlings Jackson, in the articles in *Brain* already referred to, namely, that the former answers to an action of the right hemisphere of the brain, the latter to a subsequent action of the left hemisphere. The expediting of the process of preperception in those cases where it has frequently been performed before, is clearly an illustration of the organic law that every function is improved by exercise. And the temporary disposition to perform the process due to recent imaginative activity, is explained at once on the physical side by the supposition that an actual perception and a perceptional image involve the activity of the same nervous tracts. For, assuming this to be the case, it follows, from a well-known organic law, that a recent excitation would leave a temporary disposition in these particular structures to resume that particular mode of activity.

What has here been said about visual perception will apply, *mutatis mutandis*, to other kinds. Although the eye is the organ of perception *par excellence*, our other senses are also avenues by which we intuit and recognize objects. Thus touch, especially when it is finely developed as it is in the blind, gives an immediate knowledge of objects—a more immediate knowledge, indeed, of their fundamental properties than sight. What makes the eye so vastly superior to the organ of touch as an instrument of perception, is first of all the range of its action, taking in simultaneously a large number of impressions from objects at a distance as well as near; and secondly, though this may seem paradoxical, the fact that it gives us so much indirectly, that is, by way of association and suggestion. This is the interesting side of visual perception, that, owing to the vast complex of distinguishable sensations of light and colour of various qualities and intensities, together with the muscular sensations attending the varying positions of the organ, the eye is able to recognize at any instant a whole external world with its fundamental properties and relations. The ear comes next to the eye in this respect, but only after a long interval, since its sensations (even in the case of musical combinations) do not simultaneously order themselves in an indefinitely large group of distinguishable elements, and since even the comparatively few sensations which it is capable of simultaneously receiving, being altogether passive—that is to say, having no muscular accompaniments—impart but little and vague information respecting the external order. It is plain, then, that in the study of illusion, where the indirectly known elements are the thing to be considered, the eye, and after this the ear, will mostly engage our attention.[1]

[1] Touch gives much by way of interpretation only when an individual object, for example a man's hat, is recognized by aid of this sense alone, in which case the perception distinctly involves the reproduction of a complete visual percept. I may add that the organ of smell comes next to that of hearing, with respect both to the range and definiteness of its simultaneous sensations, and to the amount of information furnished by these. A rough sense of distance as well as of direction is clearly obtainable by means of this organ. There seems to me no reason why an animal endowed with fine olfactory sensibility, and capable of an analytic separation of sense-

So much it seemed needful to say about the mechanism of perception, in order to understand the slight disturbances of this mechanism that manifest themselves in sense-illusion. It may be added that our study of these illusions will help still further to elucidate the exact nature of perception. Normal mental life, as a whole, at once illustrates, and is illustrated by, abnormal. And while we need a rough provisional theory of accurate perception in order to explain illusory perception at all, the investigation of this latter cannot fail to verify and even render more complete the theory which it thus temporarily adopts.

Illusions of Perception.

With this brief psychological analysis of perception to help us, let us now pass to the consideration of the errors incident to the process, with a view to classify them according to their psychological nature and origin.

And here there naturally arises the question, How shall we define an illusion of perception? When trying to fix the definition of illusion in general, I practically disposed of this question. Nevertheless, as the point appears to me to be of some importance, I shall reproduce and expand one or two of the considerations then brought forward.

elements, should not gain a rough perception of an external order much more complete than our auditory perception, which is necessarily so fragmentary. This supposition appears, indeed, to be the necessary complement to the idea first broached, so far as I am aware, by Professor Croom Robertson, that to such animals, visual perception consists in a reference to a system of muscular feelings defined and bounded by strong olfactory sensations, rather than by tactual sensations as in our case.

It is said by certain philosophers that perception, as a whole, is an illusion, inasmuch as it involves the fiction of a real thing independent of mind, yet somehow present to it in the act of sense-perception. But this is a question for philosophy, not for science. Science, including psychology, assumes that in perception there is something real, without inquiring what it may consist of, or what its meaning may be. And though in the foregoing analysis of perception, viewed as a complex mental phenomenon or psychical process, I have argued that a percept gets its concrete filling up out of elements of conscious experience or sensations, I have been careful not to contend that the particular elements of feeling thus represented are the *object* of perception or the thing perceived. It may be that what we mean by a single object with its assemblage of qualities is much more than any number of such sensations; and it must be confessed that, on the face of it, it seems to be much more. And however this be, the question, What is meant by object; and is the common persuasion of the existence of such an entity in the act of perception accurate or illusory? must be handed over to philosophy.

While in the following examination of sense-illusions we put out of sight what certain philosophers say about the illusoriness of perception as a whole, we shall also do well to leave out of account what physical science is sometimes supposed to tell us respecting a constant element of illusion in perception. The physicist, by reducing all external changes to "modes of motion," appears to leave no room in his world-mechanism for the secondary qualities of bodies, such as light and heat, as popularly conceived. Yet, while allowing this, I think we may still regard the attribution of qualities like colour to objects as in the main correct and answering to a real fact. When a person says an object is red, he is understood by everybody as affirming something which is true or false, something therefore which either involves an external fact or is illusory. It would involve an external fact whenever the particular sensation which he receives is the result of a physical action (ether vibrations of a certain order), which would produce a like sensation in anybody else in the same situation and endowed with the normal retinal sensibility. On the other hand, an illusory attribution of colour would imply that there is no corresponding physical agency at work in the case, but that the sensation is connected with exceptional individual conditions, as, for example, altered retinal sensibility.

We are now, perhaps, in a position to frame a rough definition of an illusion of perception as popularly understood. A large number of such phenomena may be described as consisting in the formation of percepts or quasi-percepts in the minds of individuals under external circumstances which would not give rise to similar percepts in the case of other people.

A little consideration, however, will show that this is not an adequate definition of what is ordinarily understood by an illusion of sense. There are special circumstances which are fitted to excite a momentary illusion in all minds. The optical illusions due to the reflection and refraction of light are not peculiar to the individual, but arise in all minds under precisely similar external conditions.

It is plain that the illusoriness of a perception is in these cases determined in relation to the sense-impressions of other moments and situations, or to what are presumably better percepts than the present one. Sometimes this involves an appeal from one sense to another. Thus, there is the process of verification of sight by touch, for example, in the case of optical images, a mode of perception which, as we have seen, gives a more direct cognition of external quality. Conversely, there may occasionally be a reference from touch to sight, when it is a question of discriminating two points lying very close to one another. Finally, the same sense may correct itself, as when the illusion of the stereoscope is corrected by afterwards looking at the two separate pictures.

We may thus roughly define an illusion of perception as consisting in the formation of a quasi-percept which is peculiar to an individual, or which is contradicted by another and presumably more accurate percept. Or, if we take the meaning of the word common to include both the universal as contrasted with the individual experience, and the permanent, constant, or average, as distinguished from the momentary and variable percept, we may still briefly describe an illusion of perception as a deviation from the common or collective experience.

Sources of Sense-Illusion.

Understanding sense-illusion in this way, let us glance back at the process of perception in its several stages or aspects, with the object of discovering what room occurs for illusion.

It appears at first as if the preliminary stages—the reception, discrimination, and classification of an impression—would not offer the slightest opening for error. This part of the mechanism of perception seems to work so regularly and so smoothly that one can hardly conceive a fault in the process. Nevertheless, a little consideration will show that even here all does not go on with unerring precision.

Let us suppose that the very first step is wanting—distinct attention to an impression. It is easy to see that this will favour illusion by leading to a confusion of the impression. Thus the timid man will more readily fall into the illusion of ghost-seeing than a cool-headed observant man, because he is less attentive to the actual impression of the moment. This inattention to the sense-impression will be found to be a great co-operating factor in the production of illusions.

But if the sensation is properly attended to, can there be error through a misapprehension of what is actually in the mind at the moment? To say that there can may sound paradoxical, and yet in a sense this is demonstrable. I do not mean that there is an observant mind behind and distinct from the sensation, and failing to observe it accurately through a kind of mental short-sightedness. What I mean is that the usual psychical effect of the incoming nervous process may to some extent be counteracted by a powerful reaction of the centres. In the course of our study of illusions, we shall learn that it is possible for the quality of an impression, as, for example, of a sensation of colour, to be appreciably modified when there is a strong tendency to regard it in one particular way.

Postponing the consideration of these, we may say that certain illusions appear clearly to take their start from an error in the process of classifying or identifying a present impression. On the physical side, we may say that the first stages of the nervous process, the due excitation of the sensory centre in accordance with the form of the incoming stimulation and the central reaction involved in the recognition of the sensation, are incomplete. These are so limited and comparatively unimportant a class, that it will be well to dispose of them at once.

Confusion of the Sense-Impression.

The most interesting case of such an error is where the impression is unfamiliar and novel in character. I have already remarked that in the mental life of the adult perfectly new sensations never occur. At the same time, comparatively novel impressions sometimes arise. Parts of the sensitive surface of the body which rarely undergo stimulation are sometimes acted on, and at other times they receive partially new modes of stimulation. In such cases it is plain that the process of classing the sensation or recognizing it is not completed. It is found that whenever this happens there is a tendency to exaggerate the intensity of the sensation. The very fact of unfamiliarity seems to give to the sensation a certain exciting character. As something new and strange, it for the instant slightly agitates and discomposes the mind. Being unable to classify it with its like, we naturally magnify

its intensity, and so tend to ascribe it to a dispro-
portionately large cause.

For instance, a light bandage worn about the body
at a part usually free from pressure is liable to be
conceived as a weighty mass. The odd sense of a
big cavity in the mouth, which we experience just
after the loss of a tooth, is probably another illustration of this principle. And a third example may
also be supplied from the recollection of the dentist's
patient, namely, the absurd imagination which he
tends to form as to what is actually going on in his
mouth when a tooth is being bored by a modern
rotating drill. It may be found that the same principle helps to account for the exaggerated importance
which we attach to the impressions of our dreams.

It is evident that all indistinct impressions are
liable to be wrongly classed. Sensations answering to
a given colour or form, are, when faint, easily confused
with other sensations, and so an opening occurs for
illusion. Thus, the impressions received from distant
objects are frequently misinterpreted, and, as we shall
see by-and-by, it is in this region of hazy impression
that imagination is wont to play its most startling
pranks.

It is to be observed that the illusions arising from
wrong classification will be more frequent in the case
of those senses where discrimination is low. Thus, it
is much easier in a general way to confuse two
sensations of smell than two sensations of colour.
Hence the great source of such errors is to be found
in that mass of obscure sensation which is connected
with the organic processes, as digestion, respiration, etc.,

together with those varying tactual and motor feelings
which result from what is called the subjective stimulation of the tactual nerves, and from changes in the
position and condition of the muscles. Lying commonly in what is known as the sub-conscious region
of mind, undiscriminated, vague, and ill-defined, these
sensations, when they come to be specially attended to,
readily get misapprehended, and so lead to illusion,
both in waking life and in sleep. I shall have
occasion to illustrate this later on.

With these sensations, the result of stimulations
coming from remote parts of the organism, may be
classed the ocular impressions which we receive in
indirect vision. When the eye is not fixed on an
object, the impression, involving the activity of some
peripheral region of the retina, is comparatively indistinct. This will be much more the case when the object
lies at a distance for which the eye is not at the time
accommodated. And in these circumstances, when we
happen to turn our attention to the impression, we
easily misapprehend it, and so fall into illusion. Thus,
it has been remarked by Sir David Brewster, in his
Letters on Natural Magic (letter vii.), that when looking
through a window at some object beyond, we easily
suppose a fly on the window-pane to be a larger object,
as a bird, at a greater distance.[1]

---

[1] It may be said, perhaps, that the exceptional direction of attention,
by giving an unusual intensity to the impression, causes us to exaggerate it just as in the case of a novel sensation. An effort of attention
directed to any of our vague bodily sensations easily leads us to
magnify its cause. A similar confusion may arise even in direct
vision, when the objects are looked at in a dim light, through a want
of proper accommodation. (See Sir D. Brewster, *op. cit.*, letter i.)

While these cases of a confusion or a wrong classification of the sensation are pretty well made out, there are other illusions or quasi-illusions respecting which it is doubtful whether they should be brought under this head. For example, it was found by Weber, that when the legs of a pair of compasses are at a certain small distance apart they will be felt as two by some parts of the tactual surface of the body, but only as one by other parts. How are we to regard this discrepancy? Must we say that in the latter case there are two sensations, only that, being so similar, they are confused one with another? There seems some reason for so doing, in the fact that, by a repeated exercise of attention to the experiment, they may afterwards be recognized as two.

We here come on the puzzling question, How much in the character of the sensation must be regarded as the necessary result of the particular mode of nervous stimulation at the moment, together with the laws of sensibility, and how much must be put down to the reaction of the mind in the shape of attention and discrimination? For our present purpose we may say that, whenever a deliberate effort of attention does not suffice to alter the character of a sensation, this may be pretty safely regarded as a net result of the nervous process, and any error arising may be referred to the later stages of the process of perception. Thus, for example, the taking of the two points of a pair of compasses for one, where the closest attention does not discover the error, is best regarded as arising, not from a confusion of the sense-impression, but from a wrong interpretation of a sensation, occasioned by an overlooking of the limits of local discriminative sensibility.

Misinterpretation of the Sense-Impression.

Enough has been said, perhaps, about those errors of perception which have their root in the initial process of sensation. We may now pass to the far more important class of illusions which are related to the later stages of perception, that is to say, the process of interpreting the sense-impression. Speaking generally, one may describe an illusion of perception as a misinterpretation. The wrong kind of interpretative mental image gets combined with the impression, or, if with Helmholtz we regard perception as a process of "unconscious inference," we may say that these illusions involve an unconscious fallacious conclusion. Or, looking at the physical side of the operation, it may be said that the central course taken by the nervous process does not correspond to the external relations of the moment.

As soon as we inspect these illusions of interpretation, we see that they fall into two divisions, according as they are connected with the process of *suggestion*, that is to say, the formation of the interpretative image so far as determined by links of association with the actual impression, or with an independent process of *preperception* as explained above. Thus, for example, we fall into the illusion of hearing two voices when our shout is echoed back, just because the second auditory impression irresistibly calls up the image of a second shouter. On the other hand, a man experiences the illusion of seeing spectres of familiar objects just after exciting his imagination over a ghost-story, because the mind is strongly pre-disposed to frame this kind of percept. The first class of illusions arises from without, the sense-impression being the starting-point, and the process of preperception being controlled by this. The second class arises rather from within, from an independent or spontaneous activity of the imagination. In the one case the mind is comparatively passive ; in the other it is active, energetically reacting on the impression, and impatiently anticipating the result of the normal process of preperception. Hence I shall, for brevity's sake, commonly speak of them as Passive and Active Illusions.[1]

I may, perhaps, illustrate these two classes of illusion by the simile of an interpreter poring over an old manuscript. The first would be due to some peculiarity in the document misleading his judgment, the second to some caprice or preconceived notion in the interpreter's mind.

It is not difficult to define conjecturally the physiological conditions of these two large classes of illusion. On the physical side, an illusion of sense, like a just perception, is the result of a fusion of the nervous process answering to a sensation with a nervous process answering to a mental image. In the case of passive illusions, this fusion may be said to take place in consequence of some point of connection between the two. The existence of such a connection appears to be involved in the very fact of

---

[1] They might also be distinguished as objective and subjective illusions, or as illusions *a posteriori* and illusions *a priori*.

suggestion, and may be said to be the organic result of frequent conjunctions of the two parts of the nervous operation in our past history. In the case of active illusions, however, which spring rather from the independent energy of a particular mode of the imagination, this point of organic connection is not the only or even the main thing. In many cases, as we shall see, there is only a faint shade of resemblance between the present impression and the mental image with which it is overlaid. The illusions dependent on vivid expectation thus answer much less to an objective conjunction of past experiences than to a capricious subjective conjunction of mental images. Here, then, the fusion of nervous processes must have another cause. And it is not difficult to assign such a cause. The antecedent activity of imagination doubtless involves as its organic result a powerful temporary disposition in the nervous structures concerned to go on acting. In other words, they remain in a state of sub-excitation, which can be raised to full excitation by a slight additional force. The more powerful this disposition in the centres involved in the act of imagination, the less the additional force of external stimulus required to excite them to full activity.

Considering the first division, passive illusions, a little further, we shall see that they may be broken up into two sub-classes, according to the causes of the errors. In a general way we assume that the impression always answers to some quality of the object which is perceived, and varies with this; that, for example, our sensation of colour invariably represents the quality of external colour which we attribute to the object.

Or, to express it physically, we assume that the external force acting on the sense-organ invariably produces the same effect, and that the effect always varies with the external cause. But this assumption, though true in the main, is not perfectly correct. It supposes that the organic conditions are constant, and that the organic process faithfully reflects the external operation. Neither of these suppositions is strictly true. Although in general we may abstract from the organism and view the relation between the external fact and the mental impression as direct, we cannot always do so.

This being so, it is possible for errors of perception to arise through peculiarities of the nervous organization itself. Thus, as I have just observed, sensibility has its limits, and these limits are the starting-point in a certain class of widely shared or *common* illusions. An example of this variety is the taking of the two points of a pair of compasses for one by the hand, already referred to. Again, the condition of the nervous structures varies indefinitely, so that one and the same stimulus may, in the case of two individuals, or of the same individual at different times, produce widely unlike modes of sensation. Such variations are clearly fitted to lead to gross *individual* errors as to the external cause of the sensation. Of this sort is the illusory sense of temperature which we often experience through a special state of the organ employed.

While there are these errors of interpretation due to some peculiarity of the organization, there are others which involve no such peculiarity, but arise through the special character or exceptional conformation of the environment at the moment. Of this order are the illusions connected with the reflection of light and sound. We may, perhaps, distinguish the first sub-class as organically conditioned illusions, and the second as extra-organically determined illusions. It may be added that the latter are roughly describable as common illusions. They thus answer in a measure to the first variety of organically conditioned illusions, namely, those connected with the limits of sensibility. On the other hand, the active illusions, being essentially individual or subjective, may be said to correspond to the other variety of this class—those connected with variations of sensibility.

Our scheme of sense-illusions is now complete. First of all, we shall take up the passive illusions, beginning with those which are conditioned by special circumstances in the organism. After that we shall illustrate those which depend on peculiar circumstances in the environment. And finally, we shall separately consider what I have called the active illusions of sense.

It is to be observed that these illusions of perception properly so called, namely, the errors arising from a wrong interpretation of an impression, and, not from a confusion of one impression with another are chiefly illustrated in the region of the two higher senses, sight and hearing. For it is here, as we have seen, that the interpretative imagination has most work to do in evolving complete percepts of material, tangible objects, having certain relations in space, out of a limited and homogeneous class of sensations, namely, those of light and colour, and of sound. As I have before observed, tactual perception, in so far as it is the recognition of an object of a certain size, hardness, and distance from our body, involves the least degree of interpretation, and so offers little room for error; it is only when tactual perception amounts to the *recognition* of an individual object, clothed with secondary as well as primary qualities, that an opening for palpable error occurs.

With respect, however, to the first sub-class of these illusions, namely, those arising from organic peculiarities which give a twist, so to speak, to the sensation, no very marked contrast between the different senses presents itself. So that in illustrating this group we shall be pretty equally concerned with the various modes of perception connected with the different senses.

It may be said once for all that in thus marking off from one another certain groups of illusion, I am not unmindful of the fact that these divisions answer to no very sharp natural distinctions. In fact, it will be found that one class gradually passes into the other, and that the different characteristics here separated often combine in a most perplexing way. All that is claimed for this classification is that it is a convenient mode of mapping out the subject.

CHAPTER IV.

A. *Passive Illusions (a) as determined by the Organism.*

IN dealing with the illusions which are related to certain peculiarities in the nervous organism and the laws of sensibility, I shall commence with those which are connected with certain limits of sensibility.

Limits of Sensibility.

To begin with, it is known that the sensation does not always answer to the external stimulus in its degree or intensity. Thus, a certain amount of stimulation is necessary before any sensation arises. And this will, of course, be greater when there is little or no attention directed to the impression, that is to say, no co-operating central reaction. Thus it happens that slight stimuli go overlooked, and here illusion may have its starting-point. The most familiar example of such slight errors is that of movement. When we are looking at objects, our ocular muscles are apt to execute very slight movements which escape our notice. Hence we tend, under certain circumstances, to carry over the retinal result of the movement, that is to say, the impression produced by a shifting of the parts of the retinal image to new nervous elements, to the object itself, and so to transform a "subjective" into an "objective" movement. In a very interesting work on apparent or illusory movements, Professor Hoppe has fully investigated the facts of such slight movements, and endeavoured to specify their causes.[1]

Again, even when the stimulus is sufficient to produce a conscious impression, the degree of the feeling may not represent the degree of the stimulus. To take a very inconspicuous case, it is found by Fechner that a given increase of force in the stimulus produces a less amount of difference in the resulting sensations when the original stimulus is a powerful one than when it is a feeble one. It follows from this, that differences in the degree of our sensations do not exactly correspond to objective differences. For example, we tend to magnify the differences of light among objects, all of which are feebly illuminated, that is to say, to see them much more removed from one another in point of brightness than when they are more strongly illuminated. Helmholtz relates that, owing to this tendency, he has occasionally caught himself, on a dark night, entertaining the illusion that

<hr>

[1] *Die Schein-Bewegungen*, von Professor Dr. J. I. Hoppe (1879); *cf.* an ingenious article on "Optical Illusions of Motion," by Professor Silvanus P. Thompson, in *Brain*, October, 1880. These illusions frequently involve the co-operation of some preconception or expectation. For example, the apparent movement of a train when we are watching it and expecting it to move, involves both an element of sense-impression and of imagination. It is possible that the illusion of table-turning rests on the same basis, the table-turner being unaware of the fact of exerting a certain amount of muscular force, and vividly expecting a movement of the object.

the comparatively bright objects visible in twilight were self-luminous.[1]

Again, there are limits to the conscious separation of sensations which are received together, and this fact gives rise to illusion. In general, the number of distinguishable sensations answers to the number of external causes; but this is not always the case, and here we naturally fall into the error of mistaking the number of the stimuli. Reference has already been made to this fact in connection with the question whether consciousness can be mistaken as to the character of a present feeling.

The case of confusing two impressions when the sensory fibres involved are very near one another, has already been alluded to. Both in touch and in sight we always take two or more points for one when they are only separated by an interval that falls below the limits of local discrimination. It seems to follow from this that our perception of the world as a continuum, made up of points perfectly continuous one with another may, for what we know, be illusory. Supposing the universe to consist of atoms separated by very fine intervals, then it is demonstrable that it would appear to our sensibility as a continuum, just as it does now.[2]

Two or more simultaneous sensations are indis-

---

[1] *Physiologische Optik*, p. 316.

[2] It is plain that this supposed error could only be brought under our definition of illusion by extending the latter, so as to include sense-perceptions which are contradicted by reason employing idealized elements of sense-impression, which, as Lewes has shown (*Problems of Life and Mind*, i. p. 260), make up the "extra-sensible world" of science.

tinguishable from one another, not only when they have nearly the same local origin, but under other circumstances. The blending of partial sensations of tone in a *klang*-sensation, and the coalescence in certain cases of the impressions received by way of the two retinas, are examples of this. It is not quite certain what determines this fusion of two simultaneous feelings. It may be said generally that it is favoured by similarity between the sensations; [1] by a comparative feebleness of one of the feelings; by the fact of habitual concomitance, the two sensations occurring rarely, if ever, in isolation; and by the presence of a mental disposition to view them as answering to one external object. These considerations help us to explain the coalescence of the retinal impressions and its limits, the fusion of partial tones, and so on. [2]

It is plain that this fusion of sensations, whatever its exact conditions may be, gives rise to error or wrong interpretation of the sense-impression. Thus, to take the points of two legs of a pair of compasses for one point is clearly an illusion of perception. Here is another and less familiar example. Very cold and smooth surfaces, as those of metal, often appear to be wet. I never feel sure, after wiping the blades of my skates, that they are perfectly dry, since they always

[1] An ingenious writer, M. Binet, has tried to prove that the fusion of homogeneous sensations, having little difference of local colour, is an illustration of this principle. (See the *Revue Philosophique*, September, 1880.)

[2] Even the fusion of elementary sensations of colour, on the hypothesis of Young and Helmholtz, in a seemingly simple sensation may be explained to some extent by these circumstances, more especially the identity of local interpretation.

seem more or less damp to my hand. What is the reason of this? Helmholtz explains the phenomenon by saying that the feeling we call by the name of wetness is a compound sensation consisting of one of temperature and one of touch proper. These sensations occurring together so frequently, blend into one, and so we infer, according to the general instinctive tendency already noticed, that there is one specific quality answering to the feeling. And since the feeling is nearly always produced by surfaces moistened by cold liquid, we refer it to this circumstance, and speak of it as a feeling of wetness. Hence, when the particular conjunction of sensations arises apart from this external circumstance, we erroneously infer its presence.[1]

The most interesting case of illusion connected with the fusion of simultaneous sensations is that of single vision, or the deeply organized habit of combining the sensations of what are called the corresponding points of the two retinas. This coalescence of two sensations is so far erroneous since it makes us overlook the existence of two distinct external agencies acting on different parts of the sensitive surface of the body. And this is the more striking in the case of

---

[1] The perception of lustre as a single quality seems to illustrate a like error. There is good reason to suppose that this impression arises through a difference of brightness in the two retinal images due to the regularly reflected light. And so when this inequality of retinal impression is imitated, as it may easily be by combining a black and a white surface in a stereoscope, we imagine that we are looking at one lustrous surface. (See Helmholtz, *Physiologische Optik*, p. 782, etc., and *Populäre wissenschaftliche Vorträge*, 2tes Heft, p. 80.)

looking at solid objects, since here it is demonstrable that the forces acting on the two retinas are not perfectly similar. Nevertheless, such a coalescence plainly answers to the fact that these external agencies usually arise in one and the same object, and this unity of the object is, of course, the all-important thing to be sure of.

This habit may, however, beget palpable illusion in another way. In certain exceptional cases the coalescence does not take place, as when I look at a distant object and hold a pencil just before my eyes.[1] And in this case the organized tendency to take one visual impression for one object asserts its force, and I tend to fall into the illusion of seeing two separate pencils. If I do not wholly lapse into the error, it is because my experience has made me vaguely aware that double images under these circumstances answer to one object, and that if there were really two pencils present I should have four visual impressions.

Once more, it is a law of sensory stimulation that an impression persists for an appreciable time after the cessation of the action of the stimulus. This "after sensation" will clearly lead to illusion, in so far as we tend to think of the stimulus as still at work. It forms, indeed, as will be seen by-and-by, the simplest and lowest stage of hallucination. Sometimes this becomes the first stage of a palpable error. After listening to a child crying for some time the ear

---

[1] The conditions of the production of these double images have been accurately determined by Helmholtz, who shows that the coalescence of impressions takes place whenever the object is so situated in the field of vision as to make it practically necessary that it should be recognized as one.

easily deceives itself into supposing that the noise is continued when it has actually ceased. Again, after taking a bandage from a finger, the tingling and other sensations due to the pressure sometimes persist for a good time, in which case they easily give rise to an illusion that the finger is still bound.

It follows from this fact of the reverberation of the nervous structures after the removal of a stimulus, that whenever two discontinuous stimulations follow one another rapidly enough, they will appear continuous. This fact is a fruitful source of optical illusion. The appearance of a blending of the stripes of colours on a rotating disc or top, of the formation of a ring of light by swinging round a piece of burning wood, and the illusion of the toy known as the thaumatrope, or wheel of life, all depend on this persistence of retinal impression. Many of the startling effects of sleight of hand are undoubtedly due in part to this principle. If two successive actions or sets of circumstances to which the attention of the spectator is specially directed follow one another by a very narrow interval of time, they easily appear continuous, so that there seems absolutely no time for the introduction of an intermediate step.[1]

There is another limit to sensibility which is in a manner the opposite to the one just named. It is a

---

[1] These illusions are, of course, due in part to inattention, since close critical scrutiny is often sufficient to dispel them. They are also largely promoted by a preconception that the event is going to happen in a particular way. But of this more further on. I may add that the late Professor Clifford has argued ingeniously against the idea of the world being a continuum, by extending this idea of the wheel of life. (See *Lectures and Essays*, i. p. 112, *et seq.*)

law of nervous stimulation that a continued activity of any structure results in less and less psychic result, and that when a stimulus is always at work it ceases in time to have any appreciable effect. The common illustration of this law is drawn from the region of sound. A constant noise, as of a mill, ceases to produce any conscious sensation. This fact, it is plain, may easily become the commencement of an illusion. Not only may we mistake a measure of noise for perfect silence,[1] we may misconceive the real nature of external circumstances by overlooking some continuous impression.

Curious illustrations of this effect are found in optical illusions, namely, the errors we make respecting the movement of stationary objects after continued movement of the eyes. When, for example, in a railway carriage we have for some time been following the (apparent) movement of objects, as trees, etc., and turn our eyes to an apparently stationary object, as the carpet of the compartment, this seems to move in the contrary direction to that of the trees. Helmholtz's explanation of this illusion is that when we suppose that we are fixing our eye on the carpet we are really continuing to move it over the surface by reason of the organic tendency, already spoken of, to go on doing anything that has been done. But since we are unaware of this prolonged series of ocular movements, the muscular feelings having become faint, we take the impression produced by the sliding of the

---

[1] It is supposed that in the case of every sense-organ there is always some minimum forces of stimulus at work, the effect of which on our consciousness is *nil*.

picture over the retina to be the result of a movement of the object.[1]

Another limit to our sensibility, which needs to be just touched on here, is known by the name of the specific energy of the nerves. One and the same nerve-fibre always reacts in a precisely similar way, whatever the nature of the stimulus. Thus, when the optic nerve is stimulated in any manner, whether by light, mechanical pressure, or an electric current, the same effect, a sensation of light, follows.[2] In a usual way, a given class of nerve-fibre is only stimulated by one kind of stimulus. Thus, the retina, in ordinary circumstances, is stimulated by light. Owing to this fact, there has arisen a deeply organized habit of translating the impression in one particular way. Thus, I instinctively regard a sensation received by means of the optic nerve as one caused by light.

Accordingly, whenever circumstances arise in which a like sensation is produced by another kind of stimulus, we fall into illusion. The phosphenes, or circles of light which are seen when the hinder part of the eye-

[1] See Helmholtz, *Physiologische Optik*, p. 603. Helmholtz's explanation is criticised by Dr. Hoppe, in the work already referred to (sec. vii.), though I cannot see that his own theory of these movements is essentially different. The apparent movement of objects in vertigo, or giddiness, is probably due to the loss, through a physical cause, of the impressions made by the pressure of the fluid contents of the ear on the auditory fibres, by which the sense of equilibrium and of rotation is usually received. (See Ferrier, *Functions of the Brain*, pp. 60, 61.)

[2] I do not need here to go into the question whether, as Johannes Müller assumed, this is an original attribute of nerve-structure, or whether, as Wundt suggests, it is due simply to the fact that certain kinds of nervous fibre have, in the course of evolution, been slowly adapted to one kind of stimulus.

ball is pressed, may be said to be illusory in so far as we speak of them as perceptions of light, thus referring them to the external physical agency which usually causes them. The same remark applies to those "subjective sensations," as they are called, which are known to have as their physical cause subjective stimuli, consisting, in the case of sight, in varying conditions of the peripheral organ, as increased blood-pressure. Strictly speaking, such simple feelings as these appear to be, involve an ingredient of false perception : in saying that we *perceive* light at all, we go beyond the pure sensation, interpreting this wrongly.

Very closely connected with this limitation of our sensibility is another which refers to the consciousness of the local seat, or origin of the impression. This has so far its basis in the sensation itself as it is well known that (within the limits of local discrimination, referred to above) sensations have a particular "local" colour, which varies in the case of each of the nervous fibres by the stimulation of which they arise.[1] But though this much is known through a difference in the sensibility, nothing more is known. Nothing can certainly be ascertained by a mere inspection of the sensation as to the distance the nervous process has travelled, whether from the peripheral termination of the fibre or from some intermediate point.

In a general way, we refer our sensations to the peripheral endings of the nerves concerned, according to what physiologists have called " the law of eccen-

---

[1] I here refer to what is commonly supposed to be the vague innate difference of sensation according to the local origin, before this is rendered precise, and added to by experience and association.

tricity." Thus I am said to feel the pain caused by a bruise in the foot in the member itself. This applies also to some of the sensations of the special senses. Thus, impressions of taste are clearly localized in the corresponding peripheral terminations.

With respect to the sense of smell, and still more to those of hearing and sight, where the impression is usually caused by an object at a distance from the peripheral organ, our attention to this external cause leads us to overlook in part the " bodily seat " of the sensation. Yet even here we are dimly aware that the sensation is received by way of a particular part of the sensitive surface, that is to say, by a particular sense-organ. Thus, though referring an odour to a distant flower, we perceive that the sensation of odour has its bodily origin in the nose. And even in the case of hearing and sight, we vaguely refer the impressions, as such, to the appropriate sense-organ. There is, indeed, in these cases a double local reference, a faint one to the peripheral organ which is acted on, and a more distinct one to the object or the force in the environment which acts on this.

Now, it may be said that the act of localization is in itself distinctly illusory, since it is known that the sensation first arises in connection with the excitation of the sensory *centre*, and not of the peripheral fibre.[1]

---

[1] The illusory character of this simple mode of perception is seen best, perhaps, in the curious habit into which we fall of referring a sensation of contact or discomfort to the edge of the teeth, the hair, and the other insentient structures, and even to anything customarily attached to the sentient surface, as dress, a pen, graving tool, etc. On these curious illusions, see Lotze, *Mikrokosmus*, third edit., vol. ii. p. 202, etc. ; Taine, *De l'Intelligence*, tom. ii. p. 83. *et seq.*

Yet it must at least be allowed that this localization of sensation answers to the important fact that, under usual circumstances, the agency producing the sensation is applied at this particular point of the organism, the knowledge of which point is supposed by modern psychologists to have been very slowly learnt by the individual and the race, through countless experiments with the moving organ of touch, assisted by the eye.

Similarly, the reference of the impression, in the case of hearing and sight, to an object in the environment, though, as we have seen, from one point of view illusory, clearly answers to a fact of our habitual experience; for in an immense preponderance of cases at least a visual or auditory impression does arise through the action on the sense-organ of a force (ether or air waves) proceeding from a distant object.

In some circumstances, however, even this element of practical truth disappears, and the localization of the impression, both within and without the organism, becomes altogether illusory. This result is involved in the illusions, already spoken of, which arise from the instinctive tendency to refer sensations to the ordinary kind of stimulus. Thus, when a feeling resulting from a disturbance in the optic nerve is interpreted as one of external light vaguely felt to be acting on the eye, or one resulting from some action set up in the auditory fibre as a sensation of external sound vaguely felt to be entering the ear, we see that the error of localization is a consequence of the other error already characterized.

As I have already observed, an excitation of a nerve at any other point than the peripheral termination, occurs but rarely in normal life. One familiar instance is the stimulation of the nerve running to the hand and fingers, by a sharp blow on the elbow over which it passes. As everybody knows, this gives rise to a sense of pain at the *extremities* of the nerve. The most common illustration of such errors of localization is found in subjective sensations, such as the impression we sometimes have of something creeping over the skin, of a disagreeable taste in the mouth, of luminous spots floating across the field of vision, and so on. The exact physiological seat of these is often a matter of conjecture only; yet it may safely be said that in many instances the nervous excitation originates at some point considerably short of its peripheral extremity : in which case there occurs the illusion of referring the impressions to the peripheral sense-organ, and to an external force acting on this.

The most striking instances of these errors of localization are found in abnormal circumstances. It is well known that a man who has lost a leg refers all sensations arising from a stimulation of the truncated fibres to his lost foot, and in some cases has even to convince himself of the non-existence of his lost member by sight or touch. Patients often describe these experiences in very odd language. "If," says one of Dr. Weir Mitchell's patients, "I should say I am more sure of the leg which ain't than the one which air, I guess I should be about correct."[1]

---

[1] Quoted by G. H. Lewes, *Problems of Life and Mind*, third series, p. 335. These illusions are supposed to involve an excitation of the nerve-fibres (whether sensory or motor) which run to the muscles and yield the so-called muscular sensations.

There is good reason for supposing that this source of error plays a prominent part in the illusions of the insane. Diseased centres may be accompanied by disordered peripheral structures, and so subjective sensation may frequently be the starting-point of the wildest illusions. Thus, a patient's horror of poison may have its first origin in some subjective gustatory sensation. Similarly, subjective tactual sensations may give rise to gross illusions, as when a patient "feels" his body attacked by foul and destructive creatures.

It may be well to remark that this mistaken interpretation of the seat or origin of subjective sensation is closely related to hallucination. In so far as the error involves the ascription of the sensation to a force external to the sense-organ, this part of the mental process must, when there is no such force present, be viewed as hallucinatory. Thus, the feeling of something creeping over the skin is an hallucination in the sense that it implies the idea of an object external to the skin. Similarly, the projection of an ocular impression due to retinal disturbance into the external field of vision, may rightly be named an hallucination. But the case is not always so clear as this. Thus, for example, when a gustatory sensation is the result of an altered condition of the saliva, it may be said that the error is as much an illusion as an hallucination.[1]

In a wide sense, again, all errors connected with

---

[1] It is brought out by Griesinger (*loc. cit.*) and the other writers on the pathology of illusion already quoted, that in the case of subjective sensations of touch, taste, and smell, no sharp line can be drawn between illusion and hallucination.

those subjective sensations which arise from a stimulation of the peripheral regions of the nerve may be called illusions rather than hallucinations. Or, if they must be called hallucinations, they may be distinguished as " peripheral " from those " central " hallucinations which arise through an internal automatic excitation of the sensory centre. It is plain from this that the region of subjective sensation is an ambiguous region, where illusion and hallucination mix and become confused. To this point I shall have occasion to return by-and-by.

I have now probably said enough respecting the illusions that arise through the fact of there being fixed limits to our sensibility. The *rationale* of these illusions is that whenever the limit is reached, we tend to ignore it and to interpret the impression in the customary way.

Variations of Sensibility.

We will now pass to a number of illusions which depend on something variable in the condition of our sensibility, or some more or less exceptional organic circumstance. These variations may be momentary and transient or comparatively permanent. The illusion arises in each case from our ignoring the variation, and treating a given sensation under all circumstances as answering to one objective cause.

First of all, the variation of organic state may affect our mental representation of the strength of the stimulus or external cause. Here the fluctuation may be a temporary or a permanent one. The first case is illustrated in the familiar example of taking a room to be brighter than it is when emerging from a dark one. Another striking example is that of our sense of the temperature of objects, which is known to be strictly relative to a previous sensation, or more correctly to the momentary condition of the organ. Yet, though every intelligent person knows this, the deeply rooted habit of making sensation the measure of objective quality asserts its sway, and frequently leads us into illusion. The well-known experiment of first plunging one hand in cold water, the other in hot, and then dipping them both in tepid, is a startling example of this organized tendency. For here we are strongly disposed to accept the palpable contradiction that the same water is at once warm and cool.

Far more important than these temporary fluctuations of sensibility are the permanent alterations. Excessive fatigue, want of proper nutrition, and certain poisons are well known to be causes of such changes. They appear most commonly under two forms, exalted sensibility, or hyperæsthesia, and depressed sensibility, or anæsthesia. In these conditions flagrant errors are made as to the real magnitude of the causes of the sensations. These variations may occur in normal life to some extent. In fairly good health we experience at times strange exaltations of tactual sensibility, so that a very slight stimulus, such as the contact of the bed-clothes, becomes greatly exaggerated.

In diseased states of the nervous system these variations of sensibility become much more striking. The patient who has hyperæsthesia fears to touch a perfectly smooth surface, or he takes a knock at the door to be a clap of thunder. The hypochondriac may, through an increase of organic sensibility, translate organic sensations as the effect of some living creature gnawing at his vitals. Again, states of anæsthesia lead to odd illusions among the insane. The common supposition that the body is dead, or made of wood or of glass, is clearly referable in part to lowered sensibility of the organism.[1]

It is worth adding, perhaps, that these variations in sensibility give rise not only to sensory but also to motor illusions. To take a homely instance, the last miles of a long walk seem much longer than the first, not only because the sense of fatigue leading us to dwell on the transition of time tends to magnify the apparent duration, but because the fatigued muscles and connected nerves yield a new set of sensations which constitute an exaggerated standard of measurement. A number of optical illusions illustrate the same thing. Our visual sense of direction is determined in part by the feelings accompanying the action of the ocular muscles, and so is closely connected with the perception of movement, which has already been touched on. If an ocular muscle is partially paralyzed it takes a much greater " effort " to effect a given extent of movement than when the muscle is sound. Hence any movement performed by the eye seems exaggerated. Hence, too, in this condition objects are seen in a wrong direction; for the patient reasons that they are where they would seem to be if he had executed a wider movement than he really has. This may easily be proved by asking him to try to seize

---

[1] For a fuller account of these pathological disturbances of sensibility, see Griesinger; also Dr. A. Mayer, *Die Sinnestäuschungen.*

the object with his hand. The effect is exaggerated when complete paralysis sets in, and no actual movement occurs in obedience to the impulse from within.[1]

Variations in the condition of the nerve affect not only the degree, but also the quality of the sensation, and this fact gives rise to a new kind of illusion. The curious phenomena of colour-contrast illustrate momentary alterations of sensibility. When, after looking at a green colour for a time, I turn my eye to a grey surface and see this of the complementary rose-red hue, the effect is supposed to be due to a temporary fatigue of the retina in relation to those ingredients of the total light in the second case which answer to the partial light in the first (the green rays).[2]

These momentary modifications of sensibility are

---

[1] Helmholtz, *op. cit.*, p. 600, *et seq.* These facts seem to point to the conclusion that at least some of the feelings by which we know that we are expending muscular energy are connected with the initial stage of the outgoing nervous process in the motor centres. In other pathological conditions the sense of weight by the muscles of the arms is similarly confused.

[2] Wundt (*Physiologische Psychologie*, p. 653) would exclude from illusions all those errors of sense-perception which have their foundation in the normal structure and function of the organs of sense. Thus, he would exclude the effects of colour-contrast, *e.g.* the apparent modification of two colours in juxtaposition towards their common boundary, which probably arises (according to E. Hering) from some mutual influence of the temporary state of activity of adjacent retinal elements. To me, however, these appear to be illusions, since they may be brought under the head of wrong *interpretations* of sense-impressions. When we see a grey patch as rose-red, as though it were so independently of the action of the complementary light previously or simultaneously, that is to say, as though it would appear rose-red to an eye independently of this action, we surely misinterpret.

of no practical significance, being almost instantly corrected. Other modifications are more permanent. It was found by Himly that when the retina is over-excitable every stimulus is raised in the spectrum scale of colours. Thus, violet becomes red. An exactly opposite effect is observed when the retina is torpid.[1] Certain poisons are known to affect the quality of the colour-impression. Thus, santonin, when taken in any quantity, makes all colourless objects look yellow. Severe pathological disturbances are known to involve, in addition to hyperæsthesia and anæsthesia, what has been called paræsthesia, that is to say, that condition in which the quality of sensation is greatly changed. Thus, for example, to one in this state all food appears to have a metallic taste, and so on.

If we now glance back at the various groups of illusions just illustrated, we find that they all have this feature in common : they depend on the general mental law that when we have to do with the unfrequent, the unimportant, and therefore unattended to, and the exceptional, we employ the ordinary, the familiar, and the well-known as our standard. Thus, whether we are dealing with sensations that fall below the ordinary limits of our mental experience, or with those which arise in some exceptional state of the organism, we carry the habits formed in the much wider region of average every-day perception with us. In a word, illusion in these cases always arises through what may, figuratively at least, be described as the application of a rule, valid for the majority of cases, to an exceptional case.

[1] Quoted by G. H. Lewes, *loc. cit.*, p. 257.

In the varieties of illusion just considered, the circumstance that gives the peculiarity to the case thus wrongly interpreted has been referred to the organism. In the illusions to which we now pass, it will be referred to the environment. At the same time, it is plain that there is no very sharp distinction between the two classes. Thus, the visual illusion produced by pressing the eyeball might be regarded not only as the result of the organic law of the " specific energy " of the nerves, but, with almost equal appropriateness, as the consequence of an exceptional state of things in the environment, namely, the pressure of a body on the retina. As I have already observed, the classification here adopted is to be viewed simply as a rough expedient for securing something like a systematic review of the phenomena.

CHAPTER V.

ILLUSIONS OF PERCEPTION—*continued.*

A. *Passive Illusions (b) as determined by the Environment.*

In the following groups of illusion we may look away from nervous processes and organic disturbances, regarding the effect of any external stimulus as characteristic, that is, as clearly marked off from the effects of other stimuli, and as constant for the same stimulus. The source of the illusion will be looked for in something exceptional in the external circumstances, whereby one object or condition of an object imitates the effect of another object or condition, to which, owing to a large preponderance of experience, we at once refer it.

Exceptional Relation of Stimulus to Organ.

A transition from the preceding to the following class of illusions is to be met with in those errors which arise from a very exceptional relation between the stimulus and the organ of sense. Such a state of things is naturally interpreted by help of more common and familiar relations, and so error arises.

For example, we may grossly misinterpret the intensity of a stimulus under certain circumstances. Thus, when a man crunches a biscuit, he has an uncomfortable feeling that the noise as of all the structures of his head being violently smashed is the same to other ears, and he may even act on his illusory perception, by keeping at a respectful distance from all observers. And even though he be a physiologist, and knows that the force of sensation in this case is due to the propagation of vibrations to the auditory centre by other channels than the usual one of the ear, the deeply organized impulse to measure the strength of an external stimulus by the intensity of the sensation asserts its force.

Again, if we turn to the process of perceptional construction properly so called, the reference of the sensation to a material object lying in a certain direction, etc., we find a similar transitional form of illusion. The most interesting case of this in visual perception is that of a disturbance or displacement of the organ by external force. For example, an illusory sense of direction arises by the simple action of closing one eye, say the left, and pressing the other eyeball with one of the fingers a little outwards, that is to the right. The result of this movement is, of course, to transfer the retinal picture to new nervous elements further to the right. And since, in this instance, the displacement is not produced in the ordinary way by the activity of the ocular muscle making itself known by certain feelings of movement, it is disregarded altogether, and the direction of the objects is judged as though the eye were stationary.

A somewhat similar illusion as to direction occurs in auditory perception. The sense of direction by the ear is known to be due in part to the action of the auricle, or projecting part of the ear. This collects the air-waves, and so adds to the intensity of the sounds, especially those coming from in front, and thus assists in the estimation of direction. This being so, if an artificial auricle is placed in front of the ears; if, for example, the two hands are each bent into a sort of auricle, and placed in front of the ears, the back of the hand being in front, the sense of direction (as well as of distance) is confused. Thus, sounds really travelling from a point in front of the head will appear to come from behind it.

Again, the perception of the unity of an object is liable to be falsified by the introduction of exceptional circumstances into the sense-organ. This is illustrated in the well-known experiment of crossing two fingers, say the third and fourth, and placing a marble or other small round object between them. Under ordinary circumstances, the two lateral surfaces (that is, the outer surfaces of the two fingers) now pressed by the marble, can only be acted on simultaneously by *two* objects having convex surfaces. Consequently, we cannot help feeling the presence of two objects in this exceptional instance. The illusion is analogous to that of the stereoscope, to be spoken of presently.

Exceptional External Arrangements.

Passing now to those cases where the exceptional circumstance is altogether exterior to the organ, we find a familiar example in the illusions connected with

the action of well-known physical forces, as the refraction of light, and the reflection of light and
sound. A stick half-immersed in water always *looks*
broken, however well we may know that the appearance is due to the bending of the rays of light.
Similarly, an echo always sounds as though it came
from some object in the direction in which the air-
waves finally travel to the ear, though we are perfectly
sure that these undulations have taken a circuitous
course. It is hardly necessary to remind the reader
that the deeply organized tendency to mistake the
direction of the visible or audible object in these cases
has from remote ages been made use of as a means of
popular delusion. Thus, we are told by Sir D. Brewster,
in his entertaining *Letters on Natural Magic* (letter
iv.), that the concave mirror was probably used as the
instrument for bringing the gods before the people.
The throwing of the images formed by such mirrors
upon smoke or against fire, so as to make them more
distinct, seems to have been a favourite device in the
ancient art of necromancy.

Closely connected with these illusions of direction
with respect to resting objects, are those into which we
are apt to fall respecting the movements of objects.
What looks like the movement of something across
the field of vision is made known to us either by the
feeling of the ocular muscles, if the eye follows the
object, or through the sequence of locally distinct
retinal impressions, if the eye is stationary. Now,
either of these effects may result, not only from the
actual movement of the object in a particular direction, but from our own movement in an opposite

direction; or, again, from our both moving in the first direction, the object more rapidly than ourselves; or, finally, from our both moving in an opposite direction to this, ourselves more rapidly than the object. There is thus always a variety of conceivable explanations, and the action of past experience and association shows itself very plainly in the determination of the direction of interpretation. Thus, it is our instinctive tendency to take apparent movement for real movement, except when the fact of our own movement·is clearly present to consciousness, as when we are walking, or when we are sitting behind a horse whose movement we see. And so when the sense of our own movement becomes indistinct, as in a railway carriage, we naturally drift into the illusion that objects, such as trees, telegraph posts, and so on, are moving, when they are perfectly still. Under the same circumstances, we are apt to suppose that a train which is just shooting ahead of us is moving slowly.

Similar uncertainties arise with respect to the relative movement of two objects, the eye being supposed to be fixed in space. When two objects seem to pass one another, it may be that they are both moving in contrary directions, or that one only is moving, or finally, that both are moving in the same direction, the one faster than the other. Experience and habit here again suggest the interpretation which is most easy, and not unfrequently produce illusion. Thus, when we watch clouds scudding over the face of the moon, the latter seems moving rather than the former, and the illusion only disappears when we fix the eye on the moon and recognize that it is really stationary. The probable reason of this is, as Wundt suggests, that experience has made it far easier for us to think of small objects like the moon moving rapidly, than of large masses like the clouds.[1]

The perception of distance, still more than that of direction, is liable to be illusory. Indeed, the visual recognition of distance, together with that of solidity, has been the great region for the study of " the deceptions of the senses." Without treating the subject fully here, I shall try to describe briefly the nature and source of these illusions.[2]

Confining ourselves first of all to near objects, we know that the smaller differences of distance in these cases are, if the eyes are at rest, perceived by means of the dissimilar pictures projected on the two retinas; or if they move, by this means, together with the muscular feelings that accompany different degrees of convergence of the two eyes. This was demonstrated by the famous experiments of Wheatstone. Thus, by means of the now familiar stereoscope, he was able to produce a perfect illusion of relief. The stereoscope may be

---

[1] The subject of the perception of movement is too intricate to be dealt with fully here. I have only touched on it so far as necessary to illustrate our general principle. For a fuller treatment of the subject, see the work of Dr. Hoppe, already referred to.

[2] The perception of magnitude is closely connected with that of distance, and is similarly apt to take an illusory form. I need only refer to the well-known simple optical contrivances for increasing the apparent magnitude of objects. I ought, perhaps, to add that I do not profess to give a complete account of optical illusions here, but only to select a few prominent varieties, with a view to illustrate general principles of illusion. For a fuller account of the various mechanical arrangements for producing optical illusion, I must refer the reader to the writings of Sir D. Brewster and Helmholtz.

said to introduce an exceptional state of things into the spectator's environment. It imitates, by means of two flat drawings, the dissimilar retinal pictures projected by a single solid receding object, and the lenses through which the eyes look are so constructed as to compel them to converge as though looking on a single object. And so powerful is the tendency to interpret this impression as one of solidity, that even though we are aware of the presence of the stereoscopic apparatus, we cannot help seeing the two drawings as a single solid object.

In the case of more remote objects, there is no dissimilarity of the retinal pictures or feelings of convergence to assist the eye in determining distance. Here its judgment, which now becomes more of a process of *conscious* inference, is determined by a number of circumstances which, through experience and association, have become the signs of differences of depth in space. Among these are the degree of indistinctness of the impression, the apparent or retinal magnitude (if the object is a familiar one), the relations of linear perspective, as the interruption of the outline of far objects by that of near objects, and so on. In a process so complicated there is clearly ample room for error, and wrong estimates of distance whenever unusual circumstances are present are familiar to all. Thus, the inexperienced English tourist, when in the clear atmosphere of Switzerland, where the impressions from distant objects are more distinct than at home, naturally falls into the illusion that the mountains are much nearer than they are, and so fails to realize their true altitude.

Illusions of Art.

The imitation of solidity and depth by art is a curious and interesting illustration of the mode of production of illusion. Here we are not, of course, concerned with the question how far illusion is desirable in art, but only with its capabilities of illusory presentment; which capabilities, it may be added, have been fully illustrated in the history of art. The full treatment of this subject would form a chapter in itself; here I can only touch on its main features.

Pictorial art working on a flat surface cannot, it is plain, imitate the stereoscope, and produce a perfect sense of solidity. Yet it manages to produce a pretty strong illusion. It illustrates in a striking manner the ease with which the eye conceives relations of depth or relief and solidity. If, for example, on a carpet, wall-paper, or dress, bright lines are laid on a dark colour as ground, we easily imagine that they are advancing. The reason of this seems to be that in our daily experience advancing surfaces catch and reflect the light, whereas retiring surfaces are in shadow.[1]

The same principle is illustrated in one of the means used by the artist to produce a strong sense of relief, namely, the cast shadow. A circle drawn with chalk with a powerful cast shadow on one side

---

[1] Painters are well aware that the colours at the red end of the spectrum are apt to appear as advancing, while those of the violet end are known as retiring. The appearance of relief given by a gilded pattern on a dark blue as ground, is in part referable to the principle just referred to. In addition, it appears to involve a difference in the action of the muscles of accommodation in the successive adaptations of the eye to the most refrangible and the least refrangible rays. (See Brücke, *Die Physiologie der Farben*, sec. 17.)

will, without any shading or modelling of the form, appear to stand out from the paper, thus: .

FIG. 1.

The reason is that the presence of such a shadow so forcibly suggests to the mind that the object is a prominent one intervening between the light and the shaded surface.[1]

Even without differences of light and shade, by a mere arrangement of lines, we may produce a powerful sense of relief or solidity. A striking example of this is the way in which two intersecting lines sometimes appear to recede from the eye, as the lines $a\,a'$, $b\,b'$, in the next drawing, which seem to belong to a regular pattern on the ground, at which the eye is looking from above and obliquely.

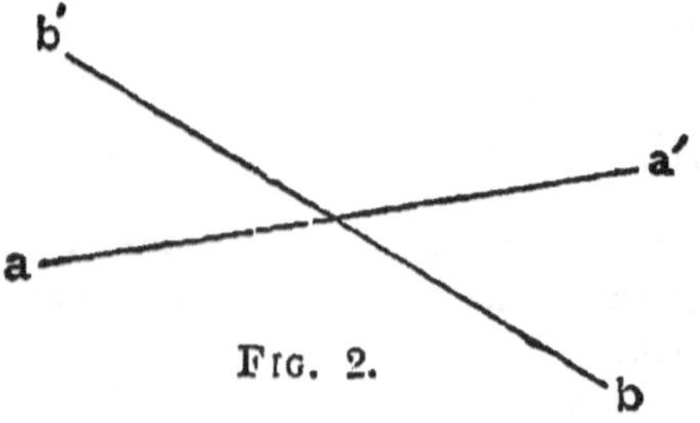

FIG. 2.

---

[1] Helmholtz tells us (*Populäre wissenschaftliche Vorträge*, 3tes Heft, p. 64) that even in a stereoscopic arrangement the presence of a wrong cast shadow sufficed to disturb the illusion.

Again, the correct delineation of the projection of a regular geometrical figure, as a cube, suffices to give the eye a sense of relief. This effect is found to be the more striking in proportion to the familiarity of the form. The following drawing of a long box-shaped solid at once seems to stand out to the eye.

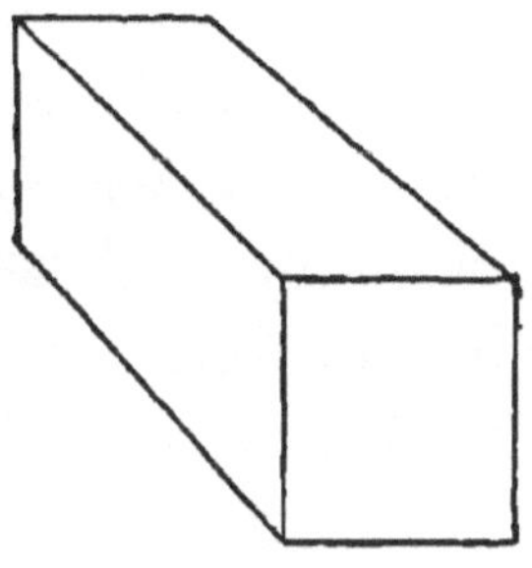

FIG. 3.

This habitual interpretation of the flat in art as answering to objects in relief, or having depth, can only be understood when it is remembered that our daily experience gives us myriads of instances in which the effect of such flat representations answers to solid receding forms. That is to say, in the case of all distant objects, in the perception of which the dissimilarity of the retinal pictures and the feeling of convergence take no part, we have to interpret solidity, and relations of nearer and further, by such signs as linear perspective and cast shadow. On the other hand, it is only in the artificial life of indoors, on our picture-covered walls, that we experience such effects without discovering corresponding realities. Hence a deeply organized habit of taking these impressions as answering to the solid and not to the flat. If our experience had been quite different;

if, for example, we had been brought up in an empty room, amid painted walls, and had been excluded from the sight of the world of receding objects outside, we might easily have formed an exactly opposite habit of taking the actual mountains, trees, etc., of the distant scene to be pictures laid on a flat surface.

It follows from this that, with respect to the distant parts of a scene, pictorial art possesses the means of perfect imitation; and here we see that a complete illusory effect is obtainable. I need but to refer to the well-known devices of linear and aerial perspective, by which this result is secured.[1] The value of these means of producing illusion at the command of the painter, may be illustrated by the following fact, which I borrow from Helmholtz. If you place two pieces of

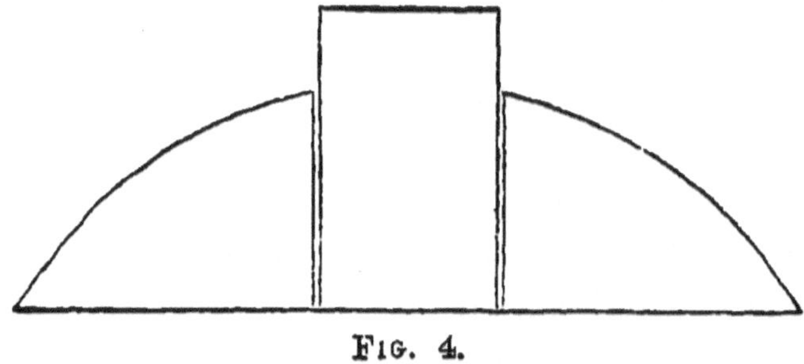

Fig. 4.

cardboard which correspond to portions of one form at the sides and in front of a third piece, in the way represented above, so as just to allow the eye to follow the contour of this last, and then look at this arrange-

---

[1] Among the means of giving a vivid sense of depth to a picture, emphasized by Helmholtz, is diminishing magnitude. It is obvious that the perceptions of real magnitude and distance are mutually involved. When, for example, a picture represents a receding series of objects, as animals, trees, or buildings, the sense of the third dimension is rendered much more clear.

ment from a point at some little distance with one eye, you easily suppose that it stands in front of the side pieces. The explanation of the illusion is that this particular arrangement powerfully suggests that the outline of the whole figure, of which the two side pieces are parts, is broken by an intervening object. Owing to the force of these and other suggestions, it is easy for the spectator, when attending to the background of a landscape painting, to give himself up for a moment to the pleasant delusion that he is looking at an actual receding scene.

In connection with pictorial delusion, I may refer to the well-known fact, that the eye in a portrait seems to follow the spectator, or that a gun, with its muzzle pointing straight outwards, appears to turn as the spectator moves.[1] These tricks of art have puzzled many people, yet their effect is easily understood, and has been very clearly explained by Sir D. Brewster, in the work already referred to (letter v.). They depend on the fact that a painting, being a flat projection only and not a solid, continues to present the front view of an object which it represents wherever the spectator happens to stand. Were the eye in the portrait a real eye, a side movement of the spectator would, it is evident, cause him to see less of the pupil and more of the side of the eyeball, and he would only continue to see the full pupil when the eye followed him. We regard the eye in the picture as a real eye having relief, and judge accordingly.

[1] A striking example of this was given in a painting, by Andsell, of a sportsman in the act of shooting, exhibited in the Royal Academy in 1879.

We may fall into similar illusions respecting distance in auditory perception. A change of wind, an unusual stillness in the air, is quite sufficient to produce the sense that sounding objects are nearer than they actually are. The art of the ventriloquist manifestly aims at producing this kind of illusion. By imitating the dull effect of a distant voice, he is able to excite in the minds of his audience a powerful conviction that the sounds proceed from a distant point. There is little doubt that ventriloquism has played a conspicuous part in the arts of divination and magic.

Misconception of Local Arrangement.

Let us now pass to a class of illusions closely related to those having to do with distance, but involving some special kind of circumstance which powerfully suggests a particular arrangement in space. One of the most striking examples of these is the erroneous localization of a quality in space, that is to say, the reference of it to an object nearer or further off than the right one. Thus, when we look through a piece of yellow glass at a dull, wintry landscape, we are disposed to imagine that we are looking at a sunny scene of preternatural warmth. A moment's reflection would tell us that the yellow tint, with which the objects appear to be suffused, comes from the presence of the glass; yet, in spite of this, the illusion persists with a curious force. The explanation is, of course, that the circumstances are exceptional, that in a vast majority of cases the impression of colour belongs to the object and not to an intervening medium,[1] and that consequently we

---

[1] This is at least true of all near objects.

tend to ignore the glass, and to refer the colour to the objects themselves.

When, however, the fact of the existence of a coloured medium is distinctly present to the mind, we easily learn to allow for this, and to recognize one coloured surface correctly through a recognized medium. Thus, we appear to ourselves to see the reflected images of the wall, etc., of a room, in a bright mahogany table, not suffused with a reddish yellow tint, as they actually are—and may be seen to be by the simple device of looking at a small bit of the image through a tube, but in their ordinary colour. We may be said to fall into illusion here in so far as we overlook the exact quality of the impression actually made on the eye. This point will be touched on presently. Here I am concerned to show that this habit of allowing for the coloured medium may, in its turn, occasionally lead to plain and palpable illusion.

The most striking example of this error is to be met with among the curious phenomena of colour-contrast already referred to. In many of these cases the appearance of the contrasting colour is, as I have observed, due to a temporary modification of the nervous substance. Yet it is found that this organic factor does not wholly account for the phenomena. For example, Meyer made the following experiment. He covered a piece of green paper by a sheet of thin transparent white paper. The colour of this double surface was, of course, a pale green. He then introduced a scrap of grey paper between the two sheets, and found that, instead of looking whitish as it really was, it looked rose-red. Whatever the colour of the under sheet the grey scrap took the complementary hue. If, however, the piece of grey paper is put outside the thin sheet, it looks grey ; and what is most remarkable is that when a second piece is put outside, the scrap inside no longer wears the complementary hue.

There is here evidently something more than a change of organic conditions; there is an action of experience and suggestion. The reason of our seeing the scrap rose-red in one case and neutral grey in another, is that in the first instance we vividly represent to ourselves that we are looking at it through a greenish veil (which is, of course, a part of the illusion) ; for rose-red seen through a greenish medium would, as a matter of fact, be light grey, as this scrap is. Even if we allow that there always exists after an impression of colour a temporary organic disposition to see the complementary hue, this does not suffice as an explanation of these cases; we have to conclude further that imagination, led by the usual run of our experience, is here a co-operant factor, and helps to determine whether the complementary tint shall be seen or not.

Misinterpretation of Form.

More complex and circumscribed associations take part in those errors which we occasionally commit respecting the particular form of objects. This has already been touched on in dealing with artistic illusion. The disposition of the eye to attribute solidity to a flat drawing is the more powerful in proportion to the familiarity of the form. Thus, an outline drawing of a building is apt to stand out with special force.

Another curious illustration of this is the phenomenon known as the conversion of the concave mould or matrix of a medal into the corresponding convex relief. If, says Helmholtz, the mould of a medal be illuminated by a light falling obliquely so as to produce strong shadows, and if we regard this with one eye, we easily fall into the illusion that it is the original raised design, illuminated from *the opposite side*. As a matter of fact, the visual impression produced by a concave form with the light falling on one side, very closely resembles that produced by a corresponding convex form with the light falling on the other side. At the same time, it is found that the opposite mode of conversion, that is to say, the transformation of the raised into the depressed form, though occurring occasionally, is much less frequent. Now, it may be asked, why should we tend to transform the concave into the convex, rather than the convex into the concave? The reader may easily anticipate the answer from what has been said about the deeply fixed tendency of the eye to solidify a plane surface. We are rendered much more familiar, both by nature and by art, with raised (*cameo*) design than with depressed design (*intaglio*), and we instinctively interpret the less familiar form by the more familiar. This explanation appears to be borne out by the fact emphasized by Schroeder that the illusion is much more powerful if the design is that of some well-known object, as the human head or figure, or an animal form, or leaves.[1]

---

[1] Helmholtz remarks (*op. cit.*, p. 628) that the difficulty of seeing the convex cast as concave is probably due to the presence of the cast shadow. This has, no doubt, some effect: yet the consideration urged in the text appears to me to be the most important one.

Another illustration of this kind of illusion recently occurred in my own experience. Nearly opposite to my window came a narrow space between two detached houses. This was, of course, darker than the front of the houses, and the receding parallel lines of the bricks appeared to cross this narrow vertical shaft obliquely. I could never look at this without seeing it as a convex column, round which the parallel lines wound obliquely. Others saw it as I did, though not always with the same overpowering effect. I can only account for this illusion by help of the general tendency of the eye to solidify impressions drawn from the flat, together with the effect of special types of experience, more particularly the perception of cylindrical forms in trees, columns, etc.

It may be added that a somewhat similar illustration of the action of special types of experience on the perception of individual form may be found in the region of hearing. The powerful disposition to take the finely graduated cadences of sound produced by the wind for the utterances of a human voice, is due to the fact that this particular form and arrangement of sound has deeply impressed itself on our minds, in connection with numberless utterances of human feeling.

Illusions of Recognition.

As a last illustration of comparatively passive illusions, I may refer to the errors which we occasionally commit in recognizing objects. As I have already observed, the process of full and clear recognition, specific and individual, involves a classing of a number of distinct aspects of the object, such as colour, form, etc. Accordingly, when in a perfectly calm state of mind we fall into illusion with respect to any object plainly visible, it must be through some accidental resemblance between the object and the other object or class of objects with which we identify it. In the case of individual identification such illusions are, of course, comparatively rare, since here there are involved so many characteristic differences. On the other hand, in the case of specific recognition there is ample room for error, especially in those kinds of more subtle recognition to which I have already referred. To " recognize " a person as a Frenchman or a military man, for example, is often an erroneous process. Logicians have included this kind of error under what they call "fallacies of observation."

Errors of recognition, both specific and individual, are, of course, more easy in the case of distant objects or objects otherwise indistinctly seen. It is noticeable in these cases that, even when perfectly cool and free from emotional excitement, we tend to interpret such indistinct impressions according to certain favourite types of experience, as the human face and figure. Our interpretative imagination easily sees traces of the human form in cloud, rock, or tree-stump.

Again, even when there is no error of recognition, in the sense of confusing one object with other objects, there may be partial illusion. I have remarked that the process of recognizing an object commonly involves an overlooking of points of diversity in the object, or aspect of the object, now present. And sometimes this inattention to what is actually present includes an error as to the actual visual sensation of the moment. Thus, for example, when I look at a sheet of white paper in a feebly lit room, I seem to see its whiteness. If, however, I bring it near the window, and let the sun fall on a part of it, I at once recognize that what I have been seeing is not white, but a decided grey. Similarly, when I look at a brick viaduct a mile or two off, I appear to myself to recognize its redness. In fact, however, the impression of colour which I receive from the object is not that of brick-red at all, but a much less decided tint; which I may easily prove by bending my head downwards and letting the scene image itself on the retina in an unusual way, in which case the recognition of the object as a viaduct being less distinct, I am better able to attend to the exact shade of the colour.

Nowhere is this inattention to the sensation of the moment exhibited in so striking a manner as in pictorial art. A picture of Meissonier may give the eye a representation of a scene in which the objects, as the human figures and horses, have a distinctness that belongs to near objects, but an apparent magnitude that belongs to distant objects. So again, it is found that the degree of luminosity or brightness of a pictorial representation differs in general enormously from that of the actual objects. Thus, according to the calculations of Helmholtz,[1] a picture representing a Bedouin's white raiment in blinding sunshine, will, when seen in a fairly lit gallery, have a degree of luminosity reaching only to about one-thirtieth of that of the actual object. On the other hand, a painting

---

[1] *Populäre wissenschaftliche Vorträge*, 3tes Heft, pp. 71, 72.

representing marble ruins illuminated by moonlight, will, under the same conditions of illumination, have a luminosity amounting to as much as from ten to twenty thousand times that of the object. Yet the spectator does not notice these stupendous discrepancies. The representation, in spite of its vast difference, at once carries the mind on to the actuality, and the spectator may even appear to himself, in moments of complete absorption, to be looking at the actual scene.

The truly startling part of these illusions is, that the direct result of sensory stimulation appears to be actually displaced by a mental image. Thus, in the case of Meyer's experiment, of looking at the distant viaduct, and of recognizing an artistic representation, imagination seems in a measure to take the place of sensation, or to blind the mind to what is actually before it.

The mystery of the process, however, greatly disappears when it is remembered that what we call a conscious "sensation" is really compounded of a result of sensory stimulation and a result of central reaction, of a purely passive impression and the mental activity involved in attending to this and classing it.[1] This being so, a sensation may be modified by anything exceptional in the mode of central reaction of the moment. Now, in all the cases just considered, we have one common feature, a powerful suggestion of the presence of a particular object or local arrangement. This suggestion, taking the form of a vivid mental image, dominates and overpowers the passive

---

[1] See, on this point, some excellent remarks by G. H. Lewes, *Problems of Life and Mind*, third series, vol. ii. p. 275.

impression. Thus, in Meyer's experiment, the mind is possessed by the supposition that we are looking at the grey spot through a greenish medium. So in the case of the distant viaduct, we are under the mastery of the idea that what we see in the distance is a red brick structure. Once more, in the instance of looking at the picture, the spectator's imagination is enchained by the vivid representation of the object for which the picture stands, as the marble ruins in the moonlight or the Bedouin in the desert.

It may be well to add that this mental uncertainty as to the exact nature of a present impression is necessitated by the very conditions of accurate perception. If, as I have said, all recognition takes place by overlooking points of diversity, the mind must, in course of time, acquire a habit of not attending to the exact quality of sense-impressions in all cases where the interpretation seems plain and obvious. Or, to use Helmholtz's words, our sensations are, in a general way, of interest to us only as signs of things, and if we are sure of the thing, we readily overlook the precise nature of the impression. In short, we get into the way of attending only to what is essential, constant, and characteristic in objects, and disregarding what is variable and accidental.[1] Thus, we attend, in the first place, to the form of objects, the most constant and characteristic element of all, being comparatively

---

[1] To some extent this applies to the changes of apparent magnitude due to altered position. Thus, we do not attend to the reduction of the height of a small object which we are wont to handle, when it is placed far below the level of the eye. And hence the error people make in judging of the point in the wall or skirting which a hat will reach when placed on the ground.

inattentive to colour, which varies with distance, atmospheric changes, and mode of illumination. So we attend to the relative magnitude of objects rather than to the absolute, and to the relative intensities of light and shade rather than to the absolute; for in so doing we are noting what is constant for all distances and modes of illumination, and overlooking what is variable. And the success of pictorial art depends on the observance of this law of perception.

These remarks at once point out the limits of these illusions. In normal circumstances, an act of imagination, however vivid, cannot create the semblance of a sensation which is altogether absent; it can only slightly modify the actual impression by interfering with that process of comparison and classification which enters into all definite determination of sensational quality.

Another great fact that has come to light in the investigation of these illusions is that oft-recurring and familiar types of experience leave permanent dispositions in the mind. As I said when describing the process of perception, what has been frequently perceived is perceived more and more readily. It follows from this that the mind will be habitually disposed to form the corresponding mental images, and to interpret impressions by help of these. The range of artistic suggestion depends on this. A clever draughtsman can indicate a face by a few rough touches, and this is due to the fact that the spectator's mind is so familiarized, through recurring experience and special interest, with the object, that it is ready to construct the requisite mental image at the slightest external suggestion. And hence the risk of hasty and illusory interpretation.

These observations naturally conduct us to the consideration of the second great group of sense-illusions, which I have marked off as active illusions, where the action of a pre-existing intellectual disposition becomes much more clearly marked, and assumes the form of a free imaginative transformation of reality.

CHAPTER VI.

B. *Active Illusions.*

WHEN giving an account of the mechanism of perception, I spoke of an independent action of the imagination which tends to anticipate the process of suggestion from without. Thus, when expecting a particular friend, I recognize his form much more readily than when my mind has not been preoccupied with his image.

A little consideration will show that this process must be highly favourable to illusion. To begin with, even if the preperception be correct, that is to say, if it answer to the perception, the mere fact of vivid expectation will affect the exact moment of the completed act of perception. And recent experiment shows that in certain cases such a previous activity of expectant attention may even lead to the illusory belief that the perception takes place before it actually does.[1]

[1] I refer to the experiments made by Exner, Wundt, and others, in determining the time elapsing between the giving of a signal to a

A more palpable source of error resides in the risk of the formation of an inappropriate preperception. If a wrong mental image happens to have been formed and vividly entertained, and if the actual impression fits in to a certain extent with this independently formed preperception, we may have a fusion of the two which exactly simulates the form of a complete percept. Thus, for example, in the case just supposed, if another person, bearing some resemblance to our expected friend, chances to come into view, we may probably stumble into the error of taking one person for another.

On the physical side, we may, agreeably to the hypothesis mentioned above, express this result by saying that, owing to a partial identity in the nervous processes involved in the anticipatory image and the impression, the two tend to run one into the other, constituting one continuous process.

There are different ways in which this independent activity of the imagination may falsify our perceptions. Thus, we may voluntarily choose to entertain a certain image for the moment, and to look at the impression in a particular way, and within certain limits such capricious selection of an interpretation is effectual in giving a special significance to an impression. Or the process of independent preperception may go on apart from our volitions, and perhaps in spite of these, in which case the illusion has something of the irresistible necessity

person and the execution of a movement in response. "It is found," says Wundt, "by these experiments that the exact moment at which a sense-impression is perceived depends on the amount of preparatory self-accommodation of attention." (See Wundt, *Physiologische Psychologie*, ch. xix., especially p. 735, *et seq.*)

of a passive illusion. Let us consider separately each mode of production.

Voluntary Selection of Interpretation.

The action of a capricious exercise of the imagination in relation to an impression is illustrated in those cases where experience and suggestion offer to the interpreting mind an uncertain sound, that is to say, where the present sense-signs are ambiguous. Here we obviously have a choice of interpretation. And it is found that, in these cases, what we see depends very much on what we wish to see. The interpretation adopted is still, in a sense, the result of suggestion, but of one particular suggestion which the fancy of the moment determines. Or, to put it another way, the caprice of the moment causes the attention to focus itself in a particular manner, to direct itself specially to certain aspects and relations of objects.

The eye's interpretation of movement, already referred to, obviously offers a wide field for this play of selective imagination. When looking out of the window of a railway carriage, I can at will picture to my mind the trees and telegraph posts as moving objects. Sometimes the true interpretation is so uncertain that the least inclination to view the phenomenon in one way determines the result. This is illustrated in a curious observation of Sinsteden. One evening, on approaching a windmill obliquely from one side, which under these circumstances he saw only as a dark silhouette against a bright sky, he noticed that the sails appeared to go, now in one direction, now in another, according as he imagined himself looking at the front or at the back of the windmill.[1]

In the interpretation of geometrical drawings, as those of crystals, there is, as I have observed, a general tendency to view the flat delineation as answering to a raised object, or a body in relief, according to the common run of our experience. Yet there are cases where experience is less decided, and where, consequently, we may regard any particular line as advancing or receding. And it is found that when we vividly imagine that the drawing is that of a convex or concave surface, we see it to be so, with all the force of a complete perception. The least disposition to see it in the other way will suffice to reverse the interpretation. Thus, in the following drawing, the reader can easily see at

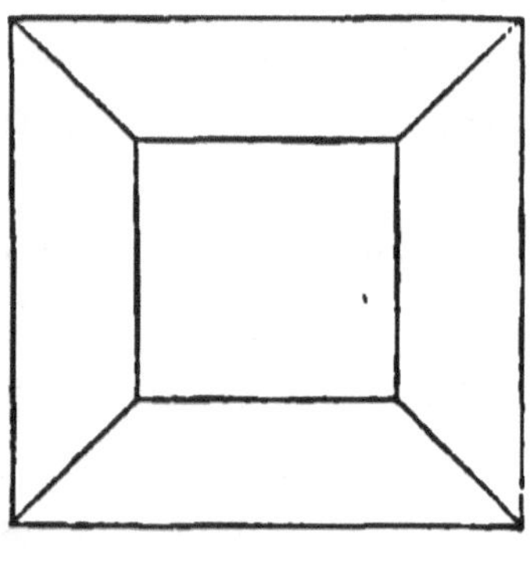

Fig. 5.

will something answering to a truncated pyramid, or to the interior of a cooking vessel.

Similarly, in the accompanying figure of a transparent solid, I can at will select either of the two surfaces which approximately face the eye and regard

---

[1] Quoted by Helmholtz, *op. cit.*, p. 626.

it as the nearer, the other appearing as the hinder surface looked at through the body.

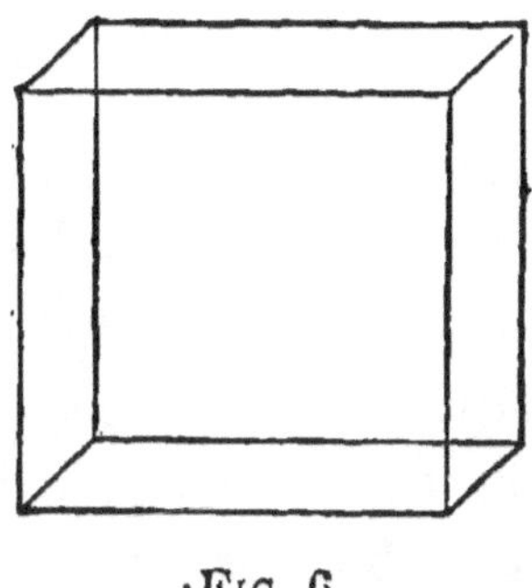

·Fig. 6.

Again, in the next drawing, taken from Schroeder, one may, by an effort of will, see the diagonal step-like pattern, either as the view from above of the edge of an advancing piece of wall at *a*, or as the view from below of the edge of an advancing (overhanging) piece of wall at *b*.

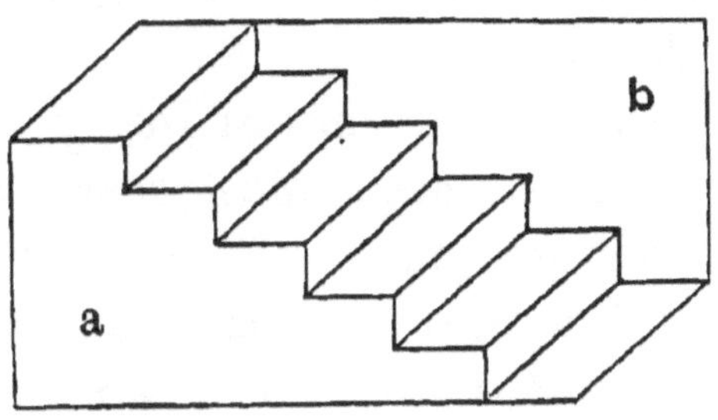

Fig. 7.

These last drawings are not in true perspective on either of the suppositions adopted, wherefore the choice is easier. But even when an outline form is in perspective, a strenuous effort of imagination may suffice to bring about a conversion of the appearance. Thus, if the reader will look at the drawing of the box-like solid (Fig. 3, p. 79), he will find that, after a trial or

two, he succeeds in seeing it as a *concave* figure representing the cover and two sides of a box as looked at
from within.[1]

Many of my readers, probably, share in my power
of variously interpreting the relative position of bands
or stripes on fabrics such as wall-papers, according
to wish. I find that it is possible to view now this
stripe or set of stripes as standing out in relief upon
the others as a ground, now these others as advancing
out of the first as a background. The difficulty of
selecting either interpretation at will becomes greater,
of course, in those cases where there is a powerful suggestion of some particular local arrangement, as, for
example, the case of patterns much brighter than the
ground, and especially of such as represent known
objects, as flowers. Yet even here a strong effort of
imagination will often suffice to bring about a conversion of the first appearance.

A somewhat similar choice of interpretation offers
itself in looking at elaborate decorative patterns.
When we strongly imagine any number of details to be
elements of one figure, they seem to become so; and a
given detail positively appears to alter in character
according as it is viewed as an element of a more or
less complex figure.

---

[1] When the drawing, by its adherence to the laws of perspective,
does not powerfully determine the eye to see it in one way rather than
in the other (as in Figs. 5 to 7), the disposition to see the one form
rather than the other points to differences in the frequency of the
original forms in our daily experience. At the same time, it is to be
observed that, after looking at the drawing for a time under each
aspect, the suggestion now of the one and now of the other forces itself
on the mind in a curious and unaccountable way.

These examples show what force belongs to a vivid preconception, if this happens to fit only very roughly the impression of the moment, that is to say, if the interpretative image is one of the possible suggestions of the impression. The play of imagination takes a wider range in those cases where the impression is very indefinite in character, easily allowing of a considerable variety of imaginative interpretation.

I referred at the beginning of this account of sense-illusions to the readiness with which the mind deceives itself with respect to the nature and causes of the vague sensations which usually form the dim background of our mental life. A person of lively imagination, by trying to view these in a particular way, and by selectively attending to those aspects of the sensation which answer to the caprice of the moment, may give a variety of interpretations to one and the same set of sensations. For example, it is very easy to get confused with respect to those tactual and motor feelings which inform us of the position of our bodily members. And so, when lying in bed, and attending to the sensations connected with the legs, we may easily delude ourselves into supposing that these members are arranged in a most eccentric fashion. Similarly, by giving special heed to the sensations arising in connection with the condition of the skin at any part, we may amuse ourselves with the strangest fancies as to what is going on in these regions.

Again, when any object of visual perception is indistinct or indefinite in form, there is plainly an opening for this capricious play of fancy in transforming the actual. This is illustrated in the well-known pastime of discovering familiar forms, such as those of the human head and animals, in distant rocks and clouds, and of seeing pictures in the fire, and so on. The indistinct and indefinite shapes of the masses of rock, cloud, or glowing coal, offer an excellent field for creative fancy, and a person of lively imagination will discover endless forms in what, to an unimaginative eye, is a formless waste. Johannes Müller relates that, when a child, he used to spend hours in discovering the outlines of forms in the partly blackened and cracked stucco of the house that stood opposite to his own.[1] Here it is plain that, while experience and association are not wholly absent, but place certain wide limits on this process of castle-building, the spontaneous activity of the percipient mind is the great determining force.

So much as to the influence of a perfectly unfettered voluntary attention on the determination of the stage of preperception, and, through this, of the resulting interpretation. Let us now pass to cases in which this direction of preperception follows not the caprice of the moment, but the leading of some fixed predisposition in the interpreter's mind. In these cases attention is no longer free, but fettered, only it is now fettered rather from within than from without; that is to say, the dominating preperception is much more the result of an independent bent of the imagination than of some suggestion forced on the mind by the actual impression of the moment.

[1] *Ueber die phantastischen Gesichtserscheinungen*, p. 45.

Involuntary Mental Preadjustment.

If we glance back at the examples of capricious selection just noticed, we shall see that they are really limited not only by the character of the impression of the time, but also by the mental habits of the spectator. That is to say, we find that his fancy runs in certain definite directions, and takes certain habitual forms. It has already been observed that the percipient mind has very different attitudes with respect to various kinds of impression. Towards some it holds itself at a distance, while towards others it at once bears itself familiarly; the former are such as answer to its previous habit and bent of imagination, the latter such as do not so answer.

This bent of the interpretative imagination assumes, as we have already seen, two forms, that of a comparatively permanent disposition, and that of a temporary state of expectation or mental preparedness. Illusion may arise in connection with either of these forms. Let us illustrate both varieties, beginning with those which are due to a lasting mental disposition.

It is impossible here to specify all the causes of illusion residing in organized tendencies of the mind. The whole past mental life, with its particular shade of experience, its ruling emotions, and its habitual direction of fancy, serves to give a particular colour to new impressions, and so to favour illusion. There is a " personal equation " in perception as in belief— an amount of erroneous deviation from the common average view of external things, which is the outcome of individual temperament and habits of mind. Thus, a naturally timid man will be in general disposed to see ugly and fearful objects where a perfectly unbiased mind perceives nothing of the kind; and the forms which these objects of dread will assume are determined by the character of his past experience, and by the customary direction of his imagination.

In perfectly healthy states of mind this influence of temperament and mental habit on the perception of external objects is, of course, very limited; it shows itself more distinctly, as we shall see, in modifying the estimate of things in relation to the æsthetic and other feelings. This applies to the mythical poetical way of looking at nature—a part of our subject to which we shall have to return later on.

Passing now from the effect of such permanent dispositions, let us look at the more striking results of temporary expectancy of mind.

When touching on the influence of such a temporary mental attitude in the process of correct perception, I remarked that this readiness of mind might assume an indefinite or a definite form. We will examine the effect of each kind in the production of illusion.

Action of Sub-Expectation.

First of all, then, our minds may at the particular moment be disposed to entertain any one of a vaguely circumscribed group of images. Thus, to return to the example already referred to, when in Italy, we are in a state of readiness to frame any of the images that we have learnt to associate with this country. We may not be distinctly anticipating any one kind of object, but are nevertheless in a condition of *sub-expectation* with reference to a large number of objects. Accordingly, when an impression occurs which answers only very roughly to one of the associated images, there is a tendency to superimpose the image on the impression. In this way illusion arises. Thus, a man, when strolling in a cathedral, will be apt to take any kind of faint hollow sound for the soft tones of an organ.

The disposition to anticipate fact and reality in this way will be all the stronger if, as usually happens, the mental images thus lying ready for use have an emotional colouring. Emotion is the great disturber of all intellectual operations. It effects marvellous things, as we shall presently see, in the region of illusory belief, and its influence is very marked in the seemingly cooler region of external perception. The effect of any emotional excitement appears to be to give a preternatural vividness and persistence to the ideas answering to it, that is to say, the ideas which are its excitants, or which are otherwise associated with it. Owing to this circumstance, when the mind is under the temporary sway of any feeling, as, for example, fear, there will be a special readiness to interpret objects by help of images congruent with the emotion. Thus, a man under the control of fear will be ready to see any kind of fear-inspiring object whenever there is any resemblance to such in the things actually present to his vision. The state of awe which the surrounding circumstances of a spiritualist *séance* inspires produces a general readiness of mind to perceive what is strange, mysterious, and apparently miraculous.

It is worth noting, perhaps, that those delightful half-illusions which imitative art seeks to produce are greatly favoured by such a temporary attitude of the interpreting imagination. In the theatre, for example, we are prepared for realizing the semblance of life that is to be unfolded before us. We come knowing that what is to be performed aims at representing a real action or actual series of events. We not improbably work ourselves into a slightly excited state in anticipation of such a representation. More than this, as the play progresses, the realization of what has gone before produces a strong disposition to believe in, the reality of what is to follow. And this effect is proportionate to the degree of coherence and continuity in the action. In this way, there is a cumulative effect on the mind. If the action is good, the illusion, as every play-goer knows, is most complete towards the end.

Were it not for all this mental preparation, the illusory character of the performance would be too patent to view, and our enjoyment would suffer. A man is often aware of this when coming into a theatre during the progress of a piece before his mind accommodates itself to the meaning of the play. And the same thing is recognizable in the fact that the frequenter of the theatre has his susceptibility to histrionic delusion increased by acquiring a habit of looking out for the meaning of the performance. Persons who first see a play, unless they be of exceptional imagination and have thought much about the theatre—as Charlotte Brontë, for instance—hardly feel the illusion at all. At least, this is true of the opera, where the departure from reality is so striking that the impression can hardly fail to be a ludicrous one, till the habit of taking the performance for what it is intended to be is fully formed.[1]

A similar effect of intellectual preadjustment is observable in the fainter degrees of illusion produced by pictorial art. Here the undeceiving circumstances, the flat surface, the surroundings, and so on, would sometimes be quite sufficient to prevent the least degree of illusion, were it not that the spectator comes prepared to see a representation of some real object. This is our state of mind when we enter a picture gallery or approach what we recognize as a picture on the wall of a room. A savage would not " realize " a slight sketch as soon as one accustomed to pictorial representation, and ready to perform the required interpretative act.[2]

So much as to the effect of an indefinite state of sub-expectation in misleading our perceptions. Let us now glance at the results of definite preimagination, including what are generally known as expectations.

[1] Another side of histrionic illusion, the reading of the imitated feelings into the actors' minds, will be dealt with in a later chapter.

[2] In a finished painting of any size this preparation is hardly necessary. In these cases, in spite of the great deviations from truth in pictorial representation already touched on, the amount of essential agreement is so large and so powerful in its effect that even an intelligent animal will experience an illusion. Mr. Romanes sends me an interesting account of a dog, that had never been accustomed to pictures, having been put into a state of great excitement by the introduction of a portrait into a room, on a level with his eye. It is not at all improbable that the lower animals, even when sane, are frequently the subjects of slight illusion. That animals dream is a fact which is observed as long ago as the age of Lucretius.

Effects of Vivid Expectation.

Such expectations may grow out of some present objective facts, which serve as signs of the expected event; or they may arise by way of verbal suggestion; or, finally, they may be due to internal spontaneous imagination.

In the first place, then, the expectations may grow out of previous perceptions, while, nevertheless, the direction of the expectation may be a wrong one. Here the interpreting imagination is, in a large sense, under the control of external suggestion, though, with respect to the particular impression that is misconstrued, it may be regarded as acting independently and spontaneously.

Illustrations of this effect in producing illusion will easily occur to the reader. If I happen to have heard that a particular person has been a soldier or clergyman, I tend to see the marks of the class in this person, and sometimes find that this process of recognition is altogether illusory. Again, let us suppose that a person is expecting a friend by a particular train. A passenger steps out of the train bearing a superficial resemblance to his friend; in consequence of which he falls into the error of false identification.

The delusions of the conjuror depend on a similar principle. The performer tells his audience that he is about to do a certain thing, for example, take a number of animals out of a small box which is incapable of holding them. The hearers, intent on what has been said, vividly represent to themselves the action described. And in this way their attention becomes bribed, so to speak, beforehand, and fails to notice the inconspicuous movements which would at once clear up the mystery. Similarly with respect to the illusions which overtake people at spiritualist *séances*. The intensity of the expectation of a particular kind of object excludes calm attention to what really happens, and the slightest impressions which answer to signs of the object anticipated are instantly seized by the mind and worked up into illusory perceptions.

It is to be noted that even when the impression cannot be made to tally exactly with the expectation, the force of the latter often effects a grotesque confusion of the perception. If, for example, a man goes into a familiar room in the dark in order to fetch something, and for a moment forgets the particular door by which he has entered, his definite expectation of finding things in a certain order may blend with the order of impressions experienced, producing for the moment a most comical illusion as to the actual state of things.

When the degree of expectation is unusually great, it may suffice to produce something like the counterfeit of a real sensation. This happens when the present circumstances are powerfully suggestive of an immediate event. The effect is all the more powerful, moreover, in those cases where the object or event expected is interesting or exciting, since here the mental image gains in vividness through the emotional excitement attending it. Thus, if I am watching a train off and know from all the signs that it is just about to start, I easily delude myself into the conviction that it has begun to start, when it is really still.[1] An intense degree of expectation may, in such cases, produce something indistinguishable from an actual sensation. This effect is seen in such common experiences as that the sight of food makes the mouth of a hungry man water; that the appearance of a surgical instrument produces a nascent sensation of pain; and that a threatening movement, giving a vivid anticipation of tickling, begets a feeling which closely approximates to the result of actual tickling.

One or two very striking instances of such imagined sensations are given by Dr. Carpenter.[2] Here is one. An officer who superintended the exhuming of a coffin rendered necessary through a suspicion of - crime, declared that he already experienced the odour of decomposition, though it was afterwards found that the coffin was empty.[3]

It is, of course, often difficult to say, in such cases as these, how far elements of actual sensation co-operate in the production of the illusions. Thus, in the case just mentioned, the odour of the earth may have been the starting-point in the illusion. In many cases, however, an imaginative mind appears to be capable of

---

[1] This kind of illusion is probably facilitated by the fact that the eye is often performing slight movements without any clear consciousness of them. See what was said about the limits of sensibility, p. 50.

[2] *Mental Physiology,* fourth edit., p. 158.

[3] In persons of very lively imagination the mere representation of an object or event may suffice to bring about such a semblance of sensation. Thus, M. Taine (*op. cit.,* vol. i. p. 94) vouches for the assertion that "one of the most exact and lucid of modern novelists," when working out in his imagination the poisoning of one of his fictitious characters, had so vivid a gustatory sensation of arsenic that he was attacked by a violent fit of indigestion.

transforming a vivid expectation into a nascent stage of sensation. Thus, a mother thinking of her sick child in an adjoining room, and keenly on the alert for its voice, will now and again fancy she really hears it when others hear nothing at all.

Transition to Hallucination.

It is plain that in these cases illusion approaches to hallucination. Imagination, instead of waiting on sensation, usurps its place and imitates its appearance. Such a " subjective " sensation produced by a powerful expectation might, perhaps, by a stretch of language, be regarded as an illusion, in the narrow sense, in so far as it depends on the suggestive force of a complete set of external circumstances; on the other hand, it is clearly an hallucination in so far as it is the production of the semblance of an external impression without any external agency corresponding to this.

In the class of illusory expectations just considered the immediately present environment still plays a part, though a much less direct part than that observable in the first large group of illusions. We will now pass to a second mode of illusory expectation, where imagination is still more detached from the present surroundings.

A common instance of this kind of expectation is the so-called " intuition," or presentiment, that something is going to happen, which expectation has no basis in fact. It does not matter whether the expectation has arisen by way of another's words or by way of personal inclinations. A strong wish for a thing will, in an exalted state of mind, beget a vivid anticipation of it. This subject will be touched on again under the Illusions of Belief. Here I am concerned to point out that such presentiments are fertile sources of sense-illusion. The history of Church miracles, visions, and the like amply illustrates the effect of a vivid anticipation in falsifying the perceptions of external things.

In persons of a lively imagination any recent occupation of the mind with a certain kind of mental image may suffice to beget something equivalent to a powerful mode of expectation. For example, we are told by Dr. Tuke that on one occasion a lady, whose imagination had been dwelling on the subject of drinking fountains, "thought she saw in a road a newly erected fountain, and even distinguished an inscription upon it, namely, 'If any man thirst, let him come unto Me, and drink.' She afterwards found that what she had actually seen was only a few scattered stones."[1] In many cases there seems to be a temporary preternatural activity of the imagination in certain directions, of which no very obvious explanation is discoverable. Thus, we sometimes find our minds dwelling on some absent friend, without being able to give any reason for this mental preoccupation. And in this way arise strong temporary leanings to illusory perception. It may be said, indeed, that all unwonted activity of the imagination, however it arises, has as its immediate result a temporary mode of expectation, definite or

---

[1] Mentioned by Dr. Carpenter (*Mental Physiology*, p. 207), where other curious examples are to be found.

indefinite, which easily confuses our perceptions of external things.

In proportion as this pre-existing imaginative impulse becomes more powerful, the amount of actual impression necessary to transform the mental image into an illusory perception becomes less; and, what is more important, this transformation of the internal image involves a larger and larger displacement of the actual impression of the moment. A man whose mind is at the time strongly possessed by one kind of image, will tend to project this outwards with hardly any regard to the actual external circumstances.

This state of things is most completely illustrated in many of the grosser illusions of the insane. Thus, when a patient takes any small objects, as pebbles, for gold and silver, under the influence of the dominant idea of being a millionaire, it is obvious that external suggestion has very little to do with the self-deception. The confusions into which the patient often falls with respect to the persons before him show the same state of mind; for in many cases there is no discoverable individual resemblance between the person actually present and the person for whom he is taken.

It is evident that when illusion reaches this stage, it is scarcely distinguishable from what is specially known as hallucination. As I have remarked in setting out, illusion and hallucination shade one into the other much too gradually for us to draw any sharp line of demarcation between them. And here we see that hallucination differs from illusion only in the proportion in which the causes are present. When the internal imaginative impulse reaches a certain strength, it becomes self-sufficient, or independent of any external impression.

This intimate relation between the extreme form of active illusion and hallucination may be seen, too, by examining the physical conditions of each. As I have already remarked, active illusion has for its physiological basis a state of sub-excitation, or an exceptional condition of irritability in the structures engaged in the act of interpretative imagination. The greater the degree of this irritability, the less will be the force of external stimulation needed to produce the effect of excitation, and the more energetic will be the degree of this excitation. Moreover, it is plain that this increase in the strength of the excitation will involve an extension of the area of excitation till, by-and-by, the peripheral regions of the nervous system may be involved just as in the case of external stimulation. This accounts for the gradual displacement of the impression of the moment by the mental image. It follows that when the irritability reaches a certain degree, the amount of external stimulus needed may become a vanishing quantity, or the state of sub-excitation may of itself develop into one of full activity.

Hallucinations.

I do not propose to go very fully into the description and explanation of hallucinations here, since they fall to a large extent under the category of distinctly pathological phenomena. Yet our study of illusions would not be complete without a glance at this part of the subject.

Hallucination, by which I mean the projection of a mental image outwards when there is no external agency answering to it, assumes one of two fairly distinct forms: it may present itself either as a semblance of an external impression with the minimum amount of interpretation, or as a counterfeit of a completely developed percept. Thus, a visual hallucination may assume the aspect of a sensation of light or colour which we vaguely refer to a certain region of the external world, or of a vision of some recognizable object. All of us frequently have incomplete visual and auditory hallucinations of the first order, whereas the complete hallucinations of the second order are comparatively rare. The first I shall call rudimentary, the second developed, hallucinations.

Rudimentary hallucinations may have either a peripheral or a central origin. They may first of all have their starting-point in those subjective sensations which, as we have seen, are connected with certain processes set up in the peripheral regions of the nervous system. Or, secondly, they may originate in a certain preternatural activity of the sensory centres, or "sensorium," in what has been called by German physiologists an automatic excitation of the central structures, which activity may probably diffuse itself downwards to the peripheral regions of the nerves. Baillarger would call hallucinations of the former class "psycho-sensorial," those of the latter class purely "psychical," hallucinations.[1]

[1] See *Annales Médico-Psychologiques,* tom. vi. p. 168, etc.; tem. vii. p. 1, etc.

It is often a matter of great difficulty to determine which part of the nervous system is originally concerned in these rudimentary hallucinations. It is probable that in normal life they are most frequently due to peripheral disturbance. And it seems reasonable to suppose that where the hallucination remains in this initial stage of a very incompletely interpreted visual or auditory impression, whether in normal or abnormal life, its real physiological source is the periphery. For the automatic excitation of the centres would pretty certainly issue in the semblance of some definite, familiar variety of sense-impression which, moreover, as a part of a complex state known as a percept, would instantly present itself as a completely formed quasi-percept. In truth, we may pretty safely argue that if it is the centre which is directly thrown into a state of activity, it will be thrown into the usual complex, that is to say, *perceptional*, mode of activity.

Let us now turn to hallucinations properly so called, that is to say, completely developed quasi-percepts. These commonly assume the form of visual or auditory hallucinations. Like the incomplete hallucinations, they may have their starting-point either in some disturbance in the peripheral regions of the nervous system or in the automatic activity of the central structures: or, to use the language of Baillarger, we may say that they are either "psycho-sensorial" or purely "psychical." A subjective visual sensation, arising from certain conditions in the retina and connected portions of the optic nerve, may by chance resemble a familiar impression, and so be at once interpreted as an effect of a particular external object.

More frequently, however, the automatic activity of the centres must be regarded, either in part or altogether, as the physiological cause of the phenomenon. This is clearly the case when, on the subjective side, the hallucination answers to a preceding energetic activity of the imagination, as in the case of the visionary and the monomaniac. Sometimes, however, as we have seen, the hallucinatory percept answers to previous prolonged acts of perception, leaving a kind of reverberation in the structures concerned; and in this case it is obviously impossible to say whether the peripheral or central regions (if either) have most to do with the hallucination.[1]

The classifications of the causes of hallucination to be met with in the works of pathologists, bear out the distinction just drawn. Griesinger tells us (*op. cit.*, pp. 94, 95) that the general causes of hallucination are: (1) Local disease of the organ of sense; (2) a state of deep exhaustion either of mind or of body; (3) morbid emotional states, such as fear; (4) outward calm and stillness between sleeping and waking; and (5) the action of certain poisons, as haschisch, opium, belladonna. The first cause points pretty distinctly to a peripheral origin, whereas the others appear to refer mainly, if not exclusively, to central derangements.

---

[1] I have already touched on the resonance of a sense-impression when the stimulus has ceased to act (see p. 55). The remarks in the text hold good of all such after-impressions, in so far as they take the form of fully developed percepts. A good example is the recurrence of the images of microscopic preparations, to which the anatomist is liable. (See Lewes, *Problems of Life and Mind*, third series, vol. ii. p. 299.) Since a complete hallucination is supposed to involve the peripheral regions of the nerve, the mere fact of shutting the eye would not, it is clear, serve as a test of the origin of the illusion.

Excessive fatigue appears to predispose the central structures to an abnormal kind of activity, and the same effect may be brought about by emotional agitation and by the action of poisons. The fourth case mentioned here, absence of external stimulation, would naturally raise the nervous structures to an exceptional pitch of excitability. Such a condition would, moreover, prove favourable to hallucination by blurring the distinction between mental image and actual impression.

Hallucinations of Normal Life.

In normal life, perfect hallucinations, in the strict sense as distinct from illusions, are comparatively rare. Fully developed persistent hallucinations, as those of Nicolai, the Berlin bookseller, and of Mrs. A——, the lady cited by Sir D. Brewster, in his *Letters on Natural Magic*, point to the presence of incipient nervous disorder. In healthy life, on the other hand, while everybody is familiar with subjective sensations such as flying spots, phosphenes, ringing in the ears, few fall into the error of seeing or hearing distinct recognizable objects in the absence of all external impressions. In the lives of eminent men we read of such phenomena as very occasional events. Malebranche, for example, is said to have heard the voice of God calling him. Descartes says that, after a long confinement, he was followed by an invisible person, calling him to pursue his search for truth. Dr. Johnson narrates that he once heard his absent mother calling him. Byron tells us that he was sometimes visited by spectres. Goethe records that he once saw an exact counterpart of himself coming towards him. Sir Walter Scott is said to have seen a phantom of the dead Byron. It is possible that all of us are liable to momentary hallucinations at times of exceptional nervous exhaustion, though they are too fugitive to excite our attention.

When not brought on by exhaustion or artificial means, the hallucinations of the sane have their origin in a preternatural power of imagination. It is well known that this power can be greatly improved by attention and cultivation. Goethe used to exercise himself in watching for ocular spectra, and could at will transform these subjective sensations into definite forms, such as flowers ; and Johannes Müller found he had the same power.[1] Stories are told of portrait painters who could summon visual images of their sitters with a vividness equal to that of reality, and serving all the purposes of their art. Mr. Galton's interesting inquiries into the power of " visualizing " would appear to prove that many people can at will sport on the confines of the phantom world of hallucination. There is good reason to think that imaginative children tend to confuse mental images and percepts.[2]

[1] That subjective sensation may become the starting-point in complete hallucination is shown in a curious instance given by Lazarus, and quoted by Taine, *op. cit.*, vol. i. p. 122, *et seq.* The German psychologist relates that, on one occasion in Switzerland, after gazing for some time on a chain of snow-peaks, he saw an apparition of an absent friend, looking like a corpse. He goes on to explain that this phantom was the product of an image of recollection which somehow managed to combine itself with the (positive) after-image left by the impression of the snow-surface.

[2] For an account of Mr. Galton's researches, see *Mind*, No. xix. Compare, however, Professor Bain's judicious observations on these

The Hallucinations of Insanity.

The hallucinations of the insane are but a fuller manifestation of forces that we see at work in normal life. Their characteristic is that they simulate the form of distinctly present objects, the existence of which is not instantly contradicted by the actual surroundings of the moment.[1] The hallucinations have their origin partly in subjective sensations, which are probably connected with peripheral disturbances, partly and principally in central derangements.[2] These include profound emotional changes, which affect the ruling mental tone, and exert a powerful influence on the course of the mental images. The hallucinations of insanity are due to a projection of mental images which have, owing to certain circumstances, gained a preternatural persistence and vividness. Sometimes it is the images that have been dwelt on with passionate longing before the disease, sometimes those which have grown most habitual through the mode of daily occupa-

results in the next number of *Mind*. The liability of children to take images for percepts, is illustrated by the experiences related in a curious little work, *Visions*, by E. H. Clarke, M.D. (Boston, U.S., 1878), pp. 17, 46, and 212.

[1] A common way of describing the relation of the hallucinatory to real objects, is to say that the former appear partly to cover and hide the latter.

[2] Griesinger remarks that the forms of the hallucinations of the insane rarely depend on sense-disturbances alone. Though these are often the starting-point, it is the whole mental complexion of the time which gives the direction to the imagination. The common experience of seeing rats and mice running about during a fit of *delirium tremens* very well illustrates the co-operation of peripheral impressions not usually attended to, and possibly magnified by the morbid state of sensibility of the time (in this case flying spots, *muscæ volitantes*), with emotional conditions. (See Griesinger, *loc. cit.*, p. 96.)

tion,[1] and sometimes those connected with some incident at or near the time of the commencement of the disease.

In mental disease, auditory hallucinations play a part no less conspicuous than visual.[2] Patients frequently complain of having their thoughts spoken to them, and it is not uncommon for them to imagine that they are addressed by a number of voices at the same time.[3]

These auditory hallucinations offer a good opportunity for studying the gradual growth of centrally originating hallucinations. In the early stages of the disease, the patient partly distinguishes his representative from his presentative sounds. Thus, he talks of sermons being composed to him *in his head*. He calls these "internal voices," or "voices of the soul." It

---

[1] Wundt (*Physiologische Psychologie*, p. 652) tells us of an insane woodman who saw logs of wood on all hands in front of the real objects.

[2] It is stated by Baillarger (*Memoires de l'Académie Royale de Médicine*, tom. xii. p. 273, etc.) that while visual hallucinations are more frequent than auditory in healthy life, the reverse relation holds in disease. At the same time, Griesinger remarks (*loc. cit.*, p. 98) that visual hallucinations are rather more common than auditory in disease also. This is what we should expect from the number of subjective sensations connected with the peripheral organ of vision. The greater relative frequency of auditory hallucinations in disease, if made out, would seem to depend on the close connection between articulate sounds and the higher centres of intelligence, which centres are naturally the first to be thrown out of working order. It is possible, moreover, that auditory hallucinations are quite as common as visual in states of comparative health, though more easily overlooked. Professor Huxley relates that he is liable to auditory though not to visual hallucinations. (See *Elementary Lessons in Physiology*, p. 267.)

[3] See Baillarger, *Memoires de l'Académie Royale de Médicine*, tom. xii. p. 273, *et seq.*

is only when the disease gains ground and the central irritability increases that these audible thoughts become distinctly projected as external sounds into more or less definite regions of the environment.   And it is exceedingly curious to notice the different directions which patients give to these sounds, referring them now to a quarter above the head, now to a region below the floor, and so on.[1]

Range of Sense-Illusions.

And now let us glance back to see the path we have traversed.   We set out with an account of perfectly normal perception, and found, even here, in the projection of our sensations of colour, sound, etc., into the environment or to the extremities of the organism, something which, from the point of view of physical science, easily wears the appearance of an ingredient of illusion.

Waiving this, however, and taking the word illusion as commonly understood, we find that it begins when the element of imagination no longer answers to a present reality or external fact in any sense of this expression.   In its lowest stages illusion closely counterfeits correct perception in the balance of the direct factor, sensation, and the indirect factor, mental reproduction or imagination.   The degree of illusion increases in proportion as the imaginative element gains

---

[1] See Baillarger, *Annales Medico-Psychologiques*, tom. vi. p. 168 *et. seq.*; also tom. xii. p. 273, *et seq.* Compare Griesinger, *op. cit.* In a curious work entitled *Du Démon de Socrate* (Paris, 1856), M. Lélut seeks to prove that the philosopher's admonitory voice was an incipient auditory hallucination symptomic of a nascent stage of mental alienation.

in force relatively to the present impression; till, in the wild illusions of the insane, the amount of actual impression becomes evanescent. When this point is reached, the act of imagination shows itself as a purely creative process, or an hallucination.

While we may thus trace the progress of illusion towards hallucination by means of the gradual increase in force and extent of the imaginative, or indirect, as opposed to the sensuous, or direct, element in perception, we have found a second starting-point for this movement in the mechanism of sensation, involving, as it does, the occasional production of "subjective sensations." Such sensations constitute a border-land between the regions of illusion in the narrow sense, and hallucination. In their simplest and least developed form they may be regarded, at least in the case of hearing and sight, as partly hallucinatory; and they serve as a natural basis for the construction of complete hallucinations, or hallucinatory percepts.

In these different ways, then, the slight, scarcely noticeable illusions of normal life lead up to the most startling hallucinations of abnormal life. From the two poles of the higher centres of attention and imagination on the one side, and the lower regions of nervous action involved in sensation on the other side, issue forces which may, under certain circumstances, develop into full hallucinatory percepts. Thus closely is healthy attached to morbid mental life. There seems to be no sudden break between our most sober every-day recognitions of familiar objects and the wildest hallucinations of the demented. As we pass from the former to the latter, we find that there is never any abrupt transition, never any addition of perfectly new elements, but only that the old elements go on combining in ever new proportions.

The connection between the illusory side of our life and insanity may be seen in another way. All illusion has as its negative condition an interruption of the higher intellectual processes, the due control of our mental representations by reflection and reason. In the case of passive illusions, the error arises from our inability to subordinate the suggestion made by some feature of the present impression to the result of a fuller inspection of the object before us, or of a wider reflection on the past. In other words, our minds are dominated by the partial and the particular, to the exclusion of the total or the general. In active illusions, again, the powers of judgment and reflection, including those of calm perception itself, temporarily vacate their throne in favour of imagination. And this same suspension of the higher intellectual functions, the stupefaction of judgment and reflection made more complete and permanent, is just what characterizes insanity.

We may, perhaps, express this point of connection between the illusions of normal life and insanity by help of a physiological hypothesis. If the nervous system has been slowly built up, during the course of human history, into its present complex form, it follows that those nervous structures and connections which have to do with the higher intellectual processes, or which represent the larger and more general relations of our experience, have been most recently evolved. Consequently, they would be the least deeply organized, and so the least stable; that is to say, the most liable to be thrown *hors de combat*. This is what happens temporarily in the case of the sane, when the mind is held fast by an illusion. And, in states of insanity, we see the process of nervous dissolution beginning with these same nervous structures, and so taking the reverse order of the process of evolution.[1] And thus, we may say that throughout the mental life of the most sane of us, these higher and more delicately balanced structures are constantly in danger of being reduced to that state of inefficiency, which in its full manifestation is mental disease.

Does this way of putting the subject seem alarming? Is it an appalling thought that our normal mental life is thus intimately related to insanity, and graduates away into it by such fine transitions? A moment's reflection will show that the case is not so bad as it seems. It is well to remind ourselves that the brain is a delicately adjusted organ, which very easily gets disturbed, and that the best of us are liable to become the victims of absurd illusion if we habitually allow our imaginations to be overheated, whether by furious passion or by excessive indulgence in the pleasures of day-dreaming, or in the intoxicating mysteries of spiritualist *séances*. But if we take care to keep our heads cool and avoid unhealthy degrees of mental excitement, we need not be very anxious on the ground of our liability to this kind of error. As I have tried to show, our most frequent illusions are necessarily connected with something exceptional, either in the

---

[1] This is well brought out by Dr. J. Hughlings Jackson, in the papers in *Brain*, already referred to.

organism or in the environment. That is to say, it is of the nature of illusion in healthy conditions of body and mind to be something very occasional and relatively unimportant. Our perceptions may be regarded as the reaction of the mind on the impressions borne in from the external world, or as a process of adjustment of internal mental relations to external physical relations. If this process is, in the main, a right one, we need not greatly trouble, because it is not invariably so. We should accept the occasional failure of the intellectual mechanism as an inseparable accompaniment of its general efficiency.

To this it must be added that many of the illusions described above can hardly be called cases of non-adaptation at all, since they have no relation to the practical needs of life, and consequently are, in a general way, unattended to. In other cases, again, namely, where the precise nature of a present sensation, being practically an unimportant matter, is usually unattended to, as in the instantaneous recognition of objects by the eye under changes of illumination, etc., the illusion is rather a part of the process of adaptation, since it is much more important to recognize the permanent object signified by the sensation than the precise nature of the present sensational "sign" itself.

Finally, it should never be forgotten that in normal states of mind there is always the possibility of rectifying an illusion. What distinguishes abnormal from normal mental life is the persistent occupation of the mind by certain ideas, so that there is no room for the salutary corrective effect of reflection on the actual impression of the moment, by which we are wont to "orientate," or take our bearings as to the position of things about us. In sleep, and in certain artificially produced states, much the same thing presents itself. Images become realities just because they are not instantly recognized as such by a reference to the actual surroundings of the moment. But in normal waking life this power of correction remains with us. We may not exercise it, it is true, and thus the illusion will tend to become more or less persistent and recurring; for the same law applies to true and to false perception: repetition makes the process easier. But if we only choose to exert ourselves, we can always keep our illusions in a nascent or imperfectly developed stage. This applies not only to those half-illusions into which we voluntarily fall, but also to the more irresistible passive illusions, and those arising from an over-excited imagination. Even persons subject to hallucinations, like Nicolai of Berlin, learn to recognize the unreal character of these phantasms. On this point the following bit of autobiography from the pen of Coleridge throws an interesting light. "A lady (he writes) once asked me if I believed in ghosts and apparitions. I answered with truth and simplicity, No, madam, I have seen far too many myself." [1] However irresistible our sense-illusions may be, so long as we are under the sway of particular impressions or mental images, we can, when resolved to do so, un-

[1] *Friend*, vol. i. p. 248. The story is referred to by Sir W. Scott in his *Demonology and Witchcraft*.

deceive ourselves by carefully attending to the actual state of things about us. And in many cases, when once the correction is made, the illusion seems an impossibility. By no effort of imagination are we able to throw ourselves back into the illusory mental condition. So long as this power of dispelling the illusion remains with us, we need not be alarmed at the number and variety of the momentary misapprehensions to which we are liable.

CHAPTER VII.

The phenomena of dreams may well seem at first sight to form a world of their own, having no discoverable links of connection with the other facts of human experience. First of all, there is the mystery of sleep, which quietly shuts all the avenues of sense and so isolates the mind from contact with the world outside. To gaze at the motionless face of a sleeper temporarily rapt from the life of sight, sound, and movement—which, being common to all, binds us together in mutual recognition and social action—has always something awe-inspiring. This external inaction, this torpor of sense and muscle, how unlike to the familiar waking life, with its quick responsiveness and its overflowing energy! And then, if we look at dreams from the inside, we seem to find but the reverse face of the mystery. How inexpressibly strange does the late night-dream seem to a person on waking! He feels he has been seeing and hearing things no less real than those of waking life; but things which belong to an unfamiliar world, an order of sights and a sequence of events quite unlike those of waking experience; and he asks himself in his perplexity where that once-visited region really lies, or by what magic power it was suddenly and for a moment created for his vision. In truth, the very name of dream suggests something remote and mysterious, and when we want to characterize some impression or scene which by its passing strangeness filled us with wonder, we naturally call it dream-like.

Theories of Dreams.

The earliest theories respecting dreams illustrate very clearly this perception of the remoteness of dream-life from waking experience. By the simple mind of primitive man this dream-world is regarded as similar in its nature or structure to our common world, only lying remote from this. The savage conceives that when he falls asleep, his second self leaves his familiar body and journeys forth to unfamiliar regions, where it meets the departed second selves of his dead ancestors, and so on. From this point of view, the experience of the night, though equal in reality to that of the day, is passed in a wholly disconnected region.[1]

A second and more thoughtful view of dreams, marking a higher grade of intellectual culture, is that these visions of the night are symbolic pictures unfolded to the inner eye of the soul by some supernatural being. The dream-experience is now, in a sense, less real than it was before, since the phantasms that wear the guise of objective realities are simply

[1] See E. B. Tylor, *Primitive Culture*, ch. xi.; *cf.* Herbert Spencer, *Principles of Sociology*, ch. x.

images spread out to the spirit's gaze, or the direct utterance of a divine message. Still, this mysterious contact of the mind with the supernatural is regarded as a fact, and so the dream assumes the appearance of a higher order of experience. Its one point of attachment to the experience of waking life lies in its symbolic function; for the common form which this supernatural view assumes is that the dream is a dim prevision of coming events. Artemidorus, the great authority on dream interpretation (*oneirocritics*) for the ancient world, actually defines a dream as "a motion or fiction of the soul in a diverse form signifying either good or evil to come;" and even a logician like Porphyry ascribes dreams to the influence of a good demon, who thereby warns us of the evils which another and bad demon is preparing for us. The same mode of viewing dreams is quite common to-day, and many who pride themselves on a certain intellectual culture, and who imagine themselves to be free from the weakness of superstition, are apt to talk of dreams as of something mysterious, if not distinctly ominous. Nor is it surprising that phenomena which at first sight look so wild and lawless, should still pass for miraculous interruptions of the natural order of events.[1]

Yet, in spite of this obvious and impressive element of the mysterious in dream-life, the scientific impulse to illuminate the less known by the better known has long since begun to play on this obscure subject. Even in the ancient world a writer might here and

---

[1] For a fuller account of the different modes of dream-interpretation, see my article "Dream," in the ninth edition of the *Encyclopædia Britannica*.

there be found, like Democritus or Aristotle, who was bold enough to put forward a natural and physical explanation of dreams. But it has been the work of modern science to provide something like an approximate solution of the problem. The careful study of mental life in its intimate union with bodily operations, and the comparison of dream-combinations with other products of the imagination, normal as well as morbid, have gradually helped to dissolve a good part of the mystery which once hung like an opaque mist about the subject. In this way, our dream-operations have been found to have a much closer connection with our waking experiences than could be supposed on a superficial view. The materials of our dreams are seen, when closely examined, to be drawn from our waking experience. Our waking consciousness acts in numberless ways on our dreams, and these again in unsuspected ways influence our waking mental life.[1] Not only so, it is found that the quaint chaotic play of images in dreams illustrates mental processes and laws which are distinctly observable in waking thought. Thus, for example, the apparent objective reality of these visions has been accounted for, without the need of resorting to any supernatural agency, in the light of a vast assemblage of facts gathered from the by-ways, so to speak, of waking mental life. I need hardly add that I refer to the illusions of sense dealt with in the foregoing chapters.

Dreams are to a large extent the semblance of

---

[1] For a fuller account of the reaction of dreams on waking consciousness, see Paul Radestock, *Schlaf und Traum*. The subject is touched on later, under the Illusions of Memory.

external perceptions. Other psychical phenomena, as self-reflection, emotional activity, and so on, appear in dream-life, but they do so in close connection with these quasi-perceptions. The name "vision," given by old writers to dreams, sufficiently points out this close affinity of the mental phenomena to sense-perception; and so far as science is concerned, they must be regarded as a peculiar variety of sense-illusion. Hence the appropriateness of studying them in close connection with the illusions of perception of the waking state. Though marked off by the presence of very exceptional physiological conditions, they are largely intelligible by help of these physiological and psychological principles which we have just been considering.

The State of Sleep.

The physiological explanation of dreams must, it is plain, set out with an account of the condition of the organism known as sleep. While there is here much that is uncertain, there are some things which are fairly well known. Recent physiological observation has gone to prove that during sleep all the activities of the organism are appreciably lowered. Thus, for example, according to Testa, the pulse falls by about one-fifth. This lowering of the organic functions appears, under ordinary circumstances, to increase towards midnight, after which there is a gradual rising.

The nervous system shares in this general depression of the vital activities. The circulation being slower, the process of reparation and nutrition of the nerves is retarded, and so their degree of excitability diminished.

This is clearly seen in the condition of the peripheral regions of the nervous system, including the sense-organs, which appear to be but very slightly acted on by their customary stimuli.

The nervous centres must participate in this lethargy of the system. In other words, the activity of the central substance is lowered, and the result of this is plainly seen in what is usually thought of as the characteristic feature of sleep, namely, a transition from vigorous mental activity or intense and clear consciousness, to comparative inactivity or faint and obscure consciousness. The cause of this condition of the centres is supposed to be the same as that of the torpidity of all the other organs in sleep, namely, the retardation of the circulation. But, though there is no doubt as to this, the question of the proximate physiological conditions of sleep is still far from being settled. Whether during sleep the blood-vessels of the brain are fuller or less full than during waking, is still a moot point. Also the qualitative condition of the blood in the cerebral vessels is still a matter of discussion.[1]

Since the effect of sleep is to lower central activity, the question naturally occurs whether the nervous centres are ever rendered inactive to such an extent as to interrupt the continuity of our conscious life. This question has been discussed from the point of view of the metaphysician, of the psychologist, and of the physiologist, and in no case is perfect unanimity to be found. The metaphysical question, whether the soul as a spiritual substance is capable of being wholly in-

---

[1] For an account of the latest physiological hypotheses as to the proximate cause of sleep, see Radestock, *op. cit.*, appendix.

active, or whether it is not in what seem the moments
of profoundest unconsciousness partially awake—the
question so warmly discussed by the Cartesians, Leib-
nitz, etc.—need not detain us here.

Of more interest to us are the psychological and
the physiological discussions. The former seeks to
settle the question by help of introspection and memory.
On the one side, it is urged against the theory of unbroken mental activity, that we remember so little of
the lowered consciousness of sleep.[1] To this it is replied
that our forgetfulness of the contents of dream-consciousness, even if this were unbroken, would be fully
accounted for by the great dissimilarity between dreaming and waking mental life. It is urged, moreover,
on this side that a sudden rousing of a man from sleep
always discovers him in the act of dreaming, and that
this goes to prove the uniform connection of dreaming
and sleeping. This argument, again, may be met by
the assertion that our sense of the duration of our
dreams is found to be grossly erroneous ; that, owing to
the rapid succession of the images, the *realization* of
which would involve a long duration, we enormously
exaggerate the length of dreams in retrospection.[2]
From this it is argued that the dream which is recalled
on our being suddenly awakened may have had its
whole course during the transition state of waking.

Again, the fact that a man may resolve, on going to
sleep, to wake at a certain hour, has often been cited in

[1] Plutarch, Locke, and others give instances of people who never
dreamt. Lessing asserted of himself that he never knew what it was
to dream.

[2] The error touched on here will be fully dealt with under
Illusions of Memory.

proof of the persistence of a degree of mental activity even in perfectly sound sleep. The force of this consideration, however, has been explained away by saying that the anticipation of rising at an unusual hour necessarily produces a slight amount of mental disquietude, which is quite sufficient to prevent sound sleep, and therefore to expose the sleeper to the rousing action of faint external stimuli.

While the purely psychological method is thus wholly inadequate to solve the question, physiological reasoning appears also to be not perfectly conclusive. Many physiologists, not unnaturally desirous of upsetting what they regard as a gratuitous metaphysical hypothesis, have pronounced in favour of an absolutely dreamless or unconscious sleep. From the physiological point of view, there is no mystery in a totally suspended mental activity. On the other hand, there is much to be said on the opposite side, and perhaps it may be contended that the purely physiological evidence rather points to the conclusion that central activity, however diminished during sleep, always retains a minimum degree of intensity. At least, one would be disposed to argue in this way from the analogy of the condition of the other functions of the organism during sleep. Possibly this modicum of positive evidence may more than outweigh any slight presumption against the doctrine of unbroken mental activity drawn from the negative circumstance that we remember so little of our dream-life.[1]

Such being the state of physiological knowledge

---

[1] For a very full, fair, and thoughtful discussion of this whole question, see Radestock, *op. cit.*, ch. iv.

respecting the immediate conditions of sleep, we cannot look for any certain information on the nature of that residual mode of cerebral activity which manifests itself subjectively in dreams. It is evident, indeed, that this question can only be fully answered when the condition of the brain as a whole during sleep is understood. Meanwhile we must be content with vague hypotheses.

It may be said, for one thing, that during sleep the nervous substance as a whole is less irritable than during waking hours. That is to say, a greater amount of stimulus is needed to produce any conscious result.[1] This appears plainly enough in the case of the peripheral sense-organs. Although these are not, as it is often supposed, wholly inactive during sleep, they certainly require a more potent external stimulus to rouse them to action. And what applies to the peripheral regions applies to the centres. In truth, it is clearly impossible to distinguish between the diminished irritability of the peripheral and that of the central structures.

At first sight it seems contradictory to the above to say that stimuli which have little effect on the centres of consciousness during waking life produce an appreciable result in sleep. Nevertheless, it will be found that this is the case. Thus organic processes which scarcely make themselves known to the mind in a waking state, may be shown to be the originators of many of our dreams. This fact can only be explained on the physical side by saying that the special cerebral

---

[1] This may be technically expressed by saying that the liminal intensity (Schwelle) is raised during sleep.

activities engaged in an act of attention are greatly liberated during sleep by the comparative quiescence of the external senses. These activities, by co-operating with the faint results of the stimuli coming from the internal organs, serve very materially to increase their effect.

Finally, it is to be observed that, while the centres thus respond with diminished energy to peripheral stimuli, external and internal, they undergo a direct, or "automatic," mode of excitation, being roused into activity independently of an incoming nervous impulse. This automatic stimulation has been plausibly referred to the action of the products of decomposition accumulating in the cerebral blood-vessels.[1] It is possible that there is something in the nature of this stimulation to account for the force and vividness of its conscious results, that is to say, of dreams.

The Dream State.

Let us now turn to the psychic side of these conditions, that is to say, to the general character of the mental states known as dreams. It is plain that the closing of the avenues of the external senses, which is the accompaniment of sleep, will make an immense difference in the mental events of the time. Instead of drawing its knowledge from without, noting its bearings in relation to the environment, the mind will now be given over to the play of internal imagination. The activity of fancy will, it is plain, be unrestricted by collision with external fact. The internal mental life will expand in free picturesque movement.

[1] See Wundt, *Physiologische Psychologie*, pp. 188-191.

To say that in sleep the mind is given over to its own imaginings, is to say that the mental life in these circumstances will reflect the individual temperament and mental history. For the play of imagination at any time follows the lines of our past experience more closely than would at first appear, and being coloured with emotion, will reflect the predominant emotional impulses of the individual mind. Hence the saying of Heraclitus, that, while in waking we all have a common world, in sleep we have each a world of our own.

This play of imagination in sleep is furthered by the peculiar attitude of attention. When asleep the voluntary guidance of attention ceases; its direction is to a large extent determined by the contents of the mind at the moment. Instead of holding the images and ideas, and combining them according to some rational end, the attention relaxes its energies and succumbs to the force of imagination. And thus, in sleep, just as in the condition of reverie or day-dreaming, there is an abandonment of the fancy to its own wild ways.

It follows that the dream-state will not appear to the mind as one of fancy, but as one of actual perception, and of contact with present reality. Dreams are clearly illusory, and, unlike the illusions of waking life, are complete and persistent.[1] And the reason of this ought now to be clear. First of all, the mind during sleep wants what M. Taine calls the corrective of a pre-

---

[1] There is, indeed, sometimes an undertone of critical reflection, which is sufficient to produce a feeling of uncertainty and bewilderment, and in very rare cases to amount to a vague consciousness that the mental experience is a dream.

sent sensation. When awake under ordinary circumstances, any momentary illusion is at once set right by a new act of orientation. The superior vividness of the external impression cannot leave us in any doubt, when calm and self-possessed, whether our mental images answer to present realities or not. On the other hand, when asleep, this reference to a fixed objective standard is clearly impossible. Secondly, we may fairly argue that the mental images of sleep approximate in character to external impressions. This they do to some extent in point of intensity, for, in spite of the diminished excitability of the centres, the mode of stimulation which occurs in sleep may, as I have hinted, involve an energetic cerebral action. And, however this be, it is plain that the image will gain a preternatural force through the greatly narrowed range of attention. When the mind of the sleeper is wholly possessed by an image or group of images, and the attention kept tied down to these, there is a maximum reinforcement of the images. But this is not all. When the attention is thus held captive by the image, it approximates in character to an external impression in another way. In our waking state, when our powers of volition are intact, the external impression is characterized by its fixity or its obdurate resistance to our wishes. On the other hand, the mental image is fluent, accommodating, and disappears and reappears according to the direction of our volitions. In sleep, through the suspension of the higher voluntary power of attention, the mental image seems to lord it over our minds just as the actual impression of waking life.

This much may suffice, perhaps, by way of a general description of the sleeping and dreaming state. Other points will make themselves known after we have studied the contents and structure of dreams in detail.

Dreams are commonly classified (*e.g.* by Wundt) with hallucinations, and this rightly, since, as their common appellation of " vision " suggests, they are for the most part the semblance of percepts in the absence of external impressions. At the same time, recent research goes to show that in many dreams something answering to the " external impression " in waking perception is the starting-point. Consequently, in order to be as accurate as possible, I shall divide dreams into illusions (in the narrow sense) and hallucinations.

Dream-Illusions.

By dream-illusions I mean those dreams which set out from some peripheral nervous stimulation, internal or external. That the organic processes of digestion, respiration, etc., act as stimuli to the centres in sleep is well known. Thus, David Hartley assigns as the second great source of dreams " states of the body." [1] But it is not so well known to what an extent our dreams may be influenced by stimuli acting on the exterior sense-organs. Let us first glance at the action of such external stimuli.

Action of External Stimuli.

During sleep the eyes are closed, and consequently the action of external light on the retina impeded.

[1] *Observations on Man*, Part I. ch. iii. sec. 5.

Yet it is found that even under these circumstances any very bright light suddenly introduced is capable of stimulating the optic fibres, and of affecting consciousness. The most common form of this is the effect of bright moonlight, and of the early sun's rays. Krauss tells a funny story of his having once, when twenty-six years old, caught himself, on waking, in the act of stretching out his arms towards what his dream-fancy had pictured as the image of his mistress. When fully awake, this image resolved itself into the full moon.[1] It is not improbable, as Radestock remarks, that the rays of the sun or moon are answerable for many of the dreams of celestial glory which persons of a highly religious temperament are said to experience.

External sounds, when not sufficient to rouse the sleeper, easily incorporate themselves into his dreams. The ticking of a watch, the stroke of a clock, the hum of an insect, the song of a bird, the patter of rain, are common stimuli to the dream-phantasy. M. Alf. Maury tells us, in his interesting account of the series of experiments to which he submitted himself in order to ascertain the result of external stimulation on the mind during sleep, that when a pair of tweezers was made to vibrate near his ear, he dreamt of bells, the tocsin, and the events of June, 1848.[2] Most of us, probably, have gone through the experience of impolitely falling asleep when some one was reading to us, and of having dream-images suggested by the sounds that were still indistinctly heard. Scherner gives an amusing case of a youth who was permitted to

---

[1] Quoted by Radestock, *op. cit.*, p. 110.
[2] *Le Sommeil et les Rêves*, p. 132, *et seq.*

whisper his name into the ear of his obdurate mistress, the consequence of which was that the lady contracted a habit of dreaming about him, which led to a felicitous change of feeling on her part.[1]

The two lower senses, smell and taste, seem to play a less important part in the production of dream-illusions. Radestock says that the odour of flowers in a room easily leads to visual images of hot-houses, perfumery shops, and so on; and it is probable that the contents of the mouth may occasionally act as a stimulus to the organ of taste, and so give rise to corresponding dreams. As Radestock observes, these lower sensations do not commonly make known their quality to the sleeper's mind. They become transformed at once into visual, instead of into olfactory or gustatory percepts. That is to say, the dreamer does not imagine himself smelling or tasting, but seeing an object.

The contact of objects with the tactual organ is one of the best recognized causes of dreams. M. Maury found that when his lips were tickled, his dream-fancy interpreted the impression as of a pitch plaster being torn off his face. An unusual pressure on any part of the body, as, for example, from contact with a fellow-sleeper, is known to give rise to a well-marked variety of dream. Our own limbs may even appear as foreign bodies to our dream-imagination, when through pressure they become partly paralyzed. Thus, on one occasion, I awoke from a miserable dream, in which I felt sure I was grasping somebody's hand in

[1] *Das Leben des Traumes*, p. 369. Other instances are related by Beattie and Abercrombie.

bed, and I was racked by terrifying conjectures as to who it might be. When fully awake, I discovered that I had been lying on my right side, and clasping the wrist of the right arm (which had been rendered insensible by the pressure of the body) with the left hand.

In close connection with these stimuli of pressure are those of muscular movement, whether unimpeded or impeded. We need not enter into the difficult question how far the "muscular sense" is connected with the activity of the motor nerves, and how far with sensory fibres attached to the muscular or the adjacent tissues. Suffice it to say that an actual movement, a resistance to an attempted movement, or a mere dis-disposition to movement, whether consequent on a surplus of motor energy or on a sensation of discomfort or fatigue in the part to be moved, somehow or other makes itself known to our minds, even when we are deprived of the assistance of vision. And these feel-ings of movement, impeded or unimpeded, are common initial impulses in our dream-experiences. It is quite a mistake to suppose that dreams are built up out of the purely passive sensations of sight and hearing. A close observation will show that in nearly every dream we imagine ourselves either moving among the objects we perceive or striving to move when some weighty obstacle obstructs us. All of us are familiar with the common forms of nightmare, in which we strive hope-lessly to flee from some menacing evil, and this dream-experience, it may be presumed, frequently comes from a feeling of strain in the muscles, due to an awkward disposition of the limbs during sleep. The common dream-illusion of falling down a vast abyss is plausibly referred by Wundt to an involuntary extension of the foot of the sleeper.

Action of Internal Stimuli.

Let us now pass from the action of stimuli lying outside the organism, to that of stimuli lying within the peripheral regions of the sense-organs. I have already spoken of the influence of subjective sensations of sight, hearing, etc., on the illusions of waking life, and it is now to be added that these sensations play an important part in our dream-life. Johannes Müller lays great prominence on the part taken by ocular spectra in the production of dreams. As he observes, the apparent rays of light, light-patches, mists of light, and so on, due to changes of blood-pressure in the retina, only manifest themselves clearly when the eyes are closed and the more powerful effect of the external stimulus cut off. These subjective spectra come into prominence in the sleepy condition, giving rise to what M. Maury calls "hallucinations hypnagogiques," and which he regards (after Gruithuisen) as the chaos out of which the dream-cosmos is evolved.[1] They are pretty certainly the starting-point in those picturesque dreams in which figure a number of bright objects, such as beautiful birds, butterflies, flowers, or angels.

That the visual images of our sleep do often involve the peripheral regions of the organ of sight, seems to be proved by the singular fact that they sometimes persist after waking. Spinoza and Jean Paul Richter

[1] *Le Sommeil et les Rêves,* p. 42, *et seq.*

both experienced this survival of dream-images. Still more pertinent is the fact that the effects of retinal fatigue are producible by dream-images. The physiologist Gruithuisen had a dream, in which the principal feature was a violet flame, and which left behind it, *after waking*, for an appreciable duration, a complementary image of a yellow spot.[1]

Subjective auditory sensations appear to be much less frequent causes of dream-illusions than corresponding visual sensations. Yet the rushing, roaring sound caused by the circulation of the blood in the ear is, probably, a not uncommon starting-point in dreams. With respect to subjective sensations of smell and taste, there is little to be said. On the other hand, subjective sensations due to varying conditions in the skin are a very frequent exciting cause of dreams. Variations in the state of tension of the skin, brought about by alteration of position, changes in the character of the circulation, the irradiation of heat to the skin or the loss of the same, chemical changes,— these are known to give rise to a number of familiar sensations, including those of tickling, itching, burning, creeping, and so on; and the effects of these sensations are distinctly traceable in our dreams. For example, the exposure of a part of the body through a loss of the bed-clothes is a frequent excitant of distressing dreams. A cold foot suggests that the sleeper is walking over snow or ice. On the other hand, if the cold foot happens to touch a warm part of the body, the

---

[1] *Beiträge sur Physiognosie und Heautognosie*, p. 256. For other cases see H. Meyer, *Physiologie der Nervenfaser*, p. 309; and Strümpell, *Die Natur und Entstehung der Träume*, p. 125.

dream-fancy constructs images of walking on burning lava, and so on.

These sensations of the skin naturally conduct us to the organic sensations as a whole; that is to say, the feelings connected with the varying condition of the bodily organs. These include the feelings which arise in connection with the processes of digestion, respiration, and circulation, and the condition of various organs according to their state of nutrition, etc. During our waking life these organic feelings coalesce for the most part, forming as the "vital sense" an obscure background for our clear discriminative consciousness, and only come forward into this region when very exceptional in character, as when respiration or digestion is impeded, or when we make a special effort of attention to single them out.[1] When we are asleep, however, and the avenues of external perception are closed, they assume greater prominence and distinctness. The centres, no longer called upon to react on stimuli coming from without the organism, are free to react on stimuli coming from its hidden recesses. So important a part, indeed, do these organic feelings take in the dream-drama, that some writers are disposed to regard them as the great, if not the exclusive, cause of dreams. Thus, Schopenhauer held that the excitants of dreams are impressions received from the internal regions of the organism through the sympathetic nervous system.[2]

---

[1] A very clear and full account of these organic sensations, or common sensations, has recently appeared from the pen of A. Horwicz in the *Vierteljahrsschrift für wissenschaftliche Philosophie*, iv. Jahrgang 3tes Heft.

[2] Schopenhauer uses this hypothesis in order to account for the apparent reality of dream-illusions. He thinks these internal sensa-

It is hardly necessary, perhaps, to give many illustrations of the effect of such organic sensations on our dreams. Among the most common provocatives of dreams are sensations connected with a difficulty in breathing, due to the closeness of the air or to the pressure of the bed-clothes on the mouth. J. Börner investigated the influence of these circumstances by covering with the bed-clothes the mouth and a part of the nostrils of persons who were sound asleep. This was followed by a protraction of the act of breathing, a reddening of the face, efforts to throw off the clothes, etc. On being roused, the sleeper testified that he had experienced a nightmare, in which a horrid animal seemed to be weighing him down.[1] Irregularity of the heart's action is also a frequent cause of dreams. It is not improbable that the familiar dream-experience of flying arises from disturbances of the respiratory and circulatory movements.

Again, the effects of indigestion, and more particularly stomachic derangement, on dreams are too well known to require illustration. It may be enough to allude to the famous dream which Hood traces to an excessive indulgence at supper. It is known that the varying condition of the organs of secretion influences our dream-fancy in a number of ways.

Finally, it is to be observed that an injury done to any part of the organism is apt to give rise to appro-

tions may be transformed by the " intuitive function " of the brain (by means of the "forms" of space, time, etc.) into quasi-realities, just as well as the subjective sensations of light, sound, etc., which arise in the organs of sense in the absence of external stimuli. (See *Versuch über das Geistersehen : Werke*, vol. **v.** p. 244, *et seq.*)

[1] *Das Alpdrücken*, pp. 8, 9, 27.

priate dream-images. In this way, very slight disturbances which would hardly affect waking consciousness may make themselves felt during sleep. Thus, for example, an incipient toothache has been known to suggest that the teeth are being extracted.[1]

It is worth observing that the interpretation of these various orders of sensations by the imagination of the dreamer takes very different forms according to the person's character, previous experience, ruling emotions, and so on. This is what is meant by saying that during sleep every man has a world of his own, whereas, when awake, he shares in the common world of perception.

Dream-Exaggeration.

It is to be noticed, further, that this interpretation of sensation during sleep is uniformly a process of exaggeration.[2] The exciting causes of the feeling of discomfort, for example, are always absurdly magnified. The reason of this seems to be that, owing to the condition of the mind during sleep, the nature of the sensation is not clearly recognizable. Even in the case of familiar external impressions, such as the sound of the striking of a clock, there appears to be wanting that simple process of reaction by which, in a waking condition of the attention, a sense-impression is instantly discriminated and classed. In sleep, as in the artifi-

---

[1] It is this fact which justifies writers in assigning a prognostic character to dreams.

[2] A part of the apparent exaggeration in our dream-experiences may be retrospective, and due to the effect of the impression of wonder which they leave behind them. (See Strümpell, *Die Natur und Entstehung der Träume.*)

cially induced hypnotic condition, the slighter differences of quality among sensations are not clearly recognized. The activity of the higher centres, which are concerned in the finer processes of discrimination and classification, being greatly reduced, the impression may be said to come before consciousness as something novel and unfamiliar. And just as we saw that in waking life novel sensations agitate the mind, and so lead to an exaggerated mode of interpretation; so here we see that what is unfamiliar disturbs the mind, rendering it incapable of calm attention and just interpretation.

This failure to recognize the real nature of an impression is seen most conspicuously in the case of the organic sensations. As I have remarked, these constitute for the most part, in waking life, an undiscriminated mass of obscure feeling, of which we are only conscious as the mental tone of the hour. And in the few instances in which we do attend to them separately, whether through their exceptional intensity or in consequence of an extraordinary effort of discriminative attention, we can only be said to perceive them, that is, recognize their local origin, very vaguely. Hence, when asleep, these sensations get very oddly misinterpreted.

The localization of a bodily sensation in waking life means the combination of a tactual and a visual image with the sensation. Thus, my recognition of a twinge of toothache as coming from a certain tooth, involves representations of the active and passive sensations which touching and looking at the tooth would yield me. That is to say, the feeling instantly calls up a compound mental image exactly answering to a visual percept. This holds good in dream-interpretation too; the interpretation is effected by means of a visual image. But since the feeling is only very vaguely recognized, this visual image does not answer to the bodily part concerned. Instead of this, the fancy of the dreamer constructs some visual image which bears a vague resemblance to the proper one, and is generally, if not always, an exaggeration of this in point of extensive magnitude, etc. For example, a sensation arising from pressure on the bladder, being dimly connected with the presence of a fluid, calls up an image of a flood, and so on.

This mode of dream-interpretation has by some writers been erected into the typical mode, under the name of dream-symbolism. Thus Scherner, in his interesting though somewhat fanciful work, *Das Leben des Traumes*, contends that the various regions of the body regularly disclose themselves to the dream-fancy under the symbol of a building or group of buildings; a pain in the head calling up, for example, the image of spiders on the ceiling, intestinal sensations exciting an image of a narrow alley, and so on. Such theories are clearly an exaggeration of the fact that the localization of our bodily sensations during sleep is necessarily imperfect.[1]

In many cases the image called up bears on its objective side no discoverable resemblance to that of the bodily region or the exciting cause of the sensation. Here the explanation must be looked for in the subjective side of the sensation and mental image, that is to say, in their emotional quality, as pleasurable or

---

[1] *Cf.* Radestock, *op. cit.*, pp. 131, 132.

painful, distressing, quieting, etc. It is to be observed,
indeed, that in natural sleep, as in the condition known
as hypnotism, while differences of specific quality in
the sense-impressions are lost, the broad difference of
the pleasurable and the painful is never lost. It is, in
fact, the subjective emotional side of the sensation that
uniformly forces itself into consciousness. This being
so, it follows that, speaking generally, the sensations of
sleep, both external and internal, or organic, will be
interpreted by what G. H. Lewes has called "an
analogy of feeling;" that is to say, by means of a
mental image having some kindred emotional character
or colouring.

Now, the analogy between the higher emotional
and the bodily states is a very close one. A sensation
of obstruction in breathing has its exact analogue in
a state of mental embarrassment, a sensation of itching
its counterpart in mental impatience, and so on. And
since these emotional experiences are deeper and
fuller than the sensations, the tendency to exaggerate
the nature and causes of these last would naturally
lead to an interpretation of them by help of these
experiences. In addition to this, the predominance of
visual imagery in sleep would aid this transformation
of a bodily sensation into an emotional experience,
since visual perceptions have, as their accompaniments
of pleasure and pain, not sensations, but emotions.[1]

---

[1] I was on one occasion able to observe this process going on in
the transition from waking to sleeping. I partly fell asleep when
suffering from toothache. Instantly the successive throbs of pain
transformed themselves into a sequence of visible movements, which
I can only vaguely describe as the forward strides of some menacing
adversary.

Since in this vague interpretation of bodily sensation the actual impression is obscured, and not taken up as an integral part into the percept, it is evident that we cannot, strictly speaking, call the process an imitation of an act of perception, that is to say, an illusion. And since, moreover, the visual image by which the sensation is thus displaced appears as a present object, it would, of course, be allowable to speak of this as an hallucination. This substitution of a more or less analogous visual image for that appropriate to the sensation forms, indeed, a transition from dream-illusion, properly so called, to dream-hallucination.

Dream-Hallucinations.

On the physical side, these hallucinations answer to cerebral excitations which are central or automatic, not depending on movements transmitted from the periphery of the nervous system. Of these stimulations some appear to be direct, and due to unknown influences exerted by the state of nutrition of the cerebral elements, or the action of the contents of the blood-vessels on these elements.

Effects of Direct Central Stimulation.

That such action does prompt a large number of dream-images may be regarded as fairly certain. First of all, it seems impossible to account for all the images of dream-fancy as secondary phenomena connected by links of association with the foregoing classes of sensation. However fine and invisible many of the threads which hold together our ideas may be, they will hardly explain the profusion and picturesque variety of dream-imagery. Secondly, we are able in certain cases to infer with a fair amount of certainty that a dream-image is due to such central stimulation. The common occurrence that we dream of the more stirring events, the anxieties and enjoyments of the preceding day, appears to show that when the cerebral elements are predisposed to a certain kind of activity, as they are after having been engaged for some time in this particular work, they are liable to be excited by some stimulus brought directly to bear on them during sleep. And if this is so, it is not improbable that many of the apparently forgotten images of persons and places which return with such vividness in dreams are excited by a mode of stimulation which is for the greater part confined to sleep. I say "for the greater part," because even in our indolent, listless moments of waking existence such seemingly forgotten ideas sometimes return as though by a spontaneous movement of their own and by no discoverable play of association.

It may be well to add that this immediate revival of impressions previously received by the brain includes not only the actual perceptions of waking life, but also the ideas derived from others, the ideal fancies supplied by works of fiction, and even the images which our unaided waking fancy is wont to shape for itself. Our daily conjectures as to the future, the communications to us by others of their thoughts, hopes, and fears,—these give rise to numberless vague fugitive images, any one of which may become distinctly revived in sleep.[1]

[1] Even the " unconscious impressions " of waking hours, that is to say, those impressions which are so fugitive as to leave no psychical

This throws light on the curious fact that we often dream of experiences and events quite unlike those of our individual life. Thus, for example, the common construction by the dream-fancy of the experience of flight in mid-air, and the creation of those weird forms which the terror of a nightmare is wont to bring in its train, seem to point to the past action of waking fancy. To imagine one's self flying when looking at a bird is probably a common action with all persons, at least in their earlier years, and images of preternaturally horrible beings are apt to be supplied to most of us some time during life by nurses or by books.

Indirect Central Stimulation.

Besides these direct central stimulations, there are others which, in contradistinction, may be called indireet, depending on some previous excitation. These are, no doubt, the conditions of a very large number of our dream-images. There must, of course, be some primary cerebral excitation, whether that of a present peripheral stimulation, or that which has been termed central and spontaneous; but when once this first link of the imaginative chain is supplied, other links may be added in large numbers through the operation of the forces of association. One may, indeed, safely say that the large proportion of the contents of every dream arise in this way.

trace behind, may thus rise into the clear light of consciousness during sleep. Maury relates a curious dream of his own, in which there appeared a figure that seemed quite strange to him, though he afterwards found that he must have been in the habit of meeting the original in a street through which he was accustomed to walk (*loc. cit.*, p. 124).

The very simplest type of dream excited by a present sensation contains these elements. To take an example, I once dreamt, as a consequence of the loud barking of a dog, that a dog approached me when lying down, and began to lick my face. Here the play of the associative forces was apparent: a mere sensation of sound called up the appropriate visual image, this again the representation of a characteristic action, and so on. So it is with the dreams whose first impulse is some central or spontaneous excitation. A momentary sight of a face or even the mention of a name during the preceding day may give the start to dream-activity ; but all subsequent members of the series of images owe their revival to a tension, so to speak, in the fine threads which bind together, in so complicated a way, our impressions and ideas.

Among the psychic accompaniments of these central excitations visual images, as already hinted, fill the most conspicuous place. Even auditory images, though by no means absent, are much less numerous than visual. Indeed, when there are the conditions for the former, it sometimes happens that the auditory effect transforms itself into a visual effect. An illustration of this occurred in my own experience. Trying to fall asleep by means of the well-known device of counting, I suddenly found myself losing my hold on the faint auditory effects, my imagination transforming them into a visual spectacle, under the form of a path of light stretching away from me, in which the numbers appeared under the grotesque form of visible objects, tumbling along in glorious confusion.

Next to these visual phantasms, certain motor

hallucinations seem to be most prominent in dreams. By a motor hallucination, I mean the illusion that we are actually moving when there is no peripheral excitation of the motor organ. Just as the centres concerned in passive sensation are susceptible of central stimulation, so are the centres concerned in muscular sensation. A mere impulse in the centres of motor innervation (if we assume these to be the central seat of the muscular feelings) may suffice to give rise to a complete representation of a fully executed movement. And thus in our sleep we seem to walk, ride, float, or fly.

The most common form of motor hallucination is probably the vocal. In the social encounters which make up so much of our sleep-experience, we are wont to be very talkative. Now, perhaps, we find ourselves zealously advocating some cause, now very fierce in denunciation, now very amusing in witty repartee, and so on. This imagination of ourselves as speaking, as distinguished from that of hearing others talking, must, it is clear, involve the excitation of the structures engaged in the production of the muscular feelings which accompany vocal action, as much as, if not more than, the auditory centres. And the frequency of this kind of dream-experience may be explained, like that of visual imagery, by the habits of waking life. The speech impulse is one of the most deeply rooted of all our impulses, and one which has been most frequently exercised in waking life.

Combination of Dream-Elements.

It is commonly said that dreams are a grotesque dissolution of all order, a very chaos and whirl of images without any discoverable connection. On the other hand, a few writers claim for the mind in sleep a power of arranging and grouping its incongruous elements in definite and even life-like pictures. Each of these views is correct within certain limits; that is to say, there are dreams in which the strangest disorder seems to prevail, and others in which one detects the action of a central control. Yet, speaking generally, sequences of dream-images will be found to be determined by certain circumstances and laws, and so far not to be haphazard or wholly chaotic. We have now to inquire into the laws of these successions; and, first of all, we may ask how far the known laws of association, together with the peculiar conditions of the sleeping state, are able to account for the various modes of dream-combination. We have already regarded mental association as furnishing a large additional store of dream-imagery; we have now to consider it as explaining the sequences and concatenations of our dream-elements.

Incoherence of Dreams.

First of all, then, let us look at the chaotic and apparently lawless side of dreaming, and see whether any clue is discoverable to the centre of this labyrinth. In the case of all the less elaborately ordered dreams, in which sights and sounds appear to succeed one another in the wildest dance (which class of dreams probably belongs to the deeper stages of sleep), the mind may with certainty be regarded as purely passive, and the mode of sequence may be referred to the action of association complicated by the ever-recurring introduction of new initial impulses, both peripheral and central. These are the dreams in which we are conscious of being perfectly passive, either as spectators of a strange pageant, or as borne away by some apparently extraneous force through a series of the most diverse experiences. The flux of images in these dreams is very much the same as that in certain waking conditions, in which we relax attention, both external and internal, and yield ourselves wholly to the spontaneous play of memory and fancy.

It is plain at a glance that the simultaneous con-currence of wholly disconnected initial impulses will serve to impress a measure of disconnectedness on our dream-images. From widely remote parts of the organism there come impressions which excite each its peculiar visual or other image according as its local origin or its emotional tone is the more distinctly present to consciousness. Now it is a subjective ocular sensation suggesting a bouquet of lovely flowers, and close on its heels comes an impression from the organs of digestion suggesting all manner of obstacles, and so our dream-fancy plunges from a vision of flowers to one of dreadful demons.

Let us now look at the way in which the laws of association working on the incongruous elements thus cast up into our dream-consciousness, will serve to give a yet greater appearance of disorder and confusion to our dream-combinations. According to these laws, any idea may, under certain circumstances, call up another, if the corresponding impressions have only once occurred together, or if the ideas have any degree of resemblance, or, finally, if only they stand in marked contrast with one another. Any accidental coincidence of events, such as meeting a person at a particular foreign resort, and any insignificant resemblance between objects, sounds, etc., may thus supply a path, so to speak, from fact to dream-fancy.

In our waking states these innumerable paths of association are practically closed by the supreme energy of the coherent groups of impressions furnished us from the world without through our organs of sense, and also by the volitional control of internal thought in obedience to the pressure of practical needs and desires. In dream-life both of these influences are withdrawn, so that delicate threads of association, which have no chance of exerting their pull, so to speak, in our waking states, now make known their hidden force. Little wonder, then, that the filaments which bind together these dream-successions should escape detection, since even in our waking thought we so often fail to see the connection which makes us pass in recollection from a name to a visible scene or perhaps to an emotional vibration.

It is worth noting that the origin of an association is often to be looked for in one of those momentary half-conscious acts of waking imagination to which reference has already been made. A friend, for example, has been speaking to us of some common acquaintance, remarking on his poor health. The language calls up, vaguely, a visual representation of the person sinking in health and dying. An association will thus be formed between this person and the idea of death. A night or two after, the image of this person somehow recurs to our dream-fancy, and we straightway dream that we are looking at his corpse, watching his funeral, and so on. The links of the chain which holds together these dream-images were really forged, in part, in our waking hours, though the process was so rapid as to escape our attention. It may be added, that in many cases where a juxtaposition of dream-images seems to have no basis in waking life, careful reflection will occasionally bring to light some actual conjunction of impressions so momentary as to have faded from our recollection.

We must remember, further, how great an apparent disorder will invade our imaginative dream-life when the binding force of resemblance has unchecked play. In waking thought we have to connect things according to their essential resemblances, classifying objects and events for purposes of knowledge or action, according to their widest or their most important points of similarity. In sleep, on the contrary, the slightest touch of resemblance may engage the mind and affect the direction of fancy. In a sense we may be said, when dreaming, to *discover* mental affinities between impressions and feelings, including those subtle links of emotional analogy of which I have already spoken. This effect is well illustrated in a dream recorded by M. Maury, in which he passed from one set of images to another through some similarity of names, as that between *corps* and *cor*. Such a movement of fancy would, of course, be prevented in full waking consciousness by a predominant attention to the meaning of the sounds.

It will be possible, I think, after a habit of analyzing one's dreams in the light of preceding experience has been formed, to discover in a good proportion of cases some hidden force of association which draws together the seemingly fortuitous concourse of our dream-atoms. That we should expect to do so in every case is unreasonable, since, owing to the numberless fine ramifications which belong to our familiar images, many of the paths of association followed by our dream-fancy cannot be afterwards retraced.

To illustrate the odd way in which our images get tumbled together through the action of occult association forces, I will record a dream of my own. I fancied I was at the house of a distinguished literary acquaintance, at her usual reception hour. I expected the friends I was in the habit of meeting there. Instead of this, I saw a number of commonly dressed people having tea. My hostess came up and apologized for having asked me into this room. It was, she said, a tea-party which she prepared for poor people at sixpence a head. After puzzling over this dream, I came to the conclusion that the missing link was a verbal one. A lady who is a connection of my friend, and bears the same name, assists her sister in a large kind of benevolent scheme. I may add that I had not, so far as I could recollect, had occasion very recently to think of this benevolent friend, but I had been thinking of my literary friend in connection with her anticipated return to town.

In thus seeking to trace, amid the superficial chaos

of dream-fancy, its hidden connections, I make no pretence to explain why in any given case these particular paths of association should be followed, and more particularly why a slender thread of association should exert a pull where a stronger cord fails to do so. To account for this, it would be necessary to call in the physiological hypothesis that among the nervous elements connected with a particular element, a, already excited, some, as m and n, are at the moment, owing to the state of their nutrition or their surrounding influences, more powerfully predisposed to activity than other elements, as b and c.

The subject of association naturally conducts us to the second great problem in the theory of dreams—the explanation of the order in which the various images group themselves in all our more elaborate dreams.

Coherence of Dreams.

A fully developed dream is a complex of many distinct illusory sense-presentations: in this respect it differs from the illusions of normal waking life, which are for the most part single and isolated. And this complex of quasi-presentations appears somehow or other to fall together into one whole scene or series of events, which, though it may be very incongruous and absurdly impossible from a waking point of view, nevertheless makes a single object for the dreamer's internal vision, and has a certain degree of artistic unity. This plastic force, which selects and binds together our unconnected dream-images, has frequently been referred to as a mysterious spiritual faculty, under the name of "creative fancy." Thus Cudworth remarks, in his *Treatise concerning Eternal and Immutable Morality:* "That dreams are many times begotten by the phantastical power of the soul itself . . . is evident from the orderly connection and coherence of imaginations which many times are continued in a long chain or series." One may find a good deal of mystical writing on the nature and activity of this faculty, especially in German literature. The explanation of this element of organic unity in dreams is, it may be safely said, the crux in the science of dreams. That the laws of psychology help us to understand the sequences of dream-images, we have seen. What we have now to ask is whether these laws throw any light on the orderly grouping of the elements so brought up in consciousness in the form of a connected experience.

It is to be remarked at the outset that a singular kind of unity is sometimes given to our dream-combinations by a total or partial coalescence of different images. The conditions of such coalescence have been referred to already.[1] Simultaneous impressions or images will always tend to coalesce with a force which varies directly as the degree of their similarity. Sometimes this coalescence is instantaneous and not made known to consciousness. Thus, Radestock suggests that if the mind of the sleeper is simultaneously invaded by an unpleasant sensation arising out of some disturbance of the functions of the skin, and a subjective visual sensation, the resulting mental image may be a combination of the two, under the form of a caterpillar creeping over the bodily surface. And the

---

[1] See p. 53.

coalescence may even be prepared by sub-conscious operations of waking imagination. Thus, for example, I once spoke about the cheapness of hares to a member of my family, who somewhat grimly suggested that they were London cats. I did not dwell on the idea, but the following night I dreamt that I saw a big hybrid creature, half hare, half cat, sniffing about a cottage. As it stood on its hind legs and took a piece of food from a window-ledge, I became sure that it was a cat. Here it is plain that the cynical observation of my relative had, at the moment, partially excited an image of this feline hare. In some dreams, again, we may become aware of the process of coalescence, as when persons who at one moment were seen to be distinct appear to our dream-fancy to run together in some third person.

A very similar kind of unification takes place between sequent images under the form of transformation. When two images follow one another closely, and have anything in common, they readily assume the form of a transmutation. There is a sort of overlapping of the mental images, and so an appearance of continuity produced in some respects analogous to that which arises in the wheel-of-life (thaumatrope) class of sense-illusions. This would seem to account for the odd transformations of personality which not unfrequently occur in dreams, in which a person appears, by a kind of metempsychosis, to transfer his physical ego to another, and in which the dreamer's own bodily phantom plays similar freaks. And the same principle probably explains those dissolving-view effects which are so familiar an accompaniment of dream-scenery.[1]

[1] See Maury, *loc. cit.*, p. 146.

But passing from this exceptional kind of unity in dreams, let us inquire how the heterogeneous elements of our dream-fancy become ordered and arranged when they preserve their separate existence. If we look closely at the structure of our more finished dreams, we find that the appearance of harmony, connectedness, or order, may be given in one of two ways. There may, first of all, be a subjective harmony, the various images being held together by an emotional thread. Or there may, secondly, be an objective harmony, the parts of the dream, though answering to no particular experiences of waking life, bearing a certain resemblance to our habitual modes of experience. Let us inquire into the way in which each kind of order is brought about.

Lyrical Element in Dreams.

The only unity that belongs to many of our dreams is a subjective emotional unity. This is the basis of harmony in lyrical poetry, where the succession of images turns mainly on their emotional colouring. Thus, the images that float before the mind of the Poet Laureate, in his *In Memoriam,* clearly have their link of connection in their common emotional tone, rather than in any logical continuity. Dreaming has been likened to poetic composition, and certainly many of our dreams are built upon a groundwork of lyrical feeling. They might be marked off, perhaps, as our lyrical dreams.

The way in which this emotional force acts in these cases has already been hinted at. We have seen that the analogy of feeling is a common link between dream-images. Now, if any shade of feeling becomes fixed and dominant in the mind, it will tend to control all the images of the time, allowing certain congruous ones to enter, and excluding others.[1] If, for example, a feeling of distress occupies the mind, distressing images will have the advantage in the struggle for existence which goes on in the world of mind as well as in that of matter. We may say that attention, which is here wholly a passive process, is controlled by the emotion of the time, and bent in the direction of congruent or harmonious images.

Now, a ground-tone of feeling of a certain complexion, answering to the sum of sensations arising in connection with the different organic processes of the time, is a very frequent foundation of our dream-structure. So frequent is it, indeed, that one might almost say there is no dream in which it is not one great determining factor. The analysis of a very large number of dreams has convinced me that traces of this influence are discoverable in a great majority.

I will give a simple illustration of this lyrical type of dream. A little girl of about four years and three-quarters went with her parents to Switzerland. On their way she was taken to the cathedral at Strasburg, and saw the celebrated clock strike, and the figures of the Apostles come out, etc. In Switzerland she stayed at Gimmelwald, near Mürren, opposite a fine mass of snowy mountains. One morning she told her father that she had had "such a lovely dream." She fancied she was on the snow-peaks with her nurse, and walked on to the sky. There came out of the sky "such

---

[1] See what was said respecting the influence of a dominant emotional agitation on the interpretation of actual sense-impressions.

beautiful things," just like the figures of the clock.
This vision of celestial things was clearly due to the
fact that both the clock and the snow-peaks touching
the blue sky had powerfully excited her imagination,
filling her with much the same kind of emotion,
namely, wonder, admiration, and longing to reach an
inaccessible height.

Our feelings commonly have a gradual rise and
fall, and the organic sensations which so often constitute the emotional basis of our lyrical dreams
generally have stages of increasing intensity. Moreover, such a persistent ground-feeling becomes rein-
forced by the images which it sustains in consciousness.
Hence a certain *crescendo* character in our emotional
dreams, or a gradual rise to some culminating point or
climax.

This phase of dream can be illustrated from the
experience of the same little girl. When just five
years old, she was staying at Hampstead, near a church
which struck the hours somewhat loudly. One morning she related the following dream to her father (I
use her own language). The biggest bells in the world
were ringing; when this was over the earth and houses
began to tumble to pieces; all the seas, rivers, and ponds
flowed together, and covered all the land with black
water, as deep as in the sea where the ships sail;
people were drowned; she herself flew above the
water, rising and falling, fearing to fall in; she then
saw her mamma drowned, and at last flew home to tell
her papa. The gradual increase of alarm and distress
expressed in this dream, having its probable cause in
the cumulative effect of the disturbing sound of the
church bells, must be patent to all.

The following rather comical dream illustrates quite as clearly the growth of a feeling of irritation and vexation, probably connected with the development of some slightly discomposing organic sensation. I dreamt I was unexpectedly called on to lecture to a class of young women, on Herder. I began hesitatingly, with some vague generalities about the Augustan age of German literature, referring to the three well-known names of Lessing, Schiller, and Goethe. Immediately my sister, who suddenly appeared in the class, took me up, and said she thought there was a fourth distin-guished name belonging to this period. I was annoyed at the interruption, but said, with a feeling of triumph, " I suppose you mean Wieland ?" and then appealed to the class whether there were not twenty persons who knew the names I had mentioned to one who knew Wie-land's name. Then the class became generally dis-orderly. My feeling of embarrassment gained in depth. Finally, as a climax, several quite young girls, about ten years and less, came and joined the class. The dream broke off abruptly as I was in the act of taking these children to the wife of an old college tutor, to protest against their admission.

It is worth noting, perhaps, that in this evolution of feeling in dreaming the quality of the emotion may vary within certain limits. One shade of feeling may be followed by another and kindred shade, so that the whole dream still preserves a degree, though a less obvious degree, of emotional unity. Thus, for example, a lady friend of mine once dreamt that she was in church, listening to a well-known novelist of the more earnest sort, preaching. A wounded soldier was brought in to be shot, because he was mortally wounded, and had distinguished himself by his bravery. He was then shot, but not killed, and, rolling over in agony, exclaimed, "How long!" The development of an extreme emotion of horror out of the vague feeling of awe which is associated with a church, gives a curious interest to this dream.

Verisimilitude in Dreams.

I must not dwell longer on this emotional basis of dreams, but pass to the consideration of the second and objective kind of unity which characterizes many of our more elaborate dream-performances. In spite of all that is fitful and grotesque in dream-combination, it still preserves a distant resemblance to our actual experience. Though no dream reproduces a particular incident or chain of incidents in this experience, though the dream-fancy invariably transforms the particular objects, relations, and events of waking life, it still makes the order of our daily experience its prototype. It fashions its imaginary world on the model of the real. Thus, objects group themselves in space, and act on one another conformably to these perceived space-relations; events succeed one another in time, and are often seen to be connected; men act from more or less intelligible motives, and so on. In this way, though the dream-fancy sets at nought the particular relations of our experience, it respects the general and constant relations. How are we to account for this?

It is said by certain philosophers that this superposition of the relations of space, time, causation, etc., on the products of our dream-fancy is due to the fact that all experience arises by a synthesis of mental forms with the chaotic matter of sense-impressions. These philosophers allow, however, that all particular connections are determined by experience. Accordingly, what we have to do here is to inquire how far this scientific method of explaining mental connections by facts of experience will carry us. In other words, we have to ask what light can be thrown on these tendencies of dream-imagination by ascertained psychological laws, and more particularly by what are known as the laws of association.

These laws tell us that of two mental phenomena which occur together, each will tend to recall the other whenever it happens to be revived. On the physiological side, this means that any two parts of the nervous structures which have acted together become in some way connected, so that when one part begins to work the other will tend to work also. But it is highly probable that a particular structure acts in a great many different ways. Thus, it may be stimulated by unlike modes of stimuli, or it may enter into very various connections with other structures. What will follow from this? One consequence would appear to be that there will be developed an organic connection between the two structures, of such a kind that whenever one is excited the other will be disposed to act somehow and anyhow, even when there is nothing in the present mode of activity of the first structure to determine the second to act in some one definite way, in other words, when this mode of activity is, roughly speaking, novel.

Let me illustrate this effect in one of the simplest cases, that of the visual organ. If, when walking out on a dark night, a few points in my retina are suddenly stimulated by rays of light, and I recognize some luminous object in a corresponding direction, I am prepared to see something above and below, to the right and to the left of this object. Why is this? There may from the first have been a kind of innate understanding among contiguous optic fibres, predisposing them to such concerted action. But however this be, this disposition would seem to have been largely promoted by the fact that, throughout my experience, the stimulation of any retinal point has been connected with that of adjoining points, either simultaneously by some second object, or successively by the same object as the eye moves over it, or as the object itself moves across the field of vision.

When, therefore, in sleep any part of the optic centres is excited in a particular way, and the images thus arising have their corresponding loci in space assigned to them, there will be a disposition to refer any other visual images which happen at the moment to arise in consciousness to adjacent parts of space. The character of these other images will be determined by other special conditions of the moment; their locality or position in space will be determined by this organic connection. We may, perhaps, call these tendencies to concerted action of some kind general associative dispositions.

Just as there are such dispositions to united action among various parts of one organ of sense, so there may be among different organs, which are either connected originally in the infant organism, or have communications opened up by frequent coexcitation of the two. Such links there certainly are between the organs of taste and smell, and between the ear and the muscular system in general, and more particularly the vocal organ.[1] A new odour often sets us asking how the object would taste, and a series of sounds commonly disposes us to movement of some kind or another. How far there may be finer threads of connection between other organs, such as the eye and the ear, which do not betray themselves amid the stronger forces of waking mental life, one cannot say. Whatever their number, it is plain that they will exert their influence within the comparatively narrow limits of dream-life, serving to impress a certain character on the images which happen to be called up by special circumstances, and giving to the combination a slight measure of congruity. Thus, if I were dreaming that I heard some lively music, and at the same time an image of a friend was anyhow excited, my dream-fancy might not improbably represent this person as performing a sequence of rhythmic movements, such as those of riding, dancing, etc.

A narrower field for these general associative dispositions may be found in the tendency, on the reception of an impression of a given character, to look for a certain kind of second impression; though the exact nature of this is unknown. Thus, for example, the

---

[1] It is proved experimentally that the ear has a much closer organic connection with the vocal organ than the eye has. Donders found that the period required for responding vocally to a sound-signal is less than that required for responding in the same way to a light-signal.

form and colour of a new flower suggest a scent, and the perception of a human form is accompanied by a vague representation of vocal utterances. These general tendencies of association appear to me to be most potent influences in our dream-life. The many strange human forms which float before our dream-fancy are apt to talk, move, and behave like men and women in general, however little they resemble their actual prototypes, and however little individual consistency of character is preserved by each of them. Special conditions determine what they shall say or do; the general associative disposition accounts for their saying or doing something.

We thus seem to find in the purely passive processes of association some ground for that degree of natural coherence and rational order which our more mature dreams commonly possess. These processes go far to explain, too, that odd mixture of rationality with improbability, of natural order and incongruity, which characterizes our dream-combinations.

Rational Construction in Dreams.

Nevertheless, I quite agree with Herr Volkelt that association, even in the most extended meaning, cannot explain all in the shaping of our dream-pictures. The " phantastical power " which Cudworth talks about clearly includes something besides. It is an erroneous supposition that when we are dreaming there is a complete suspension of the voluntary powers, and consequently an absence of all direction of the intellectual processes. This supposition, which has been maintained by numerous writers, from Dugald Stewart downwards, seems to be based on the fact that we frequently find ourselves in dreams striving in vain to move the whole body or a limb. But this only shows, as M. Maury remarks in the work already referred to, that our volitions are frustrated through the inertia of our bodily organs, not that these volitions do not take place. In point of fact, the dreamer, not to speak of the somnambulist, is often conscious of voluntarily going through a series of actions. This exercise of volition is shown unmistakably in the well-known instances of extraordinary intellectual achievements in dreams, as Condillac's composition of a part of his *Cours d'Études*. No one would maintain that a result of this kind was possible in the total absence of intellectual action carefully directed by the will. And something of this same control shows itself in all our more fully developed dreams.

One manifestation of this voluntary activity in sleep is to be found in those efforts of attention which not unfrequently occur. I have remarked that, speaking roughly and in relation to the waking condition, the state of sleep is marked by a subjection of the powers of attention to the force of the mental images present to consciousness. Yet something resembling an exercise of voluntary attention sometimes happens in sleep. The intellectual feats just spoken of, unless, indeed, they are referred to some mysterious unconscious mental operations, clearly involve a measure of volitional guidance. All who dream frequently are occasionally aware on awaking of having greatly exercised their attention on the images presented to them during sleep. I myself am often able to recall an effort to see beautiful objects, which threatened to disappear from my field of vision, or to catch faint receding tones of preternatural sweetness; and some dreamers allege that they are able to retain a recollection of the feeling of strain connected with such exercise of attention in sleep.

The main function of this voluntary attention in dream-life is seen in the selection of those images which are to pass the threshold of clear consciousness. I have already spoken of a selective action brought about by the ruling emotion. In this case, the attention is held captive by the particular feeling of the moment. Also a selective process goes on in the case of the action of those associative dispositions just referred to. But in each of these cases the action of selective attention is comparatively involuntary, passive, and even unconscious, not having anything of the character of a conscious striving to compass some end. Besides this comparatively passive play of selective attention, there is an active play, in which there is a conscious wish to gain an end; in other words, the operation of a definite motive. This motive may be described as an intellectual impulse to connect and harmonize what is present to the mind. The voluntary kind of selection includes and transcends each of the involuntary kinds. It has as its result an imitation of that order which is brought about by what I have called the associative dispositions, only it consciously aims at this result. And it is a process controlled by a feeling, namely, the intellectual sentiment of consistency, which is not a mode of emotional excitement enthralling the will, but a calm motive, guiding the activities of attention. It thus bears somewhat the same relation to the emotional selection already spoken of, as dramatic creation bears to lyrical composition.

This process of striving to seize some connecting link, or thread of order, is illustrated whenever, in waking life, we are suddenly brought face to face with an unfamiliar scene. When taken into a factory, we strive to arrange the bewildering chaos of visual impressions under some scheme, by help of which we are said to understand the scene. So, if on entering a room we are plunged in *medias res* of a lively conversation, we strive to find a clue to the discussion. Whenever the meaning of a scene is not at once clear, and especially whenever there is an appearance of confusion in it, we are conscious of a painful feeling of perplexity, which acts as a strong motive to ever-renewed attention.[1]

In touching on this intellectual impulse to connect the disconnected, we are, it is plain, approaching the question of the very foundations of our intellectual structure. That there is this impulse firmly rooted in the mature mind nobody can doubt; and that it manifests itself in early life in the child's recurring "Why?" is equally clear. But how we are to account for it, whether it is to be viewed as a mere result of the play of associated fragments of experience, or as something involved in the very process of the association of ideas itself, is a question into which I cannot here enter.

<hr>

[1] On the nature of this impulse, as illustrated in waking and in sleep, see the article by Delbœuf, "Le Sommeil et les Rêves," in the *Revue Philosophique*, June, 1880, p. 636.

What I am here concerned to show is that the search for consistency and connection in the manifold impressions of the moment is a deeply rooted habit of the mind, and one which is retained in a measure during sleep. When, in this state, our minds are invaded by a motley crowd of unrelated images, there results a disagreeable sense of confusion; and this feeling acts as a motive to the attention to sift out those products of the dream-fancy which may be made to cohere. When once the foundations of a dream-action are laid, new images must to some extent fit in with this; and here there is room for the exercise of a distinct impulse to order the chaotic elements of dream-fancy in certain forms. The perception of any possible relation between one of the crowd of new images ever surging above the level of obscure consciousness, and the old group at once serves to detain it. The concentration of attention on it, in obedience to this impulse to seek for an intelligible order, at once intensifies it and fixes it, incorporating it into the series of dream-pictures.

Here is a dream which appears to illustrate this impulse to seek an intelligible order in the confused and disorderly. After being occupied with correcting the proofs of my volume on *Pessimism*, I dreamt that my book was handed to me by my publisher, fully illustrated with coloured pictures. The frontispiece represented the fantastic figure of a man gesticulating in front of a ship, from which he appeared to have just stepped. My publisher told me it was meant for Hamlet, and I immediately reflected that this character had been selected as a concrete example of the pessimistic tendency. I may add that, on awaking, I was distinctly aware of having felt puzzled when dreaming, and of having striven to read a meaning into the dream.

The *rationale* of this dream seems to me to be somewhat as follows. The image of the completed volume represented, of course, a recurring anticipatory image of waking life. The coloured plates were due probably to subjective optical sensations simultaneously excited, which were made to fit in (with or without an effort of voluntary attention) with the image of the book under the form of illustrations. But this stage of coherency did not satisfy the mind, which, still partly confused by the incongruity of coloured plates in a philosophic work, looked for a closer connection. The image of Hamlet was naturally suggested in connection with pessimism. The effort to discover a meaning in the pictures led to the fusion of this image with one of the subjective spectra, and in this way the idea of a Hamlet frontispiece probably arose.

The whole process of dream-construction is clearly illustrated in a curious dream recorded by Professor Wundt.[1] Before the house is a funeral procession : it is the burial of a friend, who has in reality been dead for some time past. The wife of the deceased bids him and an acquaintance who happens to be with him go to the other side of the street and join the procession. After she has gone away, his companion remarks to him, " She only said that because the cholera rages over yonder, and she wants to keep this side of the street to herself." Then comes an attempt to flee from the region of the cholera. Returning to his house, he finds the procession gone, but the street strewn with

[1] *Physiologische Psychologie*, p. 660.

rich nosegays; and he further observes crowds of men who seem to be funeral attendants, and who, like himself, are hastening to join the procession. These are, oddly enough, dressed in red. When hurrying on, it occurs to him that he has forgotten to take a wreath for the coffin. Then he wakes up with beating of the heart.

The sources of this dream are, according to Wundt, as follows. First of all, he had, on the previous day, met the funeral procession of an acquaintance. Again, he had read of cholera breaking out in a certain town. Once more, he had talked about the particular lady with this friend, who had narrated facts which clearly proved her selfishness. The hastening to flee from the infected neighbourhood and to overtake the procession was prompted by the sensation of heart-beating. Finally, the crowd of red bier-followers, and the profusion of nosegays, owed their origin to subjective visual sensations, the "light-chaos" which often appears in the dark.

Let us now see for a moment how these various elements may have become fused into a connected chain of events. First of all, it is clear that this dream is built up on a foundation of a gloomy tone of feeling, arising, as it would seem, from an irregularity of the heart's action. Secondly, it owes its special structure and its air of a connected sequence of events, to those tendencies, passive and active, to order the chaotic of which I have been speaking. Let us try to trace this out in detail.

To begin with, we may suppose that the image of the procession occupies the dreamer's mind. From quite

another source the image of the lady enters consciousness, bringing with it that of her deceased husband and
of the friend who has recently been talking about her.
These new elements adapt themselves to the scene,
partly by the passive mechanism of associative dispositions, and partly, perhaps, by the activity of voluntary
selection. Thus, the idea of the lady's husband would
naturally recall the fact of his death, and this would fall
in with the pre-existing scene under the form of the
idea that he is the person who is now being buried.
The next step is very interesting. The image of the
lady is associated with the idea of selfish motives.
This would tend to suggest a variety of actions, but the
one which becomes a factor of the dream is that which
is specially adapted to the pre-existing representations,
namely, of the procession on the further side of the
street, and the cholera (which last, like the image of
the funeral, is, we may suppose, due to an independent
central excitation). That is to say, the request of the
lady, and its interpretation, are a *resultant* of a number
of adaptative or assimilative actions, under the sway
of a strong desire to connect the disconnected, and a
lively activity of attention. Once more, the feeling
of oppression of the heart, and the subjective stimulation of the optic nerve, might suggest numberless
images besides those of anxious flight and of red-clad
men and nosegays; they suggest these, and not others,
in this particular case, because of the co-operation of
the impulse of consistency, which, setting out with the
pre-existing mental images, selects from among many
tendencies of reproduction those which happen to
chime in with the scene.

The Nature of Dream-Intelligence.

It must not be supposed that this process of welding together the chaotic materials of our dreams is ever carried out with anything like the clear rational purpose of which we are conscious when seeking, in waking life, to comprehend some bewildering spectacle. At best it is a vague longing, and this longing, it may be added, is soon satisfied. There is, indeed, something almost pathetic in the facility with which the dreamer's mind can be pacified with the least appearance of a connection. Just as a child's importunate "Why?" is often silenced by a ridiculous caricature of an explanation, so the dreamer's intelligence is freed from its distress by the least semblance of a uniting order.

It thus remains true with respect even to our most coherent dreams, that there is a complete suspension, or at least a considerable retardation, of the highest operations of judgment and thought; also a great enfeeblement, to say the least of it, of those sentiments such as the feeling of consistency and the sense of the absurd which are so intimately connected with these higher intellectual operations.

In order to illustrate how oddly our seemingly rational dreams caricature the operations of waking thought, I may, perhaps, be allowed to record two of my own dreams, of which I took careful note at the time.

On the first occasion I went "in my dream" to the "Stores" in August, and found the place empty. A shopman brought me some large fowls. I asked their price, and he answered, "Tenpence a pound." I then asked their weight, so as to get an idea of their total cost, and he replied, " Forty pounds." Not in the least surprised, I proceeded to calculate their cost: $40 \times 10 = 400 \div 12 = 33\frac{1}{3}$. But, oddly enough, I took this quotient as pence, just as though I had not already divided by 12, and so made the cost of a fowl to be 2s. 9d., which seemed to me a fair enough price.

In my second dream I was at Cambridge, among a lot of undergraduates. I saw a coach drive up with six horses. Three undergraduates got out of the coach. I asked them why they had so many horses, and they said, " Because of the luggage." I then said, " The luggage is much more than the undergraduates. Can you tell me how to express this in mathematical symbols? This is the way: if x is the weight of an undergraduate, then $x + x^n$ represents the weight of an undergraduate and his luggage together." I noticed that this sally was received with evident enjoyment.[1]

We may say, then, that the structure of our dreams, equally with the fact of their completely illusory character, points to the conclusion that during sleep, just as in the moments of illusion in waking life, there

---

[1] I may, perhaps, observe, after giving two dreams which have to do with mathematical operations, that, though I was very fond of them in my college days, I have long ceased to occupy myself with these processes. I would add, by way of redeeming my dream-intelligence from a deserved charge of silliness, that I once performed a respectable intellectual feat when asleep. I put together the riddle, " What might a wooden ship say when her side was stove in? Tremendous!" (Tree-mend-us). I was aware of having tried to improve on the form of this pun. I am happy to say I am not given to punning during waking life, though I had a fit of it once. It strikes me that punning, consisting as it does essentially of overlooking sense and attending to sound, is just such a debased kind of intellectual activity as one might look for in sleep.

is a deterioration of our intellectual life. The highest intellectual activities answering to the least stable nervous connections are impeded, and what of intellect remains corresponds to the · most deeply organized connections.

In this way, our dream-life touches that childish condition of the intelligence which marks the decadence of old age and the encroachments of mental disease. The parallelism between dreams and insanity has been pointed out by most writers on the subject. Kant observed that the madman is a dreamer awake, and more recently Wundt has remarked that, when asleep, we "can experience nearly all the phenomena which meet us in lunatic asylums." The grotesqueness of the combinations, the lack of all judgment as to consistency, fitness, and probability, are common characteristics of the short night-dream of the healthy and the long day-dream of the insane.[1]

But one great difference marks off the two domains. When dreaming, we are still sane, and shall soon prove our sanity. After all, the dream of the sleeper is corrected, if not so rapidly as the illusion of the healthy waker. As soon as the familiar stimuli of light and sound set the peripheral sense-organs in activity, and call back the nervous system to its complete round of healthy action, the illusion disappears, and we smile at our alarms and agonies, saying, "Behold, it was a dream!"

On the practical side, the illusions and hallucinations of sleep must be regarded as comparatively harm-

---

[1] See Radestock, *op. cit.*, ch. ix. ; *Vergleichung des Traumes mit dem Wahnsinn.*

less.   The sleeper, in healthy conditions of sleep, ceases to be an agent, and the illusions which enthral his brain have no evil practical consequences. They may, no doubt, as we shall see in a future chapter, occasionally lead to a subsequent confusion of fiction and reality in waking recollection.   But with the exception of this, their worst effect is probably the lingering sense of discomfort which a " nasty dream " sometimes leaves with us, though this may be balanced by the reverberations of happy dream-emotions which sometimes follow us through the day.   And however this be, it is plain that any disadvantages thus arising are more than made good by the consideration that our liability to these nocturnal illusions is connected with the need of that periodic recuperation of the higher nervous structures which is a prime condition of a vigorous intellectual activity, and so of a triumph over illusion during waking life.

For these reasons dreams may properly be classed with the illusions of normal or healthy life, rather than with those of disease. They certainly lie nearer this region than the very similar illusions of the somnambulist, which with respect to their origin appear to be more distinctly connected with a pathological condition of the nervous system, and which with respect to their practical consequences may easily prove so disastrous.

After-Dreams.

In concluding this account of dreams, I would call attention to the importance of the transition states between sleeping and waking, in relation to the production of sense-illusion. And this point may be touched on here all the more appropriately, since it helps to bring out the close relation between waking and sleeping illusion. The mind does not pass suddenly and at a bound from the condition of dream-fancy to that of waking perception. I have already had occasion to touch on the " hypnagogic state," that condition of somnolence or " sleepiness " in which external impressions cease to act, the internal attention is relaxed, and the weird imagery of sleep begins to unfold itself. And just as there is this anticipation of dream-hallucination in the presomnial condition, so there is the survival of it in the postsomnial condition. As I have observed, dreams sometimes leave behind them, for an appreciable interval after waking, a vivid after-impression, and in some cases even the semblance of a sense-perception.

If one reflects how many ghosts and other miraculous apparitions are seen at night, and when the mind is in a more or less somnolent condition, the idea is forcibly suggested that a good proportion of these visions are the *débris* of dreams. In some cases, indeed, as that of Spinoza, already referred to, the hallucination (in Spinoza's case that of " a scurvy black Brazilian ") is recognized by the subject himself as a dream-image.[1] I am indebted to Mr. W. H. Pollock for a fact which curiously illustrates the position here adopted. A lady was staying at a country house. During the night and immediately on waking up she

---

[1] For Spinoza's experience, given in his own words, see Mr. F. Pollock's *Spinoza*, p. 57; *cf.* what Wundt says on his experience, *Physiologische Psychologie*, p. 648, footnote 2.

had an apparition of a strange-looking man in mediæval costume, a figure by no means agreeable, and which seemed altogether unfamiliar to her. The next morning, on rising, she recognized the original of her hallucinatory image in a portrait hanging on the wall of her bedroom, which must have impressed itself on her brain before the occurrence of the apparition, though she had not attended to it. Oddly enough, she now learnt for the first time that the house at which she was staying had the reputation of being haunted, and by the very same somewhat repulsive-looking mediæval personage that had troubled her inter-somnolent moments. The case seems to me to be typical with respect to the genesis of ghosts, and of the reputation of haunted houses.

NOTE.

THE HYPNOTIC CONDITION.

I have not in this chapter discussed the relation of dreaming to hypnotism, or the state of artificially produced quasi-sleep, because the nature of this last is still but very imperfectly understood. In this condition, which is induced in a number of ways by keeping the attention fixed on some non-exciting object, and by weak continuous and monotonous stimulation, as stroking the skin, the patient can be made to act conformably to the verbal or other suggestion of the operator, or to the bodily position which he is made to assume. Thus, for example, if a glass containing ink is given to him, with the command to drink, he proceeds to drink. If his hands are folded, he proceeds to act as if he were in church, and so on.

Braid, the writer who did so much to get at the facts of hypnotism, and Dr. Carpenter who has helped to make known Braid's careful researches, regard the actions of the hypnotized subject as analogous to ideo-motor movements; that is to say, the movements due to the tendency of an idea to act itself out apart from volition. On the other hand, one of the latest inquirers into the subject, Professor Heidenhain, of Breslau, appears to regard these actions as the outcome of "unconscious perceptions" (*Animal Magnetism*, English translation, p. 43, etc.).

In the absence of certain knowledge, it seems allowable to argue from the analogy of natural sleep that the actions of the hypnotized patient are accompanied with the lower forms of consciousness, including sensation and perception, and that they involve dream-like hallucinations respecting the external circumstances of the moment. Regarding them in this light, the points of resemblance between hypnotism and dreaming are numerous and striking. Thus, Dr. Heidenhain tells us that the threshold or liminal value of stimulation is lowered just as in ordinary sleep sense-activity as a whole is lowered. According to Professor Weinhold, the hypnotic condition begins in a gradual loss of taste, touch, and the sense of temperature; then sight is gradually impaired, while hearing remains throughout the least interfered with.[1] In

---

[1] See an interesting account of "Recent Researches on Hypnotism," by G. Stanley Hall, in *Mind*, January, 1881.

this way, the mind of the patient is largely cut off from the external world, as in sleep, and the power of orientation is lost. Moreover, there are all the conditions present, both positive and negative, for the hallucinatory transformation of mental images into percepts just as in natural sleep. Thus, the higher centres connected with the operations of reflection and reasoning are thrown *hors de combat* or, as Dr. Heidenhain has it, "inhibited."

The condition of hypnotism is marked off from that of natural sleep, first of all, by the fact that the accompanying hallucinations are wholly due to external suggestion (including the effects of bodily posture). Dreams may, as we have seen, be very faintly modified by external influences, but during sleep there is nothing answering to the perfect control which the operator exercises over the hypnotized subject. The largest quantity of our "dream-stuff" comes, as we have seen, from within and not from without the organism. And this fact accounts for the chief characteristic difference between the natural and the hypnotic dream. The former is complex, consisting of crowds of images, and continually changing: the latter is simple, limited, and persistent. As Braid remarks, the peculiarity of hypnotism is that the attention is concentrated on a remarkably narrow field of mental images and ideas. So long as a particular bodily posture is assumed, so long does the corresponding illusion endure. One result of this, in connection with that impairing of sensibility already referred to, is the scope for a curious overriding of sense-impressions by the dominant illusory percept, a process that we have seen illustrated in the active sense-illusions of waking life. Thus, if salt water is tasted and the patient is *told* that it is beer, he complains that it is sour.

In being thus in a certain rapport, though so limited and unintelligent a rapport, with the external world, the mind of the hypnotized patient would appear to be nearer the condition of waking illusion than is the mind of the dreamer. It must be remembered, however, and this is the second point of difference between dreaming and hypnotism, that the hypnotized subject tends *to act out* his hallucinations. His quasi-percepts are wont to transform themselves into actions with a degree of force of which we see no traces in ordinary sleep. Why there should be this greater activity of the motor organs in the one condition than in the other, seems to be a point as yet unexplained. All sense-impressions and percepts are doubtless accompanied by some degree of impulse to movement, though, for some reason or another, in natural and healthy sleep these impulses are restricted to the stage of faint nascent stirrings of motor activity which hardly betray themselves externally. This difference, involving a great difference in the possible practical consequences of the two conditions of natural and hypnotic sleep, clearly serves to bring the latter condition nearer to that of insanity than the former condition is brought. A strong susceptibility to the hypnotic influence, such as Dr. Heidenhain describes, might, indeed, easily prove a very serious want of " adaptation of internal to external relations," whereas a tendency to dreaming would hardly prove a maladaptation at all.

CHAPTER VIII.

WE have now, perhaps, sufficiently reviewed sense-illusions, both of waking life and of sleep. And having roughly classified them according to their structure and origin, we are ready to go forwards and inquire whether the theory thus reached can be applied to other forms of illusory error. And here we are compelled to inquire at the outset if anything analogous to sense-illusion is to be found in that other great region of presentative cognition usually marked off from external perception as internal perception, self-reflection, or introspection.

Illusions of Introspection defined.

This inquiry naturally sets out with the question: What is meant by introspection? This cannot be better defined, perhaps, than by saying that it is the mind's immediate reflective cognition of its own states as such.

In one sense, of course, everything we know may be called a mental state, actual or imagined. Thus, a sense-impression is known, exactly like any other feeling of the mind, as a mental phenomenon or mental modification. Yet we do not usually speak of introspectively recognizing a sensation. Our sense-impressions are marked off from all other feelings by having an objective character, that is to say, an immediate relation to the external world, so that in attending to one of them our minds pass away from themselves in what Professor Bain calls the attitude of objective regard. Introspection is confined to feelings which want this intimate connection with the external region, and includes sensation only so far as it is viewed apart from external objects and on its mental side as a feeling, a process which is next to impossible where the sensation has little emotional colour, as in the case of an ordinary sensation of sight or of articulate sound.

This being so, errors of introspection, supposing such to be found, will in the main be sufficiently distinguished from those of perception. Even an hallucination of sense, whether setting out from a subjective sensation or not, always contains the semblance of a sense-impression, and so would not be correctly classed with errors of introspection.

Just as introspection must be marked off from perception, so must it be distinguished from memory. It may be contended that, strictly speaking, all introspection is retrospection, since even in attending to a present feeling the mind is reflectively representing to itself the immediately preceding momentary experience of that feeling. Yet the adoption of this view does not hinder us from drawing a broad distinction between acts of introspection and acts of memory. Introspection must be regarded as confined to the knowledge of immediately antecedent mental states with reference to which no error of memory can be supposed to arise.

It follows from this that an illusion of introspection could only be found in connection with the apprehension of present or immediately antecedent mental states. On the other hand, any illusions connected with the consciousness of personal continuity and identity would fall rather under the class of mnemonic than that of introspective error.

Once more, introspection must be carefully distinguished from what I have called belief. Some of our beliefs may be found to grow out of and be compounded of a number of introspections. Thus, my conception of my own character, or my psychological conception of mind as a whole, may be seen to arise by a combination of the results of a number of acts of introspection. Yet, supposing this to be so, we must still distinguish between the single presentative act of introspection and the representative belief growing out of it.

It follows from this that, though an error of the latter sort might conceivably have its origin in one of the former; though, for example, a man's illusory opinion of himself might be found to involve errors of introspection, yet the two kinds of illusion would be sufficiently unlike. The latter would be a simple presentative error, the former a compound representative error.

Finally, in order to complete this preliminary demarcation of our subject-matter, it is necessary to distinguish between an introspection (apparent or real) of a feeling or idea, and a process of inference based on this feeling.   The term introspective knowledge must, it is plain, be confined to what is or appears to be in the mind at the moment of inspection.

By observing this distinction, we are in a position to mark off an *illusion* of introspection from a *fallacy* of introspection.   The former differs from the latter in the absence of anything like a conscious process of inference.   Thus, if we suppose that the derivation by Descartes of the fact of the existence of God from his possession of the idea to be erroneous, such a consciously performed act of reasoning would constitute a fallacy rather than an illusion of introspection.

We may, then, roughly define an illusion of introspection as an error involved in the apprehension of the contents of the mind at any moment.   If we mistake the quality or degree of a feeling or the structure of a complex mass of feeling, or if we confuse what is actually present to the mind with some inference based on this, we may be said to fall into an illusion of introspection.

But here the question will certainly be raised : How can we conceive the mind erring as to the nature of its present contents; and what is to determine, if not my immediate act of introspection, what is present in my mind at any moment?   Indeed, to raise the possibility of error in introspection seems to do away with the certainty of presentative knowledge.

If, however, the reader will recall what was said in an earlier chapter about the possibility of error in recognizing the quality of a sense-impression, he will be prepared for a similar possibility here.   What we are accustomed to call a purely presentative cognition is, in truth, partly representative. A feeling as pure feeling is not known; it is only known when it is distinguished, as to quality or degree, and so classed or brought under some representation of a kind or description of feeling, as acute, painful, and so on. The accurate recognition of an impression of colour depends, as we have seen, on this process of classing being correctly performed. Similarly, the recognition of internal feelings implies the presence of the appropriate or corresponding class-representation. Accordingly, if it is possible for a wrong representation to get substituted for the right one, there seems to be an opening for error.

Any error that would thus arise can, of course, only be determined as such in relation to some other act of introspection of the same mind. In matters of internal perception other minds cannot directly assist us in correcting error as they can in the case of external perception, though, as we shall see by-and-by, they may do so indirectly. The standard of reality directly applicable to introspective cognition is plainly what the individual mind recognizes at its best moments, when the processes of attention and classifying are accurately performed, and the representation may be regarded with certainty as answering to the feeling. In other words, in the sphere of internal, as in that of external experience, the criterion of reality is the average and perfect, as distinguished from the particular variable and imperfect act of cognition.

We see, then, that error in the process of introspection is at least conceivable. And now let us examine this process a little further, in order to find out what probabilities of error attach to it.

To begin with, then, an act of introspection, to be complete, clearly involves the apprehension of an internal feeling or idea as something mental and marked off from the region of external experience. This distinct recognition of internal states of mind as such, in opposition to external impressions, is by no means easy, but presupposes a certain degree of intellectual culture, and a measure of the power of abstract attention.

Confusion of Internal and External Experience.

Accordingly, we find that where this is wanting there is a manifest disposition to translate internal feelings into terms of external impressions. In this way there may arise a slight amount of habitual and approximately constant error. Not that the process approaches to one of hallucination; but only that the internal feelings are intuited as having a cause or origin analogous to that of sense-impressions. Thus to the uncultivated mind a sudden thought seems like an audible announcement from without. The superstitious man talks of being led by some good or evil spirit when new ideas arise in his mind or new resolutions shape themselves. To the simple intelligence of the boor every thought presents itself as an analogue of an audible voice, and he commonly describes his rough musings as saying this and that to himself. And this mode of viewing the matter is reflected even in the language of cultivated persons. Thus we say, "The idea struck me," or "was borne in on me," "I was forced to do so and so," and so on, and in this manner we tend to assimilate internal to external mental phenomena.

Much the same thing shows itself in our customary modes of describing our internal feelings of pleasure and pain. When a man in a state of mental depression speaks of having "a load" on his mind it is evident that he is interpreting a mental by help of an analogy to a bodily feeling. Similarly, when we talk of the mind being torn by doubt or worn by anxiety. It would seem as though we tended mechanically to translate mental pleasures and pains into the language of bodily sensations.

The explanation of this deeply rooted tendency to a slightly illusory view of our mental states is, I think, an easy one. For one thing, it follows from the relation of the mental image to the sense-impression that we should tend to assimilate the former to the latter as to its nature and origin. This would account for the common habit of regarding thoughts, which are of course accompanied by representatives of their verbal symbols, as internal voices, a habit which is probably especially characteristic of the child and the uncivilized man, as we have found it to be characteristic of the insane.

Another reason, however, must be sought for the habit of assimilating internal feelings to external sensations. If language has been evolved as an incident of social life, at once one of its effects and its causes, it would seem to follow that it must have first shaped itself to the needs of expressing these common objective experiences which we receive by way of our senses.

Our habitual modes of thought, limited as they are by language, retain traces of this origin. We cannot conceive any mental process except by some vague analogy to a physical process. In other words, we can even now only think with perfect clearness when we are concerned with some object of common cognition. Thus, the sphere of external sensation and of physical agencies furnishes us with the one type of thinkable thing or object of thought, and we habitually view subjective mental states as analogues of these.

Still, it may be said that these slight nascent errors are hardly worth naming, and the question would still appear to recur whether there are other fully developed errors deserving to rank along with illusions of sense. Do we, it may be asked, ever actually mistake the quality, degree, or structure of our internal feelings in the manner hinted above, and if so, what is the range of such error? In order to appreciate the risks of such error, let us compare the process of self-observation with that of external perception with respect to the difficulties in the way of accurate presentative knowledge.

Misreading of Internal Feelings.

First of all, it is noteworthy that a state of consciousness at any one moment is an exceedingly complex thing. It is made up of a mass of feelings and active impulses which often combine and blend in a most inextricable way. External sensations come in groups, too, but as a rule they do not fuse in apparently simple wholes as our internal feelings often do. The very possibility of perception depends on a clear discrimination of sense-elements, for example, the several sensations of colour obtained by the stimulation of different parts of the retina.[1] But no such clearly defined mosaic of feelings presents itself in the internal region: one element overlaps and partly loses itself in another, and subjective analysis is often an exceedingly difficult matter. Our consciousness is thus a closely woven texture in which the mental eye often fails to trace the several threads or strands. Moreover, there is the fact that many of these ingredients are exceedingly shadowy, belonging to that obscure region of sub-consciousness which it is so hard to penetrate with the light of discriminative attention. This remark applies with particular force to that mass of organic feelings which constitutes what is known as cœnæsthesis, or vital sense.

While, to speak figuratively, the minute anatomy of consciousness is thus difficult with respect to longitudinal sections of the mental column, it is no less difficult with respect to transverse sections. Under ordinary circumstances, external impressions persist so that they can be transfixed by a deliberate act of attention, and objects rarely flit over the external scene so rapidly as to allow us no time for a careful recognition of the impression. Not so in the case of the internal region of mind. The composite states of consciousness just described never remain perfectly uniform for the shortest conceivable duration. They change continually, just as the contents of the kaleidoscope vary with every shake of the instrument. Thus,

---

[1] I need hardly observe that physiology shows that there is no separation of different elementary colour-sensations which are locally identical.

one shade of feeling runs into another in such a way that it is often impossible to detect its exact quality; and even when the character of the feeling does not change, its intensity is undergoing alterations so that an accurate observation of its quantity is impracticable. Also, in this unstable shifting internal scene features may appear for a duration too short to allow of close recognition. In this way it happens that we cannot sharply divide the feeling of the moment from its antecedents and its consequents.

If, now, we take these facts in connection with what has been said above respecting the nature of the process of introspection, the probability of error will be made sufficiently clear. To transfix any particular feeling of the moment, to selectively attend to it, and to bring it under the proper representation, is an operation that requires time, a time which, though short, is longer than the fugitive character of so much of our internal mental life allows. From all of which it would appear to follow that it must be very easy to overlook, confuse, and transform, both as to quality and as to quantity, the actual ingredients of our internal consciousness.

From these sources there spring a number of small errors of introspection which, to distinguish them from others to be spoken of presently, may be called passive. These would include all errors in detecting what is in consciousness due to the intricacies of the phenomena, and not aided by any strong basis. For example, a mental state may fail to disclose its component parts to introspective attention. Thus, a motive may enter into our action which is so entangled with other feelings as to escape our notice. The fainter the feeling the greater the difficulty of detaching it and inspecting it in isolation. Again, an error of introspection may have its ground in the fugitive character of a feeling. If, for example, a man is asked whether a rapid action was a voluntary one, he may in retrospection easily imagine that it was not so, when as a matter of fact the action was preceded by a momentary volition. When a person exclaims, " I did a thing inadvertently or mechanically," it often means that he did not note the motive underlying the action. Such transitory feelings which cannot at the moment be seized by an act of attention are pretty certain to disappear at once, leaving not even a temporary trace in consciousness.

We will now pass to the consideration of other illusions of introspection more analogous to what I have called the active illusions of perception. In our examination of these we found that a pure representation may under certain circumstances simulate the appearance of a presentation, that a mental image may approximate to a sense-impression. In the case of the internal feelings this liability shows itself in a still more striking form.

The higher feelings or emotions are distinguished from the simple sense-feelings in being largely representative. Thus, a feeling of contentment at any moment, though no doubt conditioned by the bodily state and the character of the organic sensations or cœnæsthesis, commonly depends for the most part on intellectual representations of external circumstances or relations, and may be called an ideal foretaste of actual satisfactions, such as the pleasures of success, of companionship, and so on. This being so, it is easy for imagination to call up a semblance of these higher feelings. Since they depend largely on representation, a mere act of representation may suffice to excite a degree of the feeling hardly distinguishable from the actual one. Thus, to imagine myself as contented is really to see myself at the moment as actually contented. Again, the actor, though, as we shall see by-and-by, he does not feel all that the spectator is apt to attribute to him, tends, when vividly representing to himself a particular shade of feeling, to regard himself as actually feeling in this way. Thus, it is said of Garrick, that when acting Richard III., he felt himself for the moment to be a villain.

We should expect from all this that in the act of introspection the mind is apt, within certain limits, to find what it is prepared to find. And since there is in these acts often a distinct wish to detect some particular feeling, we can see how easy it must be for a man through bias and a wrong focussing of the attention to deceive himself up to a certain point with respect to the actual contents of his mind.

Let us examine one of these active illusions a little more fully. It would at first sight seem to be a perfectly simple thing to determine at any given moment whether we are enjoying ourselves, whether our emotional condition rises above the pleasure-threshold or point of indifference and takes on a positive hue of the agreeable or pleasurable. Yet there is good reason for supposing that people not unfrequently deceive themselves on this matter. It is, perhaps, hardly an exaggeration to say that most of us are capable of imagining that we are having enjoyment when we conform to the temporary fashion of social amusement. It has been cynically observed that people go into society less in order to be happy than to seem so, and one may add that in this semblance of enjoyment they may, provided they are not *blasé*, deceive themselves as well as others. The expectation of enjoyment, the knowledge that the occasion is intended to bring about this result, the recognition of the external signs of enjoyment in others—all this may serve to blind a man in the earlier stages of social amusement to his actual mental condition.

If we look closely into this variety of illusion, we shall see that it is very similar in its structure and origin to that kind of erroneous perception which arises from inattention to the actual impression of the moment under the influence of a strong expectation of something different. The representation of ourselves as entertained dislodges from our internal field of vision our actual condition, relegating this to the region of obscure consciousness. Could we for a moment get rid of this representation and look at the real feelings of the time, we should become aware of our error; and it is possible that the process of becoming *blasé* involves a waking up to a good deal of illusion of the kind.

Just as we can thus deceive ourselves within certain limits as to our emotional condition, so we can mistake the real nature of our intellectual condition. Thus, when an idea is particularly grateful to our minds, we may easily imagine that we believe it, when in point of fact all the time there is a sub-conscious process of criticism going on, which if we attended to it for a moment would amount to a distinct act of disbelief. Some persons appear to be capable of going on habitually practising this petty deceit on themselves, that is to say, imagining they believe what in fact they are strongly inclined to doubt. Indeed, this remark applies to all the grateful illusions respecting ourselves and others, which will have to be discussed by-and-by. The impulse to hold to the illusion in spite of critical reflection, involves the further introspective illusion of taking a state of doubt for one of assurance. Thus, the weak, flattered man or woman manages to keep up a sort of fictitious belief in the truth of the words which are so pleasant to the ear.

It is plain that the external conditions of life impose on the individual certain habits of feeling which often conflict with his personal propensities. As a member of society he has a powerful motive to attribute certain feelings to himself, and this motive acts as a bias in disturbing his vision of what is actually in his mind. While this holds good of lighter matters, as that of enjoyment just referred to, it applies still more to graver matters. Thus, for example, a man may easily pursuade himself that he feels a proper sentiment of indignation against a perpetrator of some mean or cruel act, when as a matter of fact his feeling is much more one of compassion for the previously liked offender. In this way we impose on ourselves, disguising our real sentiments by a thin veil of make--believe.

So far I have spoken of an illusion of introspection

as analogous to the slight misapprehensions of sense-impression which were touched on in connection with illusions of sense (Chapter III.). It is to be observed, however, that the confusing of elements of consciousness, which is so prominent a factor in introspective illusion, involves a species of error closely analogous to a complete illusion of perception, that is to say, one which involves a misinterpretation of a sense-impression.

This variety of illusion is illustrated in the case in which a present feeling or thought is confounded with some inference based on it. For example, a present thought may, through forgetfulness, be regarded as a new discovery. Its originality appears to be immediately made known in the very freshness which characterizes it. Every author probably has undergone the experience of finding that ideas which started up to his mind as fresh creations, were unconscious reminiscences of his own or of somebody else's ideas.

In the case of present emotional states this liability to confuse the present and the past is far greater. Here there is something hardly distinguishable from an active illusion of sense-perception. In this condition of mind a man often says that he has an "intuition" of something supposed to be immediately given in the feeling itself. For instance, one whose mind is thrilled by the pulsation of a new joy exclaims, "This is the happiest moment of my life," and the assurance seems to be contained in the very intensity of the feeling itself. Of course, cool reflection will tell him that what he affirms is merely a belief, the accuracy of which presupposes processes of recollection and judgment, but to the man's mind at the moment the supremacy of this particular joy is immediately intuited. And so with the assurance that the present feeling, for example of love, is undying, that it is equal to the most severe trials, and so on. A man is said to *feel* at the moment that it is so, though as the facts believed have reference to absent circumstances and events, it is plain that the knowledge is by no means intuitive.

At such times our minds are in a state of pure feeling: intellectual discrimination and comparison are no longer possible. In this way our emotions in the moments of their greatest intensity carry away our intellects with them, confusing the region of pure imagination with that of truth and certainty, and even the narrow domain of the present with the vast domain of the past and future. In this condition differences of present and future may be said to disappear and the energy of the emotion to constitute an immediate assurance of its existence absolutely.[1]

The great region for the illustration of these active illusions is that of the moral and religious life. With respect to our real motives, our dominant aspirations, and our highest emotional experiences, we are greatly liable to deceive ourselves. The moralist and the theologian have clearly recognized the possibilities of self-deception in matters of feeling and impulse. To

---

[1] This kind of error is, of course, common to all kinds of cognition, in so far as they involve comparison. Thus, the presence of the excitement of the emotion of wonder at the sight of an unusually large object, say a mountain, disposes the mind to look on it as the largest of its class. Such illusions come midway between presentative and representative illusions. They might, perhaps, be specially marked off as illusions of "judgment."

them it is no mystery that the human heart should mistake the fictitious for the real, the momentary and evanescent for the abiding. And they have recognized, too, the double bias in these errors, namely, the powerful disposition to exaggerate the intensity and persistence of a present feeling on the one hand, and on the other hand to take a mere wish to feel in a particular way for the actual possession of the feeling.

Philosophic Illusions.

The opinion of theologians respecting the nature of moral introspection presents a singular contrast to that entertained by some philosophers as to the nature of self-consciousness. It is supposed by many of these that in interrogating their internal consciousness they are lifted above all risk of error. The " deliverance of consciousness " is to them something bearing the seal of a supreme authority, and must not be called in question. And so they make an appeal to individual consciousness a final resort in all matters of philosophical dispute.

Now, on the face of it, it does not seem probable that this operation should have an immunity from all liability to error. For the matters respecting which we are directed to introspect ourselves, are the most subtle and complex things of our intellectual and emotional life. And some of these philosophers even go so far as to affirm that the plain man is quite equal to the niceties of this process.

It has been brought as a charge against some of these same philosophers that they have based certain of their doctrines on errors of introspection. This charge must, of course, be received with some sort of suspicion here, since it has been brought forward by avowed disciples of an opposite philosophic school. Nevertheless, as there is from our present disinterested and purely scientific point of view a presumption that philosophers like other men are fallible, and since it is certain·that philosopical introspection does not materially differ from other kinds, it seems permissible just to glance at some of these alleged illusions in relation to other and more vulgar forms. Further reference to them will be made at the end of our study.

These so-called philosophical illusions will be found, like the vulgar ones just spoken of, to illustrate the distinction drawn between passive and active illusions. That is to say, the alleged misreading of individual consciousness would result now from a confusion of distinct elements, including wrong suggestion, due to the intricacies of the phenomena, now from a powerful predisposition to read something into the phenomena.

A kind of illusion in which the passive element seems most conspicuous would be the error into which the interrogator of the individual consciousness is said to fall respecting simple unanalyzable states of mind. On the face of it, it is not likely that a mere inward glance at the tangle of conscious states should suffice to determine what is such a perfectly simple mental phenomenon. Accordingly, when a writer declares that an act of introspection demonstrates the simple unanalyzable character of such a feeling as the sentiment of beauty or that of moral approval, the opponent of this view clearly has some show of argument for saying that this simplicity may be altogether illusory and due to the absence of a perfect act of attention. Similarly, when it is said that the idea of space contains no representations of muscular sensation, the statement may clearly arise from the want of a sufficiently careful kind of introspective analysis.[1]

In most cases of these alleged philosophical errors, however, the active and passive factors seem to combine. There are certain intricacies in the mental phenomenon itself favouring the chances of error, and there are independent predispositions leading the mind to look at the phenomenon in a wrong way. This seems to apply to the famous declaration of a certain school of thinkers that by an act of introspection we can intuit the fact of liberty, that is to say, a power of spontaneous determination of action superior to and regulative of the influence of motives. It may be plausibly contended that this idea arises partly from

---

[1] So far as any mental state, though originating in a fusion of elements, is now unanalyzable by the best effort of attention, we must of course regard it in its present form as simple. This distinction between what is simple or complex in its present nature, and what is originally so, is sometimes overlooked by psychologists. Whether the feelings and ideas here referred to are now simple or complex, cannot, I think, yet be very certainly determined. To take the idea of space, I find that after practice I recognize the ingredient of muscular feeling much better than I did at first. And this exactly answers to Helmholtz's contention that elementary sensations as partial tones can be detected after practice. Such separate recognition may be said to depend on correct representation. On the other hand, it must be allowed that there is room for the intuitionist to say that the associationist is here reading something into the idea which does not belong to it. It is to be added that the illusion which the associationist commonly seeks to fasten on his opponent is that of confusing final with original simplicity. Thus, he says that, though the idea of space may now to all intents and purposes be simple, it was really built up out of many distinct elements. More will be said on the relation of questions of nature and genesis further on

a mixing up of facts of present consciousness with inferences from them, and partly from a natural predisposition of the mind to invest itself with this supreme power of absolute origination.[1]

In a similar way, it might be contended that other famous philosophic dicta are founded on a process of erroneous introspection of subjective mental states. In some cases, indeed, it seems a plausible explanation to regard these illusions as mere survivals in attenuated shadowy form of grosser popular illusions. But this is not yet the time to enter on these, which, moreover, hardly fall perhaps under our definition of an illusion of introspection.

Value of the Introspective Method.

In drawing up this rough sketch of the illusions of introspection, I have had no practical object in view. I have tried to look at the facts as they are apart from any conclusions to be drawn from them. The question how far the liability to error in any region of inquiry vitiates the whole process is a difficult one; and the question whether the illusions to which we are subject in introspection materially affect the value of self-knowledge as a whole and consequently of the introspective method in psychology, as many affirm, is too subtle a one to be fully treated now. All that I shall attempt here is to show that it does not do this any more than the risk of sense-illusion can be said materially to affect the value of external observation.

---

[1] I may as well be frank and say that I myself, assuming free-will to be an illusion, have tried to trace the various threads of influence which have contributed to its remarkable vitality. (See *Sensation and Intuition*, ch. v., " The Genesis of the Free-Will Doctrine.")

It is to be noted first of all that the errors of introspection are much more limited than those of sense-perception. They broadly answer to the slight errors connected with the discrimination and recognition of the sense-impression. There is nothing answering to a complete hallucination in the sphere of the inner mental life. It follows, too, from what has been said above, that the amount of active error in introspection is insignificant, since the representation of a feeling or belief is so very similar to the actual experience of it.

In brief, the errors of introspection, though numerous, are all too slight to render the process of introspection as a whole unsound and untrustworthy. Though, as we have seen, it involves, strictly speaking, an ingredient of representation, this fact does not do away with the broad distinction between presentative and representative cognition. Introspection is pre-sentative in the sense that the reality constituting the object of cognition, the mind's present feeling, is as directly present to the knowing mind as anything can be conceived to be. It may be added that the power of introspection is a comparatively new acquisition of the human race, and that, as it improves, the amount of error connected with its operation may reasonably be expected to become infinitesimal.

It is often supposed by those who undervalue the introspective method in psychology that there is a special difficulty in the detection of error in intro-spection, owing to the fact that the object of inspection is something individual and private, and not open to common scrutiny as the object of external perception.

Yet, while allowing a certain force to this objection I would point out, first of all, that even in sense-perception, what the individual mind is immediately certain of is its own sensations. The relatively perfect certainty which finally attaches to the presentative side of sense-perception is precisely that which finally attaches to the results of introspection.

In the second place, it may be said that the contrast between the inner and the outer experience is much less than it seems. In many cases our emotions are the direct result of a common external cause, and even when they are not thus attached to some present external circumstance, we are able, it is admitted, by the use of language, roughly to compare our individual feelings. And such comparison is continually bringing to light the fact that there is a continuity in our mental structure, that our highest thoughts and emotions lead us back to our common sense-impressions, and that consequently, in spite of all individual differences of temperament and mental organization, our inner experience is in all its larger features a common experience.

I may add that this supposition of the common nature of our internal experience, as a whole, not only underlies the science of psychology, but is implied in the very process of detecting and correcting errors of introspection. I do not mean that in matters of feeling "authority" is to override "private judgment." Our last resort with respect to things of the mind is, as I have said, that of careful self-inspection. And the progress of psychology and the correction of illusion proceed by means of an ever-improving exercise

of the introspective faculty.   Yet such individual
inspection can at least be *guided* by the results of
others' similar inspection, and should be so guided as
soon as a general consensus in matters of internal experience is fairly made out.   In point of fact, the
preceding discussion of illusions of introspection has
plainly rested on the sufficiently verified assumption
that the calmest and most efficient kind of introspection, in bringing to light what is permanent as compared with what is variable in the individual cognition,
points in the direction of a common body of introspected fact.

CHAPTER IX.

BESIDES the perception of external objects, and the inspection of our internal mental states, there are other forms of quasi-presentative cognition which need to be touched on here, inasmuch as they are sometimes erroneous and illusory.

In the last chapter I alluded to the fact that emotion may arise as the immediate accompaniment of a sense-impression. When this is the case there is a disposition to read into the external object a quality answering to the emotion, just as there is a disposition to ascribe to objects qualities of heat and cold answering to the sensations thus called. And such a reference of an emotional result to an external exciting cause approximates in character to an immediate intuition. The cognition of the quality is instantaneous, and quite free from any admixture of conscious inference. Accordingly, we have to inquire into the illusory forms of such intuition, if such there be.

Æsthetic Intuition.

Conspicuous among these quasi-presentative emotional cognitions is æsthetic intuition, that is to say, the perception of an object as beautiful. It is not necessary here to raise the question whether there is, strictly speaking, any quality in things answering to the sentiment of beauty in our minds : this is a philosophical and not a psychological question, and turns on the further question, what we mean by object. All that we need to assume here is that there are certain aspects of external things, certain relations of form, together with a power of exciting certain pleasurable ideas in the spectator's mind, which are commonly recognized as the cause of the emotion of beauty, and indeed regarded as constituting the embodiments of the objective quality, beauty. Æsthetic intuition thus clearly implies the immediate assurance of the existence of a common source of æsthetic delight, a source bound up with an object of common sense-perception. And so we may say that to call a thing beautiful is more or less distinctly to recognize it as a cause of a present emotion, and to attribute to it a power of raising a kindred emotion in other minds.

Æsthetic Illusion.

According to this view of the matter, an illusion of æsthetic intuition would arise whenever this power of affecting a number of minds pleasurably is wrongly attributed, by an act of " intuition," to an object of sense-perception, on the ground of a present personal feeling.

Now, this error is by no means unfrequent. Our delight in viewing external things, though agreeing up to a certain point, does not agree throughout. It is a trite remark that there is a large individual factor, a considerable " personal equation," in matters of taste, as in other matters. Permanent differences of natural sensibility, of experience, of intellectual habits, and so on, make an object æsthetically impressive and valuable to one man and not to another. Yet these differences tend to be overlooked. The individual mind, filled with delight at some spectacle, automatically projects its feeling outwards in the shape of a cause of a common sentiment. And the force of this impulse cannot be altogether explained as the effect of past experiences and of association. It seems to involve, in addition, the play of social instincts, the impulse of the individual mind to connect itself in sympathy with the collective mind.

Here, as in the other varieties of illusion already treated of, we may distinguish between a passive and an active side; only in this case the passive side must not be taken as corresponding to any common suggestions of the object, as in the case of perception proper. So far as an illusion of æsthetic intuition may be considered as passive, it must be due to the effect of circumscribed individual associations with the object.

All agree that what is called beauty consists, to a considerable extent, of a power of awaking pleasant suggestions, but in order that these should constitute a ground of æsthetic value, they must be common, participated in by all, or at least by an indefinite number. This will be the case when the association rests on our

common every-day experiences, and our common knowledge of things, as in the case of the peaceful beauty
of an ascending curl of blue smoke ·in a woody landscape, or the awful beauty of a lofty precipice.   On
the other hand, when the experience and recollections,
which are the source of the pleasure, are restricted and
accidental, any attribution of objective worth is illusory.   Thus, the ascription of beauty to one's native
village, to one's beloved friends, and so on, in so far as
it carries the conviction of objective worth, may imply
a confusion of the individual with the common experience.

The active side of this species of illusions would be
illustrated in every instance of ascribing beauty to
objects which is due, in a considerable measure at
least, to some pre-existing disposition in the mind,
whether permanent or temporary.   A man brings his
peculiar habits of thought and feeling to the con-
templation of objects, and the æsthetic impression
produced is coloured by these predispositions.   Thus,
a person of a sad and gloomy cast of mind will be
disposed to see a sombre beauty where other eyes see
nothing of the kind.   And then there are all the
effects of temporary conditions of the imagination and
the feelings.   Thus, the individual mind may be
focussed in a certain way through the suggestion of
another.   People not seldom see a thing to be beautiful because they are told that it is so.   It might not
be well to inquire too curiously how many of the
frequenters of the annual art exhibitions use their
own eyes in framing their æsthetic judgments.   Or
the temporary predisposition may reside in a purely

personal feeling or desire uppermost at the time. Our enjoyment of nature or of art is coloured by our temporary mood. There are moments of exceptional mental exhilaration, when even a commonplace scene will excite an appreciable kind of admiration. Or there may be a strong wish to find a thing beautiful begotten of another feeling. Thus, a lover desires to find beauty in his mistress ; or, having found it in her face and form, desires to find a harmonious beauty in her mind. In these different ways temporary accidents of personal feeling and imagination enter into and determine our æsthetic intuition, making it deviate from the common standard. This kind of error may even approximate in character to an hallucination of sense when there is nothing answering to a common source of æsthetic pleasure. Thus, the fond mother, through the very force of her affection, will construct a beauty in her child, which for others is altogether non-existent.

What applies to the perception of beauty in the narrow sense will apply to all other modes of æsthetic intuition, as that of the sublime and the ludicrous, and the recognition of the opposite of beauty or the ugly. In like manner, it will apply to moral intuition in so far as it is an instantaneous recognition of a certain quality in a perceived action based on, or at least conjoined with, a particular emotional effect. In men's intuitive judgments respecting the right and the wrong, the noble and base, the admirable and contemptible, and so on, we may see the same kind of illusory universalizing of personal feeling as we have seen in their judgments respecting the beautiful. And the sources of the error are the same in the two cases. Accidents of experience, giving special associations to the actions, will not unfrequently warp the individual intuition. Ethical culture, like æsthetic culture, means a continual casting aside of early illusory habits of intuition. And further, moral intuition illustrates all those effects of feeling which we have briefly traced in the case of æsthetic intuition. The perversions of the moral intuition under the sway of prejudice are too familiar to need more than a bare allusion.

Nature of Insight.

There remains one further mode of cognition which approximates in character to presentative knowledge, and is closely related to external perception. I refer to the commonly called "intuitive" process by which we apprehend the feelings and thoughts of other minds through the external signs of movement, vocal sound, etc., which make up expression and language. This kind of knowledge, which is not sufficiently marked off from external perception on the one side and intro-spection on the other, I venture to call Insight.

I am well aware that this interpretation of the mental states of others is commonly described as a process of inference involving a conscious reference to our own similar experiences. I willingly grant that it is often so. At the same time, it must be perfectly plain that it is not always so. It is, indeed, doubtful whether in its first stages in early life it is invariably so, for there seem to be good reasons for attributing to the infant mind a certain degree of instinctive or inherited capability in making out the looks and tones of others.[1] And, however this may be, it is certain that with the progress of life a good part of this interpretation comes to be automatic or unconscious, approximating in character to a sense-perception. To recognize content-ment in a placid smile is, one would say, hardly less immediate and intuitive than to recognize the coolness of a stream.

We must, of course, all allow that the fusion of the presentative and the representative element is, speaking generally, more complete in the case of sense-perception than in that here considered. In spite of Berkeley's masterly account of the *rationale* of visual perception as an interpretation of " visual language " and all that has confirmed it, the plain man cannot, at the moment of looking at an object, easily bring him-self to admit that distance is not directly present to his vision. On the other hand, on cool reflection, he will recognize that the complacent benevolent sentiment is distinct from the particular movements and changes in the eye and other features which express it. Yet, while admitting this, I must contend that there is no very hard and fast line dividing the two processes, but that the reading of others' feelings approximates in charac-ter to an act of perception.

An intuitive insight may, then, be defined as that instantaneous, automatic, or " unconscious " mode of

---

[1] I purposely leave aside here the philosophical question, whether the knowledge of others' feelings is intuitive in the sense of being altogether independent of experience, and the manifestation of a fundamental belief. The inherited power referred to in the text might, of course, be viewed as a transmitted result of ancestral experience.

interpreting another's feeling which occurs whenever the feeling is fully expressed, and when its signs are sufficiently familiar to us. This definition will include the interpretation of thoughts by means of language, though not, of course, the belief in an objective fact grounded on a recognition of another's belief. On the other hand, it will exclude all the more complex interpretations of looks and words which imply conscious comparison, reflection, and reasoning. Further, it will exclude a large part of the interpretation of actions as motived, since this, though sometimes approaching the intuitive form, is for the most part a process of conjectural or doubtful inference, and wanting in the immediate assurance which belongs to an intuitive reading of a present emotion or thought.

From this short account of the process of insight, its relation to perception and introspection becomes pretty plain. On the one hand, it closely resembles sense-perception, since it proceeds by the interpretation of a sense-impression by means of a representative image. On the other hand, it differs from sense-perception, and is more closely allied to introspection in the fact that, while the process of interpretation in the former case is a reconstruction of *external* experiences, in the latter case it is a reconstruction of *internal* experiences. To intuit another's feeling is clearly to represent to ourselves a certain kind of internal experience previously known, in its elements at least, by introspection, while these represented experiences are distinctly referred to another personality.

And now we see what constitutes the object of insight. This is, in part, a common experience, as in the case of sense-perception and æsthetic intuition, since to perceive another's feeling is implicitly to cognize the external conditions of a common insight. But this is clearly not the whole, nor even the main part of objective reality in this act of cognition. An intuitive insight differs from a sense-perception in that it involves an immediate assurance of the existence of a feeling presentatively known, though not to our own minds. The object in insight is thus a presentative feeling as in introspection, though not our own, but another's. And so it differs from the object in sense-perception in so far as this last involves sense-experiences, as muscular and tactual feelings, which are not *at the moment* presentatively known to any mind.

Illusions of Insight.

And now we are in a position, perhaps, to define an illusion of insight, and to inquire whether there is anything answering to our definition. An illusory insight is a quasi-intuition of another's feelings which does not answer to the internal reality as presentatively known to the subject himself. In spite of the errors of introspection dealt with in the last chapter, nobody will doubt that, when it is a question between a man's knowing what is at the moment in his own mind and somebody else's knowing, logic, as well as politeness, requires us to give precedence to the former.

An illusion of insight, like the other varieties of illusion already dealt with, may arise either by way of wrong suggestion or by way of a warping preconception. Let us look at each of these sources apart.

Our insights, like our perceptions, though intuitive

in form, are obviously determined by previous experience, association, and habit. Hence, on its passive side, an illusion of insight may be described as a wrong interpretation of a new or exceptional case. For example, having associated the representation of a slight feeling of astonishment with uplifted eyebrows, we irresistibly tend to see a face in which this is a constant feature as expressing this particular shade of emotion. In this way we sometimes fall into grotesque errors as to mental traits. And the most practised physiognomist may not unfrequently err by importing the results of his special circle of experiences into new and unlike cases.

Much the same thing occurs in language.. Our timbre of voice, our articulation, and our vocabulary, like our physiognomy, have about them something individual, and error often arises from overlooking this, and hastily reading common interpretations into exceptional cases. The misunderstandings that arise even among the most open and confiding friends sufficiently illustrate this liability to error.

Sometimes the error becomes more palpable, as, for example, when we visit another country. A foreign language, when heard, provokingly suggests all kinds of absurd meanings through analogies to our familiar tongue. Thus, the Englishman who visits Germany cannot, for a time, hear a lady use the expression, "Mein Mann," without having the amusing suggestion that the speaker is wishing to call special attention to the fact of her husband's masculinity. And doubtless the German who visits us derives a similar kind of amusement from such involuntary comparisons.

A fertile source of illusory insight is, of course, conscious deception on the part of others. The rules of polite society require us to be hypocrites in a small way, and we have occasionally to affect the signs of amiability, interest, and amusement, when our actual sentiment is one of indifference, weariness, or even positive antipathy. And in this way a good deal of petty illusion arises. Although we may be well aware of the general untrustworthiness of this society behaviour, such is the force of association and habit, that the bland tone and flattering word irresistibly excite a momentary feeling of gratification, an effect which is made all the more easy by the co-operation of the recipient's own wishes, touched on in the last chapter.

Among all varieties of this deception, that of the stage is the most complete. The actor is a man who has elaborately trained himself in the simulation of certain feelings. And when his acting is of the best quality, and the proper bodily attitude, gesture, tone of voice, and so on, are hit off, the force of the illusion completely masters us. For the moment we lose sight of the theatrical surroundings, and see the actor as really carried away by the passion which he so closely imitates. Histrionic illusion is as complete as any artistic variety can venture to be.[1]

I have said that our insights are limited by our own mental experience, and so by introspection. In truth, every interpretation of another's look and word

---

[1] I here assume, along with G. H. Lewes and other competent dramatic critics, that the actor does not and dares not feel what he expresses, at least not in the perfectly spontaneous way, and in the same measure in which he appears to feel it.

is determined ultimately, not by what we have previously observed in others, but by what we have personally felt, or at least have in a sense made our own by intense sympathy. Hence we may, in general, regard an illusion of insight on the active side as a hasty projection of our own feelings, thoughts, etc., into other minds.

We habitually approach others with a predisposition to attribute to them our own modes of thinking and feeling. And this predisposition will be the more powerful, the more desirous we are for sympathy, and for that confirmation of our own views which the reflection of another mind affords. Thus, when making a new acquaintance, people are in general disposed to project too much of themselves into the person who is the object of inspection. They intuitively endow him with their own ideas, ways of looking at things, prejudices of sentiment, and so on, and receive something like a shock when later on they find out how different he is from this first hastily formed and largely performed image.

The same thing occurs in the reading of literature, and the appreciation of the arts of expression generally. We usually approach an author with a predisposition to read our own habits of thought and sentiment into his words. It is probably a characteristic defect of a good deal of current criticism of remote writers to attribute to them too much of our modern conceptions and aims. Similarly, we often import our own special feelings into the utterances of the poet and of the musical composer. That much of this intuition is illusory, may be seen by a little attention to the " intuitions " of different critics. Two readers of unlike emotional organization will find incompatible modes of feeling in the same poet. And everybody knows how common it is for musical critics and amateurs to discover quite dissimilar feelings in the same composition.[1]

The effect of this active projection of personal feeling will, of course, be seen most strikingly when there is a certain variety of feeling actually excited at the time in the observer's mind. A man who is in a particularly happy mood tends to reflect his exuberant gladness on others. The lover, in the moment of exalted emotion, reads a response to all his aspirations in his mistress's eyes. Again, a man will tend to project his own present ideas into the minds of others, and so imagine that they know what he knows; and this sometimes leads to a comical kind of embarrassment, and even to a betrayal of something which it was the interest of the person to keep to himself. Once more, in interpreting language, we may sometimes catch ourselves mistaking the meaning, owing to the presence of a certain idea in the mind at the time. Thus, if I have just been thinking of Comte, and overhear a person exclaim, " I'm positive," I irresistibly tend, for the moment, to ascribe to him an avowal of discipleship to the great positivist.

Poetic Illusion.

The most remarkable example of this projection of

---

[1] The illusory nature of much of this emotional interpretation of music has been ably exposed by Mr. Gurney. (See *The Power of Sound*, p. 345, *et seq.*)

feeling is undoubtedly illustrated in the poetic interpretation of inanimate nature. The personification of
tree, mountain, ocean, and so on, illustrates, no doubt,
the effect of association and external suggestion ;
for there are limits to such personification. But
resemblance and suggestion commonly bear, in this
case, but a small proportion to active constructive
imagination. One might, perhaps, call this kind of
projection the hallucination of insight, since there is
nothing objective corresponding to the interpretative
image.

The imaginative and poetic mind is continually
on the look out for hints of life, consciousness, and
emotion in nature. It finds a certain kind of satisfaction in this half-illusory, dream-like transformation
of nature. The deepest ground of this tendency
must probably be looked for in the primitive ideas of
the race, and the transmission by inheritance of the
effect of its firmly fixed habits of mind. The undisciplined mind of early man, incapable of distinguishing the object of perception from the product of
spontaneous imagination, and taking his own double
existence as the type of all existence, actually saw the
stream, the ocean, and the mountain as living beings :
and so firmly rooted is this way of regarding objects,
that even our scientifically trained minds find it a
relief to relapse occasionally into it.[1]

While there is this general imaginative disposition
in the poetic mind to endow nature with life and con-

---

[1] The reader will note that this impulse is complementary to the
other impulse to view all mental states as analogous to impressions
produced by external things, on which I touched in the last chapter.

sciousness, there are special tendencies to project the individual feelings into objects. Every imaginative mind looks for reflections of its own deepest feelings in the world about it. The lonely embittered heart, craving for sympathy, which he cannot meet with in his fellow-man, finds traces of it in the sighing of the trees or the moaning of the sad sea-wave. Our Poet Laureate, in his great elegy, has abundantly illustrated this impulse of the imagination to reflect its own emotional colouring on to inanimate things: for example in the lines—

> " The wild unrest that lives in woe
> Would dote and pore on yonder cloud
> That rises upward always higher,
>   And onward drags a labouring breast,
>   And topples round the dreary west,
> A looming bastion fringed with fire."

So far I have been considering active illusions of insight as arising through the play of the impulse of the individual mind to project its feelings outwards, or to see their reflections in external things. I must now add that active illusion may be due to causes similar to those which we have seen to operate in the sphere of illusory perception and introspection. That is to say, there may be a disposition, permanent or temporary, to ascribe a certain kind of feeling to others in accordance with our wishes, fears, and so on.

To give an illustration of the permanent causes, it is well known that a conceited man will be disposed to attribute admiration of himself to others. On the other hand, a shy, timid person will be prone to read into other minds the opposite kind of feeling.

Coming to temporary forces, we find that any expectation to meet with a particular kind of mental trait in a new acquaintance will dispose the observer hastily and erroneously to attribute corresponding feelings to the person. And if this expectation springs out of a present feeling, the bias to illusory insight is still more powerful. For example, a child that fears its parent's displeasure will be prone to misinterpret the parent's words and actions, colouring them according to its fears. So an angry man, strongly desirous of making out that a person has injured him, will be disposed to see signs of conscious guilt in this person's looks or words. Similarly, a lover will read fine thoughts or sentiments into the mind of his mistress under the influence of a strong wish to admire.

And what applies to the illusory interpretation of others' feelings applies to the ascription of feelings to inanimate objects. This is due not simply to the impulse to expand one's conscious existence through far-reaching resonances of sympathy, but also to a permanent or temporary disposition to attribute a certain kind of feeling to an object. Thus, the poet personifies nature in part because his emotional cravings prompt him to construct the idea of something that can be admired or worshipped. Once more, the action of a momentary feeling when actually excited is seen in the "mechanical" impulse of a man to retaliate when he strikes his foot against an object, as a chair, which clearly involves a tendency to attribute an intention to hurt to the unoffending body, and the *rationale* of which odd procedure is pretty correctly expressed in the popular phrase: "It relieves the feelings."

It is worth noting, perhaps, that these illusions of insight, like those of perception, may involve an inattention to the actual impression of the moment. To erroneously attribute a feeling to another through an excess of sympathetic eagerness is often to overlook what a perfectly dispassionate observer would see, as, for example, the immobility of the features or the signs of a deliberate effort to simulate. This inattention will, it is obvious, be greatest in the poetic attribution of life and personality to natural objects, in so far as this approximates to a complete momentary illusion. To see a dark overhanging rock as a grim sombre human presence, is for the moment to view it under this aspect only, abstracting from its many obvious unlikenesses.

In the same manner, a tendency to read a particular meaning into a word may lead to the misapprehension of the word. To give an illustration: I was lately reading the fifth volume of G. H. Lewes's *Problems of Life and Mind*. In reading the first sentence of one of the sections, I again and again fell into the error of taking "The great Lagrange," for "The great Language." On glancing back I saw that the section was headed "On Language," and I at once recognized the cause of my error in the pre-existence in my mind of the representative image of the word "language."

In concluding this short account of the errors of insight, I may observe that their range is obviously much greater than that of the previously considered classes of presentative illusion. This is, indeed, involved in what has been said about the nature of the process. Insight, as we have seen, though here classed with presentative cognition, occupies a kind of border-land between immediate knowledge or intuition and inference, shading off from the one to the other. And in the very nature of the case the scope for error must be great. Even overlooking human reticence, and, what is worse, human hypocrisy, the conditions of an accurate reading of others' minds are rarely realized. If, as has been remarked by a good authority, one rarely meets, even among intelligent people, with a fairly accurate observer of external things, what shall be said as to the commonly claimed power of " intuitive insight " into other people's thoughts and feelings, as though it were a process above suspicion ? It is plain, indeed, on a little reflection, that, taking into account what is required in the way of large and varied experience (personal and social), a habit of careful in-trospection, as well as a habit of subtle discriminative attention to the external signs of mental life, and lastly, a freedom from prepossession and bias, only a very few can ever hope even to approximate to good readers of character.

And then we have to bear in mind that this large amount of error is apt to remain uncorrected. There is not, as in the case of external perception, an easy way of verification, by calling in another sense ; a mis-apprehension, once formed, is apt to remain, and I need hardly say that errors in these matters of mutual com-prehension have their palpable practical consequences. All social cohesion and co-operation rest on this com-prehension, and are limited by its degree of perfection. Nay, more, all common knowledge itself, in so far as it depends on a mutual communication of impressions, ideas, and beliefs, is limited by the fact of this great liability to error in what at first seems to be one of the most certain kinds of knowledge.

In view of this depressing amount of error, our solace must be found in the reflection that this seemingly perfect instrument of intuitive insight is, in reality, like that of introspection, in process of being fashioned. Mutual comprehension has only become necessary since man entered the social state, and this, to judge by the evolutionist's measure of time, is not so long ago. A mental structure so complex and delicate requires for its development a proportionate degree of exercise, and it is not reasonable to look yet for perfect precision of action. Nevertheless, we may hope that, with the advance of social development, the faculty is continually gaining in precision and certainty. And, indeed, this hope is already assured to us in the fact that the faculty has begun to criticise itself, to distinguish between an erroneous and a true form of its operation. In fact, all that has been here said about illusions of insight has involved the assumption that intellectual culture sharpens the power and makes it less liable to err.

CHAPTER X.

ILLUSIONS OF MEMORY.

THUS far we have been dealing with Presentative Illusions, that is to say, with the errors incident to the process of what may roughly be called presentative cognition. We have now to pass to the consideration of Representative Illusion, or that kind of error which attends representative cognition in so far as it is immediate or self-sufficient, and not consciously based on other cognition. Of such immediate representative cognition, memory forms the most conspicuous and most easily recognized variety. Accordingly, I proceed to take up the subject of the Illusions of Memory.[1]

The mystery of memory lies in the apparent immediateness of the mind's contact with the vanished past. In "looking back" on our life, we seem to ourselves for the moment to rise above the limitations of

---

[1] Errors of memory have sometimes been called "fallacies," as, for example, by Dr. Carpenter (*Human Physiology*, ch. x.). While preferring the term "illusion," I would not forget to acknowledge my indebtedness to Dr. Carpenter, who first set me seriously to consider the subject of mnemonic error.

time, to undo its work of extinction, seizing again the realities which its on-rushing stream had borne far from us. Memory is a kind of resurrection of the buried past: as we fix our retrospective glance on it, it appears to start anew into life; forms arise within our minds which, we feel sure, must faithfully represent the things that were. We do not ask for any proof of the fidelity of this dramatic representation of our past history by memory. It is seen to be a faithful imitation, just because it is felt to be a revival of the past. To seek to make the immediate testimony of memory more sure seems absurd, since all our ways of describing and illustrating this mental operation assume that in the very act of performing it we do recover a part of our seemingly " dead selves."

To challenge the veracity of a person's memory is one of the boldest things one can do in the way of attacking deep-seated conviction. Memory is the peculiar domain of the individual. In going back in recollection to the scenes of other years he is drawing on the secret store-house of his own consciousness, with which a stranger must not intermeddle. To cast doubt on a person's memory is commonly resented as an impertinence, hardly less rude than to question his reading of his own present mental state. Even if the challenger professedly bases his challenge on the testimony of his own memory, the challenged party is hardly likely to allow the right of comparing testimonies. He can in most cases boldly assert that those who differ from him are lacking in *his* power of recollection. The past, in becoming the past, has, for most people, ceased to be a common object of reference; it has become a part of the individual's own inner self, and cannot be easily dislodged or shaken.

Yet, although people in general are naturally disposed to be very confident about matters of recollection, reflective persons are pretty sure to find out, sooner or later, that they occasionally fall into errors of memory. It is not the philosopher who first hints at the mendacity of memory, but the " plain man " who takes careful note of what really happens in the world of his personal experience. Thus, we hear persons, quite innocent of speculative doubt, qualifying an assertion made on personal recollection by the proviso, " unless my memory has played me false." And even less reflective persons, including many who pride themselves on their excellent memory, will, when sorely pressed, make a grudging admission that they may, after all, be in error. Perhaps the weakest degree of such an admission, and one which allows to the conceding party a semblance of victory, is illustrated in the " last word " of one who has boldly maintained a proposition on the strength of individual recollection, but begins to recognize the instability of his position : " I either witnessed the occurrence or dreamt it." This is sufficient to prove that, with all people's boasting about the infallibility of memory, there are many who have a shrewd suspicion that some of its asseverations will not bear a very close scrutiny.

Psychology of Memory.

In order to understand the errors of memory, we must proceed, as in the case of illusions of perception, by examining a little into the nature of the normal or correct process.

An act of recollection is said by the psychologist to be purely representative in character, whereas perception is partly representative, partly presentative. To recall an object to the mind is to reconstruct the percept in the absence of a sense-impression.[1]

An act of memory is obviously distinguished from one of simple imagination by the presence of a conscious reference to the past. Every recollection is an immediate reapprehension of some past object or event. However vague this reference may be, it must be there to constitute the process one of recollection.

The every-day usages of language do not at first sight seem to consistently observe this distinction. When a boy says, " I remember my lesson," he appears to be thinking of the present only, and not referring to the past. In truth, however, there is a vague reference to the fact of retaining a piece of knowledge through a given interval of time.

Again, when a man says, " I recollect your face," this means, " Your face seems familiar to me." Here again, though there is no definite reference to the past, there is a vague and indefinite one.

It is plain from this definition that recollection is involved in all recognition or identification. Merely to be aware that I have seen a person before implies a minimum exercise of memory. Yet we may roughly distinguish the two actions of perception and recollection in the process of recognition. The mere

---

[1] From this it would appear to follow that, so far as a percept is representative, recollection must be re-representative.

recognition of an object does not imply the presence of a distinct representative or mnemonic image. In point of fact, in so far as recognition is assimilation, it cannot be said to imply a *distinct* act of memory at all. It is only when similarity is perceived amid difference, only when the accompaniments or surroundings of the object as previously seen, differencing it from the object as now seen, are brought up to the mind that we may be said distinctly to recall the past. And our state of mind in recognizing an object or person is commonly an alternation between these two acts of separating the mnemonic image from the percept and so recalling or recollecting the past, and fusing the image and the percept in what is specifically marked off as recognition.[1]

Although I have spoken of memory as a reinstatement in representative form of external experience, the term must be understood to include every revival of a past experience, whether external or internal, which is recognized as a revival. In a general way, the recallings of our internal feelings take place in close connection with the recollection of external circumstances or events, and so they may be regarded as largely conditioned by the laws of this second kind of reproduction.

The old conceptions of mind, which regarded every mental phenomenon as a manifestation of an occult spiritual substance, naturally led to the supposition that an act of recollection involves the continued, un-

---

[1] The relation of memory to recognition is very well discussed by M. Delbœuf, in connection with a definition of memory given by Descartes. (See the article " Le Sommeil et les Rêves," in the *Revue Philosophique*, April, 1880, p. 428, *et seq.*)

broken existence of the reproductive or mnemonic image in the hidden regions of the mind. To recollect is, according to this view, to draw the image out of the dark vaults of unconscious mind into the upper chamber of illumined consciousness.

Modern psychology recognizes no such pigeon-hole apparatus in unconscious mind. On the purely psychical side, memory is nothing but an occasional reappearance of a past mental experience. And the sole mental conditions of this reappearance are to be found in the circumstances of the moment of the original experience and in those of the moment of the reappearance.

Among these are to be specially noted, first of all, the degree of impressiveness of the original experience, that is to say, the amount of interest it awakened and of attention it excited. The more impressive any experience, the greater the chances of its subsequent revival. Moreover, the absence of impressiveness in the original experience may be made good either by a repetition of the actual experience or, in the case of non-recurring experiences, by the fact of previous mnemonic revivals.

In the second place, the pre-existing mental states at the time of revival are essential conditions. It is now known that every recollection is determined by some link of association, that every mnemonic image presents itself in consciousness only when it has been preceded by some other mental state, presentative or representative, which is related to the image. This relation may be one of contiguity, that is to say, the original experiences may have occurred at the same time or in close succession; or one of similarity (partial and not amounting to identity), as where the sight of one place or person recalls that of another place or person. Finally, it is to be observed that recollection is often an act, in the full sense of that term, involving an effort of voluntary attention at the moment of revival.

Modern physiology has done much towards helping us to understand the nervous conditions of memory. The biologist regards memory as a special phase of a universal property of organic structure, namely, modifiability by the exercise of function, or the survival after any particular kind of activity of a disposition to act again in that particular way. The revival of a mental impression in the weaker form of an image is thus, on its physical side, due in part to this remaining functional disposition in the central nervous tracts concerned. And so, while on the psychical or subjective side we are unable to find anything permanent in memory, on the physical or objective side we do find such a permanent substratum.

With respect to the special conditions of mnemonic revival at any time, physiology is less explicit. In a general way, it informs us that such a reinstatement of the past is determined by the existence of certain connections between the nervous structures concerned in the reviving and revived mental elements. Thus, it is said that when the sound of a name calls up in the mind a visual image of a person seen some time since, it is because connections have been formed between particular regions and modes of activity of the auditory and the visual centres.

And it is supposed that the existence of such connections is somehow due to the fact that the two regions acted simultaneously in the first instance, when the sight of the person was accompanied by the hearing of his name. In other words, the centres, as a whole, will tend to act at any future moment in the same complex way in which they have acted in past moments.

All this is valuable hypothesis so far as it goes, though it plainly leaves much unaccounted for. As to why this reinstatement of a total cerebral pulsation in consequence of the re-excitation of a portion of the same should be accompanied by the specific mode of consciousness which we call recollection of something past, it is perhaps unreasonable to ask of physiology any sort of explanation.[1]

Thus far as to the general or essential characteristics of memory on its mental and its bodily side. But what we commonly mean by memory is, on its psychical side at least, much more than this. We do not say that we properly recollect a thing unless we are able to refer it to some more or less clearly defined region of the past, and to localize it in the succession of experiences making up our mental image of the past. In other words, though we may speak of an imperfect kind of recollection where this definite reference is

---

[1] A very interesting account of the most recent physiological theory of memory is to be found in a series of articles, bearing the title, "La Mémoire comme fait biologique," published in the *Revue Philosophique*, from the pen of the editor, M. Th. Ribot. (See especially the *Revue* of May, 1880, pp. 516, *et seq.*) M. Ribot speaks of the modification of particular nerve-elements as "the static base" of memory, and of the formation of nerve-connections by means of which the modified element may be re-excited to activity as "the dynamic base of memory" (p. 535).

wanting, we mean by a perfect form of memory something which includes this reference.

Without entering just now upon a full analysis of what this reference to a particular region of the past means, I may observe that it takes place by help of an habitual retracing of the past, or certain portions of it, that is to say, a regressive movement of the imagination along the lines of our actual experience. Setting out from the present moment, I can move regressively to the preceding state of consciousness, to the penultimate, and so on. The fact that each distinct mental state is continuous with the preceding and the succeeding, and in a certain sense overlaps these, makes any portion of our experience essentially a succession of states of consciousness, involving some rudimentary idea of time. And thus, whether I anticipate a future event or recall a past one, my imagination, setting out from the present moment, constructs a sequence of experiences of which the one particularly dwelt on is the other term or boundary. And our idea of the position of this last in time, like that of an object in space, is one of a relation to our present position, and is determined by the length of the sequence of experiences thus run over by the imagination.[1] It may be added that since the imagination can much more easily follow the actual order of experience than conceive it as reversed, the retrospective act of memory naturally tends to complete itself by a return movement forwards from the remembered event to the present moment.

[1] What constitutes the difference between such a progressive and a retrogressive movement is a point that will be considered by-and-by.

In practice this detailed retracing of successive moments of mental life is confined to very recent experiences. If I try to localize in time a remote event, I am content with placing it in relation to a series of prominent events or landmarks which serves me as a rough scheme of the past. The formation of such a mnemonic framework is largely due to the needs of social converse, which proceeds by help of a common standard of reference. This standard is supplied by those objective, that is to say, commonly experienced regularities of succession which constitute the natural and artificial divisions of the years, seasons, months, weeks, etc. The habit of recurring to these fixed divisional points of the past renders a return of imagination to any one of them more and more easy. A man has a definite idea of "a year ago" which the child wants, just because he has had so frequently to execute that vague regressive movement by which the idea arises. And though, as our actual point in time moves forward, the relative position of any given landmark is continually changing, the change easily adapts itself to that scheme of time-divisions which holds good for any present point.

Few of our recollections of remote events involve a definite reference to this system of landmarks. The recollections of early life are, in the case of most people, so far as they depend on individual memory, very vaguely and imperfectly localized. And many recent experiences which are said to be half forgotten, are not referred to any clearly assignable position in time. One may say that in average cases definite localization characterizes only such supremely interesting personal experiences as spontaneously recur again and again to the mind. For the rest it is confined to those facts and events of general interest to which our social habits lead us repeatedly to go back.[1]

The consciousness of personal identity is said to be bound up with memory. That is to say, I am conscious of a continuous permanent self under all the varying surface-play of the stream of consciousness, just because I can, by an act of recollection, bring together any two portions of this stream of experience, and so recognize the unbroken continuity of the whole. If this is so, it would seem to follow from the very fragmentary character of our recollections that our sense of identity is very incomplete. As we shall see presently, there is good reason to look upon this consciousness of continuous personal existence as resting only in part on memory, and mainly on our independently formed representation of what has happened in the numberless and often huge lacunæ of the past left by memory.

Having thus a rough idea of the mechanism of memory to guide us, we may be able to investigate the illusions incident to the process.

Illusions of Memory.

By an illusion of memory we are to understand a false recollection or a wrong reference of an idea to

---

[1] It is not easy to say how far exceptional conditions may serve to reinstate the seemingly forgotten past. Yet the experiences of dreamers and of those who have been recalled to consciousness after partial drowning, whatever they may prove with respect to the revivability of remote experiences, do not lead us to imagine that the range of our definitely localizing memory is a wide one.

some region of the past. It might, perhaps, be roughly described as a wrong interpretation of a special kind of mental image, namely, what I have called a mnemonic image.

Mnemonic illusion is thus distinct from mere forgetfulness or imperfect memory. To forget or be doubtful about a past event is one thing ; to seem to ourselves to remember it when we afterwards find that the fact was otherwise than we represented it in the apparent act of recollection is another thing. Indistinctness of recollection, or the decay of memory, is, as we shall soon see, an important co-operant condition of mnemonic illusion, but does not constitute it, any more than haziness of vision or disease of the visual organ, though highly favourable to optical illusion, can be said to constitute it.

We may conveniently proceed in our detailed examination of illusions of memory, by distinguishing between three facts which appear to be involved in every complete and accurate process of recollection. When I distinctly recall an event, I am immediately sure of three things : (1) that something did really happen to me ; (2) that it happened in the way I now think ; and (3) that it happened when it appears to have happened. I cannot be said to recall a past event unless I feel sure on each of these points. Thus, to be able to say that an event happened at a particular date, and yet unable to describe how it happened, means that I have a very incomplete recollection. The same is true when I can recall an event pretty distinctly, but fail to assign it its proper date. This being so, it follows that there are three possible openings, and only three, by which errors of memory may creep in. And, as a matter of fact, each of these openings will be found to let in one class of mnemonic illusion. Thus we have (1) false recollections, to which there correspond no real events of personal history; (2) others which misrepresent the manner of happening of the events; and (3) others which falsify the date of the events remembered.

It is obvious, from a mere glance at this threefold classification, that illusions of memory closely correspond to visual illusions. Thus, class (1) may be likened to the optical illusions known as subjective sensations of light, or ocular spectra. Here we can prove that there is nothing actually seen in the field of vision, and that the semblance of a visible object arises from quite another source than that of ordinary external light-stimulation, and by what may be called an accident. Similarly, in the case of the first class of mnemonic illusions, we shall find that there is nothing actually recollected, but that the mnemonic spectra or phantoms of recollected objects can be accounted for in quite another way. Such illusions come nearest to hallucinations in the region of memory.

Again, class (2) has its visual analogue in those optical illusions which depend on effects of haziness and of the action of refracting media interposed between the eye and the object; in which cases, though there is some real thing corresponding to the perception, this is seen in a highly defective, distorted, and misleading form. In like manner, we can say that the images of memory often get obscured, distorted, and otherwise altered when they have receded into the dim distance, and are looked back upon through a long space of intervening mental experience. Finally, class (3) has its visual counterpart in erroneous perceptions of distance, as when, for example, owing to the clearness of the mountain atmosphere and the absence of intervening objects, the side of the Jungfrau looks to the inexperienced tourist at Wengernalp hardly further than a stone's throw. It will be found that when our memory falsifies the date of an event, the error arises much in the same way as a visual miscalculation of distance.

This threefold division of illusions of memory is plainly a rather superficial one, and not based on distinctions of psychological nature or origin. In order to make our treatment of the subject scientific as well as popular, it will be necessary to introduce the distinction between the passive and the active factor under each head. It will be found, I think, without forcing the analogy too far, that here, as in the case of the illusions of perception and introspection, error is attributable now to misleading suggestion on the part of the mental content of the moment, now to a process of incorporating into this content a mental image not suggested by it, but existing independently.

If we are to proceed as we did in the case of the illusions of sense, and take up the lower stages of error first of all, we shall need to begin with the third class of errors, those of localization in time, or of what may be called mnemonic perspective. It has been already observed that the definite localization of a mnemonic image is only an occasional accompaniment of what is loosely called recollection. Hence, error as to the position of an event in the past chain of events would seem to involve the least degree of violation of the confidence which we are wont to repose in memory.   After this, we may proceed to the discussion of the second class, which I may call distortions of the mnemonic picture.   And, finally, we may deal with the most signal and palpable variety of error of memory, namely, the illusions which I have called mnemonic spectra.

Illusions of Perspective: A. *Definite Localization.*

In order to understand these errors of mnemonic perspective, we shall have to inquire more closely than we have yet done into the circumstances which customarily determine our idea of the degree of propinquity or of remoteness of a past event.   And first of all, we will take the case of a complete act of recollection when the mind is able to travel back along an uninterrupted series of experiences to a definitely apprehended point.   Here there would seem, at first sight, to be no room for error, since this movement of retrospective imagination may be said to involve a direct measurement of the distance, just as a sweep of the eye over the 'ground between a spectator and an object affords a direct measurement of the intervening space.

Modern science, however, tells us that this mode of measurement is by no means the simple and accurate process which it at first seems to be.   In point of fact, there is something like a constant error in all such retrospective measurement.   Vierordt has proved experimentally, by making a person try to reproduce the varying time-intervals between the strokes of the pendulum of a metronome, that when the interval is a very small one, we uniformly tend to exaggerate it in retrospection; when a large one, to regard it, on the contrary, as less than it actually was.[1]

A mere act of reflection will convince any one that when he tries to conceive a very small interval, say a quarter of a second, he is likely to make it too great. On the other hand, when we try to conceive a year, we do not fully grasp the whole extent of the duration. This is proved by the fact that merely by spending more time over the attempt, and so recalling a larger number of the details of the period, we very considerably enlarge our first estimate of the duration. And this leads to great discrepancies in the appreciation of the relative magnitudes of past sections of time. Thus, as Wundt observes, though in retrospect both a month and a year seem too short, the latter is relatively much more shortened than the former.[2]

The cause of this constant error in the mode of reproducing durations seems to be connected with the very nature of the reproductive act. It must be borne in mind that this act is itself, like the experience which it represents, a mental process, occupying time, and that consequently it may very possibly reflect its time-character on the resulting judgment. Thus, since it certainly takes more than a quarter of a second to pass in imagination from one impression to another, it may be that we tend to confound this duration with that which we try to represent. Similarly, the fact that

[1] *Der Zeitsinn nach Versuchen*, p. 36, *et seq.*
[2] *Physiologische Psychologie*, p. 782.

in the act of reproductive imagination we under-estimate a longer interval between two impressions, say those of the slow beats of a colliery engine, may be accounted for by the supposition that the imagination tends to pass from the one impression to the succeeding one too rapidly.[1]

The gross misappreciation of duration of long periods of time, while it may illustrate the principle just touched on, clearly involves the effect of other and more powerful influences. A mere glance at what is in our mind when we recall such a period as a month or a year, shows that there is no clear concrete representation at all. Time, it has been often said, is known only so far as filled with concrete contents or conscious experiences, and a perfect imagination of any particular period of past time would involve a re-tracing of all the successive experiences which have gone to make up this section of our life. This, I need not say, never happens, both because, on the one hand, memory does not allow of a complete reproduction of any segment of our experience, and because, on the other hand, such an imaginative reproduction, even if possible, would clearly occupy as much time as the experience itself.[2]

---

[1] Wundt refers these errors to variations in the state of pre-adjustment of the attention to impressions and representations, according as they succeed one another slowly or rapidly. There is little doubt that the effects of the state of tension of the apparatus of attention are involved here, though I am disposed to think that Wundt makes too much of this circumstance. (See *Physiologische Psychologie*, pp. 782, 783. I have given a fuller account of Wundt's theory in *Mind*, No. i.)

[2] Strictly speaking, it would occupy more time, since the effort of recalling each successive link in the chain would involve a greater interval between any two images than that between the corresponding experiences.

When I call up an image of the year just closing, what really happens is a rapid movement of imagination over a series of prominent events, among which the succession of seasons probably occupies the foremost place, serving, as I have remarked, as a framework for my retrospective picture. Each of the events which I thus run over is really a long succession of shorter experiences, which, however, I do not separately represent to myself. My imaginative reproduction of such a period is thus essentially a greatly abbreviated and symbolic mode of representation. It by no means corresponds to the visual imagination of a large magnitude, say that of the length of sea horizon visible at any one moment, which is complete in an instant, and quite independent of a successive imagination of its parts or details. It is essentially a very fragmentary and defective numerical idea, in which, moreover, the real quantitative value of the units is altogether lost sight of.

Now, it seems to follow from this that there is something illusory in all our recallings of long periods of the past. It is by no means strictly correct to say that memory ever reinstates the past. It is more true to say that we see the past in retrospect as greatly foreshortened. Yet even this is hardly an accurate account of what takes place, since, when we look at an object foreshortened in perspective, we see enough to enable us imaginatively to reconstruct the actual size of the object, whereas in the case of time-perspective no such reconstruction is even indirectly possible.

It is to be added that this constant error in time-reproduction is greater in the case of remote periods than of near ones of the same length. Thus, the retrospective estimate of a duration far removed from the present, say the length of time passed at a particular school, is much more superficial and fragmentary than that of a recent corresponding period. So that the time-vista of the past is seen to answer pretty closely to a visible perspective in which the amount of apparent error due to foreshortening increases with the distance.

In practice, however, this defect in the imagination of duration leads to no error. Although, as a concrete image answering to some definite succession of experiences a year is a gross misrepresentation, as a general concept implying a collection of a certain number of similar successions of experience it is sufficiently exact. That is to say, though we cannot imagine the *absolute* duration of any such cycle of experience, we can, by the simple device of conceiving certain durations as multiples of others, perfectly well compare different periods of times, and so appreciate their *relative* magnitudes.

Leaving, then, this constant error in time-appreciation, we will pass to the variable and more palpable errors in the retrospective measurement of time. Each person's experience will have told him that in estimating the distance of a past event by a mere retrospective sense of duration, he is liable to extraordinary fluctuations of judgment. Sometimes when the clock strikes we are surprised at the rapidity of the hour. At other times the timepiece seems rather to have lagged behind its usual pace. And what is true of a short interval is still more true of longer intervals, as months and years. The understanding of these fluctuations will be promoted by our brief glance at the constant errors in retrospective time-appreciation.

And here it is necessary to distinguish between the sense of duration which we have during any period, and the retrospective sense which survives the period, for these do not necessarily agree. The former rests mainly on our prospective sense of time, whereas the latter must be altogether retrospective.[1]

Our estimate of time as it passes is commonly said to depend on the amount of consciousness which we are giving to the fact of its transition. Thus, when the mind is unoccupied and suffering from *ennui*, we feel time to move sluggishly. On the other hand, interesting employment, by diverting the thoughts from time, makes it appear to move at a more rapid pace. This fact is shown in the common expressions which we employ, such as " to kill time," and the German *Langweile*. Similarly, it is said that when we are eagerly anticipating an event, as the arrival of a friend, the mere fact of dwelling on the interval makes it appear to swell out.[2]

This view is correct in the main, and is seen, indeed, to follow from the great psychological principle that what we attend to exists for us more, has more reality, and so naturally seems greater than what we do not

---

[1] I need hardly say that there is no sharp distinction between these two modes of subjective appreciation. Our estimate of an interval as it passes is really made up of a number of renewed anticipations and recollections of the successive experiences. Yet we can say broadly that this is a prospective estimate, while that which is formed when the period has quite expired must be altogether retrospective.

[2] See an interesting paper on " Consciousness of Time," by Mr. G. J. Romanes, in *Mind* (July, 1878).

attend to.   At the same time, this principle must be supplemented by another consideration.   Suppose that I am very desirous that time should *not* pass quickly. If, for example, I am enjoying myself or indulging in idleness, and know that I have to be off to keep a not very agreeable engagement in a quarter of an hour, time will seem to pass too rapidly; and this not because my thoughts are diverted from the fact of its transition, for, on the contrary, they are reverting to it more than they usually do, but because my wish to lengthen the interval leads me to represent the unwelcome moment as further off than it actually is, in other words, to construct an ideal representation of the period in contrast with which the real duration looks miserably short.

Our estimate of duration, when it is over, depends less on this circumstance of having attended to its transition than on other considerations.   Wundt, indeed, seems to think that the feeling accompanying the actual flow of time has no effect on the surviving subjective appreciation; but this must surely be an error, since our mental image of any period is detertermined by the character of its contents.   Wundt says that when once a tedious waiting is over, it looks short because we instantly forget the feeling of tedium. My self-observation, as well as the interrogation of others, has satisfied me, on the contrary, that this feeling distinctly colours the retrospective appreciation.   Thus, when waiting at a railway station for a belated train, I am distinctly aware that each quarter of an hour looks long, not only as it passes, but when it is over.   In fact, I am disposed to express my feeling as one of disappointment that only so short an interval has passed since I last looked at my watch.

Nevertheless, I am ready to allow that, though a feeling of tedium, or the contrary feeling of irritation at the rapidity of time, will linger for an appreciable interval and colour the retrospective estimate of time, this backward view is chiefly determined by other considerations. As Wundt remarks, we have no sense of time's slowness during sleep, yet on waking we imagine that we have been dreaming for an immensely long period. This retrospective appreciation is determined by the number and the degree or intensity of the experiences, and, what comes very much to the same thing, by the amount of unlikeness, freshness, and discontinuity characterizing these experiences.

Time, as I have already hinted, is known under the form of a succession of different conscious experiences. Unbroken uniformity would give us no sense of time, because it would give us no conscious experience at all. Strictly speaking, there is no such thing as a perfectly uniform mental state extending through an appreciable duration. In looking at one and the same object, even in listening to one and the same tone, I am in no two successive fractions of a second in exactly the same state of mind. Slight alterations in the strength of the sensation,[1] in the degree or direction of attention, and in the composition of that penumbra of vague images which it calls up, occur at every distinguishable fraction of time.

---

[1] It is well known that there is, from the first, a gradual falling off in the strength of a sensation of light when a moderately bright object is looked at.

This being so, it would seem to follow that the greater the number of clearly marked changes, and the more impressive and exciting these transitions, the fuller will be our sense of time. And this is borne out by individual reflection. When striking and deeply interesting events follow one another very rapidly, as when we are travelling, duration appears to swell out.

It is possible that such a succession of stirring experiences may beget a vague consciousness of time at each successive moment, and apart from retrospection, simply by force of the change. In other words, without our distinctly attending to time, a series of novel impressions might, by giving us the consciousness of change, make us dimly aware of the numerical richness of our experiences. But, however this be, there is no doubt that, in glancing back on such a succession of exciting transitions of mental condition, time appears to expand enormously, just as it does in looking back on our dream-experience, or that rapid series of intensified feelings which, according to De Quincey and others, is produced by certain narcotics.

The reason of this is plain. Such a type of successive experience offers to the retrospective imagination a large number of distinguishable points, and since this mode of estimating time depends, as we have seen, on the extent of the process of filling in, time will necessarily appear long in this case. On the other hand, when we have been engaged in very ordinary pursuits, in which few deeply interesting or exciting events have impressed themselves on memory, our retrospective picture will necessarily be very much of a blank,

and consequently the duration of the period will seem
to be short.

I observed that this retrospective appreciation of
time depended on the degree of connection between
the successive experiences. This condition is very
much the same as the other just given, namely, the
degree of uniformity of the experiences, since the more
closely the successive stages of the experience are
connected—as when, for example, we are going through
our daily routine of work—the more quiet and un-
exciting will be the transition from each stage to its
succeeding one. And on the other hand, all novelty of
impression and exciting transition of experience clearly
involves a want of connection. Wundt thinks the
retrospective estimate of a connected series of experiences, such as those of our daily round of occupa-
tions, is defective just because the effort of attention,
which precedes even an imaginative reproduction of
an impression, so quickly accommodates itself in this
case to each of the successive steps, whereas, when the
experiences to be recalled are disconnected, the effort
requires more time. In this way, the estimate of a
past duration would be coloured by the sense of time
accompanying the reproductive process itself. This
may very likely be the case, yet I should be disposed
to attach most importance to the number of distinguishable items of experience recalled.

Our representation of the position of a given event
in the past is, as I have tried to show, determined by
the movement of imagination in going back to it from
the present. And this is the same thing as to say
that it depends on our retrospective sense of the inter-

vening space. That is to say, the sense of distance in time, as in space, is the recognition of a term to a movement. And just as the distance of an object will seem greater when there are many intervening objects affording points of measurement, than when there are none (as on the uniform surface of the sea), so the distance of an event will vary with the number of recognized intervening points.

The appreciation of the distance of an event in time does not, however, wholly depend on the character of this movement of imagination. Just as the apparent distance of a visible object depends *inter alia* on the distinctness of the retinal impression, so the apparent temporal remoteness of a past event depends in part on the degree of intensity and clearness of the mnemonic image. This is seen even in the case of those images which we are able distinctly to localize in the time-perspective. For a series of exciting experiences intervening between the present and a past event appears not only *directly* to add to our sense of distance by constituting an apparently long interval, but *indirectly* to add to it by giving an unusual degree of faintness to the recalled image. An event preceding some unusually stirring series of experiences gets thrust out of consciousness by the very engrossing nature of the new experiences, and so tends to grow more faint and ghost-like than it would otherwise have done.

The full force of this circumstance is best seen in the fact that a very recent event, bringing with it a deep mental shock and a rapid stirring of wide tracts of feeling and thought, may get to look old in a marvellously short space of time. An announcement of the loss of a dear friend, when sudden and deeply agitating, will seem remote even after an hour of such intense emotional experience. And the same twofold consideration probably explains the well-known fact that a year seems much shorter to the adult than to the child. The novel and comparatively exciting impressions of childhood tend to fill out time in retrospect, and also to throw back remote events into a dimly discernible region.

Now, this same circumstance, the degree of vividness or of faintness of the mnemonic image, is that which determines our idea of distance when the character of the intervening experiences produces no appreciable effect.[1] This is most strikingly illustrated in those imperfect kinds of recollection in which we are unable to definitely localize the mnemonic image. To the consideration of these we will now turn.

B. *Indefinite Localization.*

Speaking roughly and generally, we may say that the vividness of an image of memory decreases in proportion as the distance of the event increases. And this is the rule which we unconsciously apply in determining distance in time. Nevertheless, this rule gives us by no means an infallible criterion of distance. The very fact that different people so often dispute about the dates and the order of past events experienced in common, shows pretty plainly that images of the

---

[1] *Cf.* Hartley, *Observations on Man*, Part I. ch. iii. sec. 4 (fifth edit., p. 391).

same age tend to arise in the mind with very unequal degrees of vividness.

Sometimes pictures of very remote incidents may suddenly present themselves to our minds with a singular degree of brightness and force. And when this is the case, there is a disposition to think of them as near. If the relations of the event to other events preceding and succeeding it are not remembered, this momentary illusion will persist. We have all heard persons exclaim, "It seems only yesterday," under the sense of nearness which accompanies a recollection of a remote event when vividly excited. The most familiar instance of such lively reproduction is the feeling which we experience on revisiting the scene of some memorable event. At such a time the past may return with something of the insistence of a present perceived reality. In passing from place to place, in talking with others, and in reading, we are liable to the sudden return by hidden paths of association of images of incidents that had long seemed forgotten, and when they thus start up fresh and vigorous, away from their proper surroundings, they invariably induce a feeling of the propinquity of the events.

In many cases we cannot say why these particular images, long buried in oblivion, should thus suddenly regain so much vitality. There seems, indeed, to be almost as much that is arbitrary and capricious in the selection by memory of its vivid images as in the selection of its images as a whole; and, this being so, it is plain that we are greatly exposed to the risk of illusion from this source.

There is an opposite effect in the case of recent occurrences that, for some reason or another, have left but a faint impression on the memory; though this fact is not, perhaps, so familiar as the other. I met a friend, we will suppose, a few days since at my club, and we exchanged a few words. My mind was somewhat preoccupied at the time, and the occurrence did not stamp itself on my recollection. To-day I meet him again, and he reminds me of a promise I made him at the time. His reminder suffices to restore a dim image of the incident, but the fact of its dimness leads to the illusion that it really happened much longer ago, and it is only on my friend's strong assurances, and on reasoning from other data that it must have occurred the day he mentions, that I am able to dismiss the illusion.

The most striking examples of the illusory effect of mere vividness, involving a complete detachment of the event from the prominent landmarks of the past, are afforded by public events which lie outside the narrower circle of our personal life, and which do not in the natural course of things become linked to any definitely localized points in the field of memory. These events may be very stirring and engrossing for the time, but in many cases they pass out of the mind just as suddenly as they entered it. We have no occasion to revert to them, and if by chance we are afterwards reminded of them, they are pretty certain to look too near, just because the fact of their having greatly interested us has served to render their images particularly vivid.

A curious instance of this illusory effect was

supplied not long since by the case of the ex-detectives, the expiration of whose term of punishment (three years) served as an occasion for the newspapers to recall the event of their trial and conviction. The news that three years had elapsed since this well-remembered occurrence proved very startling to myself, and to a number of my friends, all of us agreeing that the event did not seem to be at more than a third of its real distance. More than one newspaper commented on the apparent rapidity of the time, and this shows pretty plainly that there was some cause at work, such as I have suggested, producing a common illusion.

I have treated of these illusions connected with the estimate of past time and the dating of past events as passive illusions, not involving any active predisposition on the part of the imagination. At the same time, it is possible that error in these matters may occasionally depend on a present condition of the feelings and the imagination. It seems plain that since the apparent degree of remoteness of an event not distinctly localized in the past varies inversely as the degree of vividness of the mnemonic image, any conscious concentration of mind on a recollection will tend to bring it too near. In this way, then, an illusory propinquity may be given to a recalled event through a mere desire to dwell on it, or even a capricious wish to deceive one's self.

When, for example, old friends come together and talk over the days of yore, there is a gradual reinstatement of seemingly lost experiences, which often partakes of the character of a semi-voluntary process of self-delusion. Through the cumulative effect of mutual reminder, incident after incident returns, adding something to the whole picture till it acquires a degree of completeness, coherence, and vividness that render it hardly distinguishable from a very recent experience. The process is like looking at a distant object through a field-glass. Mistiness disappears, fresh details come into view, till we seem to ourselves to be almost within reach of the object.

Where the mind habitually goes back to some painful circumstance under the impulse of a morbid disposition to nurse regret, this momentary illusion may become recurring, and amount to a partial confusion of the near and the remote in our experience. An injury long brooded on seems at length a thing that continually moves forward as we move; it always presents itself to our memories as a very recent event. In states of insanity brought on by some great shock, we see this morbid tendency to resuscitate the dead past fully developed, and remote events and circumstances becoming confused with present ones.

On the other hand, in more healthy states of mind there presents itself an exactly opposite tendency, namely, an impulse of the will to banish whatever when recalled gives pain to the furthest conceivable regions of the past. Thus, when we have lost something we cherished dearly, and the recollection of it brings fruitless longing, we instinctively seek to expel the recollection from our minds. The very feeling that what has been can never again be, seems to induce this idea of a vast remoteness of the vanished reality. When, moreover, the lost object was fitted to call forth the emotion of reverence, the impulse to magnify the remoteness of the loss may not improbably be rein-forced by the circumstance that everything belonging to the distant past is fitted on that account to excite a feeling akin to reverence. So, again, any rupture in our mental development may lead us to exaggerate the distance of some past portion of our experience. When we have broken with our former selves, either in the way of worsening or bettering, we tend to project these further into the past.

It is only when the sting of the recollection is removed, when, for example, the calling up of the image of a lost friend is no longer accompanied with the bitterness of futile longing, that a healthy mind ventures to nourish recollections of such remote events and to view these as part of its recent experiences. In this case the mnemonic image becomes transformed into a kind of present emotional possession, an element of that idealized and sublimated portion of our ex-perience with which all imaginative persons fill up the emptiness of their actual lives, and to which the poet is wont to give an objective embodiment in his verse.

Distortions of Memory.

It is now time to pass to the second group of illusions of memory, which, according to the analogy of visual errors, may be called atmospheric illusions. Here the degree of error is greater than in the case of illusions of time-perspective, since the very nature of the events or circumstances is misconceived. We do not recall the event as it happened, but see it in part only, and obscured, or bent and distorted as by a

process of refraction. Indeed, this transformation of
the past does closely correspond with the transformation of a visible object effected by intervening media.
Our minds are such refracting media, and the past
reappears to us not as it actually was when it was close
to us, but in numerous ways altered and disguised by
the intervening spaces of our conscious experience.

To begin with, what we call recollection is uniformly
a process of softening the reality. When we appear to
ourselves to realize events of the remote past, it is
plain that our representation in a general way falls
below the reality: the vividness, the intensity of our
impressions disappears. More particularly, so far as
our experiences are emotional, they tend thus to become toned down by the mere lapse of time and the
imperfections of our reproductive power. That which
we seem to see in the act of recollection is thus very
different from the reality.

Not only is there this general deficiency in
mnemonic representation, there are special deficiencies
due to the fact of oblivescence. Our memories restore
us only fragments of our past life. And just as objects
seen imperfectly at a great distance may assume a
shape quite unlike their real one, so an inadequate
representation of a past event by memory often amounts
to misrepresentation. When revisiting a place that
we have not seen for many years, we are apt to find
that our recollection of it consisted only of some insignificant details, which arranged themselves in our
minds into something oddly unlike the actual scene
So, too, some accidental accompaniment of an incident
in early life is preserved, as though it were the main

feature, serving to give quite a false colouring to the whole occurrence.

It seems quite impossible to account for these particular survivals, they appear to be so capricious. When a little time has elapsed after an event, and the attendant circumstances fade away from memory, it is often difficult to say why we were impressed with it as we afterwards prove to have been. It is no doubt possible to see that many of the recollections of our childhood owe their vividness to the fact of the exceptional character of the events; but this cannot always be recognized. Some of them seem to our mature minds very oddly selected, although no doubt there are in every case good reasons, if we could only discover them, why those particular incidents rather than any others should have been retained.

The liability to error resulting from mere oblivescence and the arbitrary selection of mental images is seen most plainly, perhaps, in our subsequent representation and estimate of whole periods of early life. Our idea of any stage of our past history, as early childhood, or school days, is built up out of a few fragmentary intellectual relics which cannot be certainly known to answer to the most important and predominant experiences of the time. When, for example, we try to decide whether our school days were our happiest days, as is so often alleged, it is obvious that we are liable to fall into illusion through the inadequacy of memory to preserve characteristic or typical features, and none but these. We cannot easily recall the ordinary every-day level of feeling of a distant period of life, but rather think of exceptional moments of rejoicing or depression.

The ordinary man's idea of the emotional experience of his school days is probably built up out of a few scrappy recollections of extraordinary and exciting events, such as unexpected holidays, success in the winning of prizes, famous "rows" with the masters, and so on.

Besides the impossibility of getting at the average and prevailing mental tone of a distant section of life, there is a special difficulty in determining the degree of happiness of the past, arising from the fact that our memory for pleasures and for pains may not be equally good. Most people, perhaps, can recall the enjoyments of the past much more vividly than the sufferings. On the other hand, there seem to be some who find the retention of the latter the easier of the two. This fact should not be forgotten in reading the narrative of early hardships which some recent autobiographies have given us.

Not only does our idea of the past become inexact by the mere decay and disappearance of essential features, it becomes positively incorrect through the gradual incorporation of elements that do not properly belong to it. Sometimes it is easy to see how these extraneous ideas get imported into our mental representation of a past event. Suppose, for example, that a man has lost a valuable scarf-pin. His wife suggests that a particular servant, whose reputation does not stand too high, has stolen it. When he afterwards recalls the loss, the chances are that he will confuse the fact with the conjecture attached to it, and say he remembers that this particular servant did steal the pin. Thus, the past activity of imagination serves to corrupt and partially falsify recollections that have a genuine basis of fact.

It is evident that this class of mnemonic illusions approximates in character to illusions of perception. When the imagination supplies the interpretation at the very time, and the mind reads this into the perceived object, the error is one of perception. When the addition is made afterwards, on reflecting upon the perception, the error is one of memory. The "fallacies of testimony" which depend on an adulteration of pure observation with inference and conjecture, as, for example, the inaccurate and wild statements of people respecting their experiences at spiritualist *séances*, while they illustrate the curious blending of both kinds of error, are probably much oftener illusions of memory than of perception.[1]

Although in many cases we can account to ourselves for this confusion of fact and imagination, in other cases it is difficult to see any close relation between the fact remembered and the foreign element imported into it. An idea of memory seems sometimes to lose its proper moorings, so to speak; to drift about helplessly among other ideas, and finally, by some chance, to hook itself on to one of these, as though it naturally belonged to it. Anybody who has had an opportunity of carefully testing the truthfulness of his recollection of some remote event in early life will have found how oddly extraneous elements become incorporated into the memorial picture. Incidents get put into wrong places, the wrong persons are introduced into a scene, and so on. Here again we may illustrate the mnemonic illusion by a visual one. When a tree standing before or behind a house and projecting above or to

[1] See Dr. Carpenter's *Mental Physiology*, fourth edit., p. 456.

the side of it is not sharply distinguished from the latter, it may serve to give it a very odd appearance.

These confusions of the mental image may arise even when only a short interval has elapsed. In the case of many of the fleeting impressions that are only half recollected, this kind of error is very easy. Thus, for example, I may have lent a book to a friend last week. I really remember the act of lending it, but have forgotten the person. But I am not aware of this. The picture of memory has unknowingly to myself been filled up by this unconscious process of shifting and rearrangement, and the idea of another person has by some odd accident got substituted for that of the real borrower. If we could go deeply enough into the matter, we should, of course, be able to explain why this particular confusion arose. We might find, for example, that the two persons were associated in my mind by a link of resemblance, or that I had dealings with the other person about the same time. Similarly, when we manage to join an event to a wrong place, we may find that it is because we heard of the occurrence when staying at the particular locality, or in some other way had the image of the place closely associated in our minds with the event. But often we are wholly unable to explain the displacement.

So far I have been speaking of the passive processes by which the past comes to wear a new face to our imaginations. In these our present habits of feeling and thinking take no part; all is the work of the past, of the decay of memory, and the gradual confusion of images. This process of disorganization may be likened to the action of damp on some old manuscript, obliterating some parts, altering the appearance of others, and even dislocating certain portions. Besides this passive process of transformation, there is a more active one in which our present minds co-operate. In memory, as in perception and introspection, there is a process of preparation or preadjustment of mind, and here will be found room for what I had called active error. This may be illustrated by the operation of " interpreting " an old manuscript which has got partially obliterated, or of " restoring " a faded picture; in each of which operations error will be pretty sure to creep in through an importation of the restorer's own ideas into the relic of the past.

Just as when distant objects are seen mistily our imaginations come into play, leading us to fancy that we see something completely and distinctly, so when the images of memory become dim, our present imagination helps to restore them, putting a new patch into the old garment. If only there is some relic of the past event preserved, a bare suggestion of the way in which it may have happened will often suffice to produce the conviction that it actually did happen in this way. The suggestions that naturally arise in our minds at such times will bear the stamp of our present modes of experience and habits of thought. Hence, in trying to reconstruct the remote past, we are constantly in danger of importing our present selves into our past selves.

The kind of illusion of memory which thus depends on the spontaneous or independent activity of present imagination is strikingly illustrated in the curious cases of mistaken identity with which the proceedings of our law courts supply us from time to time. When a witness in good faith, but erroneously, affirms that a man is the same as an old acquaintance of his, we may feel sure that there is some striking point or points of similarity between the two persons. But this of itself would only partly account for the illusion, since we often see new faces that, by a number of curious points of affinity, call up in a tantalizing way old and familiar ones. What helps in this case to produce the illusion is the preconception that the present man *is* the witness's old friend. That is to say, his recollection is partly true, though largely false. He does really recall the similar feature, movement, or tone of voice; he only seems to himself to recall the rest of his friend's appearance; for, to speak correctly, he projects the present impression into the past, and constructs his friend's face out of elements supplied by the new one. Owing to this cause, an illusion of memory is apt to multiply itself, one man's assertion of what happened producing by contagion a counterfeit of memory's record in other minds.

I said just now that we tend to project our present modes of experience into the past. We paint our past in the hues of the present. Thus we imagine that things which impressed us in some remote period of life must answer to what is impressive in our present stage of mental development. For example, a person recalls a hill near the home of his childhood, and has the conviction that it was of great height. On revisiting the place he finds that the eminence is quite insignificant. How can we account for this? For one thing, it is to be observed that to his undeveloped childish muscles the climbing to the top meant a considerable expenditure of energy, to be followed by a sense of fatigue. The man remembers these feelings, and "unconsciously reasoning" by present experience, that is to say, by the amount of walking which would now produce this sense of fatigue, imagines that the height was vastly greater than it really was. Another reason is, of course, that a wider knowledge of mountains has resulted in a great alteration of the man's standard of height.

From this cause arises a tendency generally to exaggerate the impressions of early life. Youth is the period of novel effects, when all the world is fresh, and new and striking impressions crowd in thickly on the mind. Consequently, it takes much less to produce a given amount of mental excitation in childhood than in after-life. In looking back on this part of our history, we recall for the most part just those events and scenes which deeply stirred our minds by their strangeness, novelty, etc., and so impressed themselves on the tablet of our memory ; and it is this sense of something out of the ordinary beat that gives the characteristic colour to our recollection. In other words, we remember something as wonderful, admirable, exceptionally delightful, and so on, rather than as a definitely imagined event. This being so, we unconsciously transform the past occurrence by reasoning from our present standard of what is impressive. Who has not felt an unpleasant disenchantment on revisiting some church, house, or park that seemed a wondrous paradise to his young eyes? All our feelings are capable of leading us into this kind of illusion. What seemed beautiful or awful to us as children, is now pictured in imagination as corresponding to what moves our mature minds to delight or awe. One cannot help wondering what we should think of our early heroes or heroines if we could see them again with our adult eyes exactly as they were.

While the past may thus take on an illusory hue through the very progress of our experience and our emotional life, it may become further transformed by a more conscious process, namely, the idealizing touch of a present feeling. The way in which the emotions of love, reverence, and so on, thus transform their lost objects is too well known to need illustration. Speaking generally, we may say that in healthy minds the play of these impulses of feeling results in a softening of the harsher features of the past, and in an idealization of its happier and brighter aspects. As Wordsworth says, we may assign to Memory a pencil—

> " That, softening objects, sometimes even
>   Outstrips the heart's demand ;
>
> " That smoothes foregone distress, the lines
>   Of lingering care subdues,
>   Long-vanished happiness refines,
>   And clothes in brighter hues." [1]

Enough has now been said, perhaps, to show in how many ways our retrospective imagination transforms the actual events of our past life. So thoroughly, indeed, do the relics of this past get shaken together in new kaleidoscopic combinations, so much of the

---

[1] This is, perhaps, what is meant by saying that people recall their past enjoyments more readily than their sufferings. Yet much seems to turn on temperament and emotional peculiarities. (For a fuller discussion of the point, see my *Pessimism*, p. 344.)

result of later experiences gets imported into our early years, that it may well be asked whether, if the record of our actual life were ever read out to us, we should be able to recognize it. It looks as though we could be sure of recalling only recent events with any degree of accuracy and completeness. As soon as they recede at any considerable distance from us, they are subject to a sort of atmospheric effect. Much grows indistinct and drops altogether out of sight, and what is still seen often takes a new and grotesquely unlike shape. More than this, the play of fancy, like the action of some refracting medium, bends and distorts the outlines of memory's objects, making them wholly unlike the originals.

Hallucinations of Memory.

We will now go on to the third class of mnemonic error, which I have called the spectra of memory, where there is not simply a transformation of the past event, but a complete imaginative creation of it. This class of error corresponds, as I have observed, to an hallucination in the region of sense-perception. And just as we distinguished between those hallucinations of sense which arise first of all through some peripherally caused subjective sensation, and those which want even this element of reality and depend altogether on the activity of imagination, so we may mark off two classes of mnemonic hallucination. The false recollection may correspond to something past— and to this extent be a recollection—though not to any objective fact, but only to a subjective representation of such a fact, as, for example, a dream. In this case the imitation of the mnemonic process may be very definite and complete. Or the false recollection may be wholly a retrojection of a present mental image, and so by no stretch of language be deserving of the name recollection.

It is doubtful whether by any effort of will a person could bring himself to regard a figment of his present imagination as representative of a past reality. Definite and complete hallucinations of this sort do not in normal circumstances arise. It seems necessary for a complete illusion of memory that there should be something past and recovered at the moment, though this may not be a real personal experience.[1] On the other hand, it is possible, as we shall presently see, under certain circumstances, to create out of present materials, and in a vague and indefinite shape, pure phantoms of past experience, that is to say, quasi-mnemonic images to which there correspond no past occurrences whatever.

All recollection, as we have seen, takes place by means of a present mental image which returns with a certain degree of vividness, and is instantaneously identified with some past event. In many cases this instinctive process of identification proves to be legitimate, for, as a matter of fact, real impressions

---

[1] The only exception to this that I can think of is to be found in the power which I, at least, possess, after looking at a new object, of representing it as a familiar one. Yet this may be explained by saying that in the case of every object which is clearly apprehended there must be vague revivals of *similar* objects perceived before. Cases in which recent experiences tend, owing to their peculiar nature, very rapidly to assume the appearance of old events, will be considered presently.

are the first and the commonest source of such lively mnemonic images. But it is not always so. There are other sources of our mental imagery which compete, so to speak, with the region of real personal experience. And sometimes these leave behind them a vivid image having all the appearance of a genuine mnemonic image. When this is so, it is impossible by a mere introspective glance to detect the falsity of the message from the past. We are in the same position as the purchaser in a jet market, where a spurious commodity has got inextricably mixed up with the genuine, and there is no ready criterion by which he can distinguish the true from the false. Such a person, if he purchases freely, is pretty sure to make a number of mistakes. Similarly, all of us are liable to take counterfeit mnemonic images for genuine ones; that is to say, to fall into an illusion of "recollecting" what never really took place.

But what, it may be asked, are these false and illegitimate sources of mnemonic images, these un-authorized mints which issue a spurious mental coinage, and so confuse the genuine currency? They consist of two regions of our internal mental life, which most closely resemble the actual perception of real things in vividness and force, namely, dream-consciousness and waking imagination. Each of these may introduce into the mind vivid images which afterwards tend, under certain circumstances, to assume the guise of recollections of actual events.

That our dream-experience may now and again lead us into illusory recollection has already been hinted. And it is easy to understand why this is so.

When dreaming we have, as we have seen, a mental experience which closely approximates in intensity and reality to that of waking perception. Consequently, dreams may leave behind them, for a time, vivid images which simulate the appearance of real images of memory. Most of us, perhaps, have felt this after-effect of dreaming on our waking thoughts. It is sometimes very hard to shake off the impression left by a vivid dream, as, for example, that a dead friend has returned to life. During the day that follows the dream, we have at intermittent moments something like an assurance that we have seen our lost friend; and though we immediately correct the impression by reflecting that we are recalling but a dream, it tends to revive within us with a strange pertinacity.

In addition to this proximate effect of a dream in disturbing the normal process of recollection, there is reason to suppose that dreams may exert a more remote effect on our memories. So widely different in its form is our dreaming from our waking experience, that our dreams are rarely recalled as wholes with perfect distinctness. They revive in us only as disjointed fragments, and only for brief moments when some accidental resemblance in the present happens to stir the latent trace they have left on our minds. We get sudden flashes out of our dream-world, and the process is too rapid, too incomplete for us to identify the region whence the flashes come.

It is highly probable that our dreams are, to a large extent, answerable for the sense of familiarity that we sometimes experience in visiting a new locality

or in seeing a new face. If, as we have found some of
the best authorities saying, we are, when asleep, always
dreaming more or less distinctly, and if, as we know,
dreaming is a continual process of transformation of
our waking impressions in new combinations, it is not
surprising that our dreams should sometimes take the
form of forecasts of our waking life, and that consequently objects and scenes of this life never before
seen should now and again wear a familiar look.

That some instances of this puzzling sense of familiarity can be explained in this way is proved. Thus,
Paul Radestock, in the work *Schlaf und Traum*, already
quoted, tells us: " When I have been taking a walk,
with my thoughts quite unfettered, the idea has often
occurred to me that I had seen, heard, or thought of
this or that thing once before, without being able to
recall when, where, and in what circumstances. This
happened at the time when, with a view to the pub-
lication of the present work, I was in the habit of
keeping an exact record of my dreams. Consequently,
I was able to turn to this after these impressions, and
on doing so I generally found the conjecture confirmed
that I had previously dreamt something like it."
Scientific inquiry is often said to destroy all beautiful
thoughts about nature and life; but while it destroys
it creates. Is it not almost a romantic idea that just
as our waking life images itself in our dreams, so
our dream-life may send back some of its shadowy
phantoms into our prosaic every-day world, touching
this with something of its own weird beauty ?

Not only may dreams beget these momentary
illusions of memory, they may give rise to something

like permanent illusions. If a dream serves to connect a certain idea with a place or person, and subsequent experience does not tend to correct this, we may keep the belief that we have actually witnessed the event. And we may naturally expect that this result will occur most frequently in the case of those who habitually dream vividly, as young children.

It seems to me that many of the quaint fancies which children get into their heads about things they hear of arise in this way. I know a person who, when a child, got the notion that when his baby-brother was weaned, he was taken up on a grassy hill and tossed about. He had a vivid idea of having seen this curious ceremony. He has in vain tried to get an explanation of this picturesque rendering of an incident of baby-hood from his friends, and has come to the conclusion that it was the result of a dream. If, as seems probable, children's dreams thus give rise to subsequent illusions of memory, the fact would throw a curious light on some of the startling quasi-records of childish experience to be met with in autobiographical literature.

Odd though it may at first appear, old age is said to resemble youth in this confusion of dream-recollection with the memory of waking experience. Dr. Carpenter[1] tells us of "a lady of advanced age who . . . continually dreams about passing events, and seems entirely unable to distinguish between her dreaming and her waking experiences, narrating the former with implicit belief in them, and giving directions based on them." This confusion in the case

---

[1] *Mental Physiology*, p. 456.

of the old may possibly arise not from an increase in the intensity of the dreams, but from a decrease in the intensity of the waking impressions. As Sir Henry Holland remarks,[1] in old age life approaches to the state of a dream.

The other source of what may, by analogy with the hallucinations of sense, be called the peripherally originating spectra of memory is waking imagination. In certain morbid conditions of mind, and in the case of the few healthy minds endowed with special imaginative force, the products of this mental activity, may, as we saw when dealing with illusions of perception, closely resemble dreams in their vividness and apparent actuality. When this is the case, illusions of memory may arise at once just as in the case of dreams. This will happen more easily when the imagination has for some time been occupied with the same group of ideal scenes, persons, or events. To Dickens, as is well known, his fictitious characters were for the time realities, and after he had finished his story their forms and their doings lingered with him, assuming the aspect of personal recollections. So, too, the energetic activity of imagination which accompanies a deep and absorbing sympathy with another's painful experiences, may easily result in so vivid a realization of all their details as to leave an after-sense of *personal* suffering. All highly sympathetic persons who have closely accompanied beloved friends through a great sorrow have known something of this subsequent feeling.

The close connection and continuity between nor-

---

[1] *Mental Physiology*, second edit., p. 172.

mal and abnormal states of mind is illustrated in the fact that in insanity the illusion of taking past imaginations for past realities becomes far more powerful and persistent. Abercrombie (*Intellectual Powers*, Part III. sec. iv. § 2, "Insanity") speaks of "visions of the imagination which have formerly been indulged in of that kind which we call waking dreams or castle-building recurring to the mind in this condition, and now believed to have a real existence." Thus, for example, one patient believed in the reality of the good luck previously predicted by a fortune-teller. Other writers on mental disease observe that it is a common thing for the monomaniac to cherish the delusion that he has actually gained the object of some previous ambition, or is undergoing some previously dreaded calamity.

Nor is it necessary to these illusions of memory that there should be any exceptional force of imagination. A fairly vivid representation to ourselves of anything, whether real or fictitious, communicated by others, will often result in something very like a personal recollection. In the case of works of history and fiction, which adopt the narrative tense, this tendency to a subsequent illusion of memory is strengthened by the disposition of the mind at the moment of reading to project itself backwards as in an act of recollection. This is a point which will be further dealt with in the next chapter.

In most cases, however, illusions of memory growing out of previous activities of the imagination appear only after the lapse of some time, when in the natural course of things the mental images derived from actual experience would sink to a certain degree of faintness. Habitual novel-readers often catch themselves mistaking the echo of some passage in a good story for the trace left by an actual event. A person's name, a striking saying, and even an event itself, when we first come across it or experience it, may for a moment seem familiar to us, and to recall some past like impression, if it only happens to resemble something in the works of a favourite novelist. And so, too, any recital of another's experience, whether oral or literary, if it deeply interests us and awakens a specially vivid imagination of the events described, may easily become the starting-point of an illusory recollection.

Children are in the habit of "drinking in" with their vigorous and eager imaginations what is told them and read to them, and hence they are specially likely to fall into this kind of error. Not only so: when they grow up and their early recollections lose their definiteness, becoming a few fragments saved from a lost past, it must pretty certainly happen that if any ideas derived from these recitals are preserved, they will simulate the form of memories. Thus, I have often caught myself for a moment under the sway of the illusion that I actually visited the Exhibition of 1851, the reason being that I am able to recall the descriptions given to me of it by my friends, and the excitement attending their journey to London on the occasion. It is to be added that repetition of the act of imagination will tend still further to deepen the subsequent feeling that we are recollecting something. As Hartley well observes, a man, by repeating a story, easily comes to suppose that he remembers it.[1]

____
[1] _Loc. cit._, p. 390.

Here, then, we have another source of error that we must take into account in judging of the authenticity of an autobiographical narration of the events of childhood. The more imaginative the writer, the greater the risk of illusion from this source as well as from that of dream-fancies. It is highly probable, indeed, that in such full and explicit records of very early life as those given by Rousseau, by Goethe, or by De Quincey, some part of the quasi-narrative is based on mental images which come floating down the stream of time, not from the substantial world of the writer's personal experience, but from the airy region of dream-land or of waking fancy.

It is to be added that even when the quasi-recollection does answer to a real event of childish history, it may still be an illusion. The fact that others, in narrating events to us, are able to awaken imaginations that afterwards appear as past realities, suggests that much of our supposed early recollection owes its existence to what our parents and friends have from time to time told us respecting the first stages of our history.[1] We see, then, how much uncertainty attaches to all autobiographical description of very early life.

Modern science suggests another possible source of these distinct spectra of memory. May it not happen that, by the law of hereditary transmission, which is now being applied to mental as well as bodily phenomena, ancestral experiences will now and then reflect

---

[1] This source of error has not escaped the notice of autobiographers themselves. See the remarks of Goethe in the opening passages of his *Wahrheit und Dichtung*.

themselves in our mental life, and so give rise to apparently personal recollections? No one can say that this is not so. When the infant first steadies his eyes on a human face, it may, for aught we know, experience a feeling akin to that described above, when through a survival of dream-fancy we take some new scene to be already familiar. At the age when new emotions rapidly develop themselves, when our hearts are full of wild romantic aspirations, do there not seem to blend with the eager passion of the time deep resonances of a vast and mysterious past, and may not this feeling be a sort of reminiscence of prenatal, that is, ancestral experience?

This idea is certainly a fascinating one, worthy to be a new scientific support for the beautiful thought of Plato and of Wordsworth. But in our present state of knowledge, any reasoning on this supposition would probably appear too fanciful. Some day we may find out how much ancestral experience is capable of bequeathing in this way, whether simply shadowy, undefinable mental tendencies, or something like definite concrete ideas. If, for example, it were found that a child that was descended from a line of seafaring ancestors, and that had never itself seen or heard of the " dark-gleaming sea," manifested a feeling of recognition when first beholding it, we might be pretty sure that such a thing as recollection of prenatal events does take place. But till we have such facts, it seems better to refer the " shadowy recollections " to sources which fall within the individual's own experience.

We may now pass to those hallucinations of memory which are analogous to the *centrally* excited

hallucinations of sense-perception. As I have observed, these are necessarily vague and imperfectly
developed.

I have already had occasion to touch on the fact of
the vast amount of our forgotten experience. And I
observed that forgetfulness was a common negative condition of mnemonic illusion. I have now to complete
this statement by the observation that total forgetfulness of any period or stage of our past experience
necessarily tends to a vague kind of hallucination. In
looking back on the past, we see no absolute gaps
in the continuity of our conscious life; our image
of this past is essentially one of an unbroken series
of conscious experiences. But if through forgetfulness a part of the series is effaced from memory,
how, it may be asked, is it possible to construct this
perfectly continuous line? The answer is that we fill
up such lacunæ vaguely by help of some very imperfectly imagined common type of conscious experience. Just as the eye sees no gap in its field of
vision corresponding to the "blind spot" of the retina,
but carries its impression over this area, so memory
sees no lacuna in the past, but carries its image of
conscious life over each of the forgotten spaces.

Sometimes this process of filling in gaps in the
past becomes more complete. Thus, for example, in
recalling a particular night a week or so ago, I instinctively represent it to myself as so many hours of lying
in bed with the waking sensations appropriate to the
circumstances, as those of bodily warmth and rest, and
of the surrounding silence and darkness.

It is apparent that I cannot conceive myself apart

from some mode of conscious experience. In thinking of myself in any part of the past or future in which there is actually no consciousness, or of which the conscious content is quite unknown to me, I necessarily imagine myself as consciously experiencing something. If I picture myself under any definitely conceived circumstances, I irresistibly import into my mental image the feelings appropriate to these surroundings. In this way, people tend to imagine themselves after death as lying in the grave, feeling its darkness and its chilliness. If the circumstances of the time are not distinctly represented, the conception of the conscious experience which constitutes that piece of the ego is necessarily vague, and seems generally to resolve itself into a representation of ourselves as dimly *self-conscious*. What this consciousness of self consists of is a point that will be taken up presently.

Illusions with respect to Personal Identity.

It would seem to follow from these errors in imaginatively filling up our past life, that our consciousness of personal identity is by no means the simple and exact process which it is commonly supposed to be. I have already remarked that the very fact of there being so large a region of the irrevocable in our past experience proves our consciousness of personal continuity to be largely a matter of inference, or of imaginative conjecture, and not simply of immediate recollection. Indeed, it may be said that our power of ignoring whole regions of the past and of leaping complacently over huge gaps in our memory and linking on conscious experience with conscious experience, involves an illusory sense of continuity, and so far of personal identity. Thus, our ordinary image of our past life, if only by omitting the very large fraction passed in sleep, in at least an approximately unconscious state, clearly contains an ingredient of illusion.[1]

It is to be added that the numerous falsifications of our past history, which our retrospective imagination is capable of perpetrating, make our representation of ourselves at different moments and in different stages of our past history to a considerable extent illusory. Thus, though to mistake a past dream-experience for a waking one may not be to lose or confuse the sense of identity, since our dreams are, after all, a part of our experience, yet to imagine that we have ourselves seen what we have only heard from another or read is clearly to confuse the boundaries of our identity. And with respect to longer sections of our history, it is plain that when we wrongly assimilate our remote to our present self, and clothe our childish nature with the feelings and the ideas of our adult life, we identify ourselves overmuch. In this way, through the corruption of our memory, a kind of sham self gets mixed up with the real self, so that we cannot, strictly speaking, be sure that when we project a mnemonic image into the remote past we are not really running away from our true personality.

One wonders whether those persons who, in consequence of an injury to their brain, periodically pass from a normal into an abnormal condition of mind, in each of which there is little or no memory of the contents of the other state, complete their idea of personal continuity in each state by the same kind of process as that described in the text.

So far I have been touching only on slight errors in the recognition of that identical self which is represented as persisting through all the fluctuations of conscious life. Other and grosser illusions connected with personal identity are also found to be closely related to defects or disturbances of the ordinary mnemonic process, and so can be best treated here. In order to understand these, we must inquire a little into the nature of our idea and consciousness of a persistent self. Here, again, I would remind the reader that I am treating the point only so far as it can be treated scientifically or empirically, that is to say, by examining what concrete facts or data of experience are taken up into the idea of self. I do not wish to foreclose the philosophic question whether anything more than this empirical content is involved in the conception.

My idea of myself as persisting appears to be built up of certain similarities in the succession of my experiences. Thus, my permanent self consists, on the bodily side, of a continually renewable perception of my own organism, which perception is mainly visual and tactual, and which remains pretty constant within certain limits of time. With this objective similarity is closely conjoined a subjective similarity. Thus, the same sensibilities continue to characterize the various parts of my organism. Similarly, there are the higher intellectual, emotional, and moral peculiarities and dispositions. My idea of my persistent self is essentially a collective image representing a relatively unchanging material object, endowed with unchanging sensibilities and forming a kind of support for permanent higher mental attributes.

The construction of this idea of an enduring unchanging ego is rendered very much easier by the fact that certain concrete feelings are approximately constant elements in our mental life. Among these must be ranked first that dimly discriminated mass of organic sensation which in average states of health is fairly constant, and which stands in sharp contrast to the fluctuating external sensations. These feelings enter into and profoundly colour each person's mental image of himself. In addition to this, there are the frequently recurring higher feelings, the dominant passions and ideas which approximate more or less closely to constant factors of our conscious experience.

This total image of the ego becomes defined and rendered precise by a number of distinctions, as that between my own body or that particular material object with which are intimately united all my feelings, and other material objects in general; then between my organism and other human organisms, with which I learn to connect certain feelings answering to my own, but only faintly represented instead of actually realized feelings. To these prime distinctions are added others, hardly less fundamental, as those between my individual bodily appearance and that of other living bodies, between my personal and characteristic modes of feeling and thinking and those of others, and so on.

Our sense of personal identity may be said to be rooted in that special side of the mnemonic process which consists in the linking of all sequent events together by means of a thread of common consciousness. It is closely connected with that smooth, gliding movement of imagination which appears to involve some more or less distinct consciousness of the uniting thread of similarity. And so long as this movement is possible, so long, that is to say, as retrospective imagination detects the common element, which we may specifically call the recurring consciousness of self, so long is there the undisturbed assurance of personal identity. Nay, more, even when such a recognition might seem to be difficult, if not impossible, as in linking together the very unlike selves, viewed both on their objective and subjective sides, of childhood, youth, and mature life, the mind manages, as we have seen, to feign to itself a sufficient amount of such similarity.

But this process of linking stage to stage, of discerning the common or the recurring amid the changing and the evanescent, has its limits. Every great and sudden change in our experience tends, momentarily at least, to hinder the smooth reflux of imagination. It makes too sharp a break in our conscious life, so that imagination is incapable of spanning the gap and realizing the then and the now as parts of a connected continuous tissue.[1]

These changes may be either objective or subjective. Any sudden alteration of our bodily appearance sensibly impedes the movement of imagination. A patient after a fever, when he first looks in the glass,

---

[1] The reader will remark that this condition of clear intellectual consciousness, namely, a certain degree of similarity and continuity of character in our successive mental states, is complementary to the other condition, constant change, already referred to. It may, perhaps, be said that all clear consciousness lies between two extremes of excessive sameness and excessive difference.

exclaims, "I don't know myself." More commonly the bodily changes which affect the consciousness of an enduring self are such as involve considerable alterations of cœnæsthesis, or the mass of stable organic sensation. Thus, the loss of a limb, by cutting off a portion of the old sensations through which the organism may be said to be immediately felt, and by introducing new and unfamiliar feelings, will distinctly give a shock to our consciousness of self.

Purely subjective changes, too, or, to speak correctly, such as are known subjectively only, will suffice to disturb the sense of personal unity. Any great moral shock, involving something like a revolution in our recurring emotional experience, seems at the moment to rupture the bond of identity. And even some time after, as I have already remarked, such cataclysms in our mental geology lead to the imaginative thrusting of the old personality away from the new one under the form of a "dead self." [1]

We see, then, that the failure of our ordinary assurance of personal identity is due to the recognition of difference without similarity. It arises from an act of memory—for the mind must still be able to recall the past, dimly at least—but from a memory which misses its habitual support in a recognized

---

[1] It follows that any great transformation of our environment may lead to a partial confusion with respect to self. For not only do great and violent changes in our surroundings beget profound changes in our feelings and ideas, but since the idea of self is under one of its aspects essentially that of a relation to not-self, any great revolution in the one term will confuse the recognition of the other. This fact is expressed in the common expression that we "lose ourselves" when in unfamiliar surroundings, and the process of orientation, or "taking our bearings," fails.

element of constancy. If there is no memory, that is to say, if the past is a complete blank, the mind simply feels a rupture of identity without any transformation of self. This is our condition on awaking from a perfectly forgotten period of sleep, or from a perfectly unconscious state (if such is possible) when induced by anæsthetics. Such gaps are, as we have seen, easily filled up, and the sense of identity restored by a kind of retrospective " skipping." On the other hand, the confusion which arises from too great and violent a transformation of our *remembered* experiences is much less easily corrected. As long as the recollection of the old feelings remains, and with this the sense of violent contrast between the old and the new ones, so long will the illusion of two sundered selves tend to recur.

The full development of this process of imaginative fission or cleavage of self is to be met with in mental disease. The beginnings of such disease, accompanied as they commonly are with disturbances of bodily sensations and the recurring emotions, illustrate in a very interesting way the dependence of the recognition of self on a certain degree of uniformity in the contents of consciousness. The patient, when first aware of these changes, is perplexed, and often regards the new feelings as making up another self, a foreign *Tu*, as distinguished from the familiar *Ego*. And sometimes he expresses the relation between the old and the new self in fantastic ways, as when he imagines the former to be under the power of some foreign personality.

When the change is complete, the patient is apt to

think of his former self as detached from his present, and of his previous life as a kind of unreal dream ; and this fading away of the past into shadowy unreal forms has, as its result, a curious aberration in the sense of time. Thus, it is said that a patient, after being in an asylum only one day, will declare that he has been there a year, five years, and even ten years.[1] This confusion as to self naturally becomes the starting-point of illusions of perception ; the transformation of self seeming to require as its logical correlative (for there is a crude logic even in mental disease) a trans-formation of the environment. When the disease is fully developed under the particular form of mono-mania, the recollection of the former normal self commonly disappears altogether, or fades away into a dim image of some perfectly separate personality. A new ego is now fully substituted for the old. In other and more violent forms of disease (dementia) the power of connecting the past and present may disappear altogether, and nothing but the *disjecta membra* of an ego remain

Enough has, perhaps, been said to show how much of uncertainty and of self-deception enters into the pro-cesses of memory. This much-esteemed faculty, valu-able and indispensable though it certainly is, can clearly lay no claim to that absolute infallibility which is some-times said to belong to it. Our individual recollection,

---

[1] On these disturbances of memory and self-recognition in insanity, see Griesinger, *op. cit.*, pp. 49–51; also Ribot, "Des Désordres Généraux de la Mémoire," in the *Revue Philosophique*, August, 1880. It is related by Leuret (*Fragments Psych. sur la Folie*, p. 277) that a patient spoke of his former self as " la personne de moi-même."

left to itself, is liable to a number of illusions even with regard to fairly recent events, and in the case of remote ones it may be said to err habitually and uniformly in a greater or less degree. To speak plainly, we can never be certain on the ground of our personal recollection alone that a distant event happened exactly in the way and at the time that we suppose. Nor does there seem to be any simple way by mere reflection on the contents of our memory of distinguishing what kinds of recollection are likely to be illusory.

How, then, it may be asked, can we ever be certain that we are faithfully recalling the actual events of the past? Given a fairly good, that is, a cultivated memory, it may be said that in the case of very recent events a man may feel certain that, when the conditions of careful attention at the time to what really happened were present, a distinct recollection is substantially correct. Also it is obvious that with respect to all repeated experiences our memories afford practically safe guides. When memory becomes the basis of some item of generalized knowledge, as, for example, of the truth that the pain of indigestion has followed a too copious indulgence in rich food, there is little room for an error of memory properly so called On the other hand, when an event is not repeated in our experience, but forms a unique link in our personal history, the chances of error increase with the distance of the event; and here the best of us will do well to. have resort to a process of verification or, if necessary, of correction.

In order thus to verify the utterances of memory, we must look beyond our own internal mental states to some external facts. Thus, the recollections of our early life may often be tested by letters written by ourselves or our friends at the time, by diaries, and so on. When there is no unerring objective record to be found, we may have recourse to the less satisfactory method of comparing our recollections with those of others. By so doing we may reach a rough average recollection which shall at least be free from any individual error corresponding to that of personal equation in perception. But even thus we cannot be sure of eliminating all error, since there may be a cause of illusion acting on all our minds alike, as, for example, the extraordinary nature of the occurrence, which would pretty certainly lead to a common exaggeration of its magnitude, etc., and since, moreover, this process of comparing recollections affords an opportunity for that reading back a present preconception into the past to which reference has already been made.

The result of our inquiry is less alarming than it looks at first sight. Knowledge is valuable for action, and error is chiefly hurtful in so far as it misdirects conduct. Now, in a general way, we do not need to act upon a recollection of single remote events; our conduct is sufficiently shaped by an accurate recollection of single recent events, together with those bundles of recollections of recurring events and sequences of events which constitute our knowledge of ourselves and our common knowledge of the world about us. Nature has done commendably well in endowing us with the means of cultivating our memories up to this point, and we ought not to blame her for not giving us powers which would only very rarely prove of any appreciable practical service to us.

NOTE.

MOMENTARY ILLUSIONS OF SELF-CONSCIOUSNESS.

The account of the apparent ruptures in our personal identity given in this chapter may help us to understand the strange tendency to confuse self with other objects which occasionally appears in waking consciousness and in dreams. These errors may be said generally to be due to the breaking up of the composite image of self into its fragments, and the regarding of certain of these only. Thus, the momentary occurrence of partial illusion in intense sympathy with others, including that imaginative projection of self into inanimate objects, to which reference has already been made, may be said to depend on exclusive attention to the subjective aspect of self, to the total disregard of the objective aspect. In other words, when we thus momentarily "lose ourselves," or merge our own existence in that of another object, we clearly let drop out of sight the visual representation of our own individual organism. On the other hand, when in dreams we double our personality, or represent to ourselves an external self which becomes the object of visual perception, it is probably because we isolate in imagination the objective aspect of our personality from the other and subjective aspect. It is not at all unlikely that the several confusions of self touched on in this chapter have had something to do with the genesis of the various historical theories of a transformed existence, as, for example, the celebrated doctrine of metempsychosis.

CHAPTER XI.

OUR knowledge is commonly said to consist of two large
varieties—Presentative and Representative. Representative knowledge, again, falls into two chief divisions.
The first of these is Memory, which, though not primary
or original, like presentative knowledge, is still regarded as directly or intuitively certain. The second
division consists of all other representative knowledge
besides memory, including, among other varieties, our
anticipations of the future, our knowledge of others'
past experience, and our general knowledge about
things. There is no one term which exactly hits off
this large sphere of cognition: I propose to call it
Belief. I am aware that this is by no means a perfect
word for my purpose, since, on the one hand, it suggests that every form of this knowledge must be less
certain than presentative or mnemonic knowledge,
which cannot be assumed; and since, on the other
hand, the word is so useful a one in psychology, for
the purpose of marking off the subjective fact of
assurance in all kinds of cognition. Nevertheless,
I know not what better one I could select in order to

make my classification answer as closely as a scientific treatment will allow to the deeply fixed distinctions of popular psychology.

It might at first seem as if perception, introspecs tion, and memory must exhaust all that is meant by immediate, or self-evident, knowledge, and as if what I have here called belief must be uniformly mediate, derivate, or inferred knowledge. The apprehension of something now present to the mind, externally or internally, and the reapprehension through the process of memory of what was once so apprehended, might appear to be the whole of what can by any stretch of language be called direct cognition of things. This at least would seem to follow from the empirical theory of knowledge, which regards perception and memory as the ground or logical source of all other forms of knowledge.

And even if we suppose, with some philosophers, that there are certain innate principles of knowledge, it seems now to be generally allowed that these, apart from the particular facts of experience, are merely abstractions; and that they only develop into complete knowledge when they receive some empirical content, which must be supplied either by present perception or by memory. So that in this case, too, all definite concrete knowledge would seem to be either presentative cognition, memory, or, lastly, some mode of inference from these.

A little inquiry into the mental operations which I here include under the name belief will show, however, that they are by no means uniformly processe- of inference. To take the simplest form of such knowledge, anticipation of some personal experience: this may arise quite apart from recollection, as a spontaneous projection of a mental image into the future. A person may feel "intuitively certain" that something is going to happen to him which does not resemble anything in his past experience. Not only so; even when the expectation corresponds to a bit of past experience, this source of the expectation may, under certain circumstances, be altogether lost to view, and the belief assume a secondarily automatic or intuitive character. Thus, a man may have first entertained a belief in the success of some undertaking as the result of a rough process of inference, but afterwards go on trusting when the grounds for his confidence are wholly lost sight of.

This much may suffice for the present to show that belief sometimes approximates to immediate, or self-evident, conviction. How far this is the case will come out in the course of our inquiry into its different forms. This being so, it will be needful to include in our present study the errors connected with the process of belief in so far as they simulate the immediate instantaneous form of illusion.

What I have here called belief may be roughly distinguished into simple and compound belief. By a simple belief I mean one which has to do with a single event or fact. It includes simple modes of expectation, as well as beliefs in single past facts not guaranteed by memory. A compound belief, on the other hand, has reference to a number of events or facts. Thus, our belief in the continued existence of a particular object, as well as our convictions respecting groups or classes of events, must be regarded as compound, since they can be shown to include a number of simple beliefs.

A. *Simple Illusory Belief: Expectation.*

It will be well to begin our inquiry by examining the errors connected with simple expectations, so far as these come under our definition of illusion. And here, following our usual practice, we may set out with a very brief account of the nature of the intellectual process in its correct form. For this purpose we shall do well to take a complete or definite anticipation of an event as our type.[1]

The ability of the mind to move forward, forecasting an order of events in time, is clearly very similar to its power of recalling events. Each depends on the capability of imagination to represent a sequence of events or experiences. The difference between the two processes is that in anticipation the imagination setting out from the present traces the succession of experiences in their actual order, and not in the reverse order. It would thus appear to be a more natural and easy process than recollection, and observation bears out this conclusion. Any object present to perception which is associated with antecedents and consequents with the same degree of cohesion, calls up its consequents rather than its antecedents. The spectacle of the rising of the sun carries the mind much more forcibly forwards to the advancing morn-

---

[1] In the following account of the process of belief and its errors, I am going over some of the ground traversed by my essay on *Belief, its Varieties and Conditions* ("Sensation and Intuition," ch. iv.). To this essay I must refer the reader for a fuller analysis of the subject.

ing than backwards to the receding night. And there is good reason to suppose that in the order of mental development the power of distinctly expecting an event precedes that of distinctly recollecting one. Thus, in the case of the infant mind, as of the animal intelligence, the presence of signs of coming events, as the preparation of food, seems to excite distinct and vivid expectation.[1]

As a mode of assurance, expectation is clearly marked off from memory, and is not explainable by means of this. It is a fundamentally distinct kind of conviction. So far as we are capable of analyzing it, we may say that its peculiarity is its essentially active character. To expect a thing is to have stirred the active impulses, including the powers of attention; it is to be on the alert for it, to have the attention already focussed for it, and to begin to rehearse the actions which the actual happening of the event—for example, the approach of a welcome object—would excite. It thus stands in marked contrast to memory, which is a passive attitude of mind, becoming active only when it gives rise to the expectation of a recur-rence of the event.[2]

And now let us pass to the question whether expectation ever takes the form of immediate knowledge.

---

[1] For an account of the difference of mechanism in memory and expectation, see Taine, *De l'Intelligence*, 2ième partie, livre premier, ch. ii. sec. 6.

[2] J. S. Mill distinguishes expectation as a radically distinct mode of belief from memory, but does not bring out the contrast with respect to activity here emphasized (James Mill's *Analysis of the Human Mind*, edited by J. S. Mill, p. 411, etc.). For a fuller statement of my view of the relation of belief to action, as compared with that of Professor Bain, see my earlier work.

It may, perhaps, be objected that the anticipation of something future cannot be knowledge at all in the sense in which the perception of something present or the recollection of something past is knowledge. But this objection, when examined closely, appears to be frivolous. Because the future fact has not yet come into the sphere of actual existence, it is none the less the object of a perfect assurance.[1]

But, even if it is conceded that expectation is knowledge, the objection may still be urged that it cannot be immediate, since it is the very nature of expectation to ground itself on memory. I have already hinted that this is not the case, and I shall now try to show that what is called expectation covers much that is indistinguishable from immediate intuitive certainty, and consequently offers room for an illusory form of error.

Let us set out with the simplest kind of expectation, the anticipation of something about to happen within the region of our personal experience, and similar to what has happened before. And let the coming of the event be first of all suggested by some present external fact or sign. Suppose, for example, that the sky is heavy, the air sultry, and that I have a bad headache; I confidently anticipate a thunderstorm. It would commonly be said that such an expectation is a kind of inference from the past. I remember that these appearances have been followed by a thunderstorm very often, and I infer that they will in this new case be so followed.

---

[1] For some good remarks on the logical aspects of future events as matters of fact, see Mr. Venn's *Logic of Chance*, ch. x.

To this, however, it may be replied that in most cases there is no conscious going back to the past at all. As I have already remarked, anticipation is pretty certainly in advance of memory in early life. And even after the habit of passing from the past to the future, from memory to expectation, has been formed, the number of the past repetitions of experience would prevent the mind's clearly reverting to them. And, further, the very force of habit would tend to make the transition from memory to expectation more and more rapid, automatic, and unconscious. Thus it comes about that all distinctly suggested approaching events seem to be expected by a kind of immediate act of belief. The present signs call up the representation of the coming event with all the force of a direct intuition. At least, it may be said that if a process of inference, it is one which has the minimum degree of consciousness.

It might still be urged that the mind passes from the *present* facts as signs, and so still performs a kind of reasoning process. This is, no doubt, true, and differentiates expectation from perception, in which there is no conscious transition from the presented to the represented. Still I take it that this is only a process of reasoning in so far as the sign is consciously generalized, and this is certainly not true of early expectations, or even of any expectations in a wholly uncultivated mind.

For these reasons I think that any errors involved in such an anticipation may, without much forcing, be brought under our definition of illusion. When due altogether to the immediate force of suggestion in a present object or event, and not involving any conscious transition from past to future, or from general truth to particular instance, these errors appear to me to have more of the character of illusions than of that of fallacies.

Much the same thing may be said about the vivid anticipations of a familiar kind of experience called up by a clear and consecutive verbal suggestion. When a man, even with an apparent air of playfulness, tells me that something is going to happen, and gives a consistent consecutive account of this, I have an anticipation which is not consciously grounded on any past experience of the value of human testimony in general, or of this person's testimony in particular, but which is instantaneous and quasi-immediate. Consequently, any error connected with the mental act approximates to an illusion.

So far I have supposed that the anticipated event is a recurring one, that is to say, a kind of experience which has already become familiar to us. This, however, holds good only of a very few of our experiences. Our life changes as it progresses, both outwardly and inwardly. Many of our anticipations, when first formed, involve much more than a reproduction of a past experience, namely, a complex act of constructive imagination. Our representations of these untried experiences, as, for example, those connected with a new set of circumstances, a new social condition, a new mode of occupation, and so on, are clearly at the first far from simple processes of inference from the past. They are put together by the aid of many fragmentary images, restored by distinct threads of association, yet by a process so rapid as to appear like an intuition. Indeed, the anticipation of such new experiences more often resembles an instantaneous imaginative intuition than a process of conscious transition from old experiences. In the case of these expectations, then, there would clearly seem to be room for illusion from the first.

But even supposing that the errors connected with the first formation of an expectation cannot strictly be called illusory, we may see that such simple expectation will, in certain cases, tend to grow into something quite indistinguishable from illusion. I refer to expectations of *remote* events which allow of frequent renewal. Even supposing the expectation to have originated from some rational source, as from a conscious inference from past experience, or from the acceptance of somebody's statement, the very habit of cherishing the anticipation tends to invest it with an automatic self-sufficient character. To all intents and purposes the prevision becomes intuitive, by which I mean that the mind is at the time immediately certain that something is going to happen, without needing to fall back on memory or reflection. This being so, whenever the initial process of inference or quasi-inference happens to have been bad, an illusory expectation may arise. In other words, the force of repetition and habit tends to harden what may, in its initial form, have resembled a kind of fallacy into an illusion.

And now let us proceed further. When a permanent expectation is thus formed, there arises the possibility of processes which favour illusion precisely analogous to those which we have studied in the case of memory.

In the first place, the habit of imagining a future event is attended with a considerable amount of illusion as to time or remoteness. After what has been said respecting the conditions of such error in the case of memory, a very few words will suffice here.

It is clear, then, in the first place, that the mind will tend to shorten any period of future time, and so to antedate, so to speak, a given event, in so far as the imagination is able clearly and easily to run over its probable experiences. From this it follows that repeated forecastings of series of events, by facilitating the imaginative process, tend to beget an illusory appearance of contraction in the time anticipated. Moreover, since in anticipation so much of each division of the future time-line is unknown, it is obviously easy for the expectant imagination to skip over long intervals, and so to bring together widely remote events.

In addition to this general error, there are more special errors. As in the case of recollection, vividness of mental image suggests propinquity; and accordingly, all vivid anticipations, to whatever cause the vividness may be owing, whether to powerful suggestion on the part of external objects, to verbal suggestion. or to spontaneous imagination and feeling, are apt to represent their objects as too near.

It follows that an event intensely longed for, in so, far as the imagination is busy in representing it, will seem to approach the present. At the same time, as we have seen, an event much longed for commonly appears to be a great while coming, the explanation being that there is a continually renewed contradiction between anticipation and perception. The self-adjustment of the mind in the attitude of expectant attention proves again and again to be vain and futile, and it is this fact which brings home to it the slowness of the sequences of perceived fact, as compared with the rapidity of the sequences of imagination.

When speaking of the retrospective estimate of time, I observed that the apparent distance of an event depends on our representation of the intervening time-segment. And the same remark applies to the prospective estimate. Thus, an occurrence which we expect to happen next week will seem specially near if we know little or nothing of the contents of the intervening space, for in this case the imagination does not project the experience behind a number of other distinctly represented events.

Finally, it is to be remarked that the prospective appreciation of any duration will tend to err relatively by way of excess, where the time is exceptionally filled out with clearly expected and deeply interesting experiences. To the imagination of the child, a holiday, filled with new experiences, appears to be boundless.

Thus far I have assumed that the date of the future event is a matter which might be known. It is, however, obvious, from the very nature of knowledge with respect to the future, that we may sometimes be certain of a thing happening to us without knowing with any degree of definiteness when it will happen. In the case of these temporally undefined expectations, the law already expounded holds good that all vividness of representation tends to lend the things represented an appearance of approaching events. On the other hand, there are some events, such as our own death, which our instinctive feelings tend to banish to a region so remote as hardly to be realized at all.

So much with respect to errors in the localizing of future events.

In the second place, a habit of imagining a future event or group of events will give play to those forces which tend to transform a mental image. In other words, the habitual indulgence of a certain anticipation tends to an illusory view, not only of the "when?" but also of the "how?" of the future event. These transformations, due to subtle processes of emotion and intellect, and reflecting the present habits of these, exactly resemble those by which a remembered event becomes gradually transformed. Thus, we carry on our present habits of thought and feeling into the remote future, foolishly imagining that at a distant period of life, or in greatly altered circumstances, we shall desire and aim at the same things as now in our existing circumstances. In close connection with this forward projection of our present selves, there betrays itself a tendency to look on future events as answering to our present desires and aspirations. In this way, we are wont to soften, beautify, and idealize the future, marking it off from the hard matter-of-fact present.

The less like the future experience to our past experience, or the more remote the time anticipated, the greater the scope for such imaginative transformation. And from this stage of fanciful transformation of a future reality to the complete imaginative creation of such a reality, the step is but a small one. Here we reach the full development of illusory expectation, that which corresponds to hallucination in the region of sense-perception.

In order to understand these extreme forms of illusory expectation, it will be necessary to say something more about the relation of imagination to anticipation in general. There are, I conceive, good reasons for saying that any kind of vivid imagination tends to pass into a semblance of an expectation of a coming personal experience, or an event that is about to happen within the sphere of our own observation. It has long been recognized by writers, among whom I may mention Dugald Stewart, that to distinctly imagine an event or object is to feel for the moment a degree of belief in the corresponding reality. Now, I have already said that expectation is probably a more natural and an earlier developed state of mind than memory. And so it seems probable that any mental image which happens to take hold on the mind, if not recognized as one of memory, or as corresponding to a fact in somebody else's experience, naturally assumes the form of an expectation of a personal experience. The force of the expectation will vary in general as the vividness and persistence of the mental image. Moreover, it follows, from what has been said, that this force of imagination will determine what little time-character we ever give to these wholly ungrounded illusions.

We see, then, that any process of spontaneous imagination will tend to beget some degree of illusory expectation. And among the agencies by which such ungrounded imagination arises, the promptings of feeling play the most conspicuous part. A present emotional excitement may give to an imaginative anticipation, such as that of the prophetic enthusiast, a reality which approximates to that of an actually perceived object. And even where this force of excitement is wanting, a gentle impulse of feeling may suffice to beget an assurance of a distant reality. The unknown recesses of the remote future offer, indeed, the field in which the illusory impulses of our emotional nature have their richest harvest.

> "Thus, from afar, each dim discover'd scene
> More pleasing seems than all the past hath been;
> And every form, that Fancy can repair
> From dark oblivion, glows divinely there."

The recurring emotions, the ruling aspirations, find objects for themselves in this veiled region. Feelings too shy to burst forth in unseemly anticipation of the immediate future, modestly satisfy themselves with this remote prospect of satisfaction. And thus, there arises the half-touching, half-amusing spectacle of men and women continually renewing illusory hopes, and continually pushing the date of their realization further on as time progresses and brings no actual fruition.

So far I have spoken of such expectations as refer to future personal experience only. Growing individual experience and the enlargement of this by the addition of social experience enable us to frame a number of other beliefs more or less similar to the simple expectations just dealt with. Thus, for example, I can forecast with confidence events which will occur in the lives of others, and which I shall not even witness; or again, I may even succeed in dimly descrying events, such as political changes or scientific discoveries, which will happen after my personal experience is at an end.

Once more, I can believe in something going on now at some distant and even inaccessible point of the universe, and this appears to involve a conditional expectation, and to mean that I am certain that I or anybody else would see the phenomenon, if we could at this moment be transported to the spot.

All such previsions are supposed to be formed by a process of inference from personal experience, including the trustworthiness of testimony. Even allowing, however, that this was so in the first stages of the belief, it is plain that, by dint of frequent renewal, the expectation would soon cease to be a process of inference, and acquire an apparently self-evident character. This being so, if the expectation is not adequately grounded to start with, it is very likely to develop into an illusion. And it is to be added that these permanent anticipations may have their origin much more in our own wishes or emotional promptings than in fact and experience. The mind undisciplined by scientific training is wont to entertain numerous beliefs of this sort respecting what is now going on in unvisited parts of the world, or what will happen hereafter in the distant future. The remote, and therefore obscure, in space and in time has always been the favourite region for the projection of pleasant fancies.

Once more, besides these oblique kinds of expectation, I may form other seemingly simple beliefs, to which the term expectation seems less clearly applicable. Thus, on waking in the morning and finding the ground covered with snow, my imagination moves backwards, as in the process of memory, and realizes the spectacle of the softly falling snow-flakes in the hours of the night. The oral communication of others' experience, including the traditions of the race, enables me to set out from any present point of time, and reconstruct complex chains of experience of vast length lying beyond the bounds of my own personal recollection.

I need not here discuss what the exact nature of such beliefs is. J. S. Mill identifies them with expectations. Thus, according to him, my belief in the nocturnal snowstorm is the assurance that I should have seen it had I waited up during the night. So my belief in Cicero's oratory resolves itself into the conviction that I should have heard Cicero under certain conditions of time and place, which is identical with my expectation that I shall hear a certain speaker to-morrow if I go to the House of Commons.[1] However this be, the thing to note is that such retrospective beliefs, when once formed, tend to approximate in character to recollections. This is true even of new beliefs in recent events directly made known by present objective consequences or signs, as the snowstorm. For in this case there is commonly no conscious comparison of the present signs with previously known signs, but merely a direct quasi-mnemonic passage of mind from the present fact to its antecedent. And it is still more true of long-entertained retrospective beliefs. When, for example, the original grounds of an historical hypothesis are lost sight of, and after the

----

[1] James Mill's *Analysis of the Human Mind*, edited by J. S. Mill, vol. i. p. 414, *et seq.*

belief has hardened and solidified by time, it comes to look much more like a recollection than an expectation. As a matter of fact, we have seen, when studying the illusions of memory, that our personal experience does become confused with that of others. And one may say that all long-cherished retrospective beliefs tend to become assimilated to recollections.

Here then, again, there seems to be room for illusion to arise. Even in the case of a recent past event, directly made known by present objective signs, the mind is liable to err just as in the case of forecasting an immediately approaching event. And such error has all the force of an illusion: its contradiction is almost as great a shock as that of a recollection. When, for example, I enter my house, and see a friend's card lying on the table, I so vividly represent to myself the recent call of my friend, that when I learn the card is an old one which has accidentally been put on the table, I experience a sense of disillusion very similar to that which attends a contradicted perception. The early crude stages of physical science abundantly illustrate the genesis of such illusions.

It may be added that if there be any feeling present in the mind at the time, the barest suggestion of something having happened will suffice to produce the immediate assurance. Thus, an angry person is apt to hastily accuse another of having done certain things on next to no evidence. The love of the marvellous seems to have played a conspicuous part in building up and sustaining the fanciful hypotheses which mark the dawn of physical science.

Verbal suggestion is a common mode of produc-

ing this semblance of a recollected event. By means
of the narrative style, it vividly suggests the idea
that the events described belong to the past, and ex-
cites the imagination to a retrospective construction
of them as though they were remembered events.
Hence the power of works of fiction on the ordinary
mind. Even when there is no approach to an illusion
of perception, or to one of memory in the strict sense,
the reading of a work of fiction begets at the moment
a retrospective belief that has a certain resemblance to
a recollection.

All such illusions as those just illustrated, if not
afterwards corrected, tend to harden into yet more distinctly "intuitive" errors. Thus, for example, one of
the crude geological hypotheses, of which Sir Charles
Lyell tells us,[1] would, by the mere fact of being kept
before the mind, tend to petrify into a hard fixed belief. And this process of hardening is seen strikingly
illustrated in the case of traditional errors, especially
when these fall in with our own emotional propensities.
Our habitual representations of the remote historical
past are liable to much the same kind of error as our
recollections of early personal experience. The wrong
statements of others and the promptings of our own
fancies may lead in the first instance to a filling up
of the remote past with purely imaginary shapes.
Afterwards the particular origin of the belief is forgotten, and the assurance assumes the aspect of a
perfectly intuitive conviction. The hoary traditional
myths respecting the golden age, and so on, and the

---

[1] *Principles of Geology*, ch. iii.

persistent errors of historians under the sway of a strong emotional bias, illustrate such illusions.

So much as to simple illusions of belief, or such as involve single representations only.   Let us now pass to compound illusions, which involve a complex group of representations.

B. *Compound Illusory Belief.*

A familiar example of a compound belief is the belief in a permanent or persistent individual object of a certain character.   Such an idea, whatever its whole meaning may be—and this is a disputed point in philosophy—certainly seems to include a number of particular representations, corresponding to direct personal recollections, to the recollections of others, and to numerous anticipations of ourselves and of others.   And if the object be a living creature endowed with feelings, our idea of it will contain, in addition to these represented perceptions of ourselves or of others, a series of represented insights, namely, such as correspond to the inner experience of the being, so far as this is known or imagined.

It would thus seem that the idea which we habitually carry about with us respecting a complex individual object is a very composite idea.   In order to see this more fully, let us inquire into what is meant by our belief in a person.   My idea of a particular friend contains, among other things, numbers of vague representations of his habitual modes of feeling and acting, and numbers of still more vague expectations of how he will or might feel and act in certain circumstances.

Now, it is plain that such a composite idea must have been a very slow growth, involving, in certain stages of its formation, numerous processes of inference or quasi-inference from the past to the future. But in process of time these elements fuse inseparably : the directly known and the inferred no longer stand apart in my mind; my whole conception of the individual as he has been, is, and will be, seems one indivisible cognition; and this cognition is so firmly fixed and presents itself so instantaneously to the mind when I think of the object, that it has all the appearance of an intuitive conviction.

If this is a fairly accurate description of the structure of these compound representations and of their attendant beliefs, it is easy to see how many openings for error they cover. To begin with, my representation of so complex a thing as a concrete personality must always be exceedingly inadequate and fragmentary. I see only a few facets of the person's many-sided mind and character. And yet, in general, I am not aware of this, but habitually identify my representation with the totality of the object.

More than this, a little attention to the process by which these compound beliefs arise will disclose the fact that this apparently adequate representation of another has arisen in part by other than logical processes. If the blending of memory and expectation were simply a mingling of facts with correct inferences from these, it might not greatly matter; but it is something very different from this. Not only has our direct observation of the person been very limited, even that which we have been able to see has not been perfectly mirrored in our memory. It has already been remarked that recollection is a selective process, and this truth is strikingly illustrated in the growth of our enduring representations of things. What stamps itself on my memory is what surprised me or what deeply interested me at the moment. And then there are all the risks of mnemonic illusion to be taken into account as well. Thus, my idea of a person, so far even as it is built up on a basis of direct personal recollection, is essentially a fragmentary and to some extent a misleading representation.

Nor is this all. My habitual idea of a person is a resultant of forces of memory conjoined with other forces. Among these are to be reckoned the influence of illusory perception or insight, my own and that of others. The amount of misinterpretation of the words and actions of a single human being during the course of a long acquaintance must be very considerable. To these must be, added the effect of erroneous single expectations and reconstructions of past experiences, in so far as these have not been distinctly contradicted and dissipated. All these errors, connected with single acts of observing or inferring the feelings and doings of another, have their effect in distorting the subsequent total representation of the person.

Finally, we must include a more distinct ingredient of active illusion, namely, all the complex effects of the activity of imagination as led, not by fact and experience, but by feeling and desire. Our permanent idea of another reflects all that we have fondly imagined the person capable of doing, and thus is made up of an ideal as well as a real actually known personality. And this result of spontaneous imagination must be taken to include the ideals entertained by others who are likely to have influenced us by their beliefs.[1]

Enough has probably been said to show how immensely improbable it is that our permanent cognition of so complex an object as a particular human being should be at all an accurate representation of the reality, how much of the erroneous is certain to get mixed up with the true. And this being so, we may say that our apparently simple direct cognition of a given person, our assurance of what he is and will continue to be, is to some extent illusory.

Illusion of Self-Esteem.

Let us now pass to another case of compound representation, where the illusory element is still more striking. I refer to the idea of self which each of us habitually carries about with him. Every man's opinion of himself, as a whole, is a very complex mental product, in which facts known by introspection no doubt play a part, but probably only a very subordinate part. It is obvious, from what has been said about the structure of our habitual representations of other individuals, that our ordinary representation of ourselves will be tinged with that mass of error which we have found to be connected

---

[1] To make this rough analysis more complete, I ought, perhaps, to include the effect of all the errors of introspection, memory, and spontaneous belief, into which the person himself falls, in so far as they communicate themselves to others.

with single acts of introspection, recollections of past personal experience, and illusory single expectations of future personal experiences. How large an opening for erroneous conviction here presents itself can only be understood by a reference to certain deeply fixed impulses and feelings connected with the very consciousness of self, and favouring what I have marked off as active illusion. I shall try to show very briefly that each man's intuitive persuasion of his own powers, gifts, or importance—in brief, of his own particular value, contains, from the first, a palpable ingredient of active illusion.

Most persons, one supposes, have with more or less distinct consciousness framed a notion of their own value, if not to the world generally, at least to themselves. And this notion, however undefined it may be, is held to with a singular tenacity of belief. The greater part of mankind, indeed, seem never to entertain the question whether they really possess points of excellence. They assume it as a matter perfectly self-evident, and appear to believe in their vaguely conceived worth on the same immediate testimony of consciousness by which they assure themselves of their personal existence. Indeed, the conviction of personal consequence may be said to be a constant factor in most men's consciousness. However restrained by the rules of polite intercourse, it betrays its existence and its energy in innumerable ways. It displays itself most triumphantly when the mind is suddenly isolated from other minds, when other men unite in heaping neglect and contempt on the believer's head. In these moments he proves an almost heroic strength of confidence, believing in himself and in his claims to careful consideration when all his acquaintance are practically avowing their disbelief.

The intensity of this belief in personal value may be observed in very different forms. The young woman who, quite independently of others' opinion, and even in defiance of it, cherishes a conviction that her external attractions have a considerable value; the young man who, in the face of general indifference, persists in his habit of voluble talk on the supposition that he is conferring on his fellow-creatures the fruits of profound wisdom; and the man of years whose opinion of his own social importance and moral worth is quite disproportionate to the estimation which others form of his claims—these alike illustrate the force and pertinacity of the belief.

There are, no doubt, many exceptions to this form of self-appreciation. In certain robust minds, but little given to self-reflection, the idea of personal value rarely occurs. And then there are timid, sensitive natures that betray a tendency to self-distrust of all kinds, and to an undue depreciation of personal merit. Yet even here traces of an impulse to think well of self will appear to the attentive eye, and one can generally recognize that this impulse is only kept down by some other stronger force, as, for example, extreme sensitiveness to the judgment of others, great conscientiousness, and so on. And however this be, it will be allowed that the average man rates himself highly.

It is to be noticed that this persuasion of personal value or excellence is, in common, very vague. A man may have a general sense of his own importance without in the least being able to say wherein exactly his superiority lies. Or, to put it another way, he may have a strong conviction that he stands high in the scale of morally deserving persons, and yet be unable to define his position more nearly. Commonly, the conviction seems to be only definable as an assurance of a superlative of which the positive and comparative are suppressed. At most, his idea of his moral altitude resolves itself into the proposition, "I am a good deal better than Mr. A. or Mr. B." Now, it is plain that in these intuitive judgments on his own excellence, the man is making an assertion with respect, not only to inner subjective feelings which he only can be supposed to know immediately, but also to external objective facts which are patent to others, namely, to certain active tendencies and capabilities, to the direction of external conduct in certain lines.[1] Hence, if the assertion is erroneous, it will be in plain contradiction to others' perceptions of his powers or moral endowments. And this is what we actually find. A man's self-esteem, in a large preponderance of cases, is plainly in excess of others' esteem of him. What the man conceives himself to be differs widely from what others conceive him to be.

> "Oh wad some power the giftie gie us,
> To see oursels as others see us!"

Now, whence comes this large and approximately uniform discrepancy between our self-esteem and

---

[1] In the case of a vain woman thinking herself much more pretty than others think her, the error is still more obviously one connected with a belief in objective fact.

others' esteem of us? By trying to answer this question we shall come to understand still better the processes by which the most powerful forms of illusion are generated.

It is, I think, a matter of every-day observation that children manifest an apparently instinctive disposition to magnify self as soon as the vaguest idea of self is reached. It is very hard to define this feeling more precisely than by terming it a rudimentary sense of personal importance. It may show itself in very different ways, taking now a more active form, as an impulse of self-assertion, and a desire to enforce one's own will to the suppression of others' wills, and at another time wearing the appearance of a passive emotion, an elementary form of *amour propre*. And it is this feeling which forms the germ of the self-estimation of adults. For in truth all attribution of value involves an element of feeling, as respect, and of active desire, and the ascription of value to one's self is in its simplest form merely the expression of this state of mind.

But how is it, it may be asked, that this feeling shows itself instinctively as soon as the idea of self begins to arise in consciousness? The answer to this question is to be found, I imagine, in the general laws of mental development. All practical judgments like that of self-estimation are based on some feeling which is developed before it; and, again, the feeling itself is based on some instinctive action which, in like manner, is earlier than the feeling. Thus, for example, an Englishman's judgment that his native country is of paramount value springs out of a long-existent sentiment of patriotism, which sentiment again may be regarded as having slowly grown up about the half-blindly followed habit of defending and furthering the interests of one's nation or tribe. In a similar way, one suspects, the feeling of personal worth, with its accompanying judgment, is a product of a long process of instinctive action.

What this action is it is scarcely necessary to remind the reader. Every living organism strives, or acts as if it consciously strove, to maintain its life and promote its well-being. The actions of plants are clearly related to the needs of a prosperous exist-ence, individual first and serial afterwards. The move-ments of the lower animals have the same end. Thus, on the supposition that man has been slowly evolved from lower forms, it is clear that the instinct of self-promotion must be the deepest and most ineradicable element of his nature, and it is this instinct which directly underlies the rudimentary sentiment of self-esteem of which we are now treating.

This instinct will appear, first of all, as the unre-flecting organized habit of seeking individual good, of aiming at individual happiness, and so of pushing on the action of the individual will. This impulse shows itself in distinct form as soon as the individual is brought into competition with another similarly con-stituted being. It is the force which displays itself in all opposition and hostility, and it tends to limit and counteract the gregarious instincts of the race. In the next place, as intelligence expands, this in-stinctive action becomes conscious pursuit of an end, and at this stage the thing pursued attracts to itself a sentiment. The individual now consciously desires his own happiness as contrasted with that of others, knowingly aims at enlarging his own sphere of action to the diminution of others' spheres. Here we have the nascent sentiment of self-esteem, on which all later judgments respecting individual importance are, in part at least, founded.

Thus, we see that long before man had arrived at an idea of self there had been growing up an emotional predisposition to think well of self. And in this way we may understand how it is that this sentiment of self-esteem shows itself immediately and instinctively in the child's mind as soon as its unfolding consciousness is strong enough to grasp the first rough idea of personal existence. Far down, so to speak, below the surface of distinct consciousness, in the intricate formation of ganglion-cell and nerve-fibre, the connections between the idea of self and this emotion of esteem have been slowly woven through long ages of animal development.

Here, then, we seem to have the key to the apparently paradoxical fact that a man, with all his superior means of studying his own feelings, commonly esteems himself, in certain respects at least, less accurately than a good external observer would be capable of doing. In forming an opinion of ourselves we are exposed to the full force of a powerful impulse of feeling. This impulse, acting as a bias, enters more or less distinctly into our single acts of introspection, into our attempts to recall our past doings, into our insights into the meaning of others' words and actions as related to ourselves (forming the natural disposition to enjoy flattery), and finally into our wild dreams as to our future achievements. It is thus the principal root of that gigantic illusion of self-conceit, which has long been recognized by practical sense as one of the greatest obstacles to social action; and by art as one of the most ludicrous manifestations of human weakness.

If there are all these openings for error in the beliefs we go on entertaining respecting individual things, including ourselves, there must be a yet larger number of such openings in those still more compound beliefs which we habitually hold respecting collections or classes of things. A single illusion of perception or of memory may suffice to give rise to a wholly illusory belief in a class of objects, for example, ghosts. The superstitious beliefs of mankind abundantly illustrate this complexity of the sources of error. And in the case of our every-day beliefs respecting real classes of objects, these sources contribute a considerable quota of error. We may again see this by examining our ordinary beliefs respecting our fellow-men.

A moment's consideration will show that our prevailing views respecting any section of mankind, say our fellow-countrymen, or mankind at large, correspond at best to a very loose process of reasoning. The accidents of our personal experience and opportunities of observation, the traditions which coloured our first ideas, the influence of our dominant feelings in selecting for attention and retention certain aspects of the complex object, and in idealizing this object,—these sources of passive and active illusion must, to say the least, have had as much to do with our present solidified and seemingly "intuitive" knowledge as anything that can be called the exercise of individual judgment and reasoning power.

The force of this observation and the proof that such widely generalized beliefs are in part illusory, is seen in the fact that men of unlike experience and unlike temperament form such utterly dissimilar views of the same object. Thus, as Mr. Spencer has shown,[1] in looking at things national there may be not only a powerful patriotic bias at work in the case of the vulgar Philistine, but also a distinctly anti-patriotic bias in the case of the over-fastidious seeker after culture. And I need hardly add that the different estimates of mankind held with equal assurance by the cynic, the misanthropist, and the philanthropic vindicator of his species, illustrate a like diversity of the psychological conditions of belief.

Finally, illusion may enter into that still wider collection of beliefs which make up our ordinary views of life and the world as a whole. Here there reflect themselves in the plainest manner the accidents of our individual experience and the peculiar errors to which our intellectual and emotional conformation disposes us. The world is for us what we feel it to be ; and we feel it to be the cause of our particular emotional experience. Just as we have found that our environment helps to determine our idea of self and personal continuity, so, conversely, our inner experience, our remembered or imagined joys and sorrows throw a reflection on the outer world, giving it its degree of worth. Hence the contradictory, and consequently to some extent at least illusory, views of the optimist and the pessimist,

[1] *The Study of Sociology*, ch. ix.

"intuitions" which, I have tried to show elsewhere, are connected with deeply rooted habits of feeling, and are antecedent to all reasoned philosophic systems.

If proof were yet wanted that these wide-embracing beliefs may to some extent be illusory, it would be found in the fact that they can be distinctly coloured by a temporary mood or mental tone. As I have more than once had occasion to remark, a feeling when present tends to colour all the ideas of the time. And when out of sorts, moody, and discontented, a man is prone to find a large objective cause of his dissatisfaction in a world out of joint and not moving to his mind.

It is evident that all the permanent beliefs touched on in this chapter must constitute powerful predispositions with respect to any particular act of perception, insight, introspection, or recollection. In other words, these persistent beliefs, so far as individual or personal, are but another name for those fixed habits of mind which, in the case of each one of us, constitute our intellectual bias, and the source of the error known as personal equation. And it may be added that, just as these erroneous beliefs existing in the shape of fixed prejudices constitute a bias to new error, so they act as powerful resisting forces in relation to new truth and the correction of error.

In comparing these illusions of belief with those of perception and memory, we cannot fail to notice their greater compass or range, in other words, the greater extent of the region of fact misrepresented. Even if they are less forcible and irresistible than these errors, they clearly make up for this by the area which they cover.

Another thing to be observed with respect to these comprehensive beliefs is that where, as here, so many co-operant conditions are at work, the whole amount of common objective agreement is greatly reduced. In other words, individual peculiarities of intellectual conformation, emotional temperament, and experience have a far wider scope for their influence in these beliefs than they have in the case of presentative cognitions. At the same time, it is noteworthy that error much more rapidly propagates itself here than in the case of our perceptions or recollections. As we have seen, these beliefs all include much more than the results of the individual's own experience. They offer a large field for the influence of personal ascendency, of the contagion of sympathy, and of authority and tradition. As a consequence of this, the illusions of belief are likely to be far more persistent than those of perception or of memory; for not only do they lose that salutary process of correction which comparison with the experience of others affords, but they may even be strengthened and upheld to some extent by such social influences.

And here the question might seem to obtrude itself, whether, in relation to such a fluctuating mass of belief as that just reviewed, in which there appears to be so little common agreement, we can correctly speak of anything as objectively determinable. If illusion and error as a whole are defined by a reference to what is commonly held true and certain, what, it may be asked, becomes of the so-called illusions of belief?

This question will have to be fully dealt with in the following chapter. Here it may be sufficient to remark that amid all this apparent deviation of belief from a common standard of truth, there is a clear tendency to a rational consensus. Thought, by disengaging what is really matter of permanent and common cognition, both in the individual and still more in the class,[1] and fixing this quantum of common cognition in the shape of accurate definitions and universal propositions, is ever fighting against and restraining the impulses of individual imagination towards dissociation and isolation of belief. And this same process of scientific control of belief is ever tending to correct widespread traditional forms of error, and to erect a new and better standard of common cognition.

This scientific regulation of belief only fails where the experiences which underlie the conceptions are individual, variable, and subjective. Hence there is no definite common conception of the value of life and of the world, just because the estimate of this value must vary with individual circumstances, temperament, etc. All that can be looked for here in the way of a common standard or norm is a rough average estimate. And this common-sense judgment serves practically as a sufficient criterion of truth, at least in relation to such extreme one-sidedness of view as approaches the abnormal, that is to say, one of the two poles of irrational exaltation, or "joy-madness," and

---

[1] As a matter of fact, the proportion of accurate knowledge to error is far larger in the case of classes than of individuals. Propositions with general terms for subject are less liable to be faulty than propositions with singular terms for subject.

abject melancholy, which appear among the phenomena of mental disease.[1]

[1] For a description of each of these extremes of boundless gaiety and utter despondency, see Griesinger, *op. cit.*, Bk. III. ch. i. and ii. The relation of pessimism to pathological conditions is familiar enough ; less familiar is the relation of unrestrained optimism. Yet Griesinger writes that among the insane " boundless hilarity," with " a feeling of good fortune," and a general contentment with everything, is as frequent as depression and repining (see especially p. 281, also pp. 64, 65).

CHAPTER XII.

THE foregoing study of illusions may not improbably have had a bewildering effect on the mind of the reader. To keep the mental eye, like the bodily eye, for any time intently fixed on one object is apt to produce a feeling of giddiness. And in the case of a subject like illusion, the effect is enormously increased by the disturbing character of the object looked at. Indeed, the first feeling produced by our survey of the wide field of illusory error might be expressed pretty accurately by the despondent cry of the poet—

> "Alas! it is delusion all:
> The future cheats us from afar,
> Nor can we be what we recall,
> Nor dare we think on what we are."

It must be confessed that our study has tended to bring home to the mind the wide range of the illusory and unreal in our intellectual life. In sense-perception, in the introspection of the mind's own feelings, in the reading of others' feelings, in memory, and finally in belief, we have found a large field for illusory cognition. And while illusion has thus so great a depth in the individual mind, it has a no less striking breadth or extent in the collective human mind. No doubt its grosser forms manifest themselves most conspicuously in the undisciplined mind of the savage and the rustic ; yet even the cultivated mind is by no means free from its control. In truth, most of the illusions illustrated in this work are such as can be shared in by all classes of mind.

In view of this wide far-reaching area of ascertained error, the mind naturally asks, What are the real limits of illusory cognition, and how can we be ever sure of having got beyond them? This question leads us on to philosophical problems of the greatest consequence, problems which can only be very lightly touched in this place. Before approaching these, let us look back a little more carefully and gather up our results, reflect on the method which we have been unconsciously adopting, and inquire how far this scientific mode of procedure will take us in determining what is the whole range of illusory cognition.

We have found an ingredient of illusion mixed up with all the popularly recognized forms of immediate knowledge. Yet this ingredient is not equally conspicuous in all cases. First of all, illusion varies very considerably in its degree of force and persistence. Thus, in general, a presentative illusion is more coercive than a representative ; an apparent reality present to the mind is naturally felt to be more indubitable than one absent and only represented. On the other hand, a representative illusion is often more enduring than a presentative, that is to say, less easily found out. It is to be added that a good deal of illusion is only partial, there being throughout an under-current of rational consciousness, a gentle play of self-criticism, which keeps the error from developing into a perfect self-delusion. This remark applies not only to the innocent illusions of art, but also to many of our every-day illusions, both presentative and representative. In many cases, indeed, as, for example, in looking at a reflection in a mirror, the illusion is very imperfect, remaining in the nascent stage.

Again, a little attention to the facts here brought together will show that the proportion of illusory to real knowledge is far from being the same in each class of immediate or quasi-immediate cognition. Thus, with respect to the great distinction between presentative and representative knowledge, it is to be observed that, in so far as any act of cognition is, strictly speaking, presentative, it does not appear to admit of error. The illusions of perception are connected with the representative side of the process, and are numerous just because this is so extensive. On the other hand, in introspection, where the scope of independent representation is so limited, the amount of illusion is very inconsiderable, and may in practice be disregarded. So again, to take a narrower group of illusions, we find that in the recalling of distant events the proportion of error is vastly greater than in the recalling of near events.

So much as to the extent of illusion as brought to light by our preceding study. Let us now glance at the conclusions obtained respecting its nature and its causes.

Causes of Illusion.

Looking at illusion as a whole, and abstracting from the differences of mental mechanism in the processes of perception, memory, etc., we may say that the *rationale* or mode of genesis of illusion is very much the same throughout. Speaking broadly, one may describe all knowledge as a correspondence of representation with fact or experience, or as a stable condition of the representation which cannot be disturbed by new experiences. It does not matter, for our present purpose, whether the fact represented is supposed to be directly present, as in presentative cognition; or to be absent, either as something past or future, or finally as a "general fact," that is to say, the group of facts (past and future) embodied in a universal proposition.[1]

In general this accordance between our representations and facts is secured by the laws of our intellectual mechanism. It follows from the principles of association that our simple experiences, external and internal, will tend to reflect themselves in perception, memory, expectation, and general belief, in the very time-connections in which they actually occur. To put it briefly, facts which occur together will in general be represented together, and they will be the more perfectly co-represented in proportion to the frequency of this concurrence.

---

[1] It has been seen that, from a purely psychological point of view, even what looks at first like pure presentative cognition, as, for example, the recognition of a present feeling of the mind, involves an ingredient of representation.

Illusion, as distinguished from correct knowledge, is, to put it broadly, deviation of representation from fact. This is due in part to limitations and defects in the intellectual mechanism itself, such as the imperfections of the activities of attention, discrimination, and comparison, in relation to what is present. Still more is it due to the control of our mental processes by association and habit. These forces, which are at the very root of intelligence, are also, in a sense, the originators of error. Through the accidents of our experience or the momentary condition of our reproductive power, representations get wrongly grouped with presentations and with one another; wrongly grouped, that is to say, according to a perfect or ideal standard, namely, that the grouping should always exactly agree with the order of experience as a whole, and the force of cohesion be proportionate to the number of the conjunctions of this experience.

This great source of error has been so abundantly illustrated under the head of Passive Illusions that I need not dwell on it further. It is plain that a passive error of perception, or of expectation, is due in general to a defective grouping of elements, to a grouping which answers, perhaps, to the run of the individual's actual experience, but not to a large and complete common experience.[1] Similarly, an illusory general belief is plainly a welding together of elements (here concepts, answering to innumerable representative images) in disagreement with the permanent connections of experience. Even a passive illusion of memory, in so

---

[1] See especially what was said about the *rationale* of illusions of perception, pp. 37, 38.

far as it involves a rearrangement of successive representations, shows the same kind of defect.

In the second place, this incorrect grouping may be due, not to defects in attention and discrimination, combined with insufficiently grounded association, but to the independent play of constructive imagination and the caprices of feeling. This is illustrated in what I have called Active Illusions, whether the excited perceptions and the hallucinations of sense, or the fanciful projections of memory or of expectation. Here we have a force directly opposed to that of experience. Active illusion arises, not through the imperfections of the intellectual mechanism, but through a palpable interference with this mechanism. It is a regrouping of elements which simulates the form of a suggestion by experience, but is, in reality, the outcome of the individual mind's extra-intellectual impulses.

We see, then, that, in spite of obvious differences in the form, the process in all kinds of immediate cognition is fundamentally identical. It is essentially a bringing together of elements, whether similar or dissimilar and associated by a link of contiguity, and a viewing of these as connected parts of a whole; it is a process of synthesis. And illusion, in all its forms, is bad grouping or carelessly performed synthesis. This holds good even of the simplest kinds of error in which a presentative element is wrongly classed; and it holds good of those more conspicuous errors of perception, memory, expectation, and compound belief, in which representations connect themselves in an order not perfectly answering to the objective order.

This view of the nature and causes of illusion is clearly capable of being expressed in physical language. Bad grouping of psychical elements is equivalent to imperfect co-ordination of their physical, that is to say, nervous, conditions, imperfect in the evolutionist's sense, as not exactly according with external relations. So far as illusions of suggestion (passive illusions) are concerned, the error is connected with organized tendencies, due to a limited action of experience. On the other hand, illusions of preconception (active illusions) usually involve no such deeply fixed or permanent organic connections, but merely a temporary confluence of nerve-processes.[1] The nature of the physical process is best studied in the case of errors of sense-perception. Yet we may hypothetically argue that even in the case of the most complex errors, as those of memory and of belief, there is implied a deviation in the mode of connection of nervous structures (whether the connection be permanent or temporary) from the external order of facts.

And now we are in a position to see whether illusion is ultimately distinguishable from other modes of error, namely, those incident to conscious processes of reasoning. It must have been plain to an attentive reader throughout our exposition that, in spite of our provisional distinction, no sharp line can be drawn between much of what, on the surface, looks like immediate knowledge, and consciously derived or inferred knowledge. On its objective side, reasoning may be

---

[1] I say "usually," because, as we have seen, there may sometimes be a permanent and even an inherited predisposition to active illusion in the individual temperament and nervous organization.

roughly defined as a conscious transition of mind from certain facts or relations of facts to other facts or relations recognized as similar. According to this definition, a fallacy would be a hasty, unwarranted transition to new cases not identical with the old. And a good part of immediate knowledge is fundamentally the same, only that here, through the exceptional force of association and habit, the transition is too rapid to be consciously recognized. Consequently, illusion becomes identified at bottom with fallacious inference: it may be briefly described as collapsed inference. Thus, illusory perception and expectation are plainly a hasty transition of mind from old to new, from past to present, conjunctions of experience.[1] And, as we have seen, an illusory general belief owes its existence to a coalescence of representations of known facts or connections with products of imagination which simulate the appearance of inferences from these facts.

In the case of memory, in so far as it is not aided

---

[1] See what was said on the nature of passive illusions of sense (pp. 44, 68, 70, etc.). The logical character of illusion might be brought out by saying that it resembles the fallacy which is due to reasoning from an approximate generalization as though it were a universal truth. In thus identifying illusion and fallacy, I must not be understood to say that there is, strictly speaking, any such thing as an unconscious reasoning process. On the contrary, I hold that it is a contradiction to talk of any *mental* operation as altogether unconscious. I simply wish to show that, by a kind of fiction, illusion may be described as the result of a series of steps which, if separately unfolded to consciousness (as they no longer are), would correspond to those of a process of inference. The fact that illusion arises by a process of contraction out of conscious inference seems to justify this use of language, even apart from the fact that the nervous processes in the two cases are pretty certainly the same.

by reasoning from present signs, there seems to be nothing like a movement of inference. It is evident, indeed, that memory is involved in and underlies every such transition of thought. Illusions of memory illustrate rather a process of wrong classing, that is to say, of wrongly identifying the present mental image with past fact, which is the initial step in all inference. In this way they closely resemble those slight errors of perception which are due to erroneous classing of sense-impressions. But since the intellectual process involved in assimilating mental elements is very similar to that implied in assimilating complex groups of such elements, we may say that even in these simple kinds of error there is something which resembles a wrong classing of relations, something, therefore, which approximates in character to a fallacy.

By help of this brief review of the nature and causes of illusion, we see that in general it may be spoken of as deviation of individual from common experience. This applies to passive illusion in so far as it follows from the accidents of individual experience, and it still more obviously applies to active illusion as due to the vagaries of individual feeling and constructive imagination. We might, perhaps, characterize all illusion as partial view, partial both in the sense of being incomplete, and in the other sense of being that to which the mind by its peculiar predispositions inclines. This being so, we may very roughly describe all illusion as abnormal. Just as hallucination, the most signal instance of illusion, is distinctly on the border-land of healthy and unhealthy mental life; just as dreams are in the direction of such unhealthy mental action ; so the lesser illusions of memory and so on are abnormal in the sense that they imply a departure from a common typical mode of intellectual action.

It is plain, indeed, that this is the position we have been taking up throughout our discussion of illusion. We have assumed that what is common and normal is true, or answers to what is objectively real. Thus, in dealing with errors of perception, we took for granted that the common percept—meaning by this what is permanent in the individual and the general experience—is at the same time the true percept. So in discussing the illusions of memory we estimated objective time by the judgment of the average man, free from individual bias, and apart from special circumstances favourable to error. Similarly, in the case of belief, true belief was held to be that which men in general, or in the long run, or on the average, hold true, as distinguished from what the individual under variable and accidental influences holds true. And even in the case of introspection we found that true cognition resolved itself into a consensus or agreement as to certain psychical facts.

Criterion of Illusion.

Now, it behoves us here to examine this assumption, with the view of seeing how far it is perfectly sound. For it may be that what is commonly held true does not in all cases strictly answer to the real, in which case our idea of illusion would have to be extended so as to include certain common beliefs. This question was partly opened up at the close of the last chapter.

It will be found that the full discussion of it carries us beyond the scientific point of view altogether. For the present, however, let us see what can be said about it from that standpoint of positive science to which we have hitherto been keeping.

Now, if by common be meant what has been shared by all minds or the majority of minds up to a particular time, a moment's inspection of the process of correcting illusion will show that science assumes the possibility of a common illusion. In the history of discovery, the first assault on an error was the setting up of the individual against the society. The men who first dared to say that the sun did not move round the earth found to their cost what it was to fly in the face of a common, though illusory, perception of the senses.[1]

If, however, by common be understood what is permanently and unshakably held true by men in proportion as their minds become enlightened, then science certainly does assume the truth of common perception and belief. Thus, the progress of the physical sciences may be described as a movement towards a new, higher, and more stable consensus of ideas and beliefs. In point of fact, the truths accepted by men of science already form a body of common belief for

---

[1] If we turn from the region of physical to that of moral ideas, we see this historical collision between common and individual conviction in a yet more impressive form. The teacher of a new moral truth has again and again been set down to be an illusionist by a society which was itself under the sway of a long-reigning error. As George Eliot observes, " What we call illusions are often, in truth, a wider vision of past and present realities—a willing movement of a man's soul with the larger sweep of the world's forces."

those who are supposed by all to have the means of testing the value of their convictions. And the same applies to the successive improvements in the conceptions of the moral sciences, for example, history and psychology. Indeed, the very meaning of science appears to be a body of common cognition to which all minds converge in proportion to their capabilities and opportunities of studying the particular subject-matter concerned.

Not only so, from a strictly scientific point of view it might seem possible to prove that common cognition, as defined above, must in general be true cognition. I refer here to the now familiar method of the evolutionist.

According to this doctrine, which is a scientific method in so far as it investigates the historical developments of mind or the order of mental phenomena in time, cognition may be viewed as a part of the result of the interaction of external agencies and the organism, as an incident of the great process of adaptation, physical and psychical, of organism to environment. In thus looking at cognition, the evolutionist is making the assumption which all science makes, namely, that correct views are correspondences between internal (mental) relations and external (physical) relations, incorrect views disagreements between these relations. From this point of view he may proceed to argue that the intellectual processes must tend to conform to external facts. All correspondence, he tells us, means fitness to external conditions and practical efficiency, all want of correspondence practical incompetence. Consequently, those individuals in whom the correspondence was more complete and exact would have an advantage in the struggle for existence and so tend to be preserved. In this way the process of natural selection, by separately adjusting individual representations to actualities, would make them converge towards a common meeting-point or social standard of true cognition. That is to say, by eliminating or at least greatly circumscribing the region of individual illusion, natural selection would exclude the possibility of a persistent common illusion.

Not only so, the evolutionist may say that this coincidence between common beliefs and true beliefs would be furthered by social as well as individual competition. A community has an advantage in the struggle with other communities when it is distinguished by the presence of the conditions of effective co-operation, such as mutual confidence. Among these conditions a body of true knowledge seems to be of the first importance, since conjoint action always presupposes common beliefs, and, to be effective action, implies that these beliefs are correct. Consequently, it may be argued, the forces at work in the action of man on man, of society on the individual, in the way of assimilating belief, must tend, in the long run, to bring about a coincidence between representations and facts. Thus, in another way, natural selection would help to adjust our ideas to realities, and to exclude the possibility of anything. like a permanent common error.

Yet once more, according to Mr. Herbert Spencer, the tendency to agreement between our ideas and the environment would be aided by what he calls the direct process of adaptation. The exercise of a function tends to the development of that function. Thus, our acts of perception must become more exact by mere repetition. So, too, the representations and concepts growing out of perceptions must tend to approximate to external facts by the direct action of the environment on our physical and psychical organism ; for external relations which are permanent will, in the long run, stamp themselves on our nervous and mental structure more deeply and indelibly than relations which are variable and accidental.

It would seem, from all this, that so long as we are keeping to the scientific point of view, that is to say, taking for granted that there is something objectively real answering to our perceptions and conceptions, the question of the possibility of a universal or (permanently) common illusion does not arise. Yet a little more reflection will show us that it may arise in a way. So far as the logical sufficiency of the social consensus or common belief is accepted as scientifically proved, it is open to suspicion on strictly scientific grounds. The evolutionist's proof involves one or two assumptions which are not exactly true.

In the first place, it is not strictly correct to say that all illusion involves a practical unfitness to circumstances. At the close of our investigation of particular groups of illusion, for example, those of perception and memory, it was pointed out that many of the errors reviewed were practically harmless, being either momentary and evanescent, or of such a character as not to lead to injurious action. And now, by glancing back over the field of illusion as a whole, we may see the same thing. The day-dreams in which some people are apt to indulge respecting the remote future have little effect on their conduct. So, too, a man's general view of the world is often unrelated to his daily habits of life. It seems to matter exceedingly little, in general, whether a person take up the geocentric or the heliocentric conception of the cosmic structure, or even whether he adopt an optimistic or pessimistic view of life and its capabilities.

So inadequate, indeed, does the agency of natural selection seem to be to eliminate illusion, that it may even be asked whether its tendency may not be sometimes to harden and fix rather than to dissolve and dissipate illusory ideas and beliefs. It will at once occur to the reader that the illusion of self-esteem, discussed in the last chapter, may have been highly useful as subserving individual self-preservation. In a similar way, it has been suggested by Schopenhauer that the illusion of the lover owes its force and historical persistence to its paramount utility for the preservation of the species. And to pass from a recurring individual to a permanently common belief, it is maintained by the same pessimist and his followers that what they regard as the illusion of optimism, namely, the idea that human life as a whole is good, grows out of the individual's irrational love of life, which is only the same instinctive impulse of self-preservation appearing as conscious desire. Once more, it has been suggested that the belief in free-will, even if illusory, would be preserved by the process of evolution, owing to its paramount utility in certain stages of moral development. All this seems to show at least the possibility of a kind of illusion which would tend to perpetuate itself, and to appear as a permanent common belief.

Now, so far as this is the case, so far as illusion is useful or only harmless, natural selection cannot, it is plain, be counted on to weed it out, keeping it within the narrow limits of the exceptional and individual. Natural selection gets rid of what is harmful only, and is indifferent to what is practically harmless.

It may, however, still be said that the process of direct adaptation must tend to establish such a consensus of true belief. Now, I do not wish for a moment to dispute that the growth of intelligence by the continual exercise of its functions tends to such a consensus: this is assumed to be the case by everybody. What I want to point out is that there is no scientific proof of this position.

The correspondence of internal to external relations is obviously limited by the modes of action of the environment on the organism, consequently by the structure of the organism itself. Scientific men are familiar with the idea that there may be forces in the environment which are practically inoperative on the organism, there being no corresponding mode of sensibility. And even if it be said that our present knowledge of the material world, including the doctrine of the conservation of energy, enables us to assert that there is no mode of force wholly unknown to us, it can still be contended that the environment may, for aught we know, be vastly more than the forces of which, owing to the nature of our organism, we know it to be composed. In short, since, on the evolution theory viewed as a scientific doctrine, the real external world does not directly mirror itself in our minds, but only indirectly brings our perceptions and representations into adjustment by bringing into adjustment the nervous organism with which they are somehow connected, it is plain that we cannot be certain of adequately apprehending the external reality which is here assumed to exist.

Science, then, cannot prove, but must assume the coincidence between permanent common intuitions and objective reality. To raise the question whether this coincidence is perfect or imperfect, whether all common intuitions known to be persistent are true or whether there are any that are illusory, is to pass beyond the scientific point of view to another, namely, the philosophic. Thus, our study of illusion naturally carries us on from scientific to philosophic reflection. Let me try to make this still more clear.

Transition to Philosophic View.

All science makes certain assumptions which it never examines. Thus, the physicist assumes that when we experience a sensation we are acted on by some pre-existing external object which is the cause, or at least one condition, of the sensation. While resolving the secondary qualities of light, sound, etc., into modes of motion, while representing the object very differently from the unscientific mind, he agrees with this in holding to the reality of something external, regarding this as antecedent to and therefore as independent of the particular mind which receives the sense-impression. Again, he assumes the uniformity of nature, the universality of the causal relation, and so on.

Similarly, the modern psychologist, when confining himself within the limits of positive science, and treating mind phenomenally or empirically, or, in other words, tracing the order of mental states in time and assigning their conditions, takes for granted much the same as physical science does. Thus, as our foregoing analysis of perception shows, he assumes that there is an external cause of our sensations, that there are material bodies in space, which act on our sense-organs and so serve as the condition of our sense-impressions. More than this, he regards, in the way that has been illustrated in this work, the percept itself, in so far as it is a process in time, as the normal result of the action of such external agents on our nerve-structures, in other words, as the effect of such action in the case of the healthy and perfect nervous organism with the average organized dispositions, physical and psychical; in which case he supposes the percept to correspond, in certain respects at least, with the external cause as made known by physical science. And, on the other hand, he looks on a false or illusory percept as arising in another way not involving, as its condition, the pre-existence of a corresponding material body or physical agent. And in this view of perception, as of other mental phenomena, the psychologist clearly takes for granted the principle that all mental events conform to the law of causation. Further, he assumes that the individual mind is somehow, in a way which it is not his province to inquire into, one and the same throughout, and so on.

The doctrine of evolution, too, in so far as scientific —that is, aiming at giving an account of the historical and pre-historical developments of the collective mind in time—agrees with psychology in making like assumptions. Thus, it conceives an external agency (the environment) as the cause of our common sensations and perceptions. That is to say, it represents the external world as somehow antecedent to, and so apparently independent of, the perceptions which are adjusted to it. And all this shows that science, while removed from vulgar unenlightened opinion, takes sides with popular thought in assuming the truth of certain fundamental ideas or so-called intuitive beliefs, into the exact meaning of which it does not inquire.

When the meaning of these assumptions is investigated, we pass out of the scientific into the philosophic domain. Philosophy has to critically investigate the data of popular thought and of science. It has to discover exactly what is implied in these fundamental principles. Then it has to test their value by erecting a final criterion of truth, by probing the structure of cognition to the bottom, and determining the proper organ of certain or accurate knowledge; or, to put it another way, it has to examine what is meant by reality, whether there is anything real independently of the mind, and if so, what. In doing this it inquires not only what common sense means by its object-world clothed in its variegated garment of secondary qualities, its beauty, and so on, but also what physical science means by its cosmic mechanism of sensible and extra-sensible matter in motion: whether there is any kind of objective reality belonging to the latter which does not also belong to the former; and how the two worlds are related one to another. That is to say, he asks whether the bodies in space assumed to exist by the physicist as the antecedent conditions of particular sensations and percepts are independent of mind and perception generally.[1]

In doing all this, philosophy is theoretically free to upset as much of popular belief of the persistent kind as it likes. Nor can science find fault with it so long as it keeps to its own sphere, and does not directly contradict any truth which science, by the methods proper to it, is able to establish. Thus, for example, if philosophy finds that there is nothing real independently of mind, science will be satisfied so long as it finds a meaning for its assumed entities, such as space, external things, and physical causes.[2]

The student of philosophy need not be told that these imposing-looking problems respecting cognition, making up what the Germans call the "Theory of Cognition," and the cognate problem respecting the nature of reality, are still a long way from being settled. To-day, as in the days of Plato and Aristotle, are argued, in slightly altered forms, the vexed questions, What is true cognition? Is it a mere efflux from

---

[1] To make this account of the philosophic problem of the object-world complete, I ought to touch not only on the distinction between the vulgar and the scientific view of material things, but also on the distinction, within physical science, between the less and the more abstract view roughly represented by molar and molecular physics.

[2] For an excellent account of the distinction between the scientific and the philosophic point of view, see Mr. Shadworth Hodgson's *Philosophy of Reflection*, Bk. I. chs. i. and iii.; also Bk. III. chs. vii. and viii.

sensation, a passive conformity of representation to sensation (sensualism or empiricism)? or is it, on the other hand, a construction of active thought, involving certain necessary forms of intelligence (rationalism or intuitivism)?

Again, how are we to shape to ourselves real objective existence? Is it something wholly independent of the mind (realism)? and if so, is this known to be what we—meaning here common people and men of science alike—represent it as being (natural realism), or something different (transfigured realism)? Or is it, on the contrary, something involving mind (idealism)? and if so, is it a strictly phenomenal distinction within our conscious experience (empirical idealism, phenomenalism), or one of the two poles of subject and object constituted by every act of thought (rational idealism)? These are some of the questions in philosophy which still await their final answer.

Philosophy being thus still a question and not a solution, we need not here trouble ourselves about its problems further than to remark on their close connection with our special subject, the study of illusion.

Our brief reference to some of the principal inquiries of philosophy shows that it tends to throw doubt on things which the unreflecting popular mind holds to be indubitable. Different schools of philosophy have shown themselves unequally concerned about these so-called intuitive certainties. In general it may be said that philosophy, though, as I have remarked, theoretically free to set up its own standard of certainty, has in practice endeavoured to give a meaning to, and to find a justification for the assumptions or first principles of science. On the other hand, it has not hesitated, when occasion required, to make very light of the intuitive beliefs of the popular mind as interpreted by itself. Thus, rationalists of the Platonic type have not shrunk from pronouncing individual impressions and objects illusory, an assertion which certainly seems to be opposed to the assumptions of common sense, if not to those of science. On the other hand, the modern empirical or association school is quite ready to declare that the vulgar belief in an external world, so far as it represents this as independent of mind,[1] is an illusion; that the so-called necessary beliefs respecting identity, uniformity, causation, etc., are not, strictly speaking, necessary; and so on. And in these ways it certainly seems to come into conflict with popular convictions, or intuitive certainties, as they present themselves to the unreflecting intelligence.

Philosophy seems, then, to be a continuation of that process of detecting illusion with which science in part concerns itself. Indeed, it is evident that our

---

[1] I hold, in spite of Berkeley's endeavours to reconcile his position with that of common sense, that the popular view does at least tend in this direction. That is to say, the every-day habit, when considering the external world, of abstracting from particular minds, leads on insensibly to that complete detachment of it from mind in general which expresses itself in the first stage of philosophic reflection, crude realism. The physicist appears to me, both from the first essays in Greek "nature-philosophy," as also from the not infrequent confusion even to-day between a perfectly safe "scientific materialism" and a highly questionable philosophic materialism, to share in this tendency to take separate consideration for separate existence. Each new stage of abstraction in physical science gives birth to a new attempt to find an independent reality, a thing-in-itself, hidden further away from sense

special study has a very close connection with the philosophic inquiry. What philosophy wants is something intuitively certain as its starting-point, some *point d'appui* for its construction. The errors incident to the process of reasoning do not greatly trouble it, since these can, in general, be guarded against by the rules of logic. But error in the midst of what, on the face of it, looks like intuitive knowledge naturally raises the question, Is there any kind of absolutely certain cognition, any organ for the accurate perception of truth? And this intimate relation between the scientific and the philosophic consideration of illusion is abundantly illustrated in the history of philosophy. The errors of sense, appearing in a region which to the vulgar seems so indubitable, have again and again set men thinking on the question, " What is the whole range of illusion? Is perception, as popularly understood, after all, a big hallucination? Is our life a dream?"[1]

On the other hand, if our study of the wide range of illusion is fitted to induce that temper of mind which is said to be the beginning of philosophy, that attitude of universal doubt expressed by Descartes in his famous maxim, *De omnibus dubitandum*, a consideration of the process of correction is fitted to lead the mind on to the determination of the conditions of accurate knowledge. It is evident, indeed, that the very conception of an illusion implies a criterion of certainty: to call a thing illusory, is to judge it by reference to some accepted standard of truth.

[1] See the interesting autobiographical record of the growth of philosophic doubt in the *Première Méditation* of Descartes.

The mental processes involved in detecting, resisting, and overcoming illusion, are a very interesting subject for the psychologist, though we have not space here to investigate them fully. Turning to presentative, and more particularly sense-illusions, we find that the detection of an illusion takes place now by an appeal from one sense to another, for example, from sight to touch, by way of verification;[1] now (as in Myer's experiment) by a reference from sense and presentation altogether to representation or remembered experience and a process of reasoning; and now, (as in the illusions of art) conversely, by a transition of mind from what is suggested to the actual sense-impression of the moment. In the sphere of memory, again, illusion is determined, as such, now by attending more carefully to the contents of memory, now by a process of reasoning from some presentative cognition. Finally, errors in our comprehensive general representations of things are known to be such partly by reasoning from other conceptions, and partly by a continual process of reduction of representation to presentation, the general to the particular. I may add that the correction of illusion by an act of reflection and reasoning, which brings the part into consistent relation with the whole of experience, includes throughout the comparison of the individual with the collective or social experience.[2]

---

[1] The appeal is not, as we have seen, invariably from sight to touch, but may be in the reverse direction, as in the recognition of the duality of the points of a pair of compasses, which seem one to the tactual sense.

[2] I might further remark that this "collective experience" includes previously detected illusions of ourselves and of others.

We may, perhaps, roughly summarize these operations by saying that they consist in the control of the lower automatic processes (association or suggestion) by the higher activities of conscious will. This activity of will takes the form now of an effort of attention to what is directly present to the mind (sense-impression, internal feeling, mnemonic image, etc.), now of conscious reflection, judgment, and reasoning, by which the error is brought into relation to our experience as a whole, individual and collective.

It is for the philosopher to investigate the inmost nature of these operations as they exhibit themselves in our every-day individual experience, and in the large intellectual movements of history. In no better way can he arrive at what common sense and science regard as certain cognition, at the kinds of knowledge on which they are wont to rely most unhesitatingly.

There is one other relation of our subject to philosophic problems which I have purposely left for final consideration. Our study has consisted mainly in the psychological analysis of illusions supposed to be known or capable of being known as such. Now, the modern association school professes to be able to resolve some of the so-called intuitions of common sense into elements exactly similar to those into which we have here been resolving what are acknowledged by all as illusions. This fact would seem to point to a close connection between the scientific study of illusion and the particular view of these fundamental intuitions taken by one philosophic school. In order to see whether there is really this connection, we must reflect a little further on the nature of the method which we have been pursuing.

I have already had occasion to use the expression "scientific psychology," or psychology as a positive science, and the meaning of this expression must now be more carefully considered. As a positive science, psychology is limited to the function of analyzing mental states, and of tracing their origin in previous and more simple mental states. It has, strictly speaking, nothing to do with the question of the legitimacy or validity of any mental act.

Take a percept, for example. Psychology can trace its parentage in sensation, the mode in which it has come by its contents in the laws of association. But by common consent, a percept implies a presentative apprehension of an object now present to sense. Is this valid or illusory? This question psychology, as science, does not attempt to answer. It would not, I conceive, answer it even if it were able to make out that the whole mental content in the percept can be traced back to elementary sensations and their combinations. For the fact that in the chemistry of mind elements may combine in perfectly new forms does not disprove that the forms thus arising, whether sentiments or quasi-cognitions, are invalid. Much less can psychology dispute the validity of a percept if it cannot be sure that the mind adds nothing to sensation and its grouping; that in the genesis of the perceptive state, with its intuition of something external and now present as object, nothing like a form of intelligence is superimposed on the elements of sensation, giving to the result of their coalescence the particular unity which we find. Whether psychology as a positive science can ever be sure of this: whether, that is to say, it can answer the question, "How do we come by the idea of object?" without assuming some particular philosophic or extra-scientific theory respecting the ultimate nature of mind, is a point which I purposely leave open.

I would contend, then, that the psychologist, in tracing the genesis of the percept out of previous mental experiences, no more settles the question, What is the object of perception? than the physicist settles it in referring the sense-impression (and so the percept) to a present material agent as its condition.

The same applies to our idea of self. I may discover the concrete experiences which supply the filling in of the idea, and yet not settle the question, Does intelligence add anything in the construction of the form of this idea? and still less settle the question whether there is any real unity answering to the idea.

If this is a correct distinction, if psychology, as science, does not determine questions of validity or objective meaning but only of genesis, if it looks at mental states in relation only to their temporal and causal concomitants and not to their objects, it must follow that our preceding analysis of illusion involves no particular philosophic theory as to the nature of intelligence, but, so far as accurate, consists of scientific facts which all philosophic theories of intelligence must alike be prepared to accept. And I have little doubt that each of the two great opposed doctrines, the intuitive and the associational, would claim to be in a position to take up these facts into its particular theory, and to view them in its own way.

But in addition to this scientific psychology, there is another so-called psychology, which is, strictly speaking, philosophic. This, I need hardly say, is the association philosophy. It proceeds by analyzing certain cognitions and sentiments into their elements, and straightway declaring that they mean nothing more than these. That is to say, the associationist passes from genesis to validity, from the history of a conscious state to its objective meaning. Thus, from showing that an intuitive belief, say that in causation, is not original (in the individual or at least in the race), it goes on to assert that it is not a valid immediate cognition at all. Now, I am not concerned here to inquire into the logical value of this transition, but simply to point out that it is extra-scientific and distinctly philosophic. If logically justifiable, it is so because of some plainly *philosophic* assumption, as that made by Hume, namely, that all ideas not derived from impressions are to this extent fictitious or illusory.

And now we are in a position to understand the bearing of our scientific analysis of acknowledged illusions on the associationist's treatment of the alleged illusions of common sense. There is no doubt, I think, that some of the so-called intuitions of common sense have points of analogy to acknowledged illusions. For example, the conviction in the act of perception that something external to the mind and independent of it exists, has a certain superficial resemblance to an hallucination of sense; and moreover, the associationist seeks to explain it by means of these very processes which underlie what is recognized by all as sense-illusion.[1] Again, it may be said that our notions of force and of a causal nexus in the physical world imply the idea of conscious energy as known through our muscular sensations, and so have a suspicious resemblance to those anthropomorphic illusions of which I have spoken under Illusions of Insight. Once more, the consciousness of freedom may, as I have suggested, be viewed as analogous in its form and its mode of origin to illusions of introspection. As a last example, it may be said that the mind's certain conviction of the innateness of some of its ideas resembles those illusions of memory which arise through an inability to think ourselves back into a remote past having a type of consciousness widely unlike that of the present.

But now, mark the difference. In our scientific analysis of popularly known illusions, we had something by which to determine the illusory character of the presentation or belief. We had a popularly or scientifically accepted standard of certainty, by a reference to which we might test the particular *soi-disant* cognition. But in the case of these fundamental beliefs we have no such criterion, except we adopt some particular philosophic theory, say that of the associationist himself. Hence this similarity in structure and origin cannot in itself be said to amount to a proof of equality of logical or objective value. Here again it must be remarked that origin does not carry validity or invalidity with it.[2]

---

[1] M. Taine frankly teaches that what is commonly called accurate perception is a " true hallucination " (*De l'Intelligence*, 2ième partie, Livre I. ch. i. sec. 3).

[2] It only seems to do so, apart from philosophic assumptions, in

We thus come back to our starting-point. While there are close relations, psychological and logical, between the scientific study of the ascertained facts of illusion and the philosophic determination of what is illusory in knowledge as a whole, the two domains must be clearly distinguished. On purely scientific ground we cannot answer the question, "How far does illusion extend?" The solution of this question must be handed over to the philosopher, as one aspect of his problem of cognition.

One or two remarks may, perhaps, be hazarded in concluding this account of the relation of the scientific to the philosophic problem of illusion. Science, as we have seen, takes its stand on a stable consensus, a body of commonly accepted belief. And this being so, it would seem to follow, that so far as she is allowed to interest herself in philosophic questions, she will naturally be disposed to ask, What beliefs are shared in by all minds, so far as normal and developed? In other words, she will be inclined to look at universality

certain cases where experience testifies to a uniform untrustworthiness of the origin. For example, we may, on grounds of matter of fact and experience, be disposed to distrust any belief that we recognize as springing from an emotional source, from the mind's feelings and wishes.

I may add that a so-called intuitive belief may refer to a matter of fact which can be tested by the facts of experience and by scientific methods. Thus, for example, the old and now exploded form of the doctrine of innate ideas, which declared that children were born with certain ideas ready made, might be tested by observation of childhood, and reasoning from its general intellectual condition. The same applies to the physiological theories of space-perception, supposed to be based on Kant's doctrine, put forward in Germany by Johannes Müller and the "nativistic school." (See my exposition and criticism of these doctrines in *Mind*, April, 1878, pp. 168–178 and 193–195.)

as the main thing to be determined in the region of philosophic inquiry. The metaphysical sceptic, fond of daring exploits, may break up as many accepted ideas as he likes into illusory *débris*, provided only he has some bit of reality left to take his stand on. Meanwhile, the scientific mind, here agreeing with the practical mind, will ask, " Will the beliefs thus said to be capable of being shown to be illusory ever cease to exercise their hold on men's minds, including that of the iconoclast himself? Is the mode of demonstration of such a kind as to be likely ever to materially weaken the common-sense ' intuition ' ? "

This question would seem to be most directly answerable by an appeal to individual testimony. Viewed in this light, it is a question for the present, for some few already allege that in their case philosophic reasonings exercise an appreciable effect on these beliefs. And so far as this is so, the man of scientific temper will feel that there is a question for him.

It is evident, however, that the question of the persistence of these fundamental beliefs is much more one for the future than for the present. The correction of a clearly detected illusion is, as I have more than once remarked, a slow process. An illusion such as the apparent movement of the sun will persist as a partially developed error long after it has been convicted. And it may be that the fundamental beliefs here referred to, even if presumably illusory, are destined to exercise their spell for long ages yet.

Whether this will be the case or not, whether these intuitive beliefs are destined slowly to decay and be dissolved as time rolls on, or whether they will retain an eternal youth, is a question which we of to-day seem, on a first view of the matter, to have no way of answering which does not assume the very point in question—the truth or falsity of the belief. This much may, however, be said. The associationist who resolves these erroneous intuitions into the play of association, admits that the forces at work generating and consolidating the illusory belief are constant and permanent forces, and such as are not likely to be less effective in the future than they have been in the past. Thus, he teaches that the intuition of the single object in the act of perception owes its strength to "inseparable association," according to which law the ideas of the separate "possibilities of sensation," which are all we know of the object, coalesce in the shape of an idea of a single uniting substance. He adds, perhaps, that heredity has tended, and will still tend, to fix the habit of thus transforming an actual multiplicity into an imaginary unity. And in thus arguing, he is allowing that the illusion is one which, to say the least of it, it will always be exceedingly difficult for reason to dislodge.

In view of this uncertainty, and of the possibility, if not the probability, of these beliefs remaining as they have remained, at least approximately universal, the man of science will probably be disposed to hold himself indifferently to the question. He will be inclined to say, "What does it matter whether you call such an apparently permanent belief the correlative of a reality or an illusion? Does it make any practical difference whether a universal 'intuition,' of which we cannot rid ourselves, be described as a uniformly recurring fiction of the imagination, or an integral constitutive factor of intelligence? And, in considering the historical aspect of the question, does it not come to much the same thing whether such permanent mental products be spoken of as the attenuated forms or ghostly survivals of more substantial primitive illusions (for example, anthropomorphic representations of material objects, 'animistic' representations of mind and personality), or as the slowly perfected results of intellectual evolution?"

This attitude of the scientific mind towards philosophic problems will be confirmed when it is seen that those who seek to resolve stable common convictions into illusions are forced, by their very mode of demonstration, to allow these intuitions a measure of validity. Thus, the ideas of the unity and externality attributed to the object in the act of perception are said by the associationist to answer to a matter of fact, namely, the permanent coexistence of certain possibilities of sensation, and the dependence of the single sensations of the individual on the presence of the most permanent of these possibilities, namely, those of the active or muscular and passive sensations of touch, which are, moreover, by far the most constant for all minds. Similarly, the idea of a necessary connection between cause and effect, even if illusory in so far as it expresses an *objective* necessity, is allowed to be true as an expression of that uniformity of our experience which all scientific progress tends to illustrate more and more distinctly. And even the idea of a permanent self, as distinct from particular fugitive feelings, is admitted by the associationist to be correct in so far as it expresses the fact that mind is "a series of feelings which is aware of itself as past and future." In short, these "illusory intuitions," by the showing of those who affirm them to be illusory, are by no means hallucinations having no real object as their correlative, but merely illusions in the narrow sense, and illusions, moreover, in which the ratio of truth to error seems to be a large one.

It would thus appear that philosophy tends, after all, to unsettle what appear to be permanent convictions of the common mind and the presuppositions of science much less than is sometimes imagined. Our intuitions of external realities, our indestructible belief in the uniformity of nature, in the nexus of cause and effect, and so on, are, by the admission of all philosophers, at least partially and *relatively* true; that is to say, true in relation to certain features of our common experience. At the worst, they can only be called illusory as slightly misrepresenting the exact results of this experience. And even so, the misrepresentation must, by the very nature of the case, be practically insignificant. And so in full view of the subtleties of philosophic speculation, the man of science may still feel justified in regarding his standard of truth, a stable consensus of belief, as above suspicion.

INDEX.

F.

Fallacy and illusion, 6, 335; of testimony, 265.

Familiarity, sense of, in new objects, 272, 281.

Fechner, G. T., 51.

Ferrier, Dr., 32, note [1], 58, note [1].

Fiction, as producing illusion, 278, 279, 311.

Fitness. *See* Adaptation.

Flattery, *rationale* of, 200, 222.

Forgetfulness and illusion, 278, 279, 311.

Free-will, doctrine of, 207, 342, 356.

Future. *See* Expectation.

G.

Galton, F., 117.

Ghosts. *See* Hallucination.

Goethe, 116, 117, 280 and note [1].

Griesinger, W., 13, note [1], 63, note [1], 66, note [1], 115, 118, note [2], 119, note [1], 120, note [1], 290, note [1], 327, note [1].

Gruithuisen, 143, 144.

Gurney, E., 224, note [1].

H.

Hall, G. S., 186, note [1].

Hallucination, and illusion, 11, 109, 111, 112, 121; and subjective sensation, 63, 109, 121; sensory and motor, 66; nervous conditions of, 112–114; incomplete and complete, 113; as having either central or peripheral origin, 113; causes of, classified, 115; in sane condition, 116; in insanity, 118; visual and auditory, 119; dreams regarded as, 139, 151; hypnagogic, 143; after-dreams and ghosts, 183; of memory, 271; relation of, to errors of belief, 322; intuition of external world regarded as, 355.

Happiness, feeling of, 200.

Harmful, illusion as, 188, 229, 292, 339.

Harmless, illusions as, 124, 292, 341.

Hartley, D., 139, 256, note [1], 279.

Hearing, as mode of perception, 34, 48; localization of impression in, 60; sense of direction in, 72; activity of, in sleep, 140; and muscular sense, 171.

Heidenhain, Dr., 186–188.

Helmholtz, H., 22, 23, note [1], 44, 51, 54 and note [1], 55, note [1], 57, 67, note [1], 78, note [1], 80, 85, note [1], 88, 90, 207, note [1].

Heraclitus, 137.

Heredity, and illusion of memory, 280; action of, in perpetuating intuition, 359.

Hering, E., 67, note [2].

Hodgson, Shadworth H., 347, note [2].

Holland, Sir H., 277.

Hood, Thomas, 146.

Hope, illusory. *See* Expectation.

Hoppe, Dr. J. I., 51, 58, note [1].

Horwicz, A., 145, note [1].

Hume, D., 355.

Huxley, Professor T., 119, note [1].

Hyperæsthesia, 65.

Hypnotism, 185.

Hypochondria, 65.

Hypothesis, as illusory, 310, 311.

I.

Idealism, 348.

Identity, cases of mistaken, 267.

Identity, personal, confusion of, in dreams, 163; consciousness of, 241, 267, 282, 285; illusory forms of, 283; gross disturbances of, in normal life, 287; in abnormal life, 289; momentary confusions of, 293.

Illusion, definition of, 1; varieties of, 9; extent of, 328; *rationale* of, 331, 337.

Oneirocritics, 129.

Opera, illusion connected with, 104.

Optimism, 323, 327, 342.

Organic sensations, discrimination of, 41; interpretation of, 99; in sleep, 145, 148.

Organism, conditions of illusion in, 47, 50; relation of our conception of the universe to sensibilities of, 343.

Orientation, 125, 138.

P.

Pain, recollection of, 264, 270.

Painting, representation of third dimension by, 77; apparent movement of eye in portrait, 81; discrepancies between, and object in magnitude and luminosity, 88; realization of, and mental preparation, 105; realization of, by animals, 105.

Paræsthesia, 68.

Paralysis of ocular muscles, 66.

Passive, and active factor in perception, 27; and active illusion, 45.

Percept, 22; and sense-impression, 59.

Perception, a form of immediate knowledge, 10, 13, 17, 18; external and internal, 14; philosophy of, 14, 20, 22, 36, 346, 348, 353, 355, 359; illusions of, 19, 35; psychology of, 20; and inference, 22, 26, 76; physiological conditions of, 31.

Persistent objects, representation of, 312.

Persistent self. *See* Personal identity.

Personal equation, in perception, 101; in æsthetic intuition, 214; in memory, 292; in belief, 324.

Personal identity, consciousness of, 241, 282, 285; illusions connected with, 283; disturbances in sense of, 287; sense of, in insanity, 289; momentary confusions of, 293; philosophic problem of, 285, 354, 360.

Personification of nature, 224.

Perspective, linear, 79, 97, 98; aerial, 80; of memory, 245.

Pessimism, 323, 327.

Phenomenalism, 348.

Philosophy, conception of illusion by, 7, 36, 205, 285, 349; of mind, 132, 285, 344, 348; as theory of knowledge, 295, 346; and science, 346, 348; and common sense, 347, 349; problems of, 347.

Phosphenes, 58.

Physical science. *See* Science.

Plato, 281.

Platonists, 349.

Pleasure, feeling of, 200; recollection of, 264, 270.

Plutarch, 133, note [1].

Poetry, lyrical and dreams, 164; misinterpretation of, 223; personification, 224.

Points, discrimination of, 52.

Poisons, action of, 115.

Pollock, F., 184, note [1].

Pollock, W. H., 184.

Predisposition, action of, in perception, 44, 101, 102; in æsthetic intuition, 215; in insight, 223; in recollection, 268; in belief, 305, 319; belief as, 324.

Prejudice. *See* Predisposition.

Prenatal experience, recollection of, 281.

Preperception, 27; illusions connected with, 44, 93; voluntary, 95; result of habit of mind, 101; result of temporary conditions, 102; as sub-expectation, 102; as definite expectation, 106.

Presentation and representation, 9, 10, 13, 14, 192, 234, 329, 330.

Projection, outward, of sensations, 63; of mental image, 111,